About the Authors

Louisa Heaton lives on Hayling Island, Hampshire, with her husband, four children and a small zoo. She has worked in various roles in the health industry—most recently four years as a Community First Responder, answering 999 calls. When not writing, Louisa enjoys other creative pursuits, including reading, quilting and patchwork—usually instead of the things she ought to

her passions for the outdoors, the sea and cycling.

The Single Dads

COLLECTION

July 2019

August 2019

September 2019

October 2019

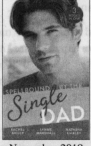

November 2019

December 2019

Fairytale with the Single Dad

LOUISA HEATON

ALISON ROBERTS

SUE MacKAY

MILLS & BOON

First Published in Great Britain 2019
By Mills & Boon, an imprint of HarperCollins*Publishers*
1 London Bridge Street, London, SE1 9GF

FAIRYTALE WITH THE SINGLE DAD
© 2019 Harlequin Books S.A.

Christmas with the Single Dad © Louisa Heaton 2016
Sleigh Ride with the Single Dad © Harlequin Books S.A. 2017
Surgeon in a Wedding Dress © Sue MacKay 2011

Special thanks and acknowledgement are given to Alison Roberts for her contribution to the Christmas in Manhattan series.

ISBN: 978-0-263-27619-0

1219

MIX
Paper from
responsible sources
FSC® C007454

This book is produced from independently certified FSC™ paper to ensure responsible forest management.

For more information visit: www.harpercollins.co.uk/green

Printed and bound in Spain
by CPI, Barcelona

CHRISTMAS WITH
THE SINGLE DAD

LOUISA HEATON

For Mrs Duff, my first English teacher, for telling me I had a wonderful imagination and that I was to never stop writing.

CHAPTER ONE

SYDNEY HARPER CONFIRMED her appointment details on the surgery's check-in touchscreen and headed into the waiting room.

It was full. Much too full. Eleven of the twelve available chairs were filled with faces she recognised. People she saw every day in the village. One or two of her own clients from the veterinary practice she ran. Were they *all* before her? Would she be sitting in this waiting room all morning to see Dr Preston? She had patients of her own waiting—it was a busy time of year. Close to Christmas. No doubt everyone was trying to see their doctor before the festive season.

With a sigh at the thought of the inevitable wait she strode in, looking for the book she always kept in her bag for situations such as this.

At the empty seat she sat down and opened the book, slipping her bookmark into her fingers. She tried to focus on the words upon the page, but her eyes were tired and she kept reading the same sentence over and over again. The words were refusing to go in and make sense.

It was happening again. Every year when it started to get close to *that date* her body rebelled and she couldn't sleep. The date would be hanging heavy in the near future, along with the dread of having to get through

Christmas again, reliving what had happened before, every moment as clear as if it had just occurred. The shock. The fear. The *guilt*.

The difficulty getting to sleep. Then the difficulty *staying* asleep. She'd keep waking, staring at the clock, staring at those bright red digits, watching them tick over, minute to minute, hour to hour. Feeling *alone*. So alone in the dark! With no one to talk to. No one to go to, to reassure herself that everyone was fine.

That first year—the first anniversary of when it had happened—she'd got up and stood in the doorway of Olivia's old room, staring at her daughter's empty bed. She'd stood there almost all night. Trying to remember what it had looked like when it had been filled with life and laughter and joy.

The second year after it had happened she'd got up again and, determined not to stand in the doorway for another night, gawking at nothing, she'd decided to make herself useful. She'd cleaned. Scrubbing the oven in the middle of the night until it shone like a new pin was perfect therapy as far as she was concerned. She could get angry with the burnt-on bits. Curse at them. Moan about the ache in her back from all the bending over. But it felt better to be focused on a real physical pain than a mental one.

Last year, when the anniversary of Olivia's death had come around, she'd decided to visit Dr Preston and he'd given her a prescription for some sleeping pills and told her to come and see him if it happened again.

This year, though her oven could no doubt do with another clean, the idea of being up all night again—alone again—just wasn't an option. She hated losing all this sleep. And it wasn't just the one night any more. She was losing sleep earlier and earlier, up to a month or more before the anniversary.

So here she was.

All she needed was a quick prescription. She could be in and out in seconds. Get back to her own patients—Fletcher the Great Dane, who needed his paw checked after a grass seed had become embedded under his pad, a health check on two new ferrets and the first set of jabs for Sara's new kitten. There were others, she knew, but they were her first three and they would be waiting. Even now. Patiently watching the clock in *her* waiting room.

The screen on the wall in front of her gave a beep and she looked up to see if she was being called in. It wasn't, but the person next to her got up out of her chair and left. Sydney was glad for the space, but it didn't last long, Mrs Courtauld, owner of a retired greyhound, settled into the newly vacant seat.

'Hello, Sydney. How nice to see you. How are you doing?'

'Mrs C! I'm fine. How are you?'

'Oh, you know. The usual aches and pains. That's why I'm here. My knees are giving me a bit of gyp. They have been ever since Prince knocked me over in the park and broke my wrist.'

'You did get quite a knock, didn't you?'

'I did! But at my age you expect a bit of wear and tear in the old joints. I'm no spring chicken now, you know. I get out and about each day if I can. It's good to keep mobile.'

Sydney nodded, smiling. 'But you're still looking great, Mrs C.'

'You're too kind, young Sydney. I do have mirrors in the house—I know how old I look. The skin on my neck is that red and saggy I'm amazed a farmer hasn't shot me, thinking I'm an escaped turkey.'

Sydney laughed. 'Ridiculous! I'd be happy to look like you if I ever make it to pensionable age.'

Mrs Courtauld snorted. 'Of course you'll make it to my age! What are you now? Thirty-three? Thirty-four?'

'Thirty-five.'

'You see? Loads of years left in you.' She thought for a moment, her eyes darkening, and she looked hard at Sydney in concern. 'Unless, of course, you're here because there's something wrong? Oh, Sydney, you're not dreadfully ill, are you?'

Mrs Courtauld's face filled with motherly concern and she laid a liver-spotted wrinkly hand on Sydney's arm.

'Just not sleeping very well.'

Mrs Courtauld nodded, looking serious. 'No. 'Course not. The anniversary is coming up again, isn't it? Little Olivia?'

Sydney swallowed hard, touched that Mrs Courtauld had realised the date was near. How many in the village had forgotten? *Don't cry.*

'Yes. It is,' she answered, her voice low. She wasn't keen on anyone else in the waiting room listening in.

Mrs Courtauld gripped Sydney's hand and squeezed it. 'Of course. Understandable. I'm the same each year when it comes round to my Alfred's birthday. Ten years since I lost him.' She paused as she looked off, as if into the distance. But then she perked up again. 'I laid some flowers at Alfred's grave the other day and I thought of you. Your little Olivia's plot is so close. I hope you don't mind, but I put an amaryllis against her headstone.'

Oh.

Sydney wasn't sure how to respond. That was sweet. It was nice to think that Olivia had a bright, beautiful flower to brighten up her plot. Nice for her to be remembered in that way.

She hadn't been to the graveyard for a while. It was just so impossibly bleak and devastating to stand there and look down at the headstone, knowing her daughter was…

She swallowed hard.

Don't even think it.

It hurt too much. Going to the grave just kept proving that she was dead, making Sydney feel helpless and lost—a feeling she couldn't bear. She'd found that by staying away, by existing in her dreams and her memories, she could still see her daughter alive and well and she never had to stare at that cold, hard, depressing ground any more.

Blinking back the tears, she was about to thank Mrs Courtauld when the computer screen that announced patient's names beeped into life and there was her name. Ms Sydney Harper. Dr Jones's room.

She got up quickly, then did a double-take, looking at the screen again. Dr *Jones?*

But she'd booked in with Dr Preston. *He* was her doctor, not this Jones person! And who was it? A locum? A new partner? If it was, and she'd been passed on to someone else…

She shoved her book back into her bag, wondering briefly if she ought to go and check with Reception and see what had happened, but the doctor was probably waiting. If she faffed around at Reception she might lose her appointment altogether—and she needed those tablets!

Clearing her throat, she pushed through the door and headed down the corridor. To the left, Dr Preston's room. To the right, Dr Jones's.

Sydney hesitated outside the door, her hand gripping the handle, afraid to go in. What if this new doctor wanted to *ask questions?* She wasn't sure she was ready to tell the story *again*. Not to a stranger. Dr Preston knew everything. There was no need to explain, no need for her to sit in front of him and embarrass herself by bursting into tears, because he *knew*. Knew what she'd gone through and was *still* going through. He often saw her in the village and would call out with a cheery wave, ask her how she was doing. She appreciated that.

A newcomer might not understand. A locum might be loath to hand out a prescription as easily.

Please don't ask me any probing questions!

She sucked in a breath and opened the door, not knowing what or who to expect. Was Dr Jones a woman? A man? Young? Old?

She strode in, her jaw set, determined to be as brief as possible so she could get her prescription and get out again but she stopped as her gaze fell upon the extremely handsome man seated behind the doctor's desk.

Her breath caught in her throat and somehow paralysed it. He was a complete shock to her system. Totally unexpected. It was like walking into a room expecting to see a normal person—some old guy in a boring shirt and tie…maybe someone bald, with old-fashioned glasses and drab brown trousers—but instead laying eyes upon a movie star in all his airbrushed glory.

The man was dressed in a well-fitting dark suit, with the brightest, bluest eyes she'd ever seen. There was a gorgeous smile of greeting upon his face. The type that stopped your heart. That stopped you breathing for a moment.

Oh, my!

Sydney had not noticed a good-looking man since Alastair had left. There was no point. Men were not on her radar. She wasn't looking for another relationship. What was the use? She'd only end up getting blamed for everything.

She was sure those men were out there. Somewhere. Even though Silverdale Village wasn't exactly overrun with hot guys. The type who ought to star in Hollywood movies or get their kits off for a charity calendar. She'd just never noticed. Living too much in her own head.

But *this* guy? Dr Jones?

I'm staring at him! Like a goldfish with my mouth hanging open! Speak, Sydney. Say something. Anything! So he knows he's not dealing with a mute.

She turned away from him to close the door, shutting her eyes to compose herself and take in a steadying breath. Hoping her cheeks had stopped flushing, hoping he hadn't noticed the effect he'd had on her.

He's just a guy.

Just.

A.

Guy.

She blew her breath out slowly before she turned around, telling herself to try and sound haughty and distant, whilst simultaneously feeling her cheeks flame hot enough to sizzle bacon. 'I…um… I don't mean to be rude, but I made an appointment to see Dr Preston…?'

An angel had walked into his consulting room.

An angel with long, luscious waves of chocolate-coloured hair and sad grey eyes. Big, sad eyes, tinged with red, in the fresh face of an English rose.

Startled, he dropped his pen, fumbling for it when it fell from his fingers and smiling in apology. What the hell had just happened? Why was he reacting like this? She was just a patient!

He'd not expected to feel suddenly...*nervous*. As if he'd never treated a patient before. Tongue-tied. Blind-sided by his physical response to this woman. He could feel his normal greeting—*Morning, take a seat, how can I help?*—stifled in his throat and he had to turn to his computer, glancing at the screen briefly to gather his thoughts before he could speak.

Sydney Harper.

Beautiful. Enchanting.

A patient!

Reel your thoughts back in and show that you know what you're doing.

He cleared his throat. 'Er...yes, you did... But he...er...got overbooked.' He paused briefly, noticing the way she hovered uncertainly at the door. The way her long cardigan covered her almost to mid-thigh, the shapeless garment hiding any figure she might have. The way her heavy tartan skirt covered her legs down to her boots. The way her fingers twisted around each other.

Curious... Why is she so frightened? Why do I get the feeling that she tries her best not to be noticed?

He could see her gaze darting about the room, as if she were looking for means of escape, and suddenly curiosity about this woman overrode any previous nervousness.

'Is that okay?'

'I'd prefer to see Dr Preston. He knows me. I'm *his* patient.'

Nathan glanced back at the computer, so that he wouldn't stare at her and make her feel even more un-comfortable. Did Dr Preston *really* know her? The last time she'd been into the surgery had been—he checked the screen—a year ago. A lot could change in a year.

He should know.

Forget that. Concentrate on your work.

He was itching to know what ailed her. What he could help her with. How to keep her in the room and not have her bolt like a skittish horse.

Purely on a professional basis, of course. I'm not interested in her in that *way.*

What had brought her to the surgery today? She looked anxious. A bit stressed. Not entirely comfortable with this change.

He gave her his best friendly smile. 'Why don't you take a seat? You never know, I might be able to help. Doctors do that.' He tried to reassure her, but she approached the chair opposite him as if she were a gazelle trying to sidle past a ravenous lion.

He waited for her to sit and then he looked her over. A little pale, though her cheeks were flushed. Her pulse was probably elevated. Her blood pressure rising. What had made her so anxious? He was intrigued. But he'd learnt a valuable trick as a doctor. Silence was a wonderful tool. People would feel compelled to fill it. They'd start talking. Eventually.

So he waited, noting how white her knuckles were as they clutched the bag upon her lap.

And he waited.

She was looking at anything *but* him. Checking out the room as if it were new to her before she finally allowed herself to glance at his face. Her cheeks reddened in the most delightful way, and she was biting her bottom lip as she finally made eye contact.

'I need some sleeping pills. Dr Preston told me to come again if I needed a repeat.'

Ah. There we go!

'You're not sleeping well?'

Her cheeks reddened some more, and again she averted her eyes. 'Not really. Look, I'm needed back at work, so if you could just write me a prescription? I don't want to keep my clients waiting.'

Nathan Jones sat back in his swivel chair and appraised her. He was curious as to why she needed them. 'Sleeping pills are really a last resort. I'll need a few details from you first of all.'

The flash of alarm in her eyes was startling to observe. And if she twisted the strap of her handbag any more it would soon snap.

Sydney shook her head. 'I don't have long.'

'Neither do I. So let's crack on, shall we? Eight minutes per patient can go by in the blink of an eye.' He was trying to keep it loose. Casual. Non-threatening. This woman was as taut as a whip.

She let out an impatient breath. 'What do you need to know?'

'Tell me about your sleep routine.'

Does your husband snore? Does he toss and turn all night, keeping you awake? Wait... What the...?

Why was he worrying about whether she had a husband or not? He wasn't looking to go *out* with this woman. She was a patient! At least for now. He had no doubt that the second she bolted from his consulting room she would make sure she never had to see him again!

'What about it?'

'Is it regular?'

'I work long days at the veterinary surgery across the road from here. I'm the only vet there, so I'm on call most nights, and since the new homes got built I've been busier than ever.'

'So you get called out a lot?'

'I do.'

He nodded and scribbled a note. 'And are you finding it difficult to drop off to sleep?'

'Yes.'

'Worried about your beeper going off? Or is it something else?'

She looked at him directly now. 'Look, Dr Preston has given me the pills before. I'm sure he won't mind if you give me some more.'

She didn't like him prying. He glanced at her records, his eyes scanning the previous note. Yes, she was correct. She'd been given sleeping pills by Dr Preston this time last year...

'...due to the sudden death of the patient's daughter three years ago, patient requested tranquillisers...'

He felt a lump of cold dread settle in his stomach as he read the notes fully.

She'd lost her *child*. Sydney Harper had lost her daughter and she couldn't sleep when the anniversary of her death got close. It happened every year. *Oh, heavens.*

He closed his eyes and gritted his teeth, mentally apologising.

'I...er...yes. I can see that in your notes.'

How terrible. The most awful thing that could ever happen to a parent. And it had happened to her and he was trying to poke around in her despair when it was clear in her notes why she needed the pills. But would he be being a good doctor just to give them to her? Or would he be a *better* doctor if he tried to stop her needing them? They could be addictive...

'I'm sure he won't mind if you give me some more tablets.'

Nathan had a daughter. Anna. She was six years old and she was all he had in this world. He couldn't imagine losing her. She was everything to him right now. What this poor woman had been through...! No wonder she looked the way she did.

'I can write you a prescription, but…' He paused. 'Have you ever been offered counselling?'

She looked directly at him, her demeanour suggesting she was about to explain something to a child. 'I was. And I did go to start with. But it didn't help me so I stopped going.'

'Perhaps you weren't ready for it then. Would you be interested in trying it again now? It might help you with this sleeping issue. I could arrange it for you.'

The computer whirred out the prescription and he grabbed it from the printer and passed it over to her.

'Counselling is not for me. I don't…talk…about what happened.'

'Maybe that's the problem?' The words were out before he could censor them. He bit his lip with annoyance. Too late to take the words back. He needed to cover their crassness. And quickly. 'Have you tried a different night-time routine? Warm milk? A bath? That kind of thing?'

But she'd stood up, was staring down at him, barely controlling the anger he could see brewing behind her eyes. 'Are you a father, Dr Jones?'

He nodded solemnly, picturing his daughter's happy, smiling face. 'I am.'

'Have you ever experienced the loss of a child?'

He could see where she was going with this, and felt horrible inside. He looked away. 'No. Thankfully.'

'Then don't tell me that *warm milk*—' she almost spat the words '—will make me better.' She spun on her heel and when she got to the door, her hand on the handle, she paused, her head low, then glanced over her shoulder, her teeth gritted. 'Thank you for my prescription.'

Then she left.

He felt as if a hurricane had blown through the room. He felt winded. Stunned. He had to get up and pace, sucking in a lungful of air, running both hands through his hair before he stood and stared out of the window at the sparrows and starlings trying to take food from the frozen feeders hanging outside. The smaller birds were carefully picking at the peanuts, whereas the starlings were tossing white breadcrumbs everywhere, making a mess.

No, he had *not* experienced the same pain that Sydney had gone through. He would never want to. But he *did* know what it felt like to realise that your life had changed for evermore.

People dealt with tragedies in different ways. Some found comfort in food. Some in drink or drugs. Some kept it all inside. Others found it easy to talk out their feelings and frustrations. A few would blindly choose to ignore it and pretend it had never happened.

He felt deflated now that she'd left his room. Sydney Harper was intense—yes—and hurting—definitely—but there was something about her. He couldn't quite put a finger on it.

It bothered him all day. Through seeing all his patients. The chest infection, the sprained ankle, a case of chicken pox, talking someone through using his asthma medication. His thoughts kept returning to his first patient at his new job.

Sydney Harper.

Beautiful. Elegant.

Fragile.

And then it came to him. The reason why he couldn't forget her. The reason he kept going over and over their interaction that morning.

I'm attracted to her.

The thought stopped him in his tracks. No. He

couldn't—*wouldn't*—be. He had nothing to offer her. Besides, he had a child to take care of. Clearly!

No. That way danger lay.

He doubted he would ever see her again. Not as his *patient*. She had clearly wanted to see Dr Preston, and the way she'd stormed from the room had left him feeling a little bit stunned. He'd *never* had a patient walk out on him like that.

A fiancée, yes.

The mother of his child, yes.

But never a patient.

Sydney strode from the room feeling mightily irritated with Dr Jones, but not knowing why. Because she had the prescription she needed. She'd obtained what she'd wanted when she'd made the appointment. But now that she was out from under Dr Jones's interested, *unsettling* gaze she felt restless and antsy. Almost angry. As if she needed to go running for a few miles to get all of that uncomfortable adrenaline out of her system. As if she needed to burn off some of the inner turmoil she was feeling. As if she needed to let out a giant enraged scream.

Averting her gaze from the people in the waiting room, she went straight back to Reception and leant over the counter towards Beattie the receptionist—the owner of a moggy called Snuggles.

'Beattie, I've just been seen by Dr Jones. Could you make a note on my records that when I make an appointment to see Dr Preston—my *actual* doctor—that I should, indeed, *see* Dr Preston?'

Beattie looked up at her in surprise. 'You didn't *like* Dr Jones?'

Her jaw almost hit the floor.

'*Like* him? Liking him has nothing to do with it. Dr

Preston is my GP and that is who I want to see when I phone to make an appointment!'

Beattie gave an apologetic smile. 'Sorry, Syd. Dr Jones offered to see you as Dr Preston was overrun and he knew you were in a rush to get back to work.'

Oh. Right. She hadn't thought of that. 'Well, that was very kind of him, but...'

It *had* been very kind of him, hadn't it? And what was she doing out here complaining? Even though she'd got what she needed.

Deflating slightly, she relaxed her tensed shoulders. 'Next time just book me in with Richard.'

'Will do. Anything else I can help you with?'

Not really. Though a niggling thought had entered her head... 'This Dr Jones that I saw today... Just a locum, is he? Just here for the day?'

She tried to make it sound casual. But it would be nice to know that she wouldn't be bumping into him in the village unless she had to. Not after she'd stormed out like that. That wasn't her normal behaviour. But something about the man had irritated her, and then he'd made that crass suggestion about warm milk...

'No, no. He's permanent.' Beattie's face filled with a huge grin. 'He moved to the village a week ago with his daughter. Into one of the homes on the new estate.'

'Oh. Right. Thank you.'

Permanent. Dr Jones would be living here. In Silverdale.

'Please don't tell me he's got an aging pet dog or anything?'

'I don't think so. But you'll run into him at the committee meetings for the Christmas market and the village nativity.'

What? She'd only just decided to return to those meetings. Had been looking forward to them!

'Why?'

Beattie looked at her oddly. 'Dr Preston is cutting down on his commitments now that he's nearly retired. He's asked Nathan to take over. You didn't like him? We all think he's gorgeous! Have you seen him smile? I tell you, that man's a heartbreaker!'

A heartbreaker? Not if *she* had anything to do with it.

Sydney grimaced, but thanked Beattie once again and left the surgery, pausing to wait for traffic to rush by so she could cross the road over to her own practice.

The new doctor was going to be on the Christmas committee. And she'd just agreed to go back. To help. She'd told them she would *be there*. Her heart sank at the thought of it as she neared her place of work.

Silverdale Veterinary Surgery was a relatively small building, comprised of two old cottages that had been knocked through inside and transformed from homes into a business.

Sydney loved it. It was clinical and businesslike, but still retained its old-world charm with white walls and large exposed oak beams and, outside, a thatched roof. There were even window boxes, which she'd learnt to tend. They overflowed with primulas and pansies in the spring, but right now were hung with dark green ivy and indigo lobelia. And *no* fairy lights. Even if everyone else seemed to think it was okay to start decorating for Christmas in *November!*

She'd never been a green-fingered person. Not before she'd got married. But when Olivia came along the little girl had loved being in the garden and growing pretty things. Although Sydney had managed to kill the first few plants they'd got, they'd eventually learned together and their flowers had begun to thrive. There'd been nothing she'd liked better than to watch Olivia use her pink tin watering can to water them each evening, when it was cool. And Syd's talent with flowers had not gone unnoticed around the village either. She'd often been in charge of the flower stalls at the Christmas market each year.

When she'd been involved, anyway.

She pushed through the door and saw that her waiting room was pleasingly busy. There was Mr Shepherd, as expected, with his Great Dane, Sara with her new kitten, and no doubt in the box by Janet's feet were her two ferrets, Apollo and Zeus.

'Morning, everyone! Sorry to keep you waiting.'

Her anxiety was gone here. This was her home turf. Her safe haven. The place that *she* controlled. Was in charge of. Where there were no surprises. Well, nothing life-changing, anyway. Not to her. Here she could cure illnesses. Make things better. As much as she could.

Her clients waved and smiled and said good morning, too. They weren't too bothered about waiting for her. And she appreciated them for that.

In the staff room, she put on her green veterinary top and prepared to start work.

This was better.

This she could do.

This she was in control of.

Nathan stood in the playground, surrounded mostly by mothers waiting for their children to come out of infant school. As always, he felt like a complete fish out of water here. All the mothers stood in little groups, chatting and laughing. They all *knew* each other. And him…? He was the lone male, feeling awkward. Sure that he was standing out like a sore thumb.

He could feel their eyes on him. Judging him. Assessing him. Were they talking about him? Could they see his awkward gait? His limp? Could they see what was wrong with him? *It feels like they can.* He almost felt as if he was carrying a huge sign naming his condition around his neck.

Silverdale Infants had seemed the perfect place for Anna when he'd first come to the village for his job interview. He'd scouted the place out and asked the headteacher to give him a tour. He'd walked through the school with her, looking in the classrooms, seeing the happy children and their paintings, listening to them singing in assembly and watching as they'd sat for storytime in their impossibly small chairs. He'd genuinely felt his daughter would be happy there. It had a good vibe. The head was a nice woman and Miss Howarth, Anna's teacher-to-be, seemed really lovely and welcoming.

Nathan had just had his first day in his new job and this had been Anna's first day at her new school. He could only hope that it had gone as well as his own day, and that she would come running out with a big smile on her face. Then, perhaps, the lump of anxiety in his stomach would disappear and they'd be able to go home and he'd cook dinner.

Nathan hated being away from Anna. Giving her into the care of someone else. But he had to work and she had to learn—and weren't schools considered *in loco parentis?*

He was grateful for the flexible hours his new job afforded him. Since Gwyneth had left them he'd had to become both father *and* mother to Anna. And he didn't think he was doing too badly. Anna seemed happy enough, only occasionally asking why she didn't have a mummy, like other children. Those days were hard.

When he could see the hurt in his daughter's eyes. And when it happened he would curse Gwyneth inwardly, whilst outwardly he would throw everything he had at making his daughter happy.

He just couldn't give her the mother that she wanted. He wasn't ready to be with someone new. To open himself up to possible hurt and betrayal. To being left again. And why put Anna through the hope of getting to know someone when they might walk away and break her heart, too?

He didn't bad-mouth Gwyneth to Anna. It wasn't up to him to tell Anna how to feel about her mother. Anna might want to find her one day and see her. Talk to her. Ask her things. Did he want Anna to grow up resentful and hating her mother? No. Even if it was hard for him. Because Gwyneth had abandoned them both. And that hurt. Not so much now, but it still caused pain whenever he thought about his and Anna's future.

He sighed as he thought about his mistake in getting involved with Gwyneth. She'd been so much fun to begin with, but—as was sometimes the way with relationships—they'd both realised something was missing. And then they'd discovered she was pregnant…

Life was short. And he would not have Anna spending hers moping about for a mother who had no interest in her whatsoever. He was only sorry that he hadn't noticed Gwyneth's shallowness earlier on. Before he'd got in too deep.

The school bell rang and he braced himself. Now he'd know. Had it gone well?

Crossing his fingers in his jacket pockets, trying not to shiver in the late November cold, he looked for her familiar face amongst the mass of children pouring out through the door, all of them almost identical in their little green jumpers and grey skirts or trousers.

Then he saw her and his heart lifted.

'Daddy!'

She was *smiling*. Beaming at him as she ran to his open arms, clutching a painting that was still slightly wet. Nathan scooped her up, hefting her onto his hip, trying not to grimace at the pain in his shoulder.

'What do we have here?' He glanced at the painting. There were daubs of brown and green that he guessed was a tree, and to one side was a large black blob with ears. 'Is that Lottie?'

Anna nodded, grinning, showing the gap where her two front teeth were missing. 'Yes!'

Lottie was their pet rabbit and his one concession to Anna's demands to fill their house with pets of all shapes and sizes. Anna *adored* animals, and ever since she'd started at nursery had plagued him with requests for cats or dogs or parrots or anything that had fur, feathers or a cute face.

Knowing that they would both be out all day—him at work, she at school—he'd not thought a dog or a cat was appropriate, but he'd given in and allowed her a rabbit. It had the added bonus of living outdoors and its presence had stopped Anna from 'rescuing' injured insects and bringing them in to be 'nursed'.

'It looks just like her.' He squinted as he saw a small daub of bright orange. 'Is that a carrot?'

'No, Daddy. Silly! That's a worm.'

'Oh, right.' He gently placed his daughter back on the ground, being careful not to grimace or wrench himself further. 'So how did it go? Was it good? Did you make friends?'

She nodded. 'Lots and lots.'

She proceeded to list them as they walked back to the car. There seemed an *awful* lot, and to his ears it sounded

as if she'd just memorised the register, but he nodded
and smiled at her as she told him about Hattie with the
bright pink glasses, and George who had held her hand
as they'd walked to assembly.

They were soon home. Nathan still had half their
life packed away in boxes after the move, but he knew
they'd get there eventually. All the important stuff was
unpacked. And Anna's room had everything. He'd done
that first. Everything else could wait for when he had the
time. He just had to decide where he wanted it all to go.

The house was brand-new, so had none of that old-
world character the rest of the cottages in the village
had. He had tiles on his roof, not thatch. A modern fake
fireplace rather than an old rustic one with real flames.
Flat, smooth walls rather than whitewashed ones with
crooked oak beams.

Still, the place would get its character eventually.

'I'm going to see if Lottie missed me.' Anna ran
through the house towards the back door, so she could
go into the garden.

'Not yet, young lady,' he called after her. 'Go upstairs
and get out of your uniform first.'

'Daddy, please!'

'It was raining this morning, Anna. I'm not having you
getting your uniform covered in mud and straw. Please
go and get changed.'

She pouted, but only briefly, and then she ran back
past him, clambering up the stairs as he took their bags
through to the kitchen, pinned her painting to the fridge
with a magnet that was shaped like a banana. He'd picked
up some vegetables from a farm shop, so he popped those
in the fridge, then switched on the kettle for a drink.

Upstairs, he heard a small *thunk* as Anna kicked off
her shoes and soon enough she was trotting back down

the stairs, wearing a weird combination of purple corduroy skirt, green tee shirt and a rather loud orange and yellow cardigan.

'Nice… I'm liking your style.' He was keen to encourage her to wear what she wanted and to pick her own clothes. He'd learned that it was important—it helped Anna to develop her independence and allowed her to express herself. And he needed Anna to be a strong character. He wanted to encourage her at all times to feel happy about herself and her own decisions. To feel valued and beautiful. Because she *was* beautiful. With her mother's good looks but thankfully none of her character.

'Will you do me a juice, Daddy?'

'Sure thing, poppet.' He watched her twist the back door key and trot out into the garden. It wasn't huge out there, and as theirs was one of the original show houses it was just plain grass, with one side border of bushes. Nothing too impressive. Nothing that needed that much work. Something he figured he'd get to later. Maybe in the New Year.

But it had the rabbit hutch. The main reason for Anna to go and play outside. He was hoping to get her a trampoline, or a bike, or something. Maybe for Christmas.

He was just diluting orange juice with some water when he heard his daughter let out a blood-curdling scream.

'Daddy!'

'Anna?' His body froze, his heart stopped beating just for a millisecond, and then he was dropping the glass into the sink and bolting for the back door. What on earth had happened? Why had she screamed? Was she hurt?

Oh, please don't let her be hurt!

'Daddy!'

She ran into his arms, crying, and he held her, puzzled. What was it? Had she fallen over? What?

'Let me look at you.' He held her out at arm's length to check her over, but she looked fine. No scuffed knees, no grazes, no cuts. Just a face flooded with tears. What the…?

'Lottie's *bleeding*!' She pointed at the hutch before burying her face in his shirt.

He looked over the top of her head and could now see that the hutch had a broken latch and poor Lottie the rabbit sat hunched within, breathing heavily and audibly, with blood all over her and in the straw around her, as if she'd been involved in some sort of weird rabbit horror movie.

'Oh…' He stood up and led Anna away and back into the kitchen, sitting her down on one of the chairs by the table. 'Stay here.'

'She's bleeding, Daddy.'

'I know, honey. We'll need to take her to the vet.'

He didn't know if the poor thing might have to be put to sleep. There was a lot of blood, and Lottie looked like she might be in shock. He dashed for the cupboard under the stairs, where they'd put Lottie's carrier and got it out. Then he grabbed some latex gloves from under the sink and headed for the garden.

'I'll get Lottie. Can you get your shoes on for me? And your coat?'

'Where are we going?'

'The vet. The animal doctor. She'll need to check her over.'

'What if she dies, Daddy?' Anna sobbed, almost hiccupping her words.

He hadn't imagined this. He'd agreed to have Lottie knowing that rabbits lived for around ten years, hoping that they wouldn't have to face this day until Anna was in her teens. But not this early. Not *now*. He wasn't sure how she'd handle a pet's death at this age.

'Let's cross that bridge when we come to it. Get your shoes on. We need to get her there quickly.'

Nathan headed into the garden, slipped on the gloves and picked up the poor, shocked rabbit and placed her in the box. Normally she fought going in the carrier. But there was no fight today. His heart sank at the thought of having to tell his daughter her rabbit might die. Had Anna not been through enough?

He pulled off the bloodied gloves and quickly discarded them in the bin.

He could only hope that the veterinary surgery was still open.

CHAPTER TWO

IT HAD BEEN a long, tiring day. After her doctor's appointment Sydney had come back to the surgery and seen her first ten patients, and then she'd got round to her surgeries—a dental clean, two spays on cats, a dog to be neutered. Lunch had been quick, and then there had been more appointments: kitten visits, puppy checks, suture removals, an elderly dog that had had to be euthanised. Then she'd returned phone calls, given owners blood test results and now she was finishing off her paperwork. Filling in records. There were three animals being kept in overnight, but Lucy, her veterinary nurse, was giving them their final check before they left for the evening.

'I'll be ready to put my feet up tonight. Have you seen my ankles?' said Lucy.

Sydney smiled sympathetically. Lucy did seem to be suffering lately.

Almost all the lights were off, except for in her office and at the surgery entrance, and Sydney was just debating whether to have a cup of tea here or go home and have it there when she heard a loud banging on the surgery's front door.

A last-minute emergency?

She hurried through, switching on the lights as she

went, and stopped when she saw who was on the other side of the door.

Dr Jones.

Oh.

Her pause was barely noticeable. At least she hoped so. Then she was rushing to the door, her cheeks flaming at having to let in the dishy doc. Though, judging by the look of worry on his face, he wasn't here to continue his conversation about warm milk.

She opened the door and Dr Jones came in, carrying a pet carrier. Behind him, a little uncertainly, followed a little girl with chestnut-brown hair in two ponytails held by pink bobbles, her face tearstained, pale and stunned. Seeing the little girl, so like Olivia—*no, so like her father*—startled her and her stomach twisted painfully. As if she'd been punched in the gut.

She dragged her gaze away from the little girl and looked over at the doctor. 'Dr Jones? Can I help?'

Am I stammering? I feel like I'm stammering.

'My daughter's rabbit. I think it's been attacked.'

He lifted up the carrier, so she could see through the barred door, but it was impossible to gauge the extent of the animal's injuries.

Sydney glanced quickly at the little girl. She looked around Olivia's age. Maybe a bit older. She wasn't sure. But she was young, and she didn't need to see Sydney examining the rabbit if it was in a bad way. There were a lot of foxes out here in Silverdale Village. It was a very rural area, surrounded by farms and woodlands. Occasionally they even saw deer. The likelihood that there were animal predators around was very high.

All business now, she took the carrier from the doctor. 'Maybe your daughter should sit in the waiting room whilst I take a look?'

The little girl slipped her tiny hand into her father's. 'Don't leave me, Daddy.'

Dr Jones looked torn, but then he nodded. 'I'll sit with you.' He looked up at Sydney. 'Is that okay? If I sit out here with Anna?'

Anna. A lovely name.

'Of course. I'll just take a quick look.'

She hurried the rabbit through to the surgery, closing the door behind her and leaning back against it for a moment whilst she gathered herself.

That's Anna. Anna! Not Olivia.

The table where she usually examined pets had already been cleaned down, so she laid the carrier upon it and opened it up.

Inside was a very scared, very shocked black rabbit. From what she could see at this stage it had injuries to the top of its head, its left eye looked damaged, and there were other fine puncture marks across its back and legs. Sydney held it gently whilst she checked it over. The ears looked okay, as did its throat, and it seemed to be breathing fine, if a little loudly. She listened to its chest through her stethoscope and tried to get a better look at the eye, but she couldn't tell if it was ruptured or not.

Poor thing.

She suspected it might die of shock. She felt for its pulse. It was slow and faint, but that was typical for an animal like this in such a situation. Its gums were pale, too and its ears cool.

There wasn't much she could do at this point. Technically, she couldn't see any *fatal* injuries. The shock itself might be the killer here. All she could do at the moment was give the rabbit a painkilling injection and some antibiotics. But she'd need to check with Dr Jones first, in case they requested euthanasia.

Sydney put the rabbit back into the carrier and secured it, then headed to the waiting room, her own heart thumping rapidly at the thought of returning to speak to him.

'Dr Jones?'

He looked up when she called his name and then patted his daughter's hand and told her to stay in her seat before he came over to her and whispered in a low voice, 'How is she?'

Sydney also kept her voice low, not wanting to upset Anna. 'She's in a great deal of shock. Can you tell me what happened?'

He shrugged. 'We're not sure. I'd been at work all day and then went to pick Anna up from school. She found Lottie like that when we got back.'

She nodded. 'She has sustained a great deal of damage to her left eye, but it's hard to see at the moment whether the eyeball itself has been ruptured. If it has, we might have to remove it, but at this stage I think we need to see if she'll survive the night.'

Dr Jones let out a heavy sigh and glanced at his daughter. 'Do you think Lottie might die?'

'It's fifty-fifty. I can give her a painkiller and some antibiotics if you wish. The bite marks are quite small and thin, possibly caused by a cat or a fox. Their mouths are filled with bacteria, so the chance of infection is high. There aren't any fatal injuries, but shock can kill an animal like this. It's up to you what measures you'd like me to take.'

She left the implication hanging. Did he want to see if the rabbit survived? Or did he want her to put the rabbit to sleep?

Dr Jones thought for a moment. 'Lottie is Anna's world. She loves animals. If there aren't any fatal injuries I think I owe it to her to see if Lottie makes it through the night. She won't be in any pain?'

'There'll be some discomfort, but the painkillers should help her an awful lot. I'll give her the injections, but if you can take her home, keep her somewhere warm and safe where she won't be disturbed. Do you have an indoor cage?'

He shook his head. 'I don't.'

'A bathroom, then. It's the safest place—somewhere there aren't any cables or wires to chew.'

'Will she want to eat?'

'You must get her to try. When a rabbit goes into shock it sometimes stops eating, and it will just lead to further complications if her digestive system shuts down. Offer her all her favourites and try to get her to drink, too. I'll need to see her first thing in the morning. Can you bring her in then?'

'Before surgery, yes. About eight?'

She nodded. 'I'll be here.'

Sydney slipped back inside her room and administered the injections. She really hoped on their behalf that Lottie would survive, but the poor thing had been through a terrible ordeal.

Back in the waiting room, she handed the carrier to Dr Jones and then, hesitantly, after thinking twice about doing so, she knelt in front of Anna. She tried not to notice the way the little girl's eyes looked into hers with so much hope. The way tears had welled in her eyes.

'Stay nice and quiet for her. No loud noises. Lottie needs to rest. Can you help her do that?'

Anna nodded. 'Yes.'

'Good.' She stood up again, frighteningly taken in by the little girl's big blue eyes. So similar to Olivia's it was unsettling. How was it possible that this little girl should remind her so strongly of her own?

Backing away, she held open the door for them, eager for them to go. So she could breathe again.

'What do I owe you?' Dr Jones glanced over at the till.

'We'll sort it in the morning. Don't worry. And good luck.'

She watched them go and backed away from the door. They were a nice family, little Anna and her father. Was there a wife at home, waiting for news? It hadn't sounded like it. *He'd* been at work, *he'd* picked his daughter up from school. No mention of anyone else.

It doesn't matter. You're not interested in him anyway. Dr Jones is off limits!

So why was she thinking about him? Just because he was handsome? No. She wasn't that shallow. It must be because of the way she'd walked out on him that morning after her consultation. She'd been rude and had not apologised for it, either. She'd been defensive. Abrupt. Even though he had suggested the most ridiculous thing. And now she'd helped with their rabbit; that was all. They'd all had a shock and she knew how that felt. She wanted it to be easier for them.

Poor rabbit.

She hoped it was still alive in the morning.

Nathan had a sleepless night. It wasn't just because of the rabbit. Though he *was* worrying about getting up in the morning and finding her dead on the floor of the bathroom. If that happened then he wanted to deal with everything before Anna saw any of it. She shouldn't have to see that.

But, no. It was his own body that had kept him from sleeping.

Yesterday he'd tried to give advice on getting a good

night's sleep to Sydney and he felt a bit hypocritical. Yes, there were tried and tested methods—relaxation, a milky drink, a warm bath, checking you had a comfortable bed—but they didn't work for him, either.

The spasticity he suffered from his multiple sclerosis kept *him* awake at night.

It wasn't as bad as it was for some people, and he knew he was lucky that no one just looking at him could guess his condition. He liked it that way. Fought to keep it so. But that didn't stop the damned stiffness that never seemed to go away. Sometimes he would lie there, trying to relax, and he would feel his muscles tightening so hard it almost felt like a vice. Then he would have to rub at his arm or his leg and hope that it would go away. It never did. And he knew it wouldn't. But that didn't stop him from trying.

So he'd spent the night alternately staring at the ceiling and getting up to check that the rabbit was still breathing.

At five a.m. he crawled out of bed, ready for a cup of tea, and checked on Lottie once more.

She's still alive. Thank goodness!

He gave her some dandelion leaves from the back garden and happily watched as she chewed them down, Her appetite was still good. Then he tried to pipette some water into her mouth—which she didn't like—so he decided to leave her a small bowl to drink from instead.

Anna was thrilled when she woke to find Lottie moving about in the bathroom. The rabbit's left eye still looked pretty mangled, though, and Anna was keen for the time to pass so she could go to the vet with her dad before school.

'You won't be at the vet, Anna. I'm dropping you at breakfast club, as normal.'

'But, Daddy, I want to go! Please?'

'No, Anna. I'm sorry.'

It was important that she kept to her routine. He hated changing things in Anna's life. And, though the incident with Lottie was out of the ordinary, it didn't mean that Anna's life had to be disturbed. It had changed enough already. Her mother had walked out on them both, not to mention that he had his diagnosis to deal with. Life for Anna would change dramatically at some point, if his condition worsened. Best to keep things as normal as he could, for however long he could. He would not have her upset unnecessarily.

Anna pouted for a bit, but got in the car happily and whispered good things to Lottie through the carrier door as he drove. 'You'll be okay, Lottie. The vet will take good care of you.'

With his daughter at breakfast club, Nathan drove to work, parked, and then walked across the road to the veterinary surgery with Lottie in her carrier once more. He was kind of proud of his daughter's little rabbit. Getting through a severe trauma and surviving. It was like finding a kindred spirit, and after getting up all night to check on her he felt he was bonding with her. And though last night he'd almost expected to have to tell Sydney to put Lottie to sleep, the fact that she'd lived... Well, he was kind of rooting for her now.

He was looking forward to seeing Sydney's reaction. She was an intriguing woman, and he was keen for her to see that the rabbit was still alive and find out her plan of action. But picturing the look of surprise on her face, or even trying to imagine what her smile might be like, was doing surprising and disturbing things to his insides. Things he didn't want to examine too closely for fear of what they might mean.

The bell above the door rang as he walked through,

clutching the carrier, and he headed over to the reception desk, where a veterinary nurse sat.

'Lottie Jones to see Sydney, please.'

'Ah, yes. Please take a seat—you'll be called through in a moment.'

He sat and waited, his nerves strangely on edge. For the rabbit? For himself? For seeing Sydney again? Last night when he'd lain awake he'd thought about her a great deal. She was very beautiful, and totally out of his league, but...she intrigued him. For all that she'd been through—the loss of her daughter—she seemed surprisingly together. A little terse, maybe, but professional and she clearly cared for her animal charges.

What made her tick? What kept her going? Her bravery in the face of immense tragedy was a very positive force, and he liked to surround himself with positive people. He needed that; he tried to stay positive himself. Perhaps just by knowing her a little bit better he might learn her secret? If she ever forgave him for what he'd said. She was a strong woman. Determined. He could see that. The complete antithesis of Gwyneth.

He shook his head as he thought of his thoughtless advice to her. *Warm milk?*

So busy was he, feeling embarrassed for what he'd said, that he wasn't ready when she opened her surgery door and called his name. 'Dr Jones?'

He looked up, startled. Today, her long brown hair was taken up into a messy ponytail. There were little wavy bits hanging free around her face, and even without make-up she looked amazing. He quickly cursed himself for noticing.

He got up, loudly cleared his throat and took the carrier through to her consulting room, determined to be distant and professional.

'She's still with us. Lottie survived the night.'

He placed the carrier onto her examination table and stood quite far back, as if the physical distance would somehow stop him stealing glances at her.

Her eyebrows rose in surprise. 'Okay. Let's have a look at her.'

He watched as Sydney's very fine hands opened the carrier and she gave Lottie a thorough assessment, listening to her chest and abdomen with her stethoscope, taking the rabbit's temperature, checking the bites and scratches and finally examining the wounded eye.

He tried not to take notice of the small beauty mark on Sydney's bared neck, her delicate cheekbones, or the way she bit her bottom lip as she concentrated. She had a very fine mouth. With full, soft-looking lips.

Dragging his eyes away from her mouth, he stared hard at Lottie. *Focus on the rabbit!*

'It's impossible for me to see if the eyeball itself has ruptured. The damage is too extensive. But until the swelling goes down I don't think we should assume that it has. I'm going to prescribe antibiotic drops for her eye, more painkillers, and a drug to keep her digestive system working which is an oral medicine. Rabbits don't like receiving oral meds, so if you can put the medicine in a food that you know she will eat you can get it into her that way.'

He nodded, keeping his gaze fixed firmly on Lottie's thick black fur so that he didn't accidentally start staring into Sydney's soft grey eyes. 'Okay. How often does she need the meds?'

'The eye drops three times a day, the oral meds four times a day. Will you be able to do that?'

He thought about his work schedule. It would be tough.

But manageable. Perhaps if he kept Lottie in her carrier at work? In an unused room?

'I'll find a way.'

'I'll need to see her in about four days' time. The swelling should have gone down by then, we'll know if the antibiotics have worked, and I'll be able to see if the eye needs to be removed.'

He risked a glance at her wide almond-shaped eyes. 'She'd cope with that?'

'Not all rabbits do well with surgery, and if we do have to remove the eye then she could be susceptible to further infection. Keep it clean. Bathe it with cooled boiled water when you can—three or four times a day.'

'Like a proper patient.' He smiled and closed the door on the carrier once again. 'Thank you, Sydney, for seeing us last night. I appreciate that you were probably closed and your staff were ready to go home.'

She glanced away, her cheeks glowing slightly, before she began typing notes into her computer. 'It was no problem.'

He watched her where she stood by the computer. It was better with her further away and not looking at him. He could think more clearly. And he wanted to make things right between them. He hated it that she'd left his consulting room feeling stressed and angry. Hated it that he'd insulted her daughter's memory with a crass piece of advice.

'I'd like to thank you properly, if I may? We got off to a bad start the other day and... Well, we both live in this village. It'd be nice to know I've not upset the first person I got to properly meet. Would you join me for a coffee some time? I'd really appreciate the chance to apologise.'

What on *earth are you doing?*

The invitation had just come out. He cursed himself

silently, knowing she would refuse him, but, hell, he kind of wanted her to say *yes*. He couldn't just see her about rabbits and sleeping tablets. Part of him wanted to know more about her. About that strong side of her that kept her going in the cruel world that had taken her daughter. That inner strength of hers…

But he also got the feeling that if they were given the chance the two of them might become friends. It had been a long time since he'd sat down and just chatted with a woman who wasn't a patient, or some cashier in a shop, someone with whom he could pass the time of day.

'Oh, I don't know. I—' She tucked a stray strand of hair behind her ear and continued typing, her fingers tripping over one another on the keyboard, so that he could see she had to tap 'delete' a few times and go back, cursing silently.

He focused on her stumbling fingers. Tried not to imagine himself reaching for her hands and stilling them. 'Just coffee. I don't have an evil plan to try and seduce you, or anything.'

Shut up, you idiot. You're making it worse!

Now she looked at him, her hands frozen over the keys. Her cheeks red. Her pause was an agonising silence before her fingers leapt into life once more, finishing her notes before she turned to him and spoke.

'That's kind of you, but—'

'Just a chat. Anna and I don't really know anyone here, and—well, I'd really like to know you.' He smiled. 'As a friend.'

It could never be anything else. Despite the fact that she was the most beautiful creature he had ever seen. Despite the fact that he could see her pulse hammering away in her throat. That her skin looked so creamy and soft. That he wanted to lift that stray strand of hair from her face and…

'I—'

'No pressure. Not a date. Just…coffee.'

He realised he was rambling, but he was confused. *She* confused him. Made him feel like he was tripping over his own words even though he wasn't. Made him surprised at what came out of his own mouth.

He'd not reached out to a woman like this since Gwyneth had left. He'd tried to become accustomed to the fact that he would spend the rest of his life alone. That he would not parade a stream of women past Anna. That he would not endanger his heart once again because on the one occasion he had given it to a woman she had ripped it apart.

The only female who would have his undying love was his daughter.

Which was as it should be.

Anna didn't need the huge change that a woman in their lives would bring. He was lucky that Gwyneth had left before Anna knew who she was or formed a bond.

But he missed being able just to sit with a woman and chat about everyday things. He missed asking about another person's day. He missed having adult company that didn't involve talks about unusual rashes, or a cough that wouldn't go away, or *could you just take a look at my boil?* And he imagined that Sydney would be interesting. Would have intelligent things to say and be the complete opposite of his ex-fiancée.

That was all he wanted.

All he *told* himself he wanted.

He waited for her to answer. Knowing she would turn him down, knowing it would hurt for some reason, but knowing that he'd had to ask because… Well, because he'd said something stupid to her the other day and he needed to apologise in the only way he knew how.

He waited.

Just a coffee?

Was there really such a thing as 'just a coffee' when a guy asked you out?

Because that was what he was doing. Asking her out. Like on a date. Right? And though he said there was no pressure, there was *always* pressure. Wasn't there?

Besides, why would she want to meet him for a drink? For a chat? This was the man who had got her so riled up yesterday, what with his probing questions and his damned twinkling eyes.

Did he not know how attractive he was? Because he seemed oblivious to it. Either that or he was a great actor. With great hair, and an irresistible charm about him, and the way he was looking at her right now... It was doing unbelievable things to her insides. Churning her up, making her stomach seem all giddy, causing her heart to thump and her mouth to go dry. She hadn't felt this way since her schoolgirl crush had asked her to the local disco. And her hands were trembling. *Trembling!*

Why had he asked her out? Why did he want to go for coffee? She had nothing to talk to him about. She didn't know this guy. Except that he was a hot doctor with effortlessly cool hair and eyes that melted her insides every time he smiled at her. Oh, and that he had a daughter. A beautiful little girl who seemed very lovely indeed, but who made her feel uncomfortable because she reminded her too much of Olivia.

If he wanted to apologise to her then why didn't he just do it? It wouldn't take a moment. No need for them to go to a coffee shop. He could say it here. Now. Then she could thank him, and then he could go, and it would all be over.

Why would she get any kind of involved with this man? He was dangerous in so many ways. Intelligent, good-looking, attractive. Not to mention his adorable daughter… She pushed the thought away. *No.*

She wanted to say, *We have nothing to talk about.* She wanted to say, *But there's no point.* She wanted to yell, *You're so perfect you look airbrushed. And I can't have coffee with you because you make me feel things that I don't want to feel and think of things I sure as hell don't want to think about!*

But she said none of those things. Instead she found herself mumbling, 'That'd be great.' Her voice almost gave out on that last word. Squeaking out of her closed throat so tightly she wondered if only dogs would have been able to hear it.

Oh, no, did I just agree to meet him?

The goofy smile he gave her in return made her temperature rise by a significant amount of degrees, and when he said goodbye and left the room she had to stand for a minute and fan her face with a piece of paper. She berated herself inwardly for having accepted. She would have to turn him down. Maybe call the surgery and leave a message for him.

This was a mistake.

A big mistake.

Nathan waited for his computer system to load up, and whilst he did he sat in his chair, staring into space and wondering just what the hell he had done.

Sydney Harper had said yes to his coffee invitation. *Yes!*

It was unbelievable. There must have been some

spike, some surge in the impulse centre of his brain that had caused his mind to short circuit or something. His leg muscles would sometimes spasm and kick out suddenly—the same must have happened with his head. And his mouth.

He had no doubt that they would get on okay. She would show up—a little late, maybe—pretend that she couldn't stay for long, have some excuse to leave sooner than she'd expected. Maybe even get a friend to call her away on an invented emergency. But...they'd get on okay. He'd apologise right away for what he'd said. Be polite as could be.

Surely it was a good thing to try and make friends when you moved to a new area? That was all he was doing.

And how many guys have you invited for coffee?

The only people he really knew in Silverdale were Dr Preston, some of the staff at the medical centre and his daughter's teacher at school, and they were more colleagues than actual friends. He'd left all his old friends behind when he'd moved from the city to this remote village. They kept in touch online. With the odd phone call and promises to meet up.

Sydney could be a *new* friend. A female friend. That was possible. How could it *not* be in today's modern age? And once he got past her prickly demeanour, made her realise he was sorry and showed her that he was no threat to her romantically, then they could both relax and they would get on like a house on fire.

He had no doubt of that.

So why, when he thought of spending time with Sydney, did he picture them kissing? Think of himself reaching for her hand across the table and lifting it to his lips while he stared deeply into her eyes. Inhaling the scent of her perfume upon her wrist…

And why did that vision remind him of Gwyneth's twisted face and her harsh words?

'I can't be with you! Why would anyone *want to be with you? You're broken. Faulty. The only thing you can offer is a lifetime of pain and despair and I didn't sign up for that!'*

Determined not to be haunted by his ex-fiancée's words, he angrily punched the keys on his keyboard, brought up his files and called in his first patient of the day.

Sam Carter was a thirty-two-year-old man who had just received a diagnosis of Huntington's Disease. His own father had died from it quite young, in his fifties, and the diagnosis had been a terrible shock to the whole family after Sam had decided to have genetic testing. Now he sat in front of Nathan, looking pale and washed out.

'What can I do for you, Sam?'

His patient let out a heavy sigh. 'I dunno. I just… need to talk to someone, I guess. Things are bad. At home. Suddenly everything in my life is about my diagnosis, and Jenny, my wife… Well…we'd been thinking about starting a family and now we don't know what to do and…'

Nathan could see Sam's eyes reddening as he fought back tears. Could hear the tremor in his patient's voice. He understood. Receiving a diagnosis for something such as Huntington's was very stressful. It changed everything. The present. The future. His own diagnosis of multiple sclerosis had changed *his* life. And Anna's. It had been the final axe to fall on his farce of a relationship.

'What did your consultant say?'

Sam sniffed. 'I can't remember. Once he said the

words—that I had Huntington's—I didn't really hear the rest. I was in shock… He gave us leaflets to take home and read. Gave us some websites and telephone numbers of people who could help, but…' He looked up at Nathan and met his eyes. 'We wanted to start a *family!* We wanted babies! And now… Now we don't know if we should. Huntington's is a terrible disease, and I'm not sure I want to pass that on to my children.'

Nathan nodded. It was a difficult thing to advise upon as a general practitioner. He didn't have a Huntington's specialty. He didn't want to give Sam the wrong advice.

'I hear what you're saying, Sam. It's a difficult situation and one that you and your wife must come to an agreement about together. I'm sure your consultant could discuss giving you two genetic counselling. A counsellor would be able to advise you better about the possibility of passing Huntington's to your children and what your options might be in terms of family planning. Have you got another appointment scheduled with your consultant soon?'

'In a month.'

'Good. Maybe use the time in between then and now to think of what questions you want to ask him. Just because you have Huntington's, and your father did too, it does not mean that any children you and Jenny have, will develop it. It's a fifty per cent chance.'

'They could be carriers, though.'

'That's a possibility, yes. Your consultant will be much better placed to talk this over with you, but if I'm right CVS—chorionic villus sampling—can be used to gain some foetal genetic material and test for the disease. And I believe there's also a blood test that can be performed on Jenny to check the cell-free foetal DNA, and that would carry no risk of miscarriage. How are you coping on a day-to-day level?'

'Fine, I guess. I have a chorea in my hand sometimes.' A chorea was a hand spasm. 'But that's all, so far.'

Nathan nodded. 'Okay. What about sleeping? Are you doing all right?'

'Not bad. I've lost some sleep, but I guess that's down to stress. My mind won't rest when I go to bed.'

'That's understandable. If it gets difficult then come and see me again and we'll look at what we can do.'

'How long do you think I've got, Dr Jones? My dad died young from this; I need to know.'

Nathan wanted to reassure him. Wanted to tell him that he would live a long life and that it would all be fine. But he couldn't know that. He had no idea how Sam's Huntington's would affect him. It affected each sufferer differently. Just like multiple sclerosis did.

'It's impossible to say. You've just got to take each day as it comes and live it the best you can. Then, when-ever the end does arrive, you'll know you lived your life to the fullest.'

Sam smiled. 'Is that *your* plan, Doc?'

Nathan smiled back. It certainly was. Living his life and trying to be happy was his number one aim. And he wanted the people around him to be happy too. The fact that he'd upset Sydney the way he had... Perhaps that was why he had asked her to coffee.

'It is.'

Sydney stared at her reflection in the mirror. 'What on earth am I doing?' she asked herself.

Her make-up was done to perfection. Her eyeliner gave a perfect sweep to the gentle curve of her eyelid. The blusher on her cheeks highlighted her cheekbones and her lipstick added a splash of colour, emphasising the fullness of her lips. Her eyelashes looked thicker and darker with a coating of mascara, making her grey eyes lighter and clearer. Her normally wavy hair had been tamed with the help of some styling spray, and the earrings in her ears dangled with the blue gems that had once belonged to her grandmother.

She looked completely different. Done up. Like a girl getting ready for a date. Like a girl who was hoping that something might happen with a special guy.

It's just coffee! Why have you put in this much effort? Is it for him?

Grabbing her facial wipes, she rubbed her face clean, angry at herself, until her skin was bare and slightly reddened by the force she'd used upon it. She stared back at her new reflection. Her normal reflection. The one she saw every day. The one bare of pretence, bare of cosmetics. Mask-free.

This is me.

She was *not* getting ready for a date! This was coffee. Just coffee. No strings attached. They were just two people meeting. Associates. She did *not* have to get all dressed up for a drink at The Tea-Total Café.

So she pulled the dress off over her head and put on her old jeans—the ones with the ripped knees—slipped on a white tee and then an oversized black fisherman's jumper and scooped her hair up into a scruffy bun, deliberately pulling bits out to give a casual effect. Then she grabbed her bag, thick coat and scarf and headed out, figuring that she'd walk there. It wasn't far. The wind might blow her hair around a bit more. She would *not* make any effort for Dr Jones.

Striding through the village, she hoped she looked confident, because she wasn't feeling it. She had more nerves in her stomach now than she'd had taking her driving test or her final exams. Her legs were weak and her nerves felt as taut as piano strings.

It was all Dr Jones's fault—that charming smile, those glinting blue eyes, that dark chestnut hair, perfectly tousled, just messy enough to make it look as if he hadn't touched it since rolling out of bed.

She swallowed hard, trying *not* to think of Dr Jones in bed. But Sydney could picture him perfectly…a white sheet just covering his modesty, his naked body, toned and virile as he gazed at her with a daring smile…beckoning her back beneath the sheets…

Stop. It.

She checked her mobile phone. Had the surgery been in touch? A last-minute patient? An emergency surgery, maybe? Something that would force her to attend work so she didn't have to go? But, no. Her phone was annoyingly clear of any recent messages or texts. She was almost tempted to call the surgery and just check that things were okay—make sure no cows on the nearby farms were about to calve. Right now she'd be much happier standing in a swamp of mud or manure with her arm in a cow's insides. Instead she was *here*.

She stood for a moment before she entered, psyching herself up.

The bell above the door rang as she went inside and she was met by a wall of heat and the aroma of freshly brewed coffee and pastries. Praying he wouldn't be there, she glanced around, ready to flash a smile of apology to the staff behind the counter before she ducked straight out again—but there he was. Dashing and handsome and tieless, dressed in a smart grey suit, the whiteness of his shirt showing the gentle tan of his skin.

He stood up, smiling, and raised a hand in greeting. 'Sydney. You made it.'

Nervous, she smiled back.

Dr Jones pulled a chair out for her and waited for her to sit before he spoke again. 'I wasn't sure what you'd like. What can I get you?'

He seemed nervous.

'Er...just tea will be fine.'

'Milk and sugar?'

She nodded, and watched as he made his way over to the counter to place her order. He looked good standing there. Tall, broad-shouldered. Sydney noticed the other women in the café checking him out. Checking *her* out and wondering why she might be with him.

You can have him, ladies, don't worry. There's nothing going on here.

He came back moments later with a tray that held their drinks and a plate of millionaire's shortbread.

She was surprised. 'Oh. They're one of my favourites.'

He looked pleased. 'Mine too. Help yourself.'

She focused on making her tea for a moment. Stirring the pot. Pouring the tea. Adding sugar. Adding milk. Stirring for a while longer. Stopping her hand from shaking. Then she took a sip, not sure what she was supposed to be talking about. She'd been quite rude to this man. Angry with him. Abrupt. Although, to be fair, she felt she'd had reason to be that way.

'So, how long have you lived in Silverdale?' he asked.

I can answer that.

'All my life. I grew up here. Went to the local schools. I left to go to university, but came back after I was qualified.'

She kept her answer short. Brief. To the point. She

wasn't going to expand this. She just wanted to hear what he had to say and then she would be gone.

'And you now run your own business? Did you start it from scratch?'

'It was my father's business. He was a vet, too.'

'Does he still live locally?'

'No. My parents moved away to be closer to the coast. They always wanted to live by the sea when they retired.'

She paused to take another sip of tea, then realised it would be even more rude of her if she didn't ask *him* a question.

'What made you come to live in Silverdale?'

'I grew up in a village. Loved it. Like you, I left for university, to do my medical training, and then after Anna was born I decided to look for a country posting, so that Anna could have the same sort of childhood I had.'

She nodded, but knew he was glossing over a lot. Where was Anna's mother? What had happened? Anna wasn't a baby any more. She was five years old, maybe six. Was this his first country posting?

Who am I kidding? I don't need to know.

Sydney gave him a polite smile and nibbled at one of the shortbreads.

'My name's Nathan, by the way.'

Nathan. A good name. Kind. She looked him up and down, from his tousled hair to his dark clean shoes. 'It suits you.'

'Thanks. I like *your* name, too.'

The compliment coupled with the eye contact was suddenly very intense and she looked away, feeling heat in her cheeks. Was it embarrassment? Was it the heat from the café's ovens and the hot tea? She wasn't sure. Her heart was beginning to pound, and she had a desperate desire to start running, but she couldn't do that.

Nor could she pretend that she was relaxed. She didn't want to be here. She'd said yes because he'd put her on the spot. Because she hadn't been able to say no. Best just to let him know and then she could go.

She leaned forward, planting her elbows on the desk and crossing her arms in a defensive posture.

'You know…this isn't right. *This*. Meeting in a coffee shop. With you. I've been through a lot and you…' she laughed nervously '…you make me *extremely* uncomfortable. When I met you yesterday, in your surgery, I was already on edge. You might have noticed that. What with your doctor's degree and your—' she looked up '—your incredible blue eyes which, quite frankly, are ridiculously much too twinkly and charming.'

She stood, grabbing her bag and slinging it over her shoulder.

'I'm happy to help you with your daughter's rabbit, and I'll be the consummate professional where that poor animal is concerned, but *this*?' She shook her head. 'This I cannot do!'

She searched in her bag to find her purse. To lay some money on the table to pay for her tea and biscuit. Then she could get out of this place and back to work. To where she felt comfortable and in control. But before she could find her purse she became aware that Nathan had stood up next to her and leaned in, enveloping her in his gorgeous scent.

'I'm sorry.'

Standing this close, with his face so near to hers, his understanding tone, his non-threatening manner, his apology… There was nothing else she could do but look into his eyes, which were a breathtaking blue up close, flecked with tones of green.

She took a step back from his gorgeous proximity. 'For what?'

'For what I said to you. In our consultation. My remark was not intended to insult you, or the memory of your daughter, by suggesting that you could get over it with the help of...' he swallowed '...warm milk. But you were my first patient, and I knew you were in a rush, and I got flustered and...' His voice trailed off as he stared into her eyes.

Sydney quickly looked away, aware that the other customers in the café might be watching them, sensing the tension, wondering what was going on.

'Sydney?'

She bit her lip, her cheeks flushing, before she turned back to meet his gaze. 'Yes?'

'I promised this was just coffee. We've had tea and shortbread which may have changed things slightly, but not greatly. So please don't go. We're just drinking tea and chomping on shortbread. Please relax. I'm not going to jump your bones.'

'Right.' She stared at him uncertainly, imagining him *actually* jumping her bones, but that was too intense an image so, giving in, she sank back into her seat and broke off a piece of shortbread and ate it.

Her cheeks were on fire. This was embarrassing. She'd reacted oddly when all he'd expected was a drink with a normal, sane adult.

She glanced up. He was smiling at her. She hadn't blown it with her crazy moment. By releasing the steam from the pressure cooker that had been her brain. He was still okay with her. It was all still okay. He wasn't about to commit her to an asylum.

'I'm out of practice with this,' she added, trying to explain her odd behaviour. 'Could you please pretend that you're having tea with a woman who behaves normally?'

He picked up his drink and smiled, his eyes twinkling with amusement. 'I'll try.'

She stared back, uncertain, and then she smiled too. She hadn't scared him off with her mini-rant—although she supposed that was because he was a doctor, and doctors knew how to listen when people ranted, or nervously skirted around the main issue they wanted to talk about. Nathan seemed like a good guy. One who deserved a good friend. And good friends admitted when they were wrong.

'I'm sorry for walking out on you like that yesterday.'

'It's not a problem.'

'It is. I was rude to you because I was unsettled. I thought you were going to ask questions that I wasn't ready to answer and I just wanted to get out of there.'

'Why?'

'Because you made me nervous.'

'Doctors make a lot of people nervous. It's called White Coat Syndrome.'

She managed a weak smile. 'It wasn't your white coat. You didn't have one.'

'No.'

'It was you. *You* made me nervous.'

He simply looked at her and smiled. He was understanding. Sympathetic. Kind. All the qualities she'd look for in a friend.

But he was also drop-dead gorgeous.

And she wasn't sure she could handle *that*.

CHAPTER THREE

HE WAS SITTING there trying to listen to Sydney, hearing her telling stories of veterinary school and some of the cases she'd worked on, but all he could think about as he sat opposite her was that she was so very beautiful and seemed completely unaware of it.

It was there even in the way she sat. The way she held her teacup—not using the handle but wrapping her hands around the whole cup, as if it was keeping her warm. The way her whole face lit up when she laughed, which he was beginning to understand was rare. He'd wondered what she would look like when she smiled and now he knew. It was so worth waiting for. Her whole face became animated, unburdened by her past. It was lighter. Purer. Joyous. And infectious. Dangerously so.

And those eyes of hers! The softest of greys, like ash.

He was unnerved. He really had just wanted to meet her for this drink and clear the air after yesterday's abrupt meeting in his surgery. And to thank her for helping Lottie after her attack. But something else was happening. He was being sucked in. Hypnotised by her. Listening to her stories, listening to her talk. He liked the sound of her voice. Her gentle tone.

He was trying—*so hard*—to keep reminding himself that this woman was just going to be a friend.

Sydney worked hard. Very hard. All her tales were of work. Of animals. Of surgeries. She'd not mentioned her daughter once and he knew *he* couldn't. Not unless she brought up the subject first. If she wanted to share that with him then it had to be *her* choice.

He understood that right now Sydney needed to keep the conversation light. This was a new thing for her. This blossoming friendship. She was like a tiny bird that was trying its hardest not to be frightened off by the large tom cat sitting watching it.

'Sounds as if you work very hard.'

She smiled, and once again his blood stirred. 'Thank you. I do. But I enjoy it. Animals give you so much. Without agenda. Unconditionally.'

'Do you have pets yourself? It must be hard not to take home all the cases that pull at your heart strings.'

'I have a cat. Just one. She's ten now. But she's very independent—like me. Magic does her own thing, and when we both get home after a long day she either curls up on my lap or in my bed.'

Her face lit up as she spoke of Magic, but she blushed as she realised she'd referenced her bed to him.

A vision crossed his mind. That long dark hair of hers spread out over a pillow. Those almond-shaped smoky eyes looking at him, relaxed and inviting, as she lay tangled in a pure white sheet...

But he pushed the thought away. As lovely as Sydney was, he couldn't go there. This was friendship. Nothing else. He had Anna to think about. And his health.

He had no idea for how long he would stay relatively unscathed by his condition. His MS had been classified as 'relapsing remitting multiple sclerosis'. Which meant that he would have clear attacks of his symptoms, which would slowly get better and go away completely—until the next attack. But he knew that as the disease progressed his symptoms might not go away at all. They would linger. Stay. Get worse with each new attack, possibly leaving him disabled. But he was holding on to the thought that it wouldn't happen soon. That he would stay in relative good health for a long time.

But he could not, in any good conscience, put anyone else through that. Who deserved that?

And he had a child to think about. A child who had already lost her mother because of him. Who did not know what it was like to have that kind of female influence in her life. Bringing someone home would be a shock to Anna. It might upset her. It might bring up all those questions about having a mother again.

Sydney Harper was just going to be his *friend*.

That was all.

He smiled as she talked, trying not to focus all of his attention on her mouth, and pushed thoughts of what it would be like to kiss her completely out of his head.

Later, he offered to walk her back to work.

'Oh, that's not necessary. You don't have to do that,' she protested.

'I might as well. I'm heading that way to pick up my pager as I'm on call tonight.'

She nodded her reluctant acceptance and swung her bag over her shoulder. Together they exited into the street.

It was a cold November day. With blue skies, just a few wispy white clouds and a chill in the air when they moved into the shade and lost the sun.

They walked along together, respectfully a few inches apart. But she was *so* aware of him and trying her hardest not to be.

Nathan Jones was delicious. Of course she was physically attracted to him. Who wouldn't be? Aside from his good looks, this man was intelligent. A good listener. Not at all judgemental. He'd seemed really interested in her. He'd asked questions without being too probing and really paid attention to her answers.

She was very much aware that although they had just spent an hour in each other's company she still didn't know much about him. They'd both edged around serious subjects. They'd both avoided talk of past traumas and upsets. And they'd both kept everything light. Unthreatening. No mention of the baggage that each of them had to be carrying.

She liked that about him. It was as if he knew what she needed.

She frowned, spotting someone from the local council up a ladder, arranging the Christmas lights. 'It gets earlier and earlier each year.'

Nathan nodded. 'I love Christmas.'

She certainly didn't want to talk to him about *that*!

She changed the subject. 'Do you know your way around Silverdale yet?' she asked him, aware that the village had many tiny roads, closes and cul-de-sacs. And now, with the new build of over two hundred new homes on the edge of Silverdale, a lot of new roads had popped up that even *she* was unfamiliar with.

'Not really. But the GPS system in the car helps.'

'If you ever need help finding your way I could help you out. I know most places. Just pop in and ask at the desk.'

He looked at her. 'Thanks. If I ever get a call-out to the middle of nowhere I'll be sure to call in and pick you up first.'

Sydney glanced at him quickly, then looked away. That

was a joke, surely? She'd meant that he could call in to her *work* and ask whoever was on Reception.

She felt his gaze upon her then, and she flushed with heat as they came to a stop outside her veterinary practice.

'Well, thank you for the tea. And the shortbread.'

'It was my pleasure.'

'I'll see you at the end of the week? When you bring in Lottie again?' she added.

The rabbit was due another check-up, so she could look at its eye and see if it needed removing or not.

'Hopefully I'll see you before that.'

Her heart pounded in her chest. What did he mean? 'Why?'

'Because we're friends now, and friends see each other any time—not just at preordained appointments.' He smiled and held out his hand.

She blushed. 'Of course.'

She took his hand in hers and tried to give him a firm handshake, but she couldn't. All she could think of was that he was touching her. And she him! And that his hand felt warm and strong. Protective. It felt good, and she briefly imagined what it might feel like if he pulled her into his arms and pressed her against his chest.

He let go, and when he did she felt an odd sense of disappointment.

Now, why am I feeling that?

She stared back at him, unsure of how to say goodbye to this new friend. Should she give a small wave and go inside? Should they just say goodbye and walk away? Or should there be some sort of kiss on the cheek?

But if I kissed him and liked it...

'Well...maybe I'll see you later, then?'

He nodded. 'Yes.'

'Right. Bye.'

'Goodbye, Sydney.'

And then, with some hesitation, he leaned in and kissed the side of her face.

She sucked in a breath. His lips had only brushed her cheek, and were gone again before she could truly appreciate it, but for the millisecond he'd made contact her body had almost imploded. Her heart had threatened to jump out of her chest. Her face must have looked as red as a stop sign.

She watched him turn and walk across the road to his place of work and she stood there, breathing heavily, her fingers pressed to her face where his lips had been, and wondered what the hell she was doing.

With this *friendship* with Dr Nathan Jones.

Technically, they hadn't done *anything*. Just shared a pot of tea. A plate of shortbread. A quick chat and a walk to work.

But all she could think of was how he'd looked when he'd smiled at her. His beautiful blue eyes. The way he'd listened, the way he'd filled the space of the cafeteria chair, all relaxed and male and virile. How attracted she was to him physically. How his lips had felt...and how frightened that made her feel.

Sydney turned and went into her own place of work.

She needed to cool down.

In more ways than one.

And she needed to stay away from Dr Nathan Jones. He was going to be trouble.

The kiss had been an impulse. To fill an awkward pause. It was just what he did when he left female friends or relatives. He kissed them goodbye.

It didn't *mean* anything. The fact that he'd breathed in

her scent as he'd leaned in...the fact that his lips had felt scorched the second they'd touched her soft cheek...the fact that he'd got a shot of adrenaline powerful enough to launch an armada meant nothing.

Did it?

It was just that it was something new. A new friendship. The fact that she was the most stunningly beautiful woman he'd met in a long time had nothing to do with it. He felt for her. She'd been through a trauma. The loss of a daughter was something he simply couldn't imagine. The fact that she was still standing, smiling and talking to people was a miracle, quite frankly. He couldn't picture going through that and having the power or strength to carry on afterwards. And she was so nice! Easy to talk to. Friendly once you got past that prickly exterior she'd erected. But he could understand why that was there.

What he felt for her was protective. That was all. And didn't friends look out for one another?

Crossing the road, he called in to the surgery and picked up his pager for the evening, along with a list of house calls that needed to be completed before he had to pick up Anna at three-thirty. He had a good few hours' worth of work ahead of him, but he was distracted.

A simple coffee had been something else.

And he was afraid to admit to himself just what it had been.

Sydney sat hunched up on her couch, clutching a mug of cold tea and worrying at a loose bit of skin on her lip. Behind her head lay Magic the cat, asleep on the back of the couch, her long black tail twitching with dreams. The house was silent except for the ticking of the clock in the hallway, and Sydney's gaze was upon the picture of her daughter in the centre of the mantelpiece.

In the picture Olivia was laughing, smiling, her little hands reaching up to catch all the bubbles that her mum was blowing through a bubble wand.

She could remember that day perfectly. It had been during the summer holiday before Olivia was due to start school and it had been a Sunday. Alastair—Sydney's husband and Olivia's father—had gone to the supermarket to do a food-shop and Sydney and Olivia had been playing in the back garden. Her daughter had been so happy. Chasing bubbles, giggling. Gasping when Sydney made a particularly large one that had floated up higher and higher until it had popped, spraying them with wetness. She'd been chasing down and splatting the smaller ones that she could reach.

'Mummy, look!' she'd said when she'd found a bubble or two resting on her clothes.

Sydney remembered the awe and excitement in her daughter's eyes. They'd been happy times. When they'd all believed that life for them was perfect. That nothing could spoil it. Olivia had been about to start infant school; Sydney had been going back to work full-time. It had been their last summer together. The last summer they'd enjoyed.

Before it had all changed. Before it had all gone dreadfully wrong.

Why did I not listen when she told me she had a headache?

She tried to keep on remembering that summer day. The sound of her daughter's deep-throated chuckles, the smile on her face. But she couldn't.

Every time she allowed herself to think of Olivia her thoughts kept dragging her back to that morning when she'd found her unconscious in her bed. To the deadly silence of the room except for her daughter's soft, yet ragged breaths. To the dread and the sickness in her stomach as she'd realised that something was desperately, deeply wrong. That her daughter wouldn't wake up no matter how much Sydney called her name. To the moment when she'd unzipped her onesie to see *that rash*.

If Olivia had lived—if meningitis had not got its sneaky grasp on her beautiful, precious child—then she would have been nine years old now. In junior school. There'd be school pictures on the mantel. Pictures that showed progress. Life. But her pictures had been frozen in time. There would be no more pictures of Olivia appearing on the walls. No more videos on her phone. No paintings on her fridge.

And I could have prevented it all if only I'd paid more attention. Alastair was right. It was all my fault.

Sydney put down her mug and hugged her knees. The anniversary of Olivia's death was getting closer. It was a day she dreaded, that relentlessly came round every year, torturing her with thoughts of what she might have done differently. Tonight she would not be able to sleep. At all.

I can't just sit here and go through that insomnia again!

She got up off the couch and looked about her for something to do. Maybe declutter a cupboard or something? Deep-clean the kitchen? Go through her books and choose some for the bookstall at the Christmas market? Something… Anything but sit there and dwell on *what ifs*!

The doorbell rang, interrupting her agonising.

She froze, then felt a rush of relief.

Thank goodness! I don't care who you are, but I'm going to talk to you. Anything to get my mind off where it's going!

She opened the door.

Nathan!

'Oh. Hi.' She'd never expected him to turn up at her door. How did he know where she lived?

Nathan looked a little uncomfortable. Uncertain. 'I... er...apologise for just turning up at your house like this.'

'Is it Lottie?'

He shook his head and scratched at his chin, looking up and down the road. 'No. I've...er...got a call-out. Nothing urgent, but...'

She'd thought that what he'd said previously about calling in on her had been a joke. Had he actually meant it?

Spending more time with the delicious Nathan since that kiss on her cheek had seemed a bad idea. She'd made a firm decision to avoid him. And now here he was!

As if in answer to her unspoken question he looked sheepish as he said, 'I looked up your home address at work. Sorry. It's just... I tried to use my GPS, but it hasn't been updated for a while and it led me to a field, so... I need your help.'

He needed to find an address! She *had* offered to help him with that, and though she'd told herself—harshly— not to spend time alone with Nathan Jones again, she was now reconsidering it. After hours of feeling herself being pulled down a dark tunnel towards all those thoughts that tortured her on a nightly basis—well, right now she welcomed his interruption. What else would she be doing anyway?

Not sleeping. That was what. The damn pills he'd given her just didn't seem to be having the desired effect. Were they different from last year's? She couldn't remember.

Nathan though was the king of light and fluffy, and that was what she needed. Plus it would be interesting to see what he did at work. And she would be helping by telling him the way to go. Anything was better than sitting in this house for another night, staring at the walls, waiting for sleep to claim her.

'Sure. I'll just get my keys.'

She tried not to be amused by the look of shock on his face when she agreed. Instead she just grabbed her coat, locked up and headed out to his car—a beat-up four-wheel drive that, quite frankly, looked as if it deserved to be in a wrecker's yard. There were dents, one panel of the car was a completely different colour from the rest of it, and where it wasn't covered in rust it was covered in mud. Even the number-plate was half hanging off, looking as if it wanted to escape.

She looked at the vehicle uncertainly. 'Does that actually work?'

He smiled fondly at it. 'She's old, but she always starts. I promise it's clean on the inside.' He rubbed the back of his neck.

Sydney almost laughed. 'Don't worry. I've got a matching one over there.' She pointed at her own vehicle and saw him notice the dried sprays of mud—not just up the bodywork, but over the back windows too.

He smiled, relaxing a little. 'That makes me feel much better.'

Sydney smiled and got into his car. 'Where are we going?'

'Long Wood Road?'

She nodded. 'I know it. It's a couple of miles from here. Take this road out of the village and when you get to the junction at the end turn right.'

'Thanks.' He gunned the engine and began to drive.

Strangely, she felt lighter. More in control. And it felt great not to be sitting in her cottage, staring at those pictures.

'Who are you going to see?'

'Eleanor Briggs?'

'I know her. She has a Russian Blue cat called Misty.'

'I'm not seeing her about Misty. I'm afraid I can't say why. Patient confidentiality prohibits me sharing that with you.'

'That's okay.' She smiled as he began heading to the outskirts of Silverdale.

It felt good next to him. Comfortable. Was that because this was business? And because he was working?

The focus isn't on me. Or us. This is just one professional helping out another.

She'd never been comfortable with being the focus of people's attention. Even as a child she'd tried to hide when she was in the school choir, or a school play. Trying her hardest not to be given a main role, trying not to be noticed. At university, when she'd had to give a solo presentation on the dangers of diabetes in dogs, she'd almost passed out from having to stand at the front of the lecture hall and present to her lecturers and tutor. The *pressure!*

But here they were, stuck in a car together, music on the radio, and she was much more relaxed. This was much better than being stuck at home, staring at old pictures that broke her heart.

Glancing at him driving, she noticed he'd rolled up his sleeves and that his forearms were lightly tanned, and filled with muscle as he changed gear. A chunky sports watch enveloped his wrist. He had good arms. *Attractive* arms. She glanced away.

A song came on that she knew and quietly she began singing and bobbing her head to the music.

Nathan looked over at her. 'You like this?'

Sydney nodded and he turned up the sound. She began to sing louder as it got to the chorus, laughing suddenly as Nathan joined in. Out of tune and clearly tone deaf.

They began to drive down a country road.

Silverdale was Sydney's whole life. A small pocket of English countryside that she felt was all hers. The place where she'd hoped to raise her daughter. In its community atmosphere where everyone looked out for one another.

Pushing the thought to one side, she turned back to Nathan. He was concentrating on the road now that the song was over and the DJ was babbling, his brow slightly furrowed, both hands gripping the wheel.

'You need to take the next left. Long Woods Road.'

Nathan indicated, following the twists and turns of her directions, and soon she was pointing out Eleanor's small cottage. They turned into the driveway and parked in front of the house. Killing the engine, he turned to her. 'Thank you. I wouldn't have got here without you.'

'And I wouldn't have had my eardrums assaulted.'

He raised an eyebrow.

'Your singing.'

'I have a lovely voice. I'll have you know that when I was in my school choir I was the only child not selected to sing a solo.'

She smirked. 'You should be proud.'

'I am.'

Then he grinned and reached for his bag, which was down by her feet. She moved slightly, out of his way, as he lifted it up and past her.

He was smiling still. Looking at her. She watched as his gaze dropped to her mouth and instantly the atmosphere changed.

Sydney looked away, pretending that something out of the window had caught her eye.

'Will you be okay for a while? I can leave the radio on.'

She didn't look at him, but dug her phone from her

pocket. 'I've got my phone. I'm playing a word game against my veterinary nurse.'

Nathan said nothing, but got out of the car. Once he was gone, she suddenly felt *alone*. His presence had filled the car, and now that he was gone it seemed so empty. The only reminder a very faint aroma of cologne. She would never have thought that spending time with Nathan would be so easy, after their coffee together. But he'd been just what she needed tonight. Bad singing included.

In the sky above stars were beginning to filter through the dark, twinkling and shining. She looked for the biggest and brightest. Olivia's star. The one she had once pointed out to her daughter as her very own special light. Just remembering that night with her daughter made her eyes sting with unshed tears, but she blinked them away.

I can't keep crying. I've got to be stronger than this!

She switched on her phone and stared at the game she no longer wanted to play.

It was pitch-black along the country roads as they followed behind another four-wheel drive that was towing a horsebox. In the back, Sydney could see a large black horse, easily fifteen hands high. Was it the Daltons? They had a horse like that. Though she guessed it could be the Webbers' horse. They had one like it too. Or maybe it wasn't anyone she knew. She didn't get called out to *all* the horses in the Silverdale area. There was a specialised equine veterinary service in Norton Town. Sometimes she worked alongside it.

As they drove back along Long Wood Road, Sydney realised she was feeling more relaxed and happy than she had for a few weeks. It was strange. Perhaps it was a good thing not to be wallowing in her memories tonight.

Perhaps getting out and about and doing something was the right thing to do.

I need a hobby. An evening class. Something. Maybe it'll be better when we start those meetings for the Christmas market and fête.

What she knew for sure was that she had felt better when she'd seen Nathan returning to the car. Seen his smile. Felt his warmth. Knowing that he wasn't the type to pry into her past. He made her feel weirdly comfortable, despite the physical response she felt. It was something she hadn't felt for a long time, and she was really glad she'd agreed to come out with him and spend some more time with him.

She was just about to say something about it—thank him for earlier—when she spotted something, off to Nathan's right, illuminated by the lights of the vehicles. It was a small herd of deer, running across the field at full pelt.

'Nathan, look!' She pointed.

There had to be seven or eight. Mostly fully grown and running hard. The lead deer had full antlers, like tree branches.

And they were heading straight for the road.

'I think I'm going to slow down.'

But as Nathan slowed their vehicle it became clear that the vehicle in front, with the horse trailer, had continued on at a normal speed.

Sydney leaned forward. 'Have they not seen them? What can we do?'

Nathan hit his horn, hoping it would make the driver ahead pay attention, or at least startle the deer into heading in another direction, but neither happened.

The biggest deer burst through the undergrowth, leaping over the ditch and straight out onto the road—right in front of the other vehicle.

Sydney watched, horrified, and brake lights lit up her face as the car in front tried to swerve at the last minute, but failed. The horsebox at the back wobbled, bouncing from left to right with the weight of the horse inside, before it tipped over and pulled the car straight into the ditch. The rest of the deer leapt by, over the road and into the next field.

Nathan hit the brakes, stopping the car. 'Call for help.'

Her heart was pounding madly in her chest. 'What are you going to do?'

'I'm going to check for casualties. After you've contacted emergency services go into the boot of the car and find the reflective triangle and put it in the road. We're on a bend here, and we need to warn other traffic. We're sitting ducks.'

Then he grabbed his bag and was gone.

She watched him run over to the car through the light of the headlamps as she dialled 999 with shaking fingers. As she watched Nathan trying to talk to someone she saw the driver fall from the driver's side. Then her gaze fell upon the horse in the horsebox. It was moving. Alive.

I have to get out there!

But she had no equipment. No bag. No medicines. She felt helpless. Useless! She'd felt this way just once before.

I'll be damned if I feel that way again!

'Which service do you require?' A voice spoke down the phone.

'*All of them*. We need them all.'

CHAPTER FOUR

SYDNEY DASHED TO the boot of Nathan's car and panicked as she struggled to open it. At first she couldn't see the reflective triangle he'd mentioned—his boot was full of *stuff*. But she rummaged through, tossing things to one side, until she found it. Then she dashed to the bend in the road and placed it down, hoping that it would be enough of a warning to stop any other vehicles that came that way from running into them.

She ran over to the ditched car and horsebox, glancing quickly at the horse in the back. It was neighing and huffing, making an awful lot of noise, stamping its hooves, struggling to find a way to stand in a box that was on its side. She couldn't see if it had any injuries. She hoped not. But there wasn't much she could do for the horse anyhow. She needed to help Nathan and the people in the car.

She'd already seen the driver was out of the vehicle. He was sitting in the road, groaning and clutching at his head. He had a bleeding laceration across his brow, causing blood to dribble down his face and eyes.

Nathan was in the ditched vehicle, assessing whoever was in the front seat.

Sydney knelt down, saw the head wound was quite deep and pulled the scarf from around her neck and tied it around the guy's scalp. 'You need to come with me. Off the road. Come and sit over here.'

She pointed at the grass verge.

'I didn't see... I didn't notice... We were arguing...' the man mumbled.

He was in shock. Sydney grabbed the man under his armpits and hauled him to his feet. Normally she wouldn't move anyone after a car accident. She knew that much. But this man had already hauled himself out of the vehicle and dropped onto the road before Nathan got there. If he'd done any damage to himself, then it was already done. The least she could do was get him out of the middle of the road and to a safer zone.

The man was heavy and dazed, but he got to his feet and staggered with her to the roadside, where she lowered him down and told him to stay. 'Don't move. Try and stay still until the ambulance gets here. I've called for help—they're on their way.'

The man looked up at her. 'My wife...*my son*!'

He tried to get up again, but Sydney held him firmly in place. 'I'll go and help them, but you *must* stay here!'

The man looked helpless and nodded, trembling as he realised there was blood all over his hands.

Sydney ran back over to the ditched car, heard a child crying and noticed that Nathan was now in the back seat. He called to her over his shoulder.

'There's a baby. In a car seat. He looks okay, but I need to get him out of the vehicle so I can sit in the back and maintain C-spine for the mother.'

Sydney nodded and glanced at the woman in the front seat. She was unconscious, and her air bag had deployed and lay crumpled and used before her. There was no bleeding that she could see, but that didn't mean a serious injury had not occurred. If a casualty was unconscious, that usually meant shock or a head injury. She hoped it was just the former.

'I'm unclipping the seatbelt.'

Sydney heard a clunk, then Nathan was backing out, holding a car seat with an indignant, crying infant inside it, bawling away.

The baby couldn't be more than nine months old, and had beautiful fluffy blond hair. But his face was red with rage and tears, and his little feet in his sleep suit were kicking in time with his crying.

'Shh… It's okay. It's okay… I've got you.' Sydney took the heavy seat with care, cooing calming words as she walked back across the road to take him to his father.

In the distance she heard the faint, reassuring sound of sirens.

'Here. Your little boy. What's his name?' she asked the man, who smiled with great relief that his son seemed physically okay.

'Brandon.'

That was good. The man's bump to the head hadn't caused amnesia or anything like that. 'And your name…?'

'Paul.'

'Okay, Paul. You're safe. And Brandon's safe—he doesn't look injured—and that man helping your wife is a doctor. She's in good hands. He knows what he's doing.'

'Is she hurt? Is Helen hurt?'

Sydney debated about how much she should reveal—should she say that Helen was unconscious? Or stay optimistic and just tell him she was doing okay? The truth won out.

'I don't know. She's unconscious, but Nathan—that's Dr Jones—is with her in the car and he's looking after her. Do you hear those sirens? More help will be with us soon.'

The sirens were much louder now, and Sydney knew she was breathing faster. Hearing them get closer and closer just reminded her of that morning when she'd had to call an ambulance for Olivia. Wishing they'd get to her faster. Feeling that they were taking for ever. Praying that they would help her daughter. She could see the same look in Paul's eyes now. The distress. The *fear*.

But this was an occasion where she actually had her wits about her and could do something.

'I need to go and help Nathan.'

She ran back across the road. The car's radiator or something must have burst, because she could hear hissing and see steam rising up through the bonnet of the vehicle. She ducked into the open door.

Nathan was in the back seat, his hands clutching Helen's head, keeping it upright and still. His face was twisted, as if *he* was in pain.

'Is she breathing still?' he managed to ask her.

Is she *breathing?* Sydney wasn't sure she wanted to check—her own shock at what had happened was starting to take effect. What if Helen wasn't breathing? What if Helen's heart had stopped?

'I—'

'Watch her chest. Is there rise and fall?'

She checked. There was movement. 'Yes, there is!'

'Count how many breaths she takes in ten seconds.'

She looked back, counting. 'Two.'

'Okay. That's good.'

She saw Nathan wince. Perhaps he had cramp, or something? There was some broken glass in the car. Perhaps he'd knelt on it? She pushed the thought to the back of her mind as vehicles flashing red and blue lights appeared. An ambulance. A fire engine, and further behind them she could see a police car.

Thank you!

Sydney got out of the car and waved them down, feeling relief flood her.

A paramedic jumped out of the ambulance and came over to her, pulling on some purple gloves. 'Can you tell me what happened?'

She gave a brief rundown of the incident, and pointed out Paul and baby Brandon, then filled him in on the woman in the car.

'Okay, let's see to her first.' The paramedic called out to his partner to look after the driver and his son whilst he checked out Helen, still in the car with Nathan.

Sydney ran back over to Paul. 'Help's here! It's okay. We're okay.' She beamed, glad that the onus of responsibility was now being shouldered by lots of other people rather than just her and Nathan.

As she stood back and watched the rescue operation she realised there were tears on her face. She wiped them away with a sleeve, aware of how frightened she'd been, and waited for Nathan to join her, shivering. She wanted to be held. To feel safe. She wanted to be comforted.

The morning she'd found Olivia she'd been on her own. Alastair had already left for work. So there'd been no one to hold her and let her know it was okay. She'd needed arms around her then and she needed them now. But Alastair had never held her again.

If she asked him, Nathan would hold her for a moment. She just knew it. Sensed it. What they'd just experienced had been traumatic. But she remained silent, clutching her coat to her. She just stood and watched the emergency services get everything sorted.

And waited.

Nathan was needed by the paramedics, and then by

the police, and by the time he was free she was not. The horse needed her—needed checking over.

She told herself a hug wasn't important and focused on the practical.

Paul and Brandon had been taken to hospital in one ambulance; Helen had been extricated and taken away in another, finally conscious. The horsebox had been righted and the horse had been led out to be checked by Sydney. It had some knocks and scrapes to its legs, mostly around its fetlocks—which, in humans, was comparable to injuries to an ankle joint—but apart from that it just seemed startled more than anything.

They'd all been very lucky, and Sydney now stood, calming the horse, whilst they waited for an animal transporter to arrive.

Nathan stood watching her. 'That horse really feels safe with you.'

She smiled. 'Makes a change. Normally horses see me coming with my vet bag and start playing up. It's nice to be able to comfort one and calm it down.'

'You're doing brilliantly.'

She looked at him. He looked a little worn out. Wearied. As if attending to the patients in the crash had physically exhausted him. Perhaps he'd had a really long day. Just like being a vet, being a doctor had to be stressful at times. Seeing endless streams of people, each with their own problems. Having to break bad news. She knew how stressful it was for her to have to tell a customer that their beloved pet was dying, or had to be put to sleep. And when she *did* euthanise a beloved pet she often found herself shedding silent tears along with the owner. She couldn't help it.

Perhaps it was the same for Nathan. Did seeing people in distress upset him? Wear him out?

'*You* did brilliantly. Knowing what to do…who to treat. How to look after Helen. I wouldn't have thought to do that.' She stroked the horse's muzzle.

'It's nothing.'

'But it is. You probably saved her life, keeping her airway open like that. She could have died.'

'At least they're in safe hands now.'

She looked at him and met his gaze. 'They were *already* in safe hands.'

She needed to let him know that what he'd done today had *mattered*. Paul still had a wife. Brandon still had a mother. Because of *him*. A while ago she'd almost lost her faith in doctors. She'd depended on them to save Olivia, and when they'd told her there was nothing they could do…

At first she hadn't wanted to believe them. Had *raged* at them. Demanded they do *something*! When they hadn't she had collapsed in a heap, hating them—and everyone—with a passion she had never known was inside her. Today, Nathan had proved to her that doctors did help.

'How do you think the horse is doing?'

Sydney could feel the animal was calmer. It had stopped stamping its hooves and snorting as they'd stood there on the side of the road, watching the clean-up operation. It had stopped tossing its head. Its breathing had become steadier.

'She's doing great.'

'Paul and Helen aren't the only ones in safe hands.' He smiled and sat down on the bank beside her, letting out a breath and rolling his shoulders.

She stared at him for a moment, shocked to realise that she wanted to sit next to him, maybe to massage his shoulders or just lean her head against his shoulder. She wanted that physical contact.

Feeling that yearning to touch him surprised her and she turned away from him, focussing on the horse. She shouldn't be feeling that for him. What was the point? It was best to focus on the horse. She knew what she was doing there.

It didn't take long for the accident to be cleared. The police took pictures, measured the road, measured the skid marks and collected debris. The car was pulled from the ditch and lifted onto a lorry to be taken away, and just as Sydney was beginning to doubt that a new horse-box would ever arrive a truck came ambling around the corner and they loaded the mare onto it to take her back to her stable.

Sydney gave the truck driver her details and told her to let Paul know that she'd be happy to come out and check on the horse, and that he was to give her a call if she was needed urgently.

Eventually she and Nathan got back into his car and she noticed that it was nearly midnight. Normally she would be lying in bed at this time, staring at the ceiling and worrying over every little thought. Wide awake.

But tonight she felt tired. Ready for her bed even without a sleeping pill. It surprised her.

Nathan started the engine. 'Let's take you home. Our little trip out lasted longer than either of us expected.'

'That's okay. I'd only have been awake anyway. At least this way I was put to good use.'

'You've not been sleeping for some time?'

She shook her head and looked away from him, out of the window. 'No.'

He seemed to ruminate on this for a while, but then he

changed the subject. 'Good thing I didn't get any more house calls.'

That was true. What would he have done if he'd got a page to say that someone was having chest pains whilst he'd been helping Helen? They'd been lucky. All of them.

It was nice and warm in Nathan's car as he drove them steadily back to Silverdale. For the first time Sydney felt the silence between them was comfortable. She didn't need to fill the silence with words. Or to feel awkward. The circumstances of the emergency had thrown them together and something intangible had changed.

It felt nice to be sitting with someone like that. Even if it *was* with a man she had at first disliked immensely.

A jolt in the road startled her, and she realised she'd almost nodded off. She sucked in a breath, shocked that she'd felt comfortable enough to fall asleep.

She glanced at Nathan just as he glanced at her, and they both quickly looked away.

Sydney smiled.

It was beginning to feel more than nice.

It was beginning to feel *good*.

Nathan pulled up outside Sydney's cottage and killed the engine. He looked out at the dark, empty street, lit only by one or two streetlamps, and watched as a cat sneaked across the road and disappeared under a hedge after being startled by his engine.

Despite the accident he'd had a good time tonight. It had felt really good to spend time with Sydney, and he felt they'd cleared the air after their misunderstandings at their first meeting and the awkward coffee.

Turning up at her door to ask for help with directions had almost been a step too far for him. He'd joked about asking her for her help, but when he'd tried to find

Eleanor's cottage on his own his stupid GPS had made him turn down a very narrow farming lane and asked him to drive through a muddy field! He'd got out and checked that there wasn't a farmhouse or something near, where he might ask for help, but there'd been nothing. Just fields. And mud. Plenty of mud!

He'd argued with himself about going to her house. Almost not gone there at all. He knew her address. He'd seen it on his computer at work and for some reason it had burnt itself into his brain. She didn't live far from her place of work, so it had been easy to find her, but he hadn't known what sort of reception he'd get. She might have slammed the door in his face.

He'd felt awkward asking for help, but thankfully she'd agreed to go with him, and it had been nice to have her with him in his car, just chatting. It had been a very long time since he'd done that with anyone. The last time had been with Gwyneth. She'd always talked when they were driving—pointing things out, forming opinions on people or places that they passed. Her judgemental approach had made him realise just how insecure she'd been, and he'd done his best to try and make her feel good about herself.

Tonight, Sydney had been invaluable at the accident site—something he knew Gwyneth would never have been. She'd not been great with blood.

Sydney had been brilliant, looking after the driver and the baby, and then she'd managed to calm the horse and check it over. He wouldn't have known how to handle such a large animal. He barely coped with looking after a rabbit, never mind a terrified horse that had been thrown around in a tin box.

Now they were back to that moment again. The one where he normally kissed people goodbye. And suddenly there was that tension again. He wasn't sure whether he should lean over and just do it. Just kiss her.

'Thanks for everything tonight. I couldn't have done it without you,' he said honestly.

She'd grabbed her handbag from the footwell on her side and sat with it on her knee. 'No problem. I couldn't have done it without you either.'

Though half her face was in shadow, he could still see her smile.

'Well…goodnight, Sydney.'

'Goodnight, Nathan.'

She stared at him for a moment, and then turned away and grabbed the latch to open the door. It wouldn't budge and she struggled with it for a moment or two.

'Sorry…sometimes it catches.'

He leant over her for the handle and she flinched as he reached past her and undid the door for her. He sat back, worried that he'd made her start.

She hurried from the vehicle without saying a word, throwing the strap of her bag over her shoulder and delving into her coat pocket for her house keys.

Disappointment filled his soul. He didn't want her to walk away feeling awkward. That flinch, it had been… He wanted…

What do I want?

'Sydney?' He was out of his car before he could even think about what he was doing. He stood there, looking over the top of his car, surprising even himself. The night air had turned chill and he could feel goosebumps trembling up his spine.

She'd turned, curious. 'Yes?'

'Um…' He couldn't think of anything to say! What was he even doing, anyway? He couldn't turn this friendship with Sydney into anything more. Neither of them was ready for that. And there was Anna to think of too. He was sure Sydney would not want to take on someone with a little girl—not after losing her own. And surely she wouldn't want to take on someone who was ill?

Gwyneth had made it quite clear that he wasn't worth *her* time and affection. That he had somehow ruined her life with his presence. Did he want to put someone else through that? Someone like Sydney? Who'd already been through so much? He'd end up needing her more than she needed him, and he'd hate that imbalance. He knew the state of his health. His condition would make him a burden. And Anna had to be his top priority. And yet...

And yet something about her *pulled* at him. Her energy. Her presence. Those grey eyes that looked so studious and wise, yet at the same time contained a hurt and a loss that even he couldn't fully understand. He'd lost his fiancée, yes, but that had been through separation. It wasn't the same as losing a child. Nowhere near it. He and Gwyneth had hardly been the love story of the century.

Even though he'd only known Sydney for a couple of days, there was something in her nature that...

'Remember to take your sleeping pill.'

Remember to take your sleeping pill? Really? That's what you come up with?

Her face filled with relief. 'Oh. Yes, I will. Thank you.'

Relief. *See?* She was being polite. She was probably desperate to get inside and away from him, because he clearly had no idea how to talk to women, having spent the last few years of his life just being a father and—

Being a father is more important than your ability to chat up women!

'You get a good night's sleep yourself. You've earned it.'

He opened his mouth to utter a reply, but she'd already slipped her key into the lock. She raised her hand

in a brief goodbye and then was inside, her door closing
with a shocking finality, and he was left standing in the
street, staring at a closed door.

Nathan watched as Sydney switched on the lights.
He ducked inside his car as she came to her window and
closed the curtains. He stared for a few minutes, then
tore his gaze away, worried about what her neighbours
might think. He started the engine, turned up the heater
and slowly drove away. Berating himself for not saying
something more inspiring, something witty—something
that would have had her...*what?*

That wasn't who he was. Those clever, witty guys,
who always had the perfect line for every occasion, lived
elsewhere. He didn't have a scriptwriter to think up clever
things for him to say that would charm her and make her
like him more. He wasn't suave, or sophisticated, or one
of those charming types who could have women at their
beck and call with a click of their fingers.

And he didn't *want* to be a man like that. He was a
single dad, with a gorgeous, clever daughter who anyone would be lucky to know. He led an uncomplicated
life. He worked hard.

What did he want to achieve with Sydney? And why
was he getting involved anyway? His own fiancée—the
woman he'd been willing to pledge his entire life to—
had walked away from him, and if someone who'd once
said they loved him could do that, then a relative stranger
like Sydney might do the same thing. She didn't strike
him as someone looking to settle down again, to start a
relationship in a ready-made family. Especially not with
another little girl after losing her own.

Did she?

No.

So why on earth could he not get her out of his head?

* * *

Nathan was fighting fatigue. Over the last few days he'd been having a small relapse in his symptoms, and he'd been suffering with painful muscle spasms, cramps, and an overwhelming tiredness that just wouldn't go away. That accident had aggravated it. It was probably stress.

As he downed some painkillers he knew he'd have to hide his discomfort from his daughter. She mustn't see him weaken. Not yet. It was still early days. He didn't want her to suspect that there was something wrong. He had to keep going for her. Had to keep being strong. Normally he could hide it. And he needed his energy for today. Anna was still too young to understand about his condition. How did you explain multiple sclerosis to a six-year-old?

Today Lottie was due for her next check-up, and he was feeling some anticipation at seeing Sydney. At work, during breaks, he often found himself itching to cross the road on some pretext, just to see if she was there, but for the life of him he couldn't think of anything to say. His inner critic kept reminding him that seeing her was probably a bad idea. The woman practically had 'Keep Out' signs hanging around her neck, and she'd certainly not divulged anything too personal to him. She hadn't even mentioned her daughter to him.

And yet…

'Anna! Come on, it's time to go.'

'Are we taking Lottie now?'

'We are. But we're walking because…' he reached for a plausible excuse '…it's a nice day.' He smiled, reaching out for the counter as a small wave of dizziness affected his balance briefly. Of all his symptoms, dizziness and feeling off-balance were the worst. He couldn't drive like this. It would be dangerous. And at least the crisp, fresh winter air would make him feel better.

'Yay!' Anna skipped off to fetch Lottie's carrier.

He managed to stop the world spinning and stood up straight, sucking in a deep breath.

The rabbit was doing quite well, Nathan thought. She was eating and drinking as normal, had come off the medication and was settled back outside. The bite wounds had healed cleanly and Lottie's eye had escaped surgery, much to both his and Anna's delight. They were hopeful for a full recovery.

With Lottie in her box, Nathan locked up and they headed to the veterinary practice. He still wasn't feeling great—quite tired and light-headed—but he tried to keep up a level of bright chatter as they walked along the village roads.

His daughter hopped alongside him, pointing out robins and magpies and on one particular occasion a rather large snail.

The walk took a while. They lived a good couple of miles from the practice and his arms ached from carrying Lottie, who seemed to get weightier with every step, but eventually they got there, and Nathan settled into a waiting room seat with much relief.

He didn't get to enjoy it for too long, though.

Sydney had opened her door. 'Do you want to bring Lottie in?'

Sydney looked well, though there were still faint dark circles beneath her eyes. It felt good to see her again. He carried Lottie through and put her onto the examination table.

'How's she doing?'

He nodded, but that upset his balance and he had to grip the examination table to centre himself.

Had Sydney noticed?

He swallowed, suppressing his nausea. 'Er...good. Eating and drinking. The eye's clean and she seems okay.' He decided to focus on Sydney's face. When he got dizzy like this it helped to focus on something close to him. She wasn't moving that much, and he needed a steady point to remain fixed on.

'Let's take a look.'

Sydney frowned, concern etched across her normally soft features as she concentrated on the examination. She was very thorough, reminding him of her capability and passion. She checked Lottie's eye, her bite wounds, her temperature and gave her a thorough going-over.

'I agree with you. She seems to have recovered well. I think we can discharge this patient.' She stood up straight again and smiled.

'That's great.'

He realised she was looking at him questioningly.

'Are you okay?'

Nathan felt another wave of nausea sweep over him as dizziness assailed him again. 'Er...not really...'

Had the walk been too much? Was he dehydrated?

Sydney glanced at Anna uncertainly, then came around the desk and took Nathan's arm and guided him over to a small stool in the corner. 'I'll get you some water.'

He sank his head into his hands as the dizziness passed, and was just starting to feel it clear a bit when she returned with a glass. He tried not to look at Anna until he was sure he could send her a reassuring smile to say everything was okay.

He took a sip of the drink. 'Thanks.'

'Missed breakfast?'

He gratefully accepted the excuse. 'Yes. Yes, I did. Must have got a bit light-headed, that's all.'

'Daddy, you had toast with jam for breakfast.' Anna contradicted.

He smiled. 'But not enough, obviously.'

'You had three slices.'

He smiled at his daughter, who was blowing his cover story quite innocently. He was afraid to look at Sydney, but she was making sure Lottie was secure in her cage.

Then she turned to look at him, staring intently, her brow lined. 'Are you safe to get home, Dr Jones?'

He stood up. 'We walked here. And I'm fine.' He didn't want to let her see how ill he felt.

'You don't look it. You look very pale.'

'Right…' He glanced at Anna. 'Perhaps I just need some more fresh air.' He took another sip of water.

Sydney stood in front of him, arms crossed. 'You don't seem in a fit state to walk home yet. Or to take care of Anna.'

'I am!' he protested.

'You had nystagmus. I know your world is spinning.'

Nystagmus was a rapid movement of the eyes in response to the semi-circular canals being stimulated. In effect, if the balance centre told you your world was spinning, your eyes tried to play catch-up in order to focus.

'Look, let me tell my next client I'll be ten minutes and I'll drive you both back.'

'No—no, it's fine! I can't disrupt your workday, that's ridiculous. I'm okay now. Besides, that would annoy your patient. I'm fine.'

He stood up to prove it, but swayed slightly, and she had to reach for him, grabbing his waist to steady him.

'Honestly. I just need to get some air for a moment. I could go and sit down across the road at the surgery, maybe. Check my blood pressure. Have a cup of sweet tea. It'll pass—it always does.' He smiled broadly, to show her he was feeling better, even though he wasn't.

She let go of him. 'You're sure?'

No.

'Absolutely.'

He saw her face fill with doubt and hesitation. 'Maybe Anna could stay here with me. She could look after the animals in the back. Give them cuddles, or something.'

Anna gasped, her smile broad. '*Could* I, Daddy?'

He didn't want to impose on Sydney. He could see it had been tough for her to offer that, and she was working. Anna should be *his* responsibility, not someone else's.

'Er... I don't know, honey. Sydney's very busy.'

'It's no problem. Olivia used to do it all the time.' She blushed and looked away.

Her daughter.

'Are you sure?'

'I'm sure. You're clearly unwell today. She can stay with me for the day and I'll drive you both home when I finish. Around four.'

Anna was jumping up and down with joy, clapping her hands together in absolute glee at this amazing turn of events.

He really didn't want to do this, but what choice did he have? Sydney was right. And hadn't he wanted to move to a village to experience this very support?

'Fine. Thank you.' He knelt to speak to his excited daughter. 'You be good for Sydney. Do what you're told and behave—yes?'

She nodded.

Standing up, he felt a little head rush. Maybe Sydney was right. Perhaps he *did* need a break.

He was just having a difficult time letting someone

help him. It irked him, gnawing away at him like a particularly persistent rodent. How could he look after his daughter if he was going to let a little dizziness affect him? And this was just the *start* of his condition. These were mild symptoms. It would get worse. And already he was relying on other people to look after his daughter—Sydney, of all people!

'Perhaps she ought to stay with—'

Sydney grabbed his arm and started to guide him towards her exit. 'Go and lie down, Dr Jones.'

Nathan grimaced hard, then kissed the top of his daughter's head and left.

It had been a delight to have Anna with her for the day. The invitation to look after Nathan's little girl had just popped out. She'd not carefully considered exactly what it would mean to look after the little girl before she'd said it, and once she had she'd felt a small amount of alarm at her offer.

But Anna had been wonderful. She was sweet, calm with the animals, with a natural affection and understanding of them that those in her care gravitated towards, allowing her to stroke them. The cats had purred. Dogs had wagged their tails or showed their bellies to be rubbed. And Anna had asked loads of questions about them, showing a real interest. She'd even told Sydney that she wanted to be a vet when she was older! That had been sweet.

Olivia had liked being with the animals, but she'd only liked the cuddling part. The oohing and aahing over cute, furry faces. Anna was different. She wanted to know what breed they were. What they were at the vet's for. How Sydney might make them better. It had been good to share her knowledge with Nathan's daughter. Good to see the differences between the two little girls.

Once they were done for the day, and the last of the records had been completed, she smiled as Lucy complained about her sore back after cleaning cages all afternoon, but then sat down to eat not one but two chocolate bars, because she felt ravenous.

They sat together, chatting about animal care, and Anna listened quietly, not interrupting, and not getting in the way.

When she'd gathered her things, Sydney told Anna it was time to go.

'Thank you for having me, Sydney.'

She eyed the little girl holding her hand as they crossed the road to collect Nathan. 'Not a problem, Anna. It was lovely to have you. Let's hope your daddy is feeling better soon, hmm?'

'Daddy always gets sick and tired. He pretends he's not, but I know when he is.'

'Perhaps he *is* just tired? He does a very important job, looking after everyone.' But something niggled at her. The way Nathan had been, and the nonchalant way Anna had mentioned that *'Daddy always gets sick and tired...'*

Was Nathan ill? And, if so, what could it be? Just a virus? Was he generally run-down? Or could it be something else? Something serious?

They quickly crossed to the surgery and collected a rather pale-looking Nathan. He insisted he was feeling much better. Suspecting he wasn't quite being truthful, she got him into the car and started the engine, glancing at Anna on the back seat through the rearview mirror.

Anna smiled, and the sight went straight to Sydney's heart. To distract herself, she rummaged in the glovebox to see if she had any of Olivia's old CDs. She found one and slid it into the CD player, and soon they were singing along with a cartoon meerkat and a warthog.

Driving through the village, she found herself smiling, amazed that she still remembered the words, and laughing at Anna singing in the back. It felt *great* to be driving along, singing together. She and Olivia had always used to do it. It was even putting a smile on Nathan's face.

Much too soon she found herself at Nathan's house, and she walked them both up to their front door, finally handing them Lottie's carrier.

Nathan smiled broadly. 'Thanks, Sydney. I really appreciate it. I got a lot of rest and I feel much better.'

'Glad to hear it. Anna was brilliant. The animals adored her.'

'They all do. Thanks again.'

'No problem. See you around.'

She began to walk away, turning to give a half wave, feeling embarrassed at doing so. She got in her car and drove away as fast as she could—before she was tempted to linger and revel in the feeling of family once again.

It felt odd to be back in the car, alone again after that short while she'd been with Anna and Nathan. The car seemed empty. The music had been silenced and returned to the glovebox.

By the time she got home her heart physically ached.

And she sat in her daughter's old room for a very long time, just staring at the empty walls.

CHAPTER FIVE

SOMEHOW IT HAD become December, and November had passed in a moment. A moment when natural sleep had continued to elude her, but her strange, mixed feelings for the new village doctor had not.

She'd listened as her own clients had chatted with her about the new doctor, smiled when they'd joked about how gorgeous he was, how heroic he was. Had she heard that he'd saved lives already? One woman in the village, who really ought to have known better, had even joked and blushed about Dr Jones giving her the kiss of life! Sydney had smiled politely, but inside her heart had been thundering.

She'd seen him fleetingly, here and there. A couple of times he'd waved at her. Once she'd bumped into him in the sandwich shop, just as a large dollop of coleslaw had squeezed itself from her crusty cob and splatted onto her top.

'Oh!' He'd laughed, rummaging in his pockets and pulling out a fresh white handkerchief. 'Here—take this.'

She'd blushed madly, accepted his hankie, and then had stood there wiping furiously at her clothes, knowing that he was standing there, staring at her. When she'd looked up to thank him *he'd* blushed, and she'd wondered what he had been thinking about.

Then they'd both gone on their way, and she'd looked over her shoulder at him at the exact moment when he'd done the same.

She felt that strange undercurrent whenever they met, or whenever she saw him. She kept trying to ignore it. Trying to ignore *him*. But it was difficult. Her head and her heart had differing reactions. Her head told her to stay away and keep her distance. But her heart and her body sang whenever he was near, as if it was saying, *Look, there he is! Give him a wave! Go and say hello! Touch him!*

Today frost covered the ground like a smattering of icing sugar, and the village itself looked very picturesque. Sydney was desperate to get out and go for a walk around the old bridleways, maybe take a few pictures with her camera, but she couldn't. There was far too much to do and she was running late for a committee meeting.

The Silverdale Christmas market and nativity was an annual festive occasion that was always held the week before Christmas. People came from all around the county, sometimes further from afield, and it was a huge financial boost to local businesses during the typically slower winter months. Unfortunately this year it was scheduled to fall on the one day that she dreaded. The anniversary of Olivia's death.

Sydney had previously been one of the organisers, but after what had happened with Olivia she hadn't been involved much. Barely at all. This year she'd decided to get back into it. She'd always been needed, especially where the animals were concerned. She'd used to judge the Best Pet show, and maintain the welfare of all the animals that got involved in the very real nativity—donkeys, sheep, cows, goats, even chickens and geese! But she'd also been in charge of the flower stalls and the food market.

It was a huge commitment, but one she had enjoyed in the past. And this year it would keep her busy. Would stop her thinking of another Christmas without her daughter. Stop her from wallowing in the fact that, yet again, she would not be buying her child any gifts to put under a non-existent tree.

She sat at the table with the rest of the committee, waiting for the last member to arrive. Dr Jones was late. Considerably so. And the more they waited, the more restless she got.

'Perhaps we should just make a start and then fill Dr Jones in if he ever gets here?' Sydney suggested.

Everyone else was about to agree when the door burst open and in he came, cheeks red from the cold outside, apologising profusely. 'Sorry, everyone, I got called out to some stomach pains—which, surprisingly, turned out to be a bouncing baby boy.'

There were surprised gasps and cheers from the others.

'Who's had a baby?' asked Malcolm, the chairman.

Nathan tucked his coat over the back of his chair. 'Lucy Carter.'

Sydney sat forward, startled. '*My* Lucy Carter? My veterinary nurse?'

His gaze met hers and he beamed a smile at her which went straight to her heart. 'The very same.'

'B-but…she wasn't pregnant!' she spluttered with indignation.

'The baby in her arms would beg to differ!'

'But…'

She couldn't believe it! Okay, Lucy had put some weight on recently, but they'd put that down to those extra chocolate bars she'd been eating… *Pregnant? That's amazing!* She felt the need to go and see her straight away. To give her a hug and maybe get a cuddle with the newborn.

'It was a shock for everyone involved. But they're both doing well and everyone's happy. She told me to let you know.'

A baby. For Lucy. That was great news. And such a surprise!

It meant more work for Sydney for a bit, of course, but she'd cope. She could get an agency member of staff in. It would be weird, not seeing Lucy at work for a while. They'd always worked together. They knew each other's ways and foibles.

She sighed. Everyone else seemed to be moving on. Lucy and her new baby. Alastair and his new bride, with a baby on the way. Everyone was getting on with their lives. And she…? She was still here. In the village she's been born in. With no child. No husband. No family of her own except her elderly parents, who lived too far away anyway.

She looked across at Nathan as he settled into his seat and felt a sudden burst of irritation towards him. She'd been looking forward to getting involved in these meetings again, getting back out there into the community, and yet now her feelings towards him were making her feel uncomfortable. Was it because he'd brought news that meant her life was going to change again?

'Let's get started, shall we?' suggested Malcolm. 'First off, I'd like to welcome Dr Nathan Jones to the committee. He has taken over the role from its previous incumbent, Dr Richard Preston.'

The group clapped, smiled and nodded a welcome for their new member. Sydney stared at him, her face impassive. He looked ridiculously attractive today. Fresh-faced. Happy. She focused on his hands. Hands that had just recently delivered a baby. And she felt guilty for having allowed herself to succumb to that brief, petty jealousy. She looked up at his face and caught him looking at her, and she looked away, embarrassed.

'I'd also like to welcome Sydney back to the committee! Sydney, as I'm sure most of you know, took a little… sabbatical, if you will, from the organisation of this annual event, and I'm most pleased to have her back in full fighting form!'

She smiled as she felt all eyes turn to her, and nodded hellos to the group members she knew well and hadn't worked with for so long. It did feel good to be back here and doing something for the community again. The Christmas market and nativity was something she hadn't been able to find any pleasure in for some time, but now she was ready.

At least she hoped she was.

'The market is going to be held in the same place as always—the centre of the village square—and I believe we've already got lots of things in place from last year. Miriam?'

Miriam, the secretary, filled them in on all the recent developments. Lots of the same stalls that came every year had rebooked. Music was going to be covered by the same brass band, and the school was going to provide a choir as well.

Sydney listened, scribbling things down on her pad that she'd need to remember, and thought of past activities. There was a lot to take in—she'd forgotten how much organising there was!—and as her list got longer and longer she almost wished she could write with both hands.

She'd also forgotten how soothing these meetings could be sometimes. The hum of voices, the opinions of everyone on how things should be done, the ebb and flow of ideas... She truly appreciated the need for all this planning and preparation. Even though sometimes the older members of the committee enjoyed their dedication to picking over details a little too much.

Briefly, she allowed her mind to wander, and the memory that sprang to her mind was of a happier year, when Olivia had played the part of Mary in the nativity. In the weeks beforehand Sydney had taught her how to ride the donkey, shown her how to behave around the other animals. She remembered holding her daughter's hand as they walked through the market stalls, making sure she didn't eat too many sweets or pieces of cake, and listening to her singing carols in the choir.

She smiled, feeling a little sad. She had those memories on camera. Alastair had videoed Olivia riding the donkey in the nativity, with her fake pregnancy bump. Olivia had loved that belly, rubbing her hands over it like a real pregnant mother soothing away imaginary kicks.

'And that brings us back to our star players for the nativity,' Malcolm continued. 'I have been reliably informed by Miss Howarth of Silverdale Infants School that our Mary this year will be played by Anna Jones, and Joseph will be Barney Brooks...'

Sydney was pulled from her reverie. *Anna? Dr Jones's Anna? She was going to play Mary?* Visions flashed through her mind. Anna wearing Olivia's costume... Anna riding Olivia's donkey... Anna being the star of the show...?

It simply hadn't occurred to her when she came back that someone else would be playing Olivia's part. But of course. There had already been new Marys in the years that she'd stayed away. She'd just not seen them, hiding away in her house every year, longing to clap her hands over her ears to blot out the sound of all those Christmas revellers. It had been torture!

It hurt to hear it. It was as if Olivia had been replaced. Had been *forgotten*...

Her chair scraped loudly on the floor as she stood, grabbing her notepad and pen, her bag and coat, and muttering apologies before rushing from the room, feeling sick.

She thought she was on her own. She thought she would get to her own car in peace. But just as she was inserting her key into the lock of her car she heard her name being called.

'Sydney!'

She didn't want to turn around. She didn't want to be polite and make small talk with whoever it was. She just wanted to go. Surely they wouldn't mind? Surely they'd understand?

She got into her seat and was about to close the door when Nathan appeared at her side, holding the car door so she couldn't close it.

'Hey! Are you okay?'

Why was he here? Why was he even bothering to ask? Why had he come after her?

'I just want to go, Nathan.'

'Something's upset you?'

'No, honestly. I just want to get home, that's all.'

'Is it Lucy? Are you worried about work?'

'No.' She slipped on her seatbelt and stared resolutely out through the windshield rather than looking at him. Her voice softened. 'I'm thrilled for Lucy. Of course I am!'

'Is it me?'

Now she looked at him, her eyes narrowing. 'Why would it be you?'

He shrugged. 'I don't know. Things haven't exactly been…straightforward. There's a…a tension, between us. We didn't exactly get off to the best start, did we?'

'It's not you,' she lied.

'Well, that's good, because they've asked me to work closely with you, seeing as I'm new and you're an established committee member.'

What? When did I miss that bit?

'Oh.'

'That's quite good, really, because—as you heard— Anna came home from school today and told me she's been picked to play the part of Mary. Apparently that means riding a donkey, and she's never done that before, so…'

'So?'

Push the memory away. Don't think about it.

'So we'll need your help.'

He smiled at her. In that way he had. Disarming her and making her feel as if she ought to oblige him with her assistance. His charming eyes twinkling.

'Know any good donkeys? Preferably something that isn't going to buck and break her neck?'

There was someone in the village who kept donkeys. They were used every year for the nativity. And she trusted the animals implicitly.

'Do you know the Bradleys? At Wicklegate Farm?'

He pretended to search his memory. 'Erm…no.'

'Do you know where Wicklegate Farm even *is*?'

He shook his head, smiling. 'No.'

Feeling some of her inner struggle fade, she smiled back. Of course he didn't. 'I suppose I'd better help you, then. Are you free next Saturday?'

'Saturday? All day.'

She nodded and started her engine. 'I'll pick you up

at ten in the morning. I know your address. Does Anna have any riding clothes?'

'Er…'

'Anything she doesn't mind getting dirty?'

'My daughter is always happy to wallow in some mud.'

'Good. Tell her I'm going to teach her how to ride a donkey.'

'Thanks.'

He stood back at last, so she could finally close her car door. She was about to drive off, eager to get home, when Nathan rapped his knuckles on her glass.

She pressed the button to wind the window down, letting in the cold evening air. 'What?'

'Lucy's at home. And waiting for your visit.'

She nodded, imagining Lucy in her small cottage, tucked up in bed, looking as proud as Punch with a big smile on her face.

'Has she picked a name for him?'

'I believe she has.'

'What is it?'

He paused, clearly considering whether to say it or not. 'She's named him Oliver.'

Oliver. So close to…

A lump filled her throat and she blinked away tears. Had Lucy chosen that name in honour of her own daughter? If she had, then…

Sydney glanced up at Nathan. 'I'll see you on Saturday.' And she quickly drove away, before he could see her cry.

Nathan had driven round to Paul and Helen's to check up on them after the accident. They lived on the outskirts of Silverdale and were pretty easy to locate, and he pulled into their driveway feeling optimistic about what he would find. Helen had been released from hospital a while ago and he only needed to remove Paul's stitches from the head laceration.

As he drove in he saw the horse grazing in a field, a blanket wrapped around its body, and smiled. They'd all been very lucky to escape as easily as they had. The accident could have been a lot worse.

But as he pulled up to the house, he spotted another vehicle.

Sydney's.

Why was she here? To check on the horse? It had to be that. It was odd that she was here at the exact same time as him, though.

Just lately she'd been in his thoughts a lot. The universe seemed to be conspiring to throw the two of them together, and whilst he didn't mind that part—she was, after all, a beautiful woman—she did tend to remind him of all his faults and of how he could never be enough for her.

His confidence had taken a knock after Gwyneth's departure. Okay, they'd only been staying in their struggling relationship because she'd learnt she was expecting a baby and Nathan had wanted to be there for her. He'd always had his doubts, and she'd been incredibly high-maintenance, but he'd honestly believed she might change the closer she got to delivering. That they both would.

She hadn't. It had still been, *Me, me, me!*

'Look at all the weight I'm putting on!'

'This pregnancy's giving me acne!'

'I'm getting varicose veins!'

'You do realise after the birth I'm going straight back to work?'

Nathan had reassured her. Had promised her it would be amazing. But it had been *his* dream. Not hers.

It had only been when she'd left him for someone else

that he'd realised how much relief he felt. It had stung that she'd left him for someone better. Someone unencumbered by ill health. Someone rich, who could give her the lifestyle she craved. But he'd felt more sorry for his baby girl, who would grow up with a mother who only had enough love for herself.

In the weeks afterwards, when he'd spent hours walking his baby daughter up and down as he tried to get her off to sleep, he'd begun to see how one-sided their relationship had always been.

Gwyneth had always been about appearances. Worrying about whether her hair extensions were the best. Whether her nails needed redoing. How much weight she was carrying. Whether she was getting promoted above someone else. She'd been a social climber—a girl who had been given everything she'd ever wanted by her parents and had come to expect the same in adulthood.

He'd fallen for her glamorous looks and the fact that in the beginning she'd seemed really sweet. But it had all been a snare. A trap. And he'd only begun to see the real Gwyneth when he'd got his diagnosis. Multiple sclerosis had scared her. The idea that she might become nursemaid to a man who wasn't strong, the way she'd pictured him, had *terrified* her.

When Nathan had discovered his illness, and Gwyneth had learned that their perfect life was not so perfect after all, her outlook had changed and she'd said some pretty harsh things. Things he'd taken to heart. That he'd believed.

He didn't want to burden Sydney with any of that.

She'd looked after his daughter for a few hours, she'd looked after and cured their rabbit, she was kind and strong…

She's the sort of woman I would go out with if I could…

But he couldn't.

She'd lost her only daughter. And where was the child's father? From what he'd heard around the village, the father had left them just a couple of months after Olivia had passed away. Shocking them all.

It seemed the whole village had thought the Harpers were strong enough to get through anything. But of course no one could know how such a tragic death would affect them.

Hadn't Sydney been through enough? He had a positive mind-set—even if he did sometimes take the things that Gwyneth had yelled at him to heart. He tried to remain upbeat. But just sometimes his mind would play tricks with him and say, *Yeah, but what if she was right?*

Besides, he wasn't sure he could trust his own judgement about those kinds of things any more. Affairs of the heart. He'd felt so sure about Gwyneth once! In the beginning, anyway. And he'd wanted to do everything for her and the baby. Had wanted the family life that had been right there in front of him. Ready and waiting.

How wrong could he have been?

He'd been floored when she'd left. She'd been high-maintenance, but not once had he suspected that she would react that way to his diagnosis. To having a baby, even. She'd been horrified at what her life had become and had been desperate to escape the drudgery she'd foreseen.

And Nathan had *known* Gwyneth. Or thought he had.

He didn't *know* Sydney. As much as he'd like to.

And he sure as hell didn't want his heart—or Anna's—broken again.

Getting out of the car, he looked up and saw Paul, Helen and Sydney coming out of the house. Helen was standing further back, her arms crossed.

'Dr Jones! Good of you to call round! You've arrived just in time. Your wife was just about to leave.'

He instantly looked at Sydney. My *wife?*

Sydney blushed madly. 'We're not married!'

Paul looked between the two of them. 'Oh, but we thought... Partners, then?'

'No. Just...friends. Associates. We just happened to be in the car together, that's all...' he explained, feeling his voice tail off when he glanced at Sydney's hot face.

'Really? You two look perfect for each other.' Paul smiled.

Nathan was a little embarrassed, but amused at the couple's mistake. 'Hello, Sydney. We seem to keep bumping into each other.'

She shook his hand in greeting. 'We do.'

'Did you get to see Lucy?'

'I did. The baby is gorgeous.'

'He is.' He was still holding her hand. Still looking at her. Someone seemed to have pressed 'pause', because for a moment he lost himself, staring into her grey eyes. It was as if the rest of the world had gone away.

Paul and Helen looked at each other and cleared their throats and Nathan dropped Sydney's hand.

'You're leaving?'

'I just came to check on the horse. No after-effects from the accident.'

'That's good. How about you, Paul? Any headaches? Anything I should be worried about?'

'No, Doc. All well and good, considering.'

'How about you, Helen?'

'I'm fine. Physically.'

'That's good.'

Sydney pulled her car keys from her pocket. 'Well, I must dash. Good to see you all so well. Paul. Helen.' She looked over at Nathan, her gaze lingering longer than it should. 'Dr Jones.'

He watched her go. Watched as she started her engine, reversed, turned and drove out of the driveway. He even watched as her car disappeared out of sight, up the lane.

Suddenly remembering that he was there to see Paul and Helen, he turned back to them, feeling embarrassed. 'Shall we go in? Get those stitches seen to?'

Paul nodded, draping his arm around Nathan's shoulder conspiratorially. 'Just friends, huh?'

He felt his cheeks colour. They'd caught him watching her. Seen how distracted she made him.

'Just friends.'

Inside the house, Helen disappeared into the kitchen to make a cup of tea.

'So, Paul... How are you?' He noted the stitches in his scalp. He'd certainly got a nasty laceration there, but apart from that obvious injury he seemed quite well.

'I'm good, Doc, thanks.' Paul settled into the chair opposite.

They had a lovely home. It was a real country cottage, with lots of character and tons of original features. There was a nice fire crackling away in the fireplace. It looked as if they were in the process of putting some Christmas decorations up.

'So I need to remove your stitches. How many days have they been in?'

'Too long! I'm really grateful for you coming out like this. I was going to make an appointment to come and say thanks to you. For saving me and Helen. And Brandon, too, of course.'

'It wasn't a problem. We were just in the right place at the right time.'

'You were in the perfect place.' He looked down at

the floor and then got his next words out in a quiet rush, after he'd turned to check that Helen wasn't listening. 'Helen and I didn't see that deer coming across the field because we were arguing.'

'Oh?' Nathan sensed a confession coming.

'I...er...hadn't reacted very well to the fact that... well...' He looked uncomfortable. 'Helen had had a miscarriage. Two weeks earlier. The hospital said they'd send you a letter... We hadn't even known she was pregnant, but she had this bleed that wouldn't stop, and we ended up at A&E one night, and they found out it was an incomplete miscarriage. She needed a D&C.'

Nathan felt a lurch in his stomach. 'I'm very sorry to hear that.'

'Yeah, well...apparently *I* wasn't sorry enough. Helen got mad with me because I wasn't upset about losing the baby. But neither of us had even *known* about the pregnancy! How could I get upset over a baby I didn't know about?' Paul let out a heavy breath. 'She thought I didn't care. We were arguing about that. Yelling...screaming at each other—so much so that Brandon started too. We didn't notice the deer because I wasn't paying attention.' He sounded guilty. 'And now, because I didn't notice the deer running in front of us, and because I didn't notice my wife was pregnant, *I'm* the bad guy who nearly got us all killed.'

How awful for them! To lose a baby like that and then to have a serious accident on top of it. They were both very lucky to have got out alive. Brandon, too. It could all have gone so terribly wrong.

'Well, I can sort your stitches for you. And I'm not so sure I would *want* to stop Helen being mad. She's had a terrible loss, Paul. You both have. And she needs to work through it.'

'I know, but...'

'There are support groups. Ones specifically for women who have suffered miscarriage. I can give you some information if you drop by the surgery. Or maybe I could ask Helen if she wants to come in and have a chat with me? You may not have known about the pregnancy, but she still lost a baby. A D&C can be a traumatic event in itself, when you think about what it is, and it can help some women to talk about things. She's had a loss and she needs to work her way through it. And I'm sure, in time, so will you.'

Paul rubbed at his bristly jaw. 'But even *she* didn't know.'

'It doesn't matter. It was still a baby, Paul. Still a loss. A terrible one. And she knows *now*. She probably feels a lot of guilt, and the easiest person to take that out on is you.'

'Does she think *I've* not been hurt too? To not even know she was pregnant and then to see her so scared when she wouldn't stop bleeding? And then to learn the reason why?' He shook his head, tears welling in his eyes. '*Why* didn't I know?'

'You're not to blame. It's difficult in those early weeks.'

'I keep thinking there must have something else I could have done for her. Something I could have said. To see that pain in her eyes... It broke my heart.'

Nathan laid a hand on Paul's shoulder.

'It *has* hurt me. I *am* upset. And I feel guilty at trying to make her get over something when she's just not ready to. Guilty that I won't get to hold that baby in my arms...'

'Grief takes time to heal. For both of you.'

Paul glanced at his hands. 'But she won't talk to me. She doesn't talk to me about any of the deep stuff because she thinks I don't care. She never shares what she's feeling. How are you supposed to be in a relationship with someone who won't tell you what's really going on?'

With great difficulty.

He looked at Paul. 'You wait. Until she's ready. And when she is…you listen.'

Nathan was so glad he'd never had to go through something like this with Gwyneth. They'd come close, when she'd thought there might still be time for an abortion, but the thought of losing his child…? It was too terrible even to think about.

Sydney would understand.

Just thinking about her now made him realise just how strong she was to have got through her daughter's death. And on her own, too.

'So I've just got to take her anger, then?'

'Be there for her. Be ready to talk when she is. She's grieving.'

Was Sydney still grieving? Was that why she wasn't able to talk to him about what had happened? Should he even *expect* her to open up to him?

He opened his doctor's bag and pulled out a small kit to remove Paul's stitches. There were ten of them, and he used a stitch-cutter and tweezers to hold the knots each time he removed them. The wound had healed well, but Paul would be left with a significant scar for a while.

'That's you done.'

'Thanks. So I've just got to wait it out, then?'

'Or you could raise the subject if *you* feel the need. I can see that you're upset at the loss, too. Let her know she can talk to you. That you're ready to talk whenever she is.'

Paul nodded and touched the spot where his stitches

had been. 'Maybe I will. I know I've lost a baby, but I'm even more scared of losing my wife.'

Nathan just stared back at him.

Sydney felt odd. She had to call round to Nathan's house in a minute, so she could take them to Wicklegate Farm and teach Anna how to ride the donkey. But for some reason she was standing in front of her wardrobe, wondering what to wear?

It shouldn't matter!

Deliberately she grabbed at a pair of old jeans, an old rugby shirt that was slightly too big for her and thick woolly socks to wear inside her boots.

I have no reason to dress up for Dr Jones.

However, once dressed, she found herself staring at her reflection in the mirror, messing with her hair. Up? Down?

She decided to leave her hair down and then added a touch of make-up. A bit of blush. Some mascara.

Her reflection stared back at her in question.

What are you doing?

Her mirror image gave no response. Obviously. But that still didn't stop her waiting for one, hoping she would see something in the mirror that would tell her the right thing to do.

She even looked at Magic. 'Am I being stupid about this?'

Magic blinked slowly at her.

She *liked* Nathan, and that was the problem. She liked it that he was comfortable to be with. She liked it that he was great to talk to. That he was very easy on the eye.

There was some small security in the fact that his little girl would be there, so it was hardly going to be a seduction, but... But a part of her—a small part, admittedly—

wondered what it would be like if something were to happen with them spending time together. What, though? A kiss? On the cheek? *The lips?* That small part of her wanted to know what it would feel like to close her eyes and feel his lips press against hers. To inhale his scent, to feel his hands upon her. To sink into his strong caress.

Alastair, in those last few months, made me feel like I had the plague. That I was disgusting to him. It would be nice to know that a man could still find me desirable.

She missed that physical connection with someone. She missed having someone in her bed in the morning. Someone to read the papers with. To talk to over a meal. She missed the comfort of sitting in the same room as another person and not even having to talk. Of sharing a good book recommendation, of watching a movie together snuggled under an old quilt and feeding each other popcorn. Coming home and not finding the house empty.

But so what? Just because she missed it, it didn't mean she had to make it happen. No matter how much she fantasised about it. Nathan was a man. And in her experience men let you down. Especially when you needed them the most. She'd already been rejected once, when she was at her lowest, and she didn't want to go through that again.

It was too hard.

So no matter how nice Nathan was—no matter how attractive, no matter how much she missed being *held*—nothing was going to happen. Today was about Anna. About donkeys and learning how to ride.

She remembered teaching Olivia. It had taken her ages to get her balance, and she'd needed a few goes at it before she'd felt confident. She hadn't liked pulling at the reins, had been worried in case it hurt the donkey.

Thinking about the past made her think of the present. Her ex-husband, Alastair, had moved on. He'd found someone new. Was making a new family. How had he moved on so quickly? It was almost insulting. Had she meant nothing to him? Had the family they'd had meant less to him than she'd realised? Perhaps that was why he'd walked away so easily?

Everyone in the village had been shocked. *Everyone.* Well, she'd make sure that everyone knew *she* wasn't moving on. Keeping Nathan and Anna at arm's length was the right thing to do, despite what she was feeling inside.

She considered cancelling. Calling him and apologising. Telling him that an emergency had cropped up. But then she'd realised that if she did she would still have to meet him again at some point. It was best to get it over and done with straight away. Less dilly-dallying. Besides, she didn't want to let Anna down. She was a good kid.

She held her house keys in her hand for a moment longer, debating with her inner conscience, and her gaze naturally strayed to a photograph of Olivia. She was standing with her head back, looking up to the sun, her eyes closed, smiling at the feel of warmth on her face. It was one of Sydney's favourite pictures: Olivia embracing the warmth of the sun.

She always enjoyed life. Even the small things.

Sydney stepped outside and locked up the cottage. She needed to drive to Nathan's house. The new estate and the road he lived on was about two miles away.

It was interesting to drive through the new builds. The houses were very modern, in bright brick, with cool grey slate tiles on their roofs and shiny white UPVC windows. They were uniformly identical, but she could see Nathan's muddy jalopy parked on his driveway and she pulled in behind it, letting out a breath. Releasing her nerves.

I can do this!

She strode up to the front door, trying to look businesslike, hoping that no one could see how nervous she suddenly felt inside. She rang the bell and let out a huge breath, trying to calm her scattered nerves.

The door opened and Nathan stood there. Smiling. 'Sydney—hi. Come on in.' he stepped back.

Reluctant to enter his home, and therefore create feelings of intimacy, she stepped back. 'Erm…shouldn't we just be off? I told the owners we'd be there in about ten minutes.'

'I'm just waiting for Anna to finish getting ready. You know what young girls are like.'

She watched his cheeks colour as he realised what he'd said, and to let him off the hook decided to step in, but keeping herself as far away from him physically as she could.

'I do…yes. Anna?' she called up the stairs.

Sydney heard some thumps and bumps and then Anna was at the top of the stairs. 'Hi, Sydney! I can't decide what to wear. Could you help me? *Please?*'

Anna wheedled out the last word, giving the cutest face that she could.

The look was so reminiscent of Olivia that Sydney had to catch her breath.

'Erm…' she glanced at Nathan, who shrugged.

'By all means…'

'Right.'

Sydney ascended the stairs, feeling sweat break out down her spine. She turned at the top and went into Anna's room. Her breath was taken away by how *girly* it was. A palace of pink. A pink feather boa hung over the mirror on a dresser, there were fairy lights around the headboard, bubblegum-coloured beanbags, a blush-pink carpet and curtains, a hammock in the corner filled with all manner of soft, cuddly toys and a patchwork quilt upon the bed.

And in front of a large pink wardrobe that had a crenelated top, like a castle, Anna stood, one hand on one hip, the other tapping her finger against her lips.

'I've never ridden a donkey. Or a horse! I don't know what would be best.'

Sydney swallowed hard as she eyed the plethora of clothes in every colour under the sun. 'Erm...something you don't mind getting dirty. Trousers or jeans. And a tee shirt? Maybe a jumper?'

Anna pulled out a mulberry-coloured jumper that was quite a thick knit, with cabling down the front. 'Like this?'

Syd nodded. 'Perfect. Trousers?'

'I have these.' Anna pulled a pair of jeans from a pile. They had some diamanté sequins sewn around the pockets. 'And this?' She pointed at the tee shirt she was already wearing.

'Those will be great. I'll go downstairs whilst you're getting dressed.'

'Could you help me, Sydney? I can never do the buttons.'

Sydney stood awkwardly whilst Anna changed her clothes, and then knelt in front of the little girl to help her do up her clothes. It had been ages since she'd had to do this. Olivia had always struggled with buttons. These two girls might almost have been made out of the same mould. Of course there were so differences between the girls, but sometimes the similarities were disturbing. Painful.

She stood up again. 'Ready?'

Anna nodded and dashed by her to run downstairs. 'I'll get my boots on!'

She sat at the bottom of the stairs and pulled on bright green wellington boots that had comical frog eyes poking out over the toes.

Sydney stood behind her, looking awkwardly at Nathan.

'Will I need boots, too?' he asked.

She nodded. 'It's a working farm...so, yes.'

She watched as they both got ready, and it was so reminiscent of standing waiting for Olivia and Alastair to get ready so they could go out that she physically felt an ache in her chest.

They had been good together. Once. When she and Alastair had married she'd truly believed they would be in each other's arms until their last days. Shuffling along together. One of those old couples you could see in parks, still holding hands.

But then it had all gone wrong.

Alastair hadn't been able to cope with losing his little girl and he'd blamed her. For not noticing that Olivia was truly ill. For not acting sooner. The way he'd blanked her, directed his anger towards her, had hurt incredibly. The one time she'd needed her husband the most had been the one time he'd failed her completely.

When Nathan and Anna were both ready she hurried them out of the door and got them into her car.

'Can you do your seatbelt, Anna?'

'Yes!' the little girl answered, beaming. 'I can't wait to ride the donkey! Did Daddy tell you I'm going to be Mary? That's the most important part in the play. Well... except for baby Jesus...but that's just going to be a doll, so...' She trailed off.

Sydney smiled into the rearview mirror. How many times had she driven her car with Olivia babbling away in the back seat? Too many times. So often, in fact, that she would usually be thinking about all the things she had to do, tuning her daughter out, saying *hmm*...or *right*...in all the right places, whenever her daughter paused for breath.

And now...? With Anna chatting away...? She wanted to listen. Wanted to show Nathan's little girl that she heard her.

I can't believe I ignored my daughter! Even for a second!

How many times had she not truly listened? How many times had she not paid attention? Thinking that she had all the time in the world to talk to her whenever she wanted? To chat about things that hadn't meant much to her but had meant the world to her daughter?

'All eyes will be on you, Anna. I'm sure you'll do a great job.'

Nathan glanced over at her. 'I appreciate you arranging this. I don't suppose you're a dab hand with a sewing machine, are you?'

She was, actually. 'Why?'

'The costume for Mary is looking a bit old. The last incumbent seems to have dragged it through a dump before storing it away and now it looks awful. Miriam has suggested that I make another one.'

She glanced over at him. 'And you said...?'

'I said yes! But that was when I thought a bedsheet and a blue teacloth over the head was all that was needed.'

'You know... I might still have Olivia's old outfit. She played Mary one year.'

'She did?' Nathan was looking at her closely.

'I still have some of her stuff in boxes in the attic. Couldn't bear to part with it. Give me a day or two and I'll check.'

'That's very kind of you.'

She kept her eyes on the road, trying not to think too

hard about going up into the attic to open those boxes. Would the clothes still have Olivia's scent? Would seeing them, touching them, be too painful? There was a reason they were still in the attic. Unsorted.

She'd boxed everything up one day, after a therapist at one of her grief counselling sessions had told her it might be a good thing to do. That it might be cathartic, or something.

It hadn't been.

She'd felt that in boxing up her daughter's clothes and putting them somewhere they couldn't be seen she was also been getting rid of all traces of her daughter. That she was hiding Olivia's memory away. And she'd not been ready. She'd drunk an awful lot of wine that night, and had staggered up into the attic to drag all the boxes back downstairs, but Alastair had stopped her. Yelled at her that it was a *good* thing, and that if she touched those boxes one more time then he would walk out the door.

She'd sobered up and the next morning had left the boxes up there—even though she'd felt bereft and distraught. And dreadfully hungover.

Alastair had left eventually, of course. Just not then. It had taken a few more weeks. By then it had been too late to drag the boxes back down. Too scary.

'What was she like?'

'Hmm?' She was pulled back to the present by his question. 'What?'

'What was Olivia like?' he asked again.

She glanced over at him quickly. He sounded as if he really wanted to know, and no one had asked her that question for years. All this time she'd stayed away from people, not making connections or getting close because she hadn't wanted to talk about Olivia. It had been too painful. But now she *wanted* to talk about her.

Was thrilled that he'd asked, because she was *ready* to talk about her. He'd made it easy to do so.

'She was…amazing.'

'Who's Olivia?' asked Anna from the back seat.

Sydney glanced in the rearview mirror once again and smiled.

The donkey was called Bert and he had a beautiful dark brown coat. The farmer had already got him saddled before their arrival and he stood waiting patiently, nibbling at some hay, as Sydney gave Anna instructions.

'Okay, it's quite simple, Anna. You don't need Bert to go fast, so you don't need to nudge him with your feet or kick at his sides. A slow plod is what we want, and Bert here is an expert at the slow plod and the Christmas nativity.'

'Will he bite me?'

She shook her head. 'No. He's very gentle and he is used to children riding him. Shall I lift you into the saddle?'

Anna nodded.

Sydney hefted Anna up. 'Put your hands here, on the pommel. I'll lead him with the reins—the way we'll get the boy playing Joseph to do it.'

'Okay.'

'Verbal commands work best, and Bert responds to *Go on* when you want him to start walking and *Stop* when you want him to stand still. Got that?'

Anna nodded again.

'Why don't you give that a try?'

Anna smiled. 'Go on, Bert!'

Bert started moving.

'He's doing it, Sydney! He's *doing* it! Look, Daddy— I'm riding!'

'That's brilliant, sweetheart.'

Sydney led Bert down the short side of the field. She turned to check on Anna. 'That's it. Keep your back straight…don't slouch.'

They walked up and down. Up and down. Until Sydney thought Anna was ready to try and do it on her own. She'd certainly picked it up a lot more quickly than Olivia had!

'Okay, Anna. Try it on your own. Head to the end of the field and use the reins to turn him and make him come back. Talk to him. Encourage him. Okay?'

She knew Anna could do it. The little girl had connected with the donkey in a way no other had, and the animal responded brilliantly to her. Sydney really didn't think Anna would have a problem on the night of the nativity. Bert was putty in her hands.

They both stood and watched as Anna led Bert confidently away from them and down the field. Sydney almost felt proud. In fact, she *was* proud.

She became aware that Nathan was staring at her, and then suddenly, almost in a blink, she felt his fingers sliding around hers.

'Thank you, Sydney.'

She turned to him and looked into his eyes. The intensity of the moment grew. It felt as if her heart had sped up but her breathing had got really slow. Her fingers in his felt protected and safe, and he stroked the back of her hand with his thumb in slow, sweeping strokes that were doing strange, chaotic things to her insides, turning her legs to jelly.

'What for?' she managed to say.

'For helping me when it's difficult for you. I appreciate the time you're giving me and my daughter. I…'

He stopped talking as he took a step closer to her, and

as he drew near her breathing stopped completely and she looked up into his handsome blue eyes.

He's going to kiss me!

Hadn't she thought about this? Hadn't she wondered what it might be like? Hadn't she missed the physical contact that came with being in a relationship? And now here was this man—this incredibly *attractive* man—holding her hand and making her stomach do twirls and swirls as his lips neared hers, as he leaned in for a kiss...

Sydney closed her eyes, awaiting the press of his lips against hers.

Only there was no kiss.

She felt him pull his hand free from hers and heard him clearing his throat and apologising before he called out, 'You're doing brilliantly, Anna! Turn him round now—come on. We need to go home.'

Sydney blinked. What had happened? He'd been about to kiss her, hadn't he? And she'd stood there, like an idiot, waiting for him to do it.

How embarrassing!

Anna brought Bert to a halt beside them, beaming widely.

'I think that's enough for today. You've done really well, Anna.'

Anna beamed as her father helped her off the donkey, and then she ran straight to Sydney and wrapped her arms around her. 'Thanks, Sydney! You're the best!'

Sydney froze at the unexpected hug, but then she relaxed and hugged the little girl back, swallowing back her surprise and...for some reason...her tears. 'So are you.'

The farmer took Bert back to his field with the other donkeys, once he'd removed the saddle and tack, and Sydney and Anna said goodbye. Then they all got back into Sydney's car and she started to drive them home.

'Thank you for...er...what you've done for Anna today,' said Nathan.

She took a breath and bit back the retort she wanted to give. 'No problem.'

'You know...taking time out of your weekend...'

'Sydney could stay for dinner, couldn't she Daddy? We're having fajitas!' Anna invited from the back.

She would have loved nothing more than to stay. Her time spent with Anna had been wonderful, and the times when she'd looked across at Nathan and caught him looking at her had been weirdly wonderful and exciting too.

But after what had just happened—the almost-kiss... He'd been going to do it. She knew it! But something had stopped him. Had got in the way.

Was it because he'd suddenly remembered Anna was there? Had he not wanted to risk his daughter seeing them kissing? Or was it something else?

She was afraid of getting carried away and reading too much into this situation. She'd helped out. That was all. She'd felt a connection that Nathan hadn't. Getting too involved with this single dad was perhaps a step too far. Where would it end? If she spent too much time with them, where would she be?

She shivered, even though the car heater was pumping out plenty of hot air. 'I'm sorry, I can't. I've got a...a thing later.'

'Maybe another time?' Nathan suggested, looking embarrassed.

As well you might!

'Sure.'

There can't ever be another time, no.

She watched them clamber from her car when she dropped them off. Nathan lingered at the open window of the car, as if he had something else to say, but then he looked away and simply said goodbye, before following his daughter up the path.

Sydney drove off before he could turn around and say anything else.

I really like them. Both of them.

But was it what they represented that she liked? This dad. This little girl. They were a ready-made family. Being with them might give her back some of what she'd lost. They offered a chance of starting again. So was it the *situation* that she liked? Or *them* as individuals?

Nathan was great. Gorgeous, charming, someone she enjoyed being around. And Anna was cute as a button, with her sing-song voice and happy-go-lucky personality.

Was it wrong to envy them? To envy them because they still had each other?

Was it wrong to have wanted—to have *craved*—Nathan's kiss?

Feeling guilty, she drove home, and she was just about to park up when she got a text. A cat was having difficulties giving birth and she needed to get to the surgery immediately to prep for a Caesarean section.

Suddenly all business—which was easy because she knew what she was doing—she turned the car around and drove to the surgery.

Nathan sent Anna upstairs to get changed into some clean clothes that didn't smell of donkey and farm. Then he headed into the kitchen, switching on the kettle and sinking into a chair as he waited for it to boil.

What the hell had he done?

Something crazy—something not *him*—had somehow slipped through his defences and he'd found himself taking hold of Sydney's hand, staring into her sad grey eyes. And he had been about to *kiss her*!

Okay, so he'd been fighting that urge for a while, and it was hardly a strange impulse, but he *had* thought that he'd got those impulses under control.

Standing there, looking down into her face, at her smooth skin, her slightly rosy cheeks, those soft, inviting lips, he'd wanted to so badly! And she'd wanted him to do it. He'd wanted to, but...

But Anna hadn't been far away, and he'd suddenly heard that horrid voice in his head that still sounded remarkably like Gwyneth, telling him that no one, and especially not Sydney, would want him. Not with his faulty, failing body. Not with his bad genes. Not with a child who wasn't hers...

How could he ask her to take on that burden—especially with the threat of his MS always present? He knew the chances of the MS killing him were practically zero. Okay, there would be difficulties, and there would be complications—there might even be comorbidities such as thyroid disease, autoimmune conditions or a meningioma. But the MS on its own...? It was unlikely.

But it had been enough to make him hesitate. To think twice. And once he'd paused too long he'd known it was too late to kiss her so he'd stepped away. Had called out to Anna...said they needed to go.

Sydney deserved a strong man. A man who would look out for her and care for her and protect her. What if he couldn't do that?

Fear. That was what it had been. Fear of putting himself out there. Of getting involved. Of exposing himself to the hurt and pain that Gwyneth had caused once. How could he go through again? How could he expose Anna to that now that she was older? She would be aware now if she grew to love someone and then that someone decided it was all too much and wanted out.

Anna being a baby had protected her from the pain of losing her mother. And today he had saved himself from finding out if he could be enough for someone like Sydney. Gwyneth had made him doubt what he had to offer. She had probably been right in what she'd said. He didn't know what his future would be like. He couldn't be certain, despite trying his best to remain positive. But it was hard sometimes. Dealing with a chronic illness… sometimes it could get to you.

The kettle boiled and he slowly made himself a cup of tea. He heard Anna come trotting back down the stairs and she came into the kitchen.

'Can I have a biscuit, Daddy?'

'Just one.'

She reached into the biscuit barrel and took out a plain biscuit. 'I loved riding Bert. He was so cute! I love donkeys. Do *you* love donkeys, Daddy?'

He thought for a moment. 'I do. Especially Bert.'

She smiled at him, crumbs dropping onto the floor. 'And do you love Sydney?'

His gaze swung straight round to his daughter's face. 'What?'

'I think you like her.'

'What makes you say that?' he asked in a strangled voice.

'Your eyes go all funny.' She giggled. 'Joshua in my class—he looks at Gemma like that and he *loves* her. They're boyfriend and girlfriend.'

Nathan cleared his throat. 'Aren't they a little young to be boyfriend and girlfriend?'

Anna shrugged, and then skipped off into the other room. He heard the television go on.

She noticed quite a lot, did Anna.

Curious, he followed her through to the lounge and

stood and watched her for a moment as she chose a channel to watch.

'Anna?'

'Yes?'

'If I did like Sydney...how would you feel about that?'

Anna tilted her head to one side and smiled, before turning back to the television. 'Fine. Then you wouldn't be all alone.'

Nathan stared at his daughter. And smiled.

CHAPTER SIX

IT HAD BEEN a long time since Sydney had had to play 'mother', and now she had the pleasure once again. The cat she'd raced to had recovered from its surgery, but had disowned her kittens afterwards. It happened sometimes with animals, when they missed giving birth in the traditional way and there just wasn't that bond there for them.

The four kittens—three black females and a black and white male—were kicking off their December in a small cat carrier at her home and she was on round-the-clock feeding every two hours.

Sydney was quite enjoying it. It gave her purpose. It gave her a routine. But mostly it gave her something to do during the long hours of the lonely nights. Even if she *was* still torturing herself with what might have happened between her and Nathan.

I wanted him to kiss me and I made that perfectly clear!

She'd hardly fought it, had she? Standing there all still, eyes closed, awaiting his kiss like some stupid girl in a fairytale. He must have thought she was a right sap. Perhaps that was what had put him off…

Disturbed from her reverie by the sound of her doorbell, she glanced at the clock—it was nearly eight in the morning—and went to answer the door.

It didn't cross her mind that she'd been up all night, hadn't combed her hair or washed her face, or that she was still wearing yesterday's clothes and smelt slightly of antiseptic and donkey at the same time.

She opened the door to see Nathan and Anna standing there. 'Er… Hi… Sorry, had we arranged to meet?' She felt confused by their being there. And so early, too.

'We were out getting breakfast,' Nathan explained. 'Anna wanted croissants and jam. We didn't have any and…' He blinked, squirming slightly. 'I thought you might like to share some with us.'

He raised a brown paper bag that was starting to show grease spots and she suddenly realised how hungry she was.

Her mouth watered and her stomach ached for the food and nourishment. Warm, buttery croissants sounded delicious!

Even though she still felt embarrassed after yesterday, the lure of the food overpowered the feeling.

'Sure. Come on in.' She stepped back, biting her lip as they passed, wondering if she was making a huge mistake in accepting. Hadn't this man humiliated her just yesterday? Unintentionally, perhaps, but still… And today she was letting him in to her house? She had no idea where her boundaries were with them any more.

Following the scent of food to her kitchen, she washed her hands and got out some plates, then butter from the fridge.

'I don't have any jam…'

'We do!' Anna chirruped. 'Blackberry, apricot and strawberry!' She put a small bag holding the jars onto the kitchen counter.

Sydney nodded. 'Wow! You *do* come prepared, don't

you? There can't be many people wandering around with a full condiments selection.'

Nathan grinned. 'We weren't sure which one you liked, so...'

He was trying to say sorry. She could see that. The croissants, the jam, the sudden breakfast—these were all part of his white flag. His olive branch. His truce. She would be cruel to reject it. Especially as it was going to be so nice. When had she last had a breakfast like this?

'I like apricot, so thank you for getting it for me.'

She smiled and mussed Anna's hair, and then indicated they should all sit at the table. Sydney filled the kettle, and poured some juice for Anna, and then they all settled down to eat.

Her home was filled with laughter, flaky pastries and the wonderful sound of happiness. It was as if her kitchen had been waiting for this family to fill it, and suddenly it no longer seemed the cold empty room she knew, but a room full of life and purpose and identity.

For an hour she forgot her grief. She let down her barriers and her walls and allowed them in. Despite her uncertainty, they were good for her. Anna was wonderfully bright and cheerful and giggly. And those differences between her and Olivia were growing starker by the minute. Anna liked looking at flowers, but had no interest in growing them. She knew what she wanted to be when she was grown up. She liked building things and being hands-on. She was such a sweet little girl, and so endearing, and Nathan...

They just got on well together. It was easy for them all.

Sydney was licking the last of the croissant crumbs from her fingers when Nathan said, 'How come you don't have any Christmas decorations?'

His question was like a bucket of ice-cold water being

thrown over her. It was a reality check. It pulled her back to her *actual* life and not the temporarily happy one she'd been enjoying.

'I don't do Christmas.'

He held her gaze, trying to see beyond her words. Trying to learn her reasons.

Anna looked at her in shock. 'Don't you believe in Santa Claus?'

Sydney smiled at her. If only it were that simple. 'Of course I do. Santa is a very good reason to enjoy Christmas.' She thought for a moment. 'Anna, why don't you go and take a look at what's in the blue cat carrier in my lounge? Be gentle, though.'

Anna gasped and ran into the other room, and Sydney turned back to face Nathan. She sucked in a breath to speak but nothing came out. Thankfully he didn't judge or say anything. He just waited for her to speak. And suddenly she could.

'Olivia died just before Christmas. It seems wrong to celebrate it.'

He swallowed. 'Do you want to talk about it?'

She did…but after the way he'd been with her yesterday… Did she want to share the innermost pain in her heart with a man who could blow so hot and cold? What would be the point in telling him if he wasn't going to stick around? If he wasn't going to be the kind of person she needed in her life? Because she was beginning to think that maybe there *could* be someone. One day. Maybe.

Could the person be Nathan?

She didn't want to feel vulnerable again, or helpless. But sitting in her home night after night, *alone*, was making her feel more vulnerable than she'd ever realised. Yet still she wasn't sure whether to tell him everything.

He stared at her intently, focusing on her eyes, her lips, then on her eyes again. What was he trying to see? What was he trying to decide?

He soon let her know, by confiding something of his own.

'I have MS—multiple sclerosis. To be exact, I have relapsing remitting multiple sclerosis. I have attacks of symptoms that come on suddenly and then go away again.'

She leaned forward, concerned. Intrigued. Was this what had been wrong with him the other day? When he'd been all dizzy at the veterinary surgery? And that time at the accident site?

'MS...?'

'I was diagnosed the week before Anna was born. It was a huge shock—nothing compared to losing a child, but it had tremendous repercussions. Not only my life, but Anna's too. Anna's mother walked out on us both during a time in which I was already reeling. Only a couple of weeks after we'd had Anna, Gwyneth left us...but it doesn't stop us from celebrating Anna's birthday each year. She gets presents, a cake, a party, balloons. You *should* enjoy Christmas. You *should* celebrate. There aren't many times in our lives where we can really enjoy ourselves, but Christmas is one of them.'

Sydney stood up and began to clear away the breakfast things. She'd heard what he'd said, but his story hardly touched hers. 'That's completely different.'

He got up and followed her into the kitchen, grabbed her arm. 'No, it isn't.'

She yanked her arm free. 'Yes, it is! My child *died*. Your girlfriend walked out. There's a *big* difference.'

'Sydney—'

'Do you think I can *enjoy* being reminded every year

that my daughter is dead? Every time Christmas be-
gins—and it seems to get earlier every year—everywhere I look people are putting up decorations and trees
and lights, buying presents for each other, and they're all
in a happy mood. All I can see is my daughter, lying in
a hospital bed with tubes coming out of her, and myself
being told that I need to say goodbye! Do you have *any*
idea of how that feels? To know that everybody else is
happy because it's that time of year again?'

He shook his head. 'No. I couldn't possibly know.'

'No.' She bit back her tears and slumped against the
kitchen units, lost in memories of that hospital once
again. Feeling the old, familiar pain and grief. 'I became the saddest I could ever be at this time of year—
when everyone else is at their happiest. I can't sleep. It's
hard for me. I could *never* celebrate.'

Nathan stood in front of her and took one of her hands
in his, looking down at their interlocked fingers. 'Perhaps you need to stop focusing on the day that she died
and instead start focusing on all the days that she lived...'

His words stunned her. A swell of anger like a giant
wave washed over her and she had to reach out to steady
herself. It was that powerful.

How *dared* he tell her how she ought to grieve? How
she ought to remember her daughter! He had no idea of
how she felt and here he was—another *doctor*—telling
her what she needed to do, handing out advice.

She inhaled a deep breath through her nose, feeling
her shoulders rise up and her chin jut out in defiance as
she stared at him, feeling her fury seethe out from her
every pore.

'*Get out.*'

'Sydney—'

He tried to reach for her arm, but seeing his hand

stretched out towards her, without her permission, made her feel even more fury and she batted him away.

'You don't get to tell me how to deal with my grief. You don't get to tell me how I should be thinking. You don't get to tell me anything!'

She stormed away from him—out of her kitchen, down the hallway, towards her front door, which she wrenched open. Then she stood there, arms folded, as tears began to break and her bottom lip began to wobble with the force of her anger and upset.

She felt as if she could tackle anything with the strength of feeling she had inside her right now. Wrestle a lion? *Bring it on*. Take down a giant? *Bring it on*. Chuck someone out of her home? *Bring. It. On!*

Nathan followed her, apology written all over his features. 'Look, Syd, I'm sorry. I—'

She held up a finger, ignoring the fact that it was shaking and trembling with her rage. 'Don't. Don't you *dare*. I don't want to hear any of it. Not from you. You with your *"drink warm milk"* advice and your *"why not try grief counselling?"* and your *"focus on the days she lived"* advice. You couldn't *possibly* understand what I am going through! You couldn't even kiss me, Dr Nathan Jones, so you don't get to tell me how to live.'

He stared back at her, his Adam's apple bobbing up and down as he swallowed hard. Then he sighed and called out for his daughter. 'Anna? We need to go.'

They both heard Anna make a protest at having to leave. She was obviously having far too much fun with the orphaned kittens.

But she showed up in the doorway and looked at both her father and Sydney. 'Are we leaving?'

''Fraid so.' Nathan nodded and gave her a rueful smile. 'We need to head back now. Sydney's got things to do.'

'Not fair, Daddy! I want to stay with the kittens. Sydney, can I stay for a little bit—*pleeeeeease*?' She added a sickly sweet smile and clutched her hands before her like she was begging for a chance of life before a judge.

Nathan steered her out through the front door. 'Another time, honey.' As he moved out of the door he turned briefly to Sydney. 'I'm sorry I've upset you. I didn't mean anything by it.'

She closed the door, and as it slammed, as she shut out the sight of Nathan and Anna walking away down her front path, she sank to the floor and put her head in her hands and sobbed. Huge, gulping sobs. Sobs that caused her to hiccup. Sobs that took ages to fade away, leaving her crouched in the hallway just breathing in a silence broken only by the ticking clock.

Finally she was able to get to her feet, and listlessly she headed back to the kitchen to clear away the breakfast things.

Sydney had felt numb for a few hours. It was a strange feeling. Having got that angry, that upset, it was as if she'd used up a year's worth of emotions all in a few minutes, and now her body and her mind had become completely exhausted, unable to feel anything.

Now she sat in her empty home, looking at the pictures of her daughter, and felt...*nothing*. No sadness. No joy. She couldn't even bring herself to try and remember the days on which they'd been taken, and when she tried to remember the sound of her daughter's chuckles she couldn't conjure it up.

It was like being frozen. Or as if she could move, breathe, live, exist, but the rest of the world was seen through a filter somehow. It was as if her memories were gone—as if her feelings had been taken away and in their place a giant nothingness remained.

She didn't like it. It made her feel even more isolated than she had been before. Lonely. She didn't even have her daughter's memories to accompany her in the silence.

She wasn't ready to forget her daughter. To lose her. She needed to remind herself again. To reconnect.

Sydney looked up. Olivia's things were in the attic. Her clothes. Her toys. Her books. Everything. She hadn't been able to go up in the loft for years because of them, but perhaps she needed to at this moment.

So, despite the tiredness and the lethargy taking over every limb, muscle and bone, she headed up the stairs and opened up the attic, sliding down the metal ladder and taking a deep breath before she headed up the steps.

There was a stillness in the attic. As if she'd entered a sacred, holy space. But instead of vaulted ceilings with regal columns and priceless holy relics gleaming in soft sunlight there was loft insulation, piles of boxes and a single bulb that was lit by pulling a hanging chain.

She let out a long, slow breath as some of her numbness began to dissipate, and in its place she felt a nervous anxiety begin to build.

Was she right to be doing this? She hadn't looked through these things for so long!

Am I strong enough? What if it's too much?

But then there was another voice in her head. A logical voice.

It's only clothes. Books. Toys. Nothing here can hurt you.

Doubt told her that something might. But she edged towards the first box, labelled *'Costumes'*, and began to unfold the top, not realising that she was biting into her bottom lip until she felt a small pain.

The contents of the box were topped with taffeta. A dress of some sort. Sydney lifted it out to look at it, to try and force a memory. And this time it came.

Olivia had wanted a 'princess dress' for a party. They'd gone shopping into Norton town centre together, her daughter holding on to her hand as she'd skipped alongside her. They'd gone from shop to shop, looking for the perfect dress, and she'd spotted this one. With a beautiful purple velvet bodice and reams upon reams of lilac taffeta billowing out from the waist.

Olivia had looked perfect in it! Twirling in front of the mirror, this way and that, swishing the skirt, making it go this way, then that way around her legs.

'Look, Mummy! It's so pretty! Can I have it?'

Sydney smiled as she pulled out outfit after outfit. A mermaid tail, another princess dress, this time in pink, a Halloween costume festooned with layers and layers of black and orange netting. Sydney hesitated as she dipped into the box and pulled out a onesie made of brown fur. It had a long tail, and ears on the hood. Sydney pressed it to her nose and inhaled, closing her eyes as tears leaked from the corners of them.

Olivia had loved this onesie. She'd used to sleep in it. She'd been wearing it when... The memory came bursting to the fore.

The morning I found you.

She smiled bravely as she inhaled the scent of the onesie once again. It had been washed, but she was convinced it still had her daughter's scent.

An image of that awful morning filled her head. The day before Olivia had said she had a headache. She hadn't wanted to go to school. But Sydney had had a long day of surgeries, and Alastair had had work, so they'd needed their daughter to go in.

At the end of the day, when Sydney had gone to pick her up, Olivia had seemed in a very low mood—not her normal self. When they'd got home she'd said she was tired and that her head still hurt, so Sydney had given her some medicine and a drink and told her she could go to bed. She'd kept checking on her, but her daughter had been sleeping, so she'd just put it down to some virus.

When Alastair had got home he'd been celebrating a success at work, and that night they'd gone to bed and made love. The next morning Alastair had left early. Sydney had called for Olivia to come down for breakfast but she hadn't answered. So she'd gone up to get her and instantly known something was wrong. The second she'd walked into her daughter's bedroom.

She'd not been able to wake her. She'd called her name, shaken her shoulders—nothing. Olivia had been hot, and Sydney had gone to unzip the onesie, and that was when she'd seen the rash and called 999.

Sydney laid the onesie down. This was the last thing that Olivia had worn. It was too sad to focus on. Too painful.

She dug further into the box and pulled out a pirate costume.

Now, this has a happier memory!

There'd been a World Book Day and all the school's children had been asked to come in as one of their favourite characters. At the time Olivia had been into pirate stories, but none of the characters had been girl pirates, so she'd decided that she would be a pirate anyway. Sydney had rolled up a pair of blue jeans to Olivia's calves, bought a red and white striped tee shirt and a tricorne hat, and used an eye patch that they'd been gifted in an old party bag.

Olivia had spent all day answering every question Sydney had asked her with, *'Arr!'* and, *'Aye, Captain!'*

Sydney laughed at the memory, her heart swelling with warmth and feeling once again. Seeing her daughter happy in her mind's eye, hearing that chuckle, seeing her smile, feeling her—

She stopped.

Oh... Could Nathan be right? That I need to focus on the days she lived?

No. No, he couldn't be right. He hadn't experienced grief like this—he didn't know what he was talking about.

But I do feel good when I remember the good times...

Perhaps holding on to the grief, on to the day she died, on to the *pain* was the thing that anchored Sydney in the past? Maybe she was holding herself back? Isolating herself so that she could wallow in her daughter's memory. Was that why Alastair had moved on? Had he been able to let go of the misery and instead chosen to remember his daughter's vibrant life, not just her death?

Stunned, she sat there for a moment, holding the pirate tee shirt and wondering. Her gaze travelled to the other boxes. Books. Toys. Clothes. Was holding on to her daughter like this the thing that was keeping her from moving on? Perhaps keeping her daughter's things in the attic had kept Olivia trapped in a place that tortured them both.

I know I have to try to move on...but by letting go of my past will I lose my daughter?

The thought that maybe she ought to donate some of Olivia's stuff to a charity shop entered her head, and she immediately stood up straight and stared down at the open box.

Give her things away?

No. Surely not. If she gave Olivia's things away, how on earth would she remember her?

You've remembered her just fine with all this stuff packed away in the attic for four years...

She let out a breath. Then another. Steadier. It calmed her racing heart. What if she didn't do it all in one go? What if she just gave away a few pieces? Bit by bit? It might be easier that way. She'd keep the stuff that mattered, though. The onesie. Olivia's favourite toys—her doll and her teddy bear Baxter. Maybe one or two of her daughter's favourite books. The last one they'd been reading, for sure.

Maybe...

She saw the look on Nathan's face as he'd left. *'I'm sorry I upset you...'*

I need to apologise.

Guilt filled her and she suddenly felt sick. Gripping her stomach, she sat down and clutched the onesie for strength. For inspiration.

She would have to apologise. Make it up to him. Explain.

If he even wants to listen.

But then she thought, *He will listen.* He was a doctor. He was good at that. And she needed to let him know that she cared.

As she thought of how she could make it up to him she saw some other boxes, further towards the back of the attic. She frowned, wondering what they were, and, crouching, she shuffled over to them, tore off the tape and opened them up.

Christmas decorations.

Perhaps she could show Nathan in more than one way that she was trying to make things right...

She'd used to love Christmas. Olivia had *adored* it.

What child didn't? It was a season of great fun and great food, rounded off with a day full of presents.

She particularly remembered the Christmas before Olivia had died. She'd asked for a bike and Sydney and Alastair had found her a sparkly pink one, with tassels on the handlebars and a basket on the front adorned with plastic flowers.

Olivia had spent all that Christmas Day peddling up and down on the pathways and around the back garden, her little knees going up and down, biting her bottom lip as she concentrated on her coordination. And then later that day, after they'd all eaten their dinner, pulled crackers, told each other bad jokes and were sitting curled up on the sofa together, Olivia had asked if next Christmas she could have a little brother or sister.

Sydney's gaze alighted on the bike, covered by an old brown blanket...

She swallowed the lump in her throat. Olivia would have loved a sibling. A little baby to play with. What would she have made of Anna? No doubt the girls would have been best friends.

Thinking of Anna made her think of Nathan. She was so very grateful for him coming over today. Offering his olive branch. He had given her a new way of thinking. And how had she reacted? Badly! She'd seen it as an attack on her rather than seeing the kind and caring motivation behind it.

She could see now what he'd been trying to say. And she had missed it completely. It was true. She had been focusing so much on her daughter's death that she had forgotten to focus on her daughter's life.

And Nathan had also told her about his MS. It had been so brave of him to share that with her, and it must have been troubling him for some time. It must have been why he'd been so ill that day she'd looked after Anna. And hadn't Anna said her daddy was always sick and tired?

Poor Nathan. But at least he knew what he was fighting. It had a name. It had a treatment plan. She would have to look it up online and see what relapsing remitting multiple sclerosis really was. Especially if—as she was starting to hope—they were going to be involved with each other. It would be good to know what to expect and how to help.

Nathan had given her a gift. A way to try and lift the burden that she'd been feeling all this time. The guilt. The grief. He'd given her something else to think about. Told her to try and remember Olivia in a different way. A less heartbreaking way.

Could she do it?

Maybe she could start by honouring the season…

Sydney lifted up a box of decorations and began to make her way back down the ladder.

CHAPTER SEVEN

MRS COURTAULD HAD arrived for her appointment. She was there for a blood pressure check, and though she could have made an appointment to see the practice nurse to get it done she'd deliberately made a doctor's appointment to see Nathan.

She came into his room, shuffling her feet, and settled down into a chair with a small groan.

He forced a smile. 'Mrs Courtauld...how are you?'

'Oh, I'm good, Doctor, thank you. I must say *you* look a bit glum. I've been round the block enough times to know when someone's *pretending* to be okay.'

He laughed. 'I'm sorry. I'll try to do better. Are you ready for Christmas?'

Sydney's rejection of him had hurt terribly. Although he didn't think she'd rejected him because of his health—unlike Gwyneth—the way she'd thrown him out still stung.

'Of course I am! Not that there's much preparation for me to do...not with my Alfred gone, God rest his soul. But my son is going to pick me up on Christmas Eve and I'm going to his house to spend the season.'

'Sounds great. Let someone else look after you and do all the work. Why not?'

'I've brought those things that you asked for.' She

reached down into her shopping trolley and pulled out a small packet wrapped in a brown paper bag and passed it across the table to him. 'I asked around and so many people wanted to help. I hope it's the kind of thing you were after. Surprisingly, there was quite a bit that people had.'

He peeked inside and smiled. It *was* rather a lot. More than he could have hoped for. But would it be any good now?

'Perfect. Thank you, Mrs C. I appreciate all the trouble you went to to coordinate this. Now, shall we check your blood pressure?'

She began to remove her coat. 'Anything for our Sydney.' She looked at him slyly. 'Will you be spending Christmas together, then?'

He felt his face colour, but smiled anyway, even though he suspected that the chance of his spending Christmas with Sydney had about the same odds as his MS disappearing without trace. Choosing not to answer, he wheeled his chair over to his patient.

Mrs Courtauld couldn't know that they'd had a falling out. He'd been trying to help Sydney, but maybe it had come out wrong? He'd been going over and over what he'd said, trying to remember the *way* he'd said it as well as *what* he'd said, and he'd got angry at himself.

His patient rolled up her sleeve, staring at him, assessing him. 'She deserves some happiness, young Sydney. She's had her sadness, and she's paid her dues in that respect. Enough grief to last a thousand lifetimes. It's her turn to be happy.' She looked up at him and made him meet her gaze. 'And you could do that for her, Doctor. You and that little girl of yours.'

'Thanks, Mrs C.'

'Call me Elizabeth.'

He smiled and checked her blood pressure.

* * *

A bell rang overhead as Sydney walked into the charity shop. There was only one in Silverdale, and sales from it aided the local hospice. She hadn't been in for a long time, but was reassured to see a familiar face behind the counter.

'Syd! Long time, no see! How are you?'

Sydney made her way to the counter with her two bags of clothes. It wasn't much. But it was a start. 'Oh, you know. Ambling on with life.'

'We've missed seeing you in here. We could always rely on you to come in most weekends, looking for a new book or two.'

'I'm sorry it's been a while.' She paused for a moment. She could back out if she wanted to. She didn't have to hand these items over. 'I've…er…brought in a few things. Children's clothes.'

'Children's…? Oh, wait…not *Olivia's*?'

Her cheeks flushed with heat and she nodded. 'Just one or two outfits. Thought I'd better start sorting, you know.'

Lisa nodded sadly. 'Sometimes it's what we need to do, to move forward.'

She didn't want to cry. Wasn't that what Nathan had said in a roundabout way? And look at how she had treated him for it! Perhaps everyone had been thinking the same, but she'd been the only one not to know.

'It's all been laundered and pressed. You should be able to put it straight out.' She placed the two bags on the counter and Lisa peered inside, her fingers touching the fabric of a skirt that Olivia had worn only once, because she'd been going through a growth spurt.

'That's grand, Syd. I'll have a sort through and maybe make a window display with them. Launch them with style, eh?'

Unable to speak, Sydney nodded. Then, blinking back tears, she hurriedly left the shop.

Outside in the cold air she began to breathe again, sucking in great lungsful of the crisp air and strangely feeling a part of her burden begin to lift.

It had been a difficult thing to do, but she'd done it. She'd made a start. Hopefully next time it would be easier. But doing it in little instalments was better than trying to get rid of it all in one go. She knew that wasn't the way for her. Slow and steady would win this race.

But now she had a really hard thing to do. She had to see Nathan. Apologise. There was one last committee meeting tonight and perhaps there, on neutral ground, she could let him know that she'd been in the wrong. That it would be nice if he could forgive her. But if not...

She dreaded to think of *if not*...

Those hours in the attic—those hours spent sorting her daughter's clothes for donation—had made her begin to see just how much she had begun to enjoy and even to depend upon Nathan's friendship.

She'd been a fool to react so badly.

She could only hope he would forgive her in a way Alastair had never been able to.

It was the last committee meeting before the big day. The Christmas market and nativity—and the anniversary of Olivia's death—were just two days away, and this was their last chance to make sure that everything was spick and span and organised correctly. That there were no last-minute hiccups.

There was palpable excitement in the room, and Miriam had even gone to the trouble to supply them with chocolate biscuits to help fuel their discussion.

Sydney sat nervously at one end of the table, far from

Nathan, anxious to get the opportunity to talk to him and put things right. Her mind buzzed with all the things she needed to say. Wanted to say. She'd hoped she'd have a chance to talk to him before the meeting started, but he'd come in late once again and grabbed his place at the table without looking at her.

'The marquees are all organised and will be delivered tomorrow and erected on-site. Items for the tombola are all sorted, and Mike has promised us the use of his PA and sound system this year.' Miriam beamed.

'How are we doing regarding the food stalls? Sydney?'

She perked up at the sound of her name and riffled through her notes, her hands shaking. 'The WI ladies in the village are in full cake-making mode and most will bring their cakes down in the morning for arrangement. The manageress of The Tea-Total Café has promised us a gingerbread spectacular, whatever that may be.'

'Sounds intriguing. Any entries this year for the Best Pet competition?'

She nodded. 'The usual suspects. I'm sure Jim will be hoping to win back the trophy from Gerry this year.' She smiled, hoping Nathan would look at her so she could catch his eye, but he just kept gazing down at his own notes.

She could almost feel her heart breaking. Had she hurt him so much with her words the other day that he couldn't even *look* at her now? Was she shut out of his world completely? It hurt to think so.

But then he looked up, glanced at her. 'Can I enter Lottie?'

She turned to him and smiled hopefully. 'You can.'

Though they were seated two chairs apart, she itched to reach for his hand across the table. To squeeze his fingers. Let him know that she was sorry. That she hadn't meant what she'd said. That she'd had a knee-jerk reaction because she was frightened of letting go.

But then he looked away again as he scribbled something into his notes.

Her heart sank.

Malcolm filled them in on what was happening with the beer tent, the businesses that had applied to have a stall and sell their wares, who'd be covering first aid and said that licences for closing the road to the council had been approved.

'All that's left that's out of our hands is the nativity. Dr Jones, I believe your daughter is going to be the star attraction this year? Any idea how rehearsals are going?'

'Miss Howarth and Anna assure me that it's all going very well.'

'And I've arranged a small area for the donkey and other farm animals to be kept in whilst they're not performing,' added Sydney, hoping to join in on his contribution.

'Excellent, excellent!' Malcolm enthused.

Once the meeting was over Sydney quickly gathered her things and hurried out into the cold after Nathan. She *had* to catch up with him. She couldn't just let him go. Not like this.

The village had already gone full-force on Christmas decorations. The main street was adorned with fairy lights, criss-crossing from one side to the other, so as people walked along at night it was like being in a sparkly tunnel. Trees were lit and shining bright from people's homes, and some residents had really gone to town, decorating their gardens and trees into small grottos. It didn't hurt her any more to see it.

'Nathan!'

He turned, and when he saw her his face darkened. She saw him glance at the floor.

Standing in front of him, she waited until he looked up and met her gaze. 'Thank you for waiting. I...er...really need to apologise to you. For how I reacted—well, *overreacted* to what you said.'

He stood staring at her, saying nothing.

'I was so in the wrong. I wasn't ready to hear what you said, and I thought you were telling me I needed to be over Olivia's death, and...you weren't. You were telling me to focus on the good times and not the bad, and that was something completely different to saying, *Get over it Sydney!*'

She was wringing her hands, over and over.

'You were trying to help me. Trying to make me see that if I could just try and look at it in another way then it needn't be so painful. So sad. That it was trapping me in the past—'

He reached out and steadied her hands, holding them in his. 'It's okay.'

Relieved that he was talking to her, she had to apologise even more. 'It's not. I behaved abominably. I kicked you out of my house! You *and* Anna! I feel so terrible about that...so inhuman and abysmal and—'

He silenced her with a kiss.

It was so unexpected. One moment she was pouring her heart out, blurting out her apologies, her regrets for her mistake, hoping he would understand, hoping he would forgive her, and the next his lips were on hers. His glorious lips! Warm and tender and so, so forgiving...

She could have cried. The beginnings of tears stung her eyes at first, but then ebbed away as the wondrousness of their kiss continued.

He cradled her face in his hands as he kissed her and

he breathed her in. Sydney moaned—a small noise in the back of her throat as she sank against him. This was… amazing! This was what they could have had the other day if he hadn't thought otherwise and backed off. What they could have had if only she hadn't got angry or scared or whatever it was she had been, so that tricks were playing in her head.

Why had they delayed doing this? They fitted so perfectly!

His tongue was searching out hers as he kissed her deeper and deeper. She almost couldn't breathe. She'd forgotten how to. All she knew right now was that she was so happy he'd forgiven her. He must have done. Or surely he wouldn't be kissing her like this.

And just when she thought she was seeing stars, and that her lungs were about to burst, he broke away from her and stared deeply into her eyes.

She gazed back into his and saw a depth of raw emotion there, a passion that could no longer be bridled. He wanted her.

And she him.

'Drive me home,' she said.

He nodded once and they got into the car.

It didn't take them long to reach her bedroom. Once inside, their giggles faded fast as they stood for a moment, just looking at each other.

Had she ever needed to be with a man this much?

Sydney needed to touch him. Needed to feel his hands upon her. She knew that he would not make the first move unless she showed him that this was what she wanted.

She reached up and, keeping eye contact, began to undo the buttons of his shirt.

He sucked in a breath. 'Sydney…'

'I need you, Nathan.' She pulled his shirt out from his trousers and then her hands found his belt buckle.

Nathan's mouth came down to claim hers, his tongue delicately arousing as he licked and tasted her lips.

She pulled his belt free and tossed it to the floor. She undid the button, unzipped the zipper, and as his trousers fell to the floor he stepped out of them and removed his shirt.

'Now me,' she urged him.

She felt his hands take the hem of her jumper and lift it effortlessly over her head, and then he did the same with her tee shirt, his eyes darkening with desire as her long dark hair spread over her milky-white shoulders. His hands cupped her breasts, his thumbs drifting over her nipples through the lace, and she groaned, arching her back so that her breasts pressed into his hands.

His mouth found her neck, her shoulders, her collarbone, all the while causing sensations on her skin that she had not experienced for a very long time, awakening her body, making her crave his every touch.

He undid her jeans, sliding them down her long legs. His lips kissed their way down her thighs and then came slowly back up to find the lace of her underwear. Then he was breathing in her scent and kissing her once again through the lace.

She almost lost it.

When had she *ever* felt this naked? This vulnerable? And yet...she revelled in it. Gloried in it. She knew she needed to show him her vulnerability, show that despite that she still wanted to be with him. To trust him. After the way she'd treated him the other day, she needed him to know that she couldn't be without him.

'You're so beautiful...' he breathed, and the heat of his breath sent goosebumps along her skin.

His hands were at her sides, going round to her back. He found the clip on her bra and undid it. She shrugged it off easily, groaning at the feel of his hands cupping her breasts, properly this time, at the feel of his mouth, his kisses.

'Nathan...'

She could feel his arousal, hard against her, and she unhooked his boxers, sliding them to the floor.

As he lay back on the bed she looked at him in triumph. This beautiful, magnificent man was all hers. And she'd so very nearly cast him aside!

She groaned as she thought of what she might have lost and lay beside him, wrapping her limbs around him so that they were entwined as their mouths joined together once more.

All he'd ever done was listen to her. Understand her. Give her space and time to be ready to talk to him. Where else would she find a man that patient? That understanding and empathetic?

He rolled her under him and breathed her name as his hands roamed her body, creating sensations that she had forgotten she'd ever felt before. She needed him so much. Longed to be *part* of him.

She pulled him closer, urging him on as he began to make love to her.

This was what life was about! Really living. Being a *part* of life—not merely existing. It was about celebrating a relationship, sharing fears and desires and finding that one person you could do that with. About opening up to another person and being okay about that.

Nathan had shared his own vulnerability, his multiple sclerosis. It must have taken him a great deal of courage. And he had shared Anna with her. Letting her get to know his daughter. He couldn't have known that they would get on like this. Must have been worried that Sydney might reject them both once she got to know them.

I nearly did.

She suddenly understood how much pain he must have felt when she'd kicked him out and she pulled him to her once more, hoping as he cried out and gripped the headboard that he would finally see just how much he'd been right to trust her, after all.

She wrapped him safely in her arms and held on tight.

Afterwards, they lay in bed in each other's arms.

Sydney's head was resting in the crook of Nathan's shoulder and he lay there, lazily stroking the skin on her arms. 'I really missed you, you know...'

She turned and kissed his chest. 'I missed you, too. I hated what I did.'

'I understood. You were lashing out because what I said hurt you. You thought I was asking you to give up even *thinking* about your daughter.' He planted a kiss on the top of her head. 'I gave you the advice someone gave me once.'

She turned, laying her chin upon his chest and staring up into his face. 'What do you mean?'

'When I got my diagnosis I was in complete shock. It was like I was mourning my old life. The life in which I could do anything whenever I wanted, without having to think about muscle weakness or spasms or taking medication every day. I mourned the body that I thought would slowly deteriorate until it was useless, and I couldn't get over that.'

'What happened?'

'Anna was born. I was euphoric about that. But then I started thinking about all the ways I might let her down as a father. What if I missed school shows, or parents' evenings, or birthdays…? And then Gwyneth left, totally appalled by the fact that she'd got involved with someone with this illness, and that made me feel under even more pressure from myself. I *couldn't* let Anna down! She only had me to rely on. I *had* to be well. I *had* to be positive. But something kept pulling me back towards feeling sorry for myself. I'd lost my partner and my health and I couldn't get past that.'

She kissed his chest. 'I'm so sorry.'

'I went to a counselling group. It was led by a really good therapist. She helped me see that I was mourning a loss. I was mourning my future. She told me to look at it in a different way. Not to focus on what I'd lost, but on what I'd gained. I didn't necessarily have a bad life in front of me, that—I had a beautiful baby daughter who loved me unconditionally and I knew what my limits might be. But they weren't necessarily there. I had to celebrate the new me rather than mourn the old me. Does that make sense?'

She nodded, laying her head back down against his beautifully strong chest. 'It does.'

'Gwyneth leaving wasn't about me. It was about her and what *she* could deal with. I couldn't control her reaction, but I could control mine. And that's why I decided to focus on the good that was coming. On what I could learn about myself in the process. Discovering hidden depths of strength.'

'Did you find them?'

'Oh, yes!' He laughed, squeezing her to him. Then he paused for a moment and rolled above her, staring deeply into her grey eyes. 'Have you?'

She nodded silently, feeling tears of joy welling in her eyes.

'I think I'm starting to. Because of you.'

He smiled and kissed her.

CHAPTER EIGHT

IT WAS THE afternoon of the Christmas market and nativity and Anna was incredibly excited.

Nathan hadn't been able to get in touch with Sydney yesterday, being busy at work, but at least now he felt better about the direction they were heading in.

It was all going well.

When she'd slammed the door on the two of them and he'd had to walk away it had been the hardest thing he had ever done. Even harder still was the fact that Anna had been full of chatter about the kittens. When could she go and visit them again? Would Sydney mind if they went round every day?

He'd managed to distract her by getting her to read through her lines for her part in the nativity, and he'd been grateful when she'd gone quiet in the back of the car as she read her little script.

But now…? Everything was going well for them. He hoped he would get a moment to talk to Sydney, because he knew that this day would be hard for her.

She'd told him it was the anniversary of Olivia's death. That she'd always faced this day alone in the past. He tried for a moment to imagine what it would be like if he was mourning Anna, but it was too dreadful. He dashed the thought away instantly.

There was so much to do. He'd promised to help out with setting up the marquees and organising the stands, and said he'd be a general dogsbody for anyone who needed him.

Surely Sydney would be there too. She had stalls to organise. The Best Pet show to judge. He hoped he'd get a moment to talk to her, to make sure she was okay.

He parked in the pub car park and walked down to the square that already looked as if it was heaving with people and noise. Right now it seemed like chaos, but he hoped that by the afternoon, and for the nativity in the evening, it would all run smoothly and everyone would be entertained.

He searched for Sydney's familiar long chocolate hair in the crowd, but he couldn't see her amongst all the people bustling about.

This was his and Anna's first Christmas in Silverdale, and he was looking forward to making new connections with people that he'd only ever met as patients. He wanted to let people see him as someone other than a doctor. To let them see that he was a father. A neighbour. A friend.

Tonight was going to go really well. He knew it. And hopefully some of the villagers who didn't know him yet would get the opportunity to meet him and welcome him as a valued member of their community.

'Dr Jones! How good to see you. Are you doing anything at the moment?'

Nathan noticed Miriam, the secretary of the committee, loitering within an empty marquee that had tables set up but nothing else. 'No. How can I help?'

'I'm running the tombola, and all the donated items are in boxes in the van, but I can't lift them with my arthritis. Would you be able to?'

He smiled. This he could do. He was a strong man.

He could lift and carry whatever she asked of him and he would do it. 'A pleasure, Miriam. Where's the van?'

Miriam pointed at a white van parked on the edge of the barriers. 'You are a dear. A real bonus to our committee. We needed some new blood!'

He waved away her compliment. 'I'm sure Dr Preston is hugely missed. I just hope I can fill his shoes.'

Miriam beamed at him. 'You far surpass Richard Preston already, Dr Jones, just by my looking at you!'

Nathan grinned. 'If I was thirty years older, Miriam...'

'Thirty? Oh, you're too kind! *Much* too kind!'

Nathan headed to her van, opened it up and started pulling out boxes. Some were very light, and he assumed they were full of teddy bears and the like. But others were considerably heavier and he struggled to carry one or two.

Whatever were people giving away—boulders?

He lugged the boxes over to the marquee, and just as he set down the last one he heard Sydney's laugh.

Instantly his heart began to pound. She was *laughing*. She was *here*. She was helping out. Same as him. Just as she'd promised she would.

He looked about for her, and once he'd made sure Miriam was okay to empty out the boxes by herself found himself heading over to the pen that Sydney was building along with Mr Bradley from Wicklegate Farm—the owner of Bert the donkey.

'Sydney!'

She turned at the sound of his voice. 'Nathan!'

He kissed her on the lips in greeting—a gesture that earned a wry smile from Mr Bradley.

'How are you doing? I meant to call you earlier—'

'I'm fine!' she answered brightly.

'Really? You don't have to pretend. I know today must be difficult for you. I thought that—'

'Nathan… Honestly. I'm doing great.'

He tried to see if she was just being brave for him, but he couldn't see any deception in her eyes. Perhaps she *was* doing okay? He stood back as she continued to build the pen, fastening some nuts on the final fence with a spanner.

'It's for Bert and the goats and things. What do you think?'

'Erm… I'm no expert on animal holding pens, but these look good to me.'

She kissed him on the cheek. 'I've got lots to do. Off you go! I know you're busy, too. You don't have to hold my hand. I'm doing okay. I've got through this day before.'

He stilled her hands. 'You were on your own before.'

'And I'm not now. I promise if I have a problem, or get upset, I'll come and find you.'

'If you're sure…?'

'I'm sure.' She smiled at him. 'I appreciate your concern. Oh, I almost forgot—I have Olivia's costume for Anna.' She stepped out of the pen and over to her car, opening the boot and bringing back a small bag. 'It should fit. It's all loose robes, and she can tie it tighter with the belt.'

He nodded, accepting the bag. 'Thanks. She nearly had to wear what I'd made her.'

He would just have to trust her. She knew he would be in her corner if she needed him.

'I'm around. Just give me a shout and maybe we can grab a snack later? Before it all kicks off?'

She blew him a kiss. 'I'll come and find you.'

'I'll hold you to it.' He smiled and waved, and then, tearing himself away, headed off to deliver the costume to his daughter.

* * *

Sydney did as she'd promised. A few hours later, when the market was all set up and ready to open to the public, she sought out Nathan, She found him at the bakery tent, manhandling a giant gingerbread grotto scene to place it on a table, and they headed off to sit on the steps around the village Christmas tree.

Nathan paid for a couple of cups of tea for them both and then joined her, wrapping his arm around her shoulders in the cold evening air.

The Christmas market looked picture-postcard-perfect. The marquees were all bedecked with Christmas lighting, carols were being played over the PA system in readiness and—oh, the aromas! The scent of hot dogs, fried onions, candy floss, roasting chestnuts, gingerbread and freshly brewed coffee floated in the air, causing their mouths to water.

'Looks amazing, doesn't it?' she said, looking out at all their hard work. It felt good to be appreciating—finally—the magic of Christmas once again.

'It certainly does. Worth all those meetings we had to sit through.'

She laughed. 'When it all comes together like this it's hard to believe we managed to achieve it.' She paused. 'Did you get the costume to Anna? Did it fit?'

He nodded. 'Perfectly. Thank you.'

They sat in companionable silence for a while, sipping their tea and just enjoying the sensation of *being*. Enjoying the moment. It was nice to sit there together, watching everyone else beavering away.

Nathan took her hand in his and smiled at her as she snuggled into his arms. But then she sat forward, peering into the distance.

'Look! They're letting everyone in. Come on—we

have stations to man!' She tossed her paper teacup into a nearby bin and headed off to her first job of the evening.

Nathan watched her go.

Was she really as unaffected by this day as she seemed?

He doubted it.

Frowning, he followed after her.

Silverdale was brimming with activity and the centre of the high street looked amazing. Sydney would have liked to truly immerse herself in the marvel of the beautiful fairy lights everywhere. To listen to the carol singers and their music. To taste the wonderfully aromatic food on display and talk to all the visitors and customers. Enjoy the floral displays.

But she couldn't.

She knew she had work to do, but she was beginning to feel guilty.

Was she really pretending that today wasn't *the day?* Had she deliberately tried to ignore it because she already knew how guilty she now felt? She hadn't mourned as much. She hadn't *remembered* her daughter the way she usually did today.

She felt bad—even if *'usually'* mostly involved staring at photographs all day and often ended with her being a crumpled, sobbing heap.

Her heart felt pained. Just breathing seemed to be exhausting. And yet she had to keep up a steady stream of false smiles and fake jollity for everyone she met or saw.

Was she lying to Nathan? Or to herself?

The stallholders were doing lively business, and she could see money changing hands wherever she looked. People she knew walked their dogs, or pushed buggies, or stood arm in arm looking in wonder and awe at their hard-worked-for Christmas Market. And now crowds were gathering at the main stage for the crowning glory of the evening—the nativity play.

She wandered through the tent with her clipboard, viewing the animals entered for the Best Pet competition. Their owners stood by, looking at her hopefully as she met each one, asked a little about their animal, remembering to remark on their colouring or lovely temperament and scribbling her thoughts on paper.

But she was doing it on automatic pilot.

Until she got to a black rabbit.

Lottie.

Lottie sat in her cage quite calmly, oblivious to all the hubbub going on around her. Her eye had healed quite well, and apart from a slight grey glaze to it no one would be able to guess that she had been attacked and almost blinded.

Sydney stared at the rabbit, her pen poised over her score sheet, remembering the first time Nathan had brought Lottie to her. How hard it had been to fight her feelings for him. How she'd tried to tell herself to stay away from him and not get involved. She hadn't listened to herself. He'd wormed his way into her affections somehow, with those cheeky twinkling eyes of his—*and, my goodness, it had felt so good to lie in his arms. Protected. Coveted. Cherished.*

And he was making her forget. Wasn't he?

No! Not forget. Just deal with it in a different way.

Losing Olivia had hurt like nothing she could ever have imagined. One minute her daughter had been lively, full of life, giggling and happy, and the next she'd wound up in a hospital bed, and Sydney had sat by her bedside for every moment, hoping for a miracle.

She'd felt so helpless. A mother was meant to protect her children—but how on earth were you meant to defend them against things you couldn't see? Bacteria. Viruses. Contagion. They were all sneaky. Taking hold of young, healthy, vital bodies and tearing them asunder. All she'd been able to do was sit. And pray. And talk to her daughter who could no longer hear her. Beg her to fight. Beg her to hold on for a little while longer.

It had all been useless.

She felt a bit sick.

What am I doing here?

'We need the result, Sydney. The nativity is about to start.'

Sydney nodded to Malcolm absently. She wanted to see the nativity. She'd promised Anna she would watch her and cheer her on as she rode in on Bert.

She marked a score for Lottie and then passed her results to Malcolm, who took them over to his small stand in the tent.

Pet owners gathered anxiously—all of them smiling, all of them hopeful for a win. There were some lovely animals, from little mice to Fletcher the Great Dane. Fletcher was a big, lolloping giant of a dog, with the sweetest nature.

Malcolm cleared his throat. 'In third place, with six points, we have Montgomery! A gorgeous example of a golden Syrian hamster.'

Everyone applauded as a little girl stepped forward to receive a purple ribbon for Montgomery.

'In second place, with eight points, we have Jonesy—a beautiful ginger tom.'

Again there was applause, and a young boy came forward to collect his ribbon.

'And in first place, with ten points, we have Lottie the rabbit!'

There were more cheers. More applause.

'Lottie's owner can't be here to collect her prize as she's preparing for her role in the nativity. So perhaps our judge—our fabulous Silverdale veterinary surgeon— would like to give us a few words as to why Lottie has won tonight's contest? Everyone... I give you Sydney Harper!'

Reluctantly, Sydney stepped over to address the crowd—a sea of faces of people she recognised. People she knew from many years of living in this community. There was Miss Howarth, Olivia's schoolteacher. And Cara the lollipop lady, who'd used to help Olivia cross the road outside school. Mr Franklin, who would always talk to Olivia as they walked to school each morning...

'Thank you, Mr Speaker.'

She tried to gather her thoughts as she stood at the microphone. She'd been in a daze for a while. Now it was time to focus. Time to ignore the sickness she could feel building in her stomach.

'There were some amazing entries in this year's competition, and it was great to see such a broad variety of much-loved animals, who all looked fantastic, I'm sure you agree.'

She paused to force a smile.

'I was looking for a certain something this year. I have the honour of knowing a lot of these animals personally. I think I can honestly say I've seen most of them in my surgery, so I know a little about them all. But Lottie won my vote this year because... Well...she's been through a lot. She went through a difficult time and almost lost her life. Instead she lost her eye, but despite that...despite the horror that she has experienced this year, she has stayed strong.'

Her gaze fell upon Nathan, who had appeared at the back of the crowd.

'She fought. And tonight, when I saw her in her cage, looking beautiful in her shiny black coat and with a quiet dignity, I knew I had found my winner. Prizes shouldn't always go to the most attractive, or the most well-behaved, or the most well-groomed. Animals, like people, are more than just their looks. There's something beneath that. A character. A *strength*. And Lottie has that—in bucketloads.'

She nodded and stepped back, indicating that she had finished.

Malcolm led the applause, thanked her, and then urged everyone to make their way to the main stage for the nativity.

Sydney waited for the main crowd to go, and when there was a clearing she walked out of the marquee, feeling a little light-headed.

She felt a hand on her arm. 'Thank you.'

Nathan.

'Oh…it was nothing.'

'Anna will be thrilled Lottie won. She didn't want to miss it, but she's getting ready for the show.'

'Make sure you collect your voucher from Malcolm later.'

'I will.'

'Right. Well…' She wanted to head for the stage. But it seemed Nathan still had something to say.

'You know, you were right just then.'

'Oh…?'

'About people having depths that you can't see. You know, you're a lot like that little rabbit. You have that inner strength.'

She didn't feel like it right now. 'We…er…we need to get going.'

'Wait!' He pulled something from behind his back. 'I got you this.'

He handed over a small parcel, wrapped in shiny paper and tied with an elaborate bow.

'It's for Christmas. Obviously.' He smiled at her. 'But I thought it was important to give it to you today.'

'What is it?'

He laughed. 'I can't tell you that! It's a surprise. Hopefully…a good one. Merry Christmas.'

Suddenly felt this was wrong. Much too wrong! She shouldn't be getting *presents*. Not *today*.

Nathan was wrong.

Today was the worst day to give her his gift.

'I… I don't know what to say.'

'I believe thank you is traditional.'

He smiled and went to kiss her, but she backed off.

'I can't do this,' she muttered.

'Syd? What's the—?'

'You shouldn't give me a gift. Not today. A present? Today? You know what this day is. You know what it means.'

'Of course! Which is why I wanted to give it to you now. To celebrate you moving forward, to give you an incentive to—'

It was too much. Sydney couldn't stand there a moment longer. She had to get away. She had to leave. She—

I promised Anna I'd watch her in the nativity.

Torn, she stood rooted to the spot, angst tearing its way through her as grief and guilt flooded in. This was *not* the way she should be on the anniversary of her daughter's death! She ought to be showing respect. She ought to be remembering her daughter. *Olivia.* Not Anna. Or Nathan. They couldn't be Olivia's replacements. They could never be what her daughter had been to her. Or mean as much.

Could they?

Her heart told her they might, even as the agony of this indecision almost made her cry out.

'Syd...?'

'Nathan, please don't! I can't do this. I can't be with you—'

'Sydney—'

'It's over. Nathan? Do you hear me? I'm done.'

He let go of her arms and stepped back from her as if she'd just slapped him.

She'd never felt more alone.

Nathan just stood there, looking at her, sadness and hurt in his eyes.

'You should remember what you said about Lottie. You're strong, too, you know... You've been through something...*unimaginable* and you're still here. But if you can't see it in yourself...if you can't feel it...believe it...then I need to keep my distance, too. I need to think about Anna. I can't mess her around. If you can't commit to us the way I need you to—'

'I never wanted to hurt you or Anna.'

'I know.' He looked away at the happy crowds. 'But... you did. Please let Anna see you before you leave.'

And he walked away.

Sydney gulped back a grief-racked sob, wondering what the hell she'd just done.

Sydney stood at the front of the crowd, waiting for Anna's big moment. She'd split up from Nathan as he'd headed backstage to give his daughter one last pep talk.

Guilt and shame were filling her. Today was the anniversary of her daughter's death. And she'd kept busy— tried her hardest not to think about her. She hadn't even gone to the cemetery to put down some flowers for her. She hadn't been for so long. Who knew what her daughter's grave looked like now? Mrs C had laid a flower there in November—was it still there? Dead and brittle? Covered by fallen leaves or weeds?

And she was here, waiting to applaud another little girl. What was she *doing*? She'd even given Anna Olivia's old costume. She'd be riding Bert, too. Saying the same lines. It would be too much to bear.

And now she'd hurt Nathan. Played around with that man's heart because she hadn't known whether she was ready to accept it completely.

Feeling sick, she was about to turn and push her way through the crowds when she noticed Bert the donkey come into view, with Anna perched proudly on his back.

Sydney gasped. She'd been expecting to be tormented with memories. But it was *so* clear now. Anna was *nothing* like Olivia. The shape of her face was different. She had her father's jawline, her father's eyes.

If I'd continued with Nathan I wouldn't have been just taking him on, but Anna, too. I'd have let them both down. And now I've broken his heart, and Anna's too...

Overwhelmed by shock and guilt, Sydney stood silently and watched. Suddenly she was smiling with encouragement as Anna's gaze met her own. She felt so proud of Anna. Almost as proud of her as she had been of Olivia, doing the same thing.

How can that be?

As she watched the little girl ride Bert over to his mark by the hay bale, dismount and then take the hand of her Joseph, Sydney felt sadness seize her once more. She could recall Olivia doing that very thing. She'd taken Joseph's hand and been led into the stable too.

'And Joseph and Mary could find nowhere to stay. The only place left to them was with the animals in the stable. And in the place where lambs were born Mary gave birth to baby Jesus...' A small boy at the side of the stage intoned his words into a microphone.

Anna reappeared, this time without her pregnancy bump and holding a doll, swaddled in a thick white blanket, which she lay down into a manger.

Why am I crying?

Sydney blinked a few times and dabbed at her eyes with the back of her hand. Was she being like the innkeeper of Bethlehem? Telling Nathan and Anna there was no room for them in her home? Her heart?

She'd felt there *was* room. It had been there. She'd felt it. Even now she could feel it.

Sydney turned and pushed her way through the crowds, tears streaming freely down her face, unable to look. Unable to face the future she would have had if she'd stayed with Nathan. Unable to believe that she had that inner strength Nathan had said she had!

It was too difficult to move on like this. Accepting Nathan and Anna would be like forgetting her own daughter, and she couldn't have that. Not ever.

Free of the crowds, she strode away from the nativity. She couldn't stay there any longer. She couldn't watch the end. All she wanted at that point was to be at home. To be surrounded by the things that made her feel calm again.

Back at her cottage, she threw her keys onto the table by the door and headed straight for the lounge, casting the still wrapped present from Nathan under the tree. She slumped into her favourite couch, settling her gaze upon her pictures of Olivia, on the one on the mantel of her daughter reaching up for those bubbles, which was now surrounded by Christmas holly and mistletoe.

She stared at it for a moment, and then sat forward and spoke out loud. 'She's not you. She could *never* replace you.'

Despite the heartache he was feeling at Sydney's abrupt departure, Nathan gave Anna a huge hug. She'd acted her part in the nativity brilliantly, and it had gone without a hitch. All those people who said you should never work with children or animals were wrong. Bert had done everything Anna had asked of him, and most importantly of all he had kept her safe.

Scooping her up into his arms, Nathan hitched her onto his hip and kissed her cheek. 'Well done, pumpkin.'

'Thanks, Daddy. Did you see me at the end? With my golden halo?'

'I did! Very impressive.'

'I made it in class.'

'It looked very professional.'

'I saw Sydney.'

He frowned, feeling his stomach plummet with dread. What had Anna seen? That Sydney had looked sick? That she'd run?

He'd almost gone after her. One moment she'd been there, and then the next...

'You did? She got called away, I think, towards the end. But she *did* see you, and she was smiling, so she was very proud.'

Anna beamed. 'I'm hungry, Daddy. Can we get something to eat?'

He nodded. 'Sure. I think the hot dog stand may just have a few left if we're quick.'

Putting her back down on the ground, he walked with her over to the fast food stall. He wasn't hungry. Not at all. All he could see was the look on Sydney's face just before she'd turned and bolted.

He'd been too far away to chase after her. Not that he could have done. He'd needed to be here for Anna, just as he'd promised. But he kept replaying in his mind the change that had come over Sydney's features. The brave smile she'd tried to give to his daughter before her face had fallen and she'd gone.

As they passed them various villagers stopped to compliment them and to tell Anna how well she'd done.

'Hey, guess what?' he said, determined to keep things happy and bright for his daughter.

'What?'

'Lottie won the Best Pet competition!'

'She *did*? Yay!' Anna jumped up and down with glee. 'Can we go and get her?'

'Let's eat these first.' He handed her a hot dog, covered with a healthy dollop of fried onions, ketchup and mustard. 'And then we will. Malcolm's looking after the pets at the moment, so she's not on her own.'

Anna bit into her hot dog and wiped her mouth when a piece of fried onion tried to escape. 'Did she get a ribbon?'

'I think she did.'

'And a prize?'

'I think so. She was very lucky, wasn't she?'

He was finding this difficult. Pretending everything was okay when all he wanted to do was sit alone and allow himself to feel miserable. Had he pushed Sydney too hard by giving her that present? Had he tried to make her accept things she wasn't ready to work through yet?

I should never have got involved! I should have kept my distance!

'We had the judge on our side.' Anna smiled and took another bite.

Did we? Maybe only briefly.

He bit into his own hot dog, but he didn't really want it. The smell of the onions only turned his stomach.

She'd not been gone long, but already he ached for her. Missed her. He'd thought for a moment that they had a future together. He'd pictured waking up in the mornings and seeing her next to him. Her grey eyes twinkling at him from her pillow. He'd imagined them taking country walks together, hand in hand, and having picnics in the summer—Sydney laughing in the warm sun, her hair glinting.

He'd imagined nights watching movies together and sharing a bucket of popcorn. Feeding each other tasty morsels and titbits from the fridge before running upstairs, giggling, as he chased her before they fell into bed. And then moments when they'd just talk. He'd hold her hand. Trace the lines on her palm. He'd imagined them making love. Maybe even having a family of their own together...

They could have had it all.

He'd had his heart broken again, and this time he felt even more distraught.

He'd known Gwyneth was selfish. Had always had to have things her own way. She'd always had the perfect life, and a disabled partner had not been for her. Even the promise of a new family, the child they'd made together, hadn't been enough for her. It had never been enough for her. His diagnosis had just been the last thing she'd needed before she walked away. He'd never expected that she would walk away from her own child, too, but she had.

Sydney was looking out for herself too, but in a different way. Her child—Olivia—had been the centre of her life. Her world. And her world had been taken from her. Her sun had been stolen so that she'd only been living in darkness.

Nathan had thought that he'd brightened that darkness for a while.

'Is Sydney coming to our house on Christmas Day?' Anna asked, finishing off her bun in a final mouthful.

'Er... I really don't know, Anna. She's a bit sad at the moment.'

'Because she doesn't have her little girl any more?'

Nathan looked at his daughter, surprised at her insight. 'Yes. I think that's it.'

But what if it wasn't just that?

'We could go to hers and try to cheer her up. It *is* Christmas, and Miss Howarth says it's the season of goodwill. We learnt that at school for the play.'

How simple it was in a child's world. Everything was so black and white. 'We'll see. You might be busy playing with all your new things.'

'Sydney could come and play with me.'

He sighed. 'I don't know, Anna. Perhaps we need to give her some space for a while.'

'I want to thank her for giving Lottie first prize. Can we go and see her now? Before Christmas Day? Before she gets sad?'

Nathan felt touched by his daughter's compassion. She was doing her best to understand. 'She's already sad. Maybe we'll see her in the village. Come on…let's get Lottie and go home.'

He took her sticky hand in his and together they headed off to the animal tent.

CHAPTER NINE

IT WAS CHRISTMAS MORNING. A day on which Sydney should have been woken by an excited child bouncing on her bed and urging her to go downstairs. Instead, she was woken by the sound of rain against her window, and she lay in bed for a moment, not wanting to move.

Christmas Day.

The house was full of decorations. Encouraged by Nathan, and feeling positive and optimistic, she had adorned the house throughout, sure in the knowledge that this season she would have a reason to celebrate. People she loved to celebrate *with*.

Only it hadn't worked out that way.

She stared at the ceiling and once again asked herself if she was really doing the right thing.

Nathan was a kind-hearted man. Compassionate, caring. And she felt sure he had strong feelings for her. Looking at the pillows beside her, she remembered that night they'd made love. How good he'd made her feel. The brief time that they'd had together had been exquisite. Being made love to, being cherished, being as *treasured* as he had made her feel, had made her realise all that had been missing from her life.

I'm alone.

He'd not come after her after the nativity. He hadn't

shown up in the few days afterwards either. She'd thought that he might, and she'd been prepared not to answer the door. To hide. But he hadn't come.

She'd always believed that by keeping her distance from romantic entanglements she was keeping herself safe—and, yes, she supposed she was. But she was also keeping herself in a prison of loneliness. It was a kind of solitary confinement. All she had was Magic, her cat. Her only interactions were with the people and the animals at work and the friendly faces she saw in the shops. When she returned home all she had left were herself and her memories.

Unless I choose Nathan's way of thinking.

Christmas was a time for family. She could be sharing the day with Nathan. With Anna. Darling, sweet little Anna, whom she also adored. And she was letting fear keep her away. Her fear of being vulnerable again. Of losing Nathan. Losing Anna. Of not being enough for either of them!

'I'm losing you if I do nothing!' she said out loud, angry at herself.

Putting on her slippers and grabbing her robe, she headed downstairs.

The Christmas tree twinkled in the corner, with just a few presents underneath it. There was that gift from Nathan. Something from her parents. A couple of gifts from faithful long-term customers at work. The gift she'd placed there in Olivia's memory.

There could have been more. There could have been something for Nathan. For Anna. There could have been happiness in this house again. The day could have been spent the way Christmas is supposed to be spent.

She could be cooking Christmas breakfast for them

all right now. Scrambled egg and smoked salmon. Maybe a little Bucks Fizz.

She sat by the tree and picked up the parcel from her mum and dad. It was soft and squidgy, and when she half-heartedly tugged at the wrapping she discovered they'd got her a new pair of fleece pyjamas. She smiled at the pattern—little penguins on tiny icebergs. The other gifts were a bottle of wine, some chocolates, a book…

All that was left was the gift from Nathan and the one for her own daughter that would never be opened.

She picked up the gift from Nathan and glanced at the card.

Merry Christmas, Sydney!
Lots of love, Nathan xxx

What would it be? She had no idea. Part of her felt that it would be wrong to open it now. They weren't together any more. He'd made that clear. She hesitated.

He'd wanted her to have it.

Sydney tore at the wrapping and discovered a plain white box. Frowning, she picked at the tape holding the end closed, getting cross when it wouldn't come free and having to use a pen from her side table to pierce it and break the seal. Inside, something was wrapped in bubble wrap.

She slid it out and slowly unwrapped the plastic. It was a picture frame, and taped to the front, was a small white envelope. There was something inside. A memory card…

It's a digital photo frame.

She plugged it into the mains, inserted the memory card and switched it on, wondering what there could be on it…and gasped.

There, right before her eyes, were pictures of Olivia

that she had never even seen before! Some were close-ups, some were group shots, some were of her with other people or children, most she recognised as people from Silverdale.

Olivia in a park on a swing set next to another little boy, who was grinning at the photographer. Olivia at a birthday party with her face all smudged with chocolate cake. Olivia in the front row of the school choir.

She watched in shocked awe as picture after picture of her daughter appeared on the screen.

Where had Nathan got these? They must have come from other people! People in the village who had taken their own photos and captured Olivia in them too. And somehow—amazingly—he had gathered all these pictures together and presented them to her like this!

Tears pricked at her eyes as she gazed at the beautiful images. And then it flicked to another picture, and this one was moving. A video. Of a school play. She remembered it clearly. It had been Olivia's first play and she'd been dressed as a ladybird in a red top that Sydney had spent ages making, sewing on little black dots and then making her a bobble headband for her antennae.

The video showed the last few moments. It captured the applause of the crowd, the kiddies all lining up in a row, taking a bow. A boy near Olivia waved madly at the camera, and then Olivia waved at someone just off to the left of the screen and called out, *'I love you, Mummy!'*

Sydney heard the words and burst into tears, her hands gripping the frame like a lifeline. She'd forgotten that moment. She'd been there. She remembered the play very well; she'd been so proud of Olivia for not forgetting any of her words, and she'd been a true actress, playing her part with aplomb. And at the end she'd seen Sydney in the crowd, and Sydney had waved at her madly and called out to her.

She pressed 'pause'. Then 'rewind'. And watched it again.

Sydney had always believed that she would never get any new photos of Olivia. That her daughter had been frozen in time. But Nathan had given her a gift that she could never have foreseen!

Surely he loved her? What man would do something so thoughtful and as kind as this if he didn't? He would have to know just what this would mean to her.

When the video ended and the frame went back to the beginning of its cycle of photos again, Sydney rushed upstairs to get dressed. She had to see him. She had to... what? Thank him?

'I don't want to thank him. I want to be with him,' she said aloud to Magic, who lay curled on her bed, blinking in irritation at her racing into the bedroom and disturbing her slumber. 'I've been so stupid!'

She yanked off her robe and her pyjamas and kicked off her slippers so hard they flew into the mirror on the wardrobe door.

She pulled on jeans, a tee shirt and a thick fisherman's jumper and twisted her hair up into a rough ponytail. She gave her teeth a quick scrub and splashed her face with some water. Once she'd given it a cursory dry with a towel she raced downstairs and headed for her car, gunning the engine and screeching off down the road.

She hadn't even locked her own front door.

But before she could go to Nathan's house there was somewhere else she needed to go first.

Silverdale Cemetery and Memorial Gardens was a peaceful place. But for a long time it had been somewhere that

Sydney had avoided. It had always hurt too much, and for a long time she hadn't come. She'd not felt she had the inner strength to get through a visit.

But today she felt able to be there.

She *wanted* to be.

Today she felt closer to her daughter than on any other day so far. Perhaps it had something to do with what Nathan had said. Perhaps it was because he had helped lift her guilt. Perhaps it was because he had given her that new way of thinking. But now Sydney felt able to go to the site where her daughter was buried, and she knew that she wouldn't stand there staring down at the earth and thinking of her daughter lying there, cold and alone and dead.

Because Olivia wasn't there any more. She wasn't in the ground, cold and dead.

Olivia was alive in her heart. And in her mind. Sydney's head was full of images long since forgotten. Memories were washing over her with the strength of a tsunami, pounding into her with laughter and delight and warm feelings of a life well-lived and enjoyed.

Olivia had been a happy little girl, and Sydney had forgotten that. Focusing too much on her last day. The day on which she'd been dying. Unconscious. Helpless. In pain.

Now Sydney had a new outlook on her daughter's life. And it was an outlook she knew Olivia would approve of. So the cemetery was no longer a place for her to fear but a place in which she could go and sit quietly for a moment, after laying some flowers. Bright, colourful winter blooms that her daughter had helped her to plant years before.

The headstone was a little dirty, so she cleaned it off with her coat sleeve and made sure her daughter's name was clear and bright. Her eyes closed as she pictured her daughter watering the flowers in the back garden with her pink tin watering can.

'I'm sorry I haven't visited for a while,' she said, her eyes still closed. 'But I got caught up in feeling sorry for myself. You wouldn't have approved.' She laughed slightly and smiled, feeling tears prick at her eyes. 'But I think I'm overcoming that. A new friend—a *good* friend—taught me a valuable lesson. I was stuck, you see, Olivia. Stuck on missing you. Stuck on taking the blame because I felt someone had to.'

She opened her eyes and smiled down at the ground and the headstone.

'I don't have to do that any more. I'm not stuck. I'm free. And because I'm free you are too. I can see you now. In my head. In here…' She tapped her chest, over her heart. 'I can see you so clearly! I can hear you and smell you and feel you in my arms.'

She paused, gathering her breath.

'You'd like Nathan. He's a doctor. He's a good man. And Anna…his daughter…you'd love her too. I know you would. I guess I just wanted to say that I… I *love* you, Olivia. I'm sorry I was gone for a while, but I'm back, and now I have someone looking out for me, and he's given me the ability to get *you* back the way I should have from the beginning.'

She touched the headstone.

'I'll be back more often from now on. And…er… I've put up a tree. I'm celebrating Christmas this year. There's something for you under it. You won't ever be forgotten.'

She sniffed in the cold, crisp December air and looked about her. Two headstones away was the grave of one Alfred Courtauld, and she remembered his wife telling her about how she'd once laid a flower on Olivia's grave.

Sydney picked up a flower from Olivia's bouquet and laid it on Alfred's stone. 'Thanks for looking after Olivia whilst I've been away.'

And then she slowly walked back to her car.

Nathan watched as Anna unwrapped her brand-new bike, her hands ripping off the swathes of reindeer-patterned paper that he'd wrapped it in, smiling warmly at her cries of joy and surprise.

'A *bike!*' she squealed, swinging her leg over the frame and getting onto the seat. 'Can I ride it? Can I take it outside?'

'Course you can.' He helped her take the bike out to the back garden and watched as she eagerly began to pedal, wobbling alarmingly at the beginning, but then soon getting the hang of it.

'Look, Daddy!'

'I'm watching, baby.'

He stood in the doorway, holding his mug of coffee, watching his daughter cycle up and down, but feeling sad that he couldn't give her more. He'd hoped this Christmas to be sharing the day with Sydney. To be opening presents together, giving Anna the feel of a *real* family, so the three of them could enjoy the day together because they were meant to be together.

But Sydney had kept her distance. She'd not dumped him as unceremoniously as Gwyneth had, but she'd still broken his heart.

It wasn't just Christmas he felt sad about. It was all of it. Every day. Christmas was a time for family, but so was the rest of the year. Waking every morning *together*. Listening to each other talk about their day each evening. Laughing. *Living.*

He'd hoped that Sydney could be in their lives, and he

knew that Anna still hoped for that, too. She'd kept going on about it last night before she went to bed.

'Will Sydney be coming tomorrow, Daddy?'

But, sadly, the answer had been no. She would not be coming.

As he headed into the kitchen to make himself a fresh drink he briefly wondered if she had opened his present. It had taken a lot of organising, but Mrs Courtauld had helped—reaching out to people, contacting them on her walks around the village with her greyhound Prince, asking everyone to check their photos and see if any of them had Olivia in them.

He'd dared to hope there would be one or two, but he had been surprised at how many they had got. Fourteen new pictures of Olivia and a video, in which she was saying the exact words he knew would gladden Sydney's heart.

Because that was what he wanted for her most of all. For her to be happy. For her heart to swell once again with love. He'd hoped that her love would include him, but…

His doorbell buzzed. *Who on earth…?*

It was Christmas morning. It couldn't be a door-to-door salesman, or anyone like that. Perhaps someone had been taken ill? Perhaps he was needed as a doctor?

He hurried to the front door, unlocked it and swung it open.

'Sydney?'

She looked out of breath, edgy and anxious. 'Can I come in?'

Did he want her to? Of course he did! He'd missed her terribly. But if she was just here to rehash everything they'd said the other night then he wasn't sure he wanted to hear it.

But something in her eyes—a brightness, a *hope*—made him give her one last audience.

He stepped back. 'Please.'

He watched as she brushed past and then followed her into the kitchen, from where she could see Anna, playing happily in the back garden.

'You got her a bike?'

He smiled as he looked at his daughter, happily pedalling away. 'Yes. It was what she wanted.'

Sydney turned to him. 'And what do *you* want, Nathan? For Christmas?'

Nathan stared at her, trying to gauge the exact reason for her turning up like this on Christmas Day. It wouldn't be a trick or a game. Sydney wasn't like that. *Had she opened his gift to her?*

He couldn't answer her. Couldn't tell her what he *really* wanted. So he changed the subject. 'Did you like your present?'

Tears filled her eyes then and she nodded, the movement of her head causing the tears to run freely down her cheeks. She wiped them away hurriedly. 'I can't believe what you did. How you managed that… I'm…speechless.'

He gave a small smile. 'I wanted to make you happy. Just tell me it didn't make you sad.'

'It didn't.' She took a quick step towards him, then stopped. 'I've come to apologise. I made a mistake.'

Nathan frowned. 'What do you mean?'

'Us. I made the wrong choice.'

He didn't say anything. He didn't want to make this go wrong. He needed to hear what she had to say.

'I got frightened. The day…the evening we were together I…panicked. And then, when I saw Anna on the donkey, I don't know what it was… I started feeling guilty. I felt that if I forgot Olivia on her most important day I would be losing her. But then today—earlier—I realised that it *wasn't* her most important day. The day she died. Her most important day was the day she was born! I can remember Olivia in a different way, just like you said, and by doing so I can also have a future. And so can she. Because my grief was trapping Olivia too. I kept her in pain all that time. Remembering the day she left me...when she was suffering. When I couldn't help her. I kept her there. Trapped in time. But not any more. Not any more,' she said firmly.

He shook his head. 'Love isn't what hurts people, Sydney. *Losing* someone hurts. *Grief* hurts. *Pain* hurts. But love? Love is the greatest thing we can experience.'

'I know. Because I feel love for Olivia. I feel love for...' She paused and stepped closer, laying a hand upon his chest, over his heart. 'For you. I've felt more helpless in the last few days being sat alone at home than I have ever felt. I need to be with you.'

He laid his hand over hers, feeling his heart pound in his ribcage as if it was a wild animal, trying desperately to escape. 'What are you saying?'

'I'm saying I want us to be together. You. Me. Anna. I think we can do it. I think that together we can be strong enough to fight whatever is coming in the future.'

'You mean it?' he asked, hope in his voice.

'I do. I've missed you so much! I've been in pain because I don't have you. I didn't realise what was missing from my life until I met you.'

Nathan smiled and kissed her, meeting her lips with a kiss that burned with fervour. Devouring her, tasting her, enjoying her with a passion that he could barely contain.

She wanted him! She wanted him back and she was willing to take a chance on their future.

It was all he'd ever wanted.

None of them knew what his future would be. How his disease would progress. Whether it would get worse. Just because that happened to a lot of people with MS, it didn't mean it would happen to him. He might be one of the lucky ones. It could stay as relapsing remitting. Who knew?

And even if it did progress he now felt braver about facing it. Because he would have Sydney at his side. And Anna, too. His daughter would not be burdened by carrying the weight of her father's illness all alone on her young shoulders. She would be able to share her worries. With a mother figure. With *Sydney*. And he knew Anna adored Sydney. They could be a perfect family. Or at least they could try!

They broke apart at the sound of his daughter's footsteps running towards the house.

'Sydney!' Anna barrelled into them both, enveloping them with her arms. 'Are you here for Christmas dinner?'

Sydney smiled at Nathan, and he answered. 'She's here for *every* dinner, I think. Aren't you?'

He looked into her grey eyes and saw happiness there. And joy.

'If you'll have me.'

Anna squeezed her tight and beamed.

Nathan pulled her close, so they were both wrapped in his embrace.

'Always.'

* * * * *

SLEIGH RIDE WITH THE SINGLE DAD

ALISON ROBERTS

CHAPTER ONE

As an omen, this wasn't good.

It could have been the opening scene to a horror movie, in fact.

Grace Forbes, in her crisp, clean set of scrubs—her stethoscope slung around her neck along with the lanyard holding her new Manhattan Mercy ID card—walking towards Charles Davenport who, as chief of Emergency Services, was about to give her an official welcome to her new job.

An enormous clap of thunder rolled overhead from a storm that had to be directly on top of central New York and big enough for the sound to carry into every corner of this huge building.

And then the lights went out.

Unexpectedly, the moment Grace had been bracing herself for became an anti-climax. It was no longer important that this was the first time in more than a decade that her path was about to cross with that of the man who'd rocked her world back in the days of Harvard Medical School. Taking control of a potential crisis in a crowded emergency room was the only thing that mattered.

In the brief, shocked silence that followed both the

clap of thunder, a terrified scream from a child and the startling contrast of a virtually windowless area bathed in bright, neon lighting being transformed instantly into the shadowed gloom of a deep cave, Charles Davenport did exactly that.

'It's just a power outage, folks.' He raised his voice but still sounded calm. 'Stay where you are. The emergency generators will kick in any minute.'

Torch apps on mobile phones flickered on like stars appearing in a night sky and beams of light began to sweep the area as people tried to see what was going on. The noise level rose and rapidly got louder and louder. Telephones were ringing against the backdrop of the buzz of agitated conversations. Alarms sounded to warn of the power disruption to medical equipment. Staff, including the administrative clerks from the waiting area, triage nurses and technicians were moving towards the central desk to await instructions and their movements triggered shouts from people desperate for attention.

'Hey, come back…where are you going?'

'Help…I need *help*.'

'Nurse…over *here*…please?'

'I'm scared, Mommy…I want to go *home*…'

Grace stayed where she was, her gaze fixed on Charles. The dramatic change in the lighting had softened the differences that time had inevitably produced and, for a heartbeat, he looked exactly as he had that night. Exactly like the haunting figure that had walked through her mind and her heart so often when sleep had opened portals to another time.

Tall and commanding. Caring enough to come after her and find out what was wrong so he could do something about making it better…

Which was pretty much what he was doing right now. She could see him assessing the situation and dealing with the most urgent priorities, even as he took in information that was coming at him from numerous directions.

'Miranda—check any alarms coming from cardiac monitors.'

'Get ready to put us on bypass for incoming patients. If we don't get power back on fast, we'll have a problem.'

'Put the trauma team on standby. If this outage is widespread, we could be in for a spate of accidents.'

Sure enough, people manning the telephones and radio links with the ambulance service were already taking calls.

'Traffic lights out at an intersection on Riverside Drive. Multi-vehicle pile-up. Fire service called for trapped patients. Cyclist versus truck incoming, stat.'

'Fall down stairs only two blocks away. Possible spinal injury. ETA two minutes.'

'Estates need to talk to you, Dr Davenport. Apparently there's some issue with the generators and they're prioritising Theatres and ICU...'

Charles nodded tersely and began issuing orders rapidly. Staff dispersed swiftly to cover designated areas and calm patients. A technician was dispatched to find extra batteries that might be needed for backup for equipment like portable ultrasound and X-ray machines. Flashlights were found and given to orderlies, security personnel and even patients' relatives to hold. Finally, Charles had an instruction specifically directed to Grace.

'Come with me,' he said. 'I need someone to head the trauma team if I have to troubleshoot other stuff.' He noticed heads turning in his direction. 'This is Dr

Grace Forbes,' he announced briskly. 'Old colleague of mine who's come from running her own emergency department in outback Australia. She probably feels right at home in primitive conditions like this.'

A smile or two flashed in Grace's direction as her new workmates rushed past to follow their own orders. The smile Charles gave her was distinctly wry. Because of the unusual situation she was being thrown into? Or was it because he knew that describing her as an old colleague was stretching the truth more than a little? It was true that she and Charles had worked in the same hospital more than once in that final year of medical school but their real relationship had been that of fierce but amicable rivals for the position of being the top student of their year. The fact that Charles knew where she'd been recently, when he hadn't been present for the interview she'd had for this job, was another indication that he was on top of his position of being head of this department. No wonder he'd won that final battle of the marks, even though it had only been by a small margin.

'Welcome to Manhattan Mercy, Grace... Trauma One is this way...'

It was hardly the best way to welcome a new member of staff but maybe it was better this way, with so many things to think about that Charles couldn't allow any flashes of memory to do more than float past the edges of his conscious mind.

He hadn't seen Grace since he'd noticed her in the audience when he'd walked onto the stage to accept the trophy for being the top student of their graduation party from medical school.

He hadn't spoken to her since...since *that* night...

'Warn people that waiting times are going to go through the roof for anything non-urgent,' he told the senior member of the administrative team as he passed her. 'But don't push them out the door. By the sound of this storm, it's not safe out there.'

A flicker in the ambient light filtering into the department suggested a flash of lightning outside and another roll of thunder could be heard only a second later so they were still right underneath it. Fingers crossed that the worst of the storm would cross the central city quickly but how long would it be before the power disruption was sorted? And how many problems would it cause?

The weather alone would give them a huge spike in traffic accidents. A sudden plunge into darkness could cause all sorts of trauma like that fall down stairs already on its way. And what about the people on home oxygen who could find themselves in severe respiratory distress with the power outage cutting off their support? They needed to be ready for anything in the ER and he needed to clear space for the potential battleground of dodging unexpected missiles of incoming cases and whatever ambush could be in store with equipment that might not be functioning until power came back on.

He hadn't faced a challenge like this for a long time but he had learned way back how to multi-task when the proverbial was hitting the fan and Charles knew he could function effectively on different levels at the same time.

Like knowing which patients could be sidelined for observation well away from centre-stage and directing staff members to transfer them as he passed their ed cubicles at the same time as fending off a request from a television crew who happened to be in the area and wanted to cover the fallout from what was apparently a record-breaking storm.

'Keep them out of here,' he growled. 'We're going to have more than enough to deal with.'

It never took long for the media to get their teeth into something, did it? Memories of how much damage had been done to his own family all those years ago had left Charles with a mistrust bordering on paranoia. It was a time of his life he had no desire to revisit so it was perhaps unfortunate that the arrival of Grace Forbes in his department had the ability to stir those memories.

And others...

A glance over his shoulder showed him that Grace was following his slightly circuitous route to Trauma One as he made sure he knew what was happening everywhere at the moment. The expression on her face was serious and the focus in those dark grey eyes reminded him of how capable he knew she was. And how intelligent. He'd had to fight hard back at medical school to keep his marks on the same level as Grace and, while they'd never moved in the same social circles, he'd had enormous respect for her. A respect that had tipped into something very different when he'd discovered that she had a vulnerable side, mind you, but he wasn't going to allow the memory of that night to surface.

No way. Even if this situation wasn't making it completely unacceptable to allow such a personal distraction, he wouldn't go there. It was in the same, forbidden territory that housed flirting and he had never been tempted to respond to opportunities that were only becoming more blatant as time crept on.

No. He couldn't go there. It would still feel like he was being unfaithful...

Nobody could ever accuse Charles Davenport of being less than totally loyal. To his family and to his work.

And that was exactly where his entire focus had to be right now. It didn't matter a damn that this was a less than ideal welcome to a new staff member. Grace would have to jump into the deep end and do her bit to get Manhattan Mercy's ER through this unexpected crisis.

Just as he was doing.

Other staff members were already in the area assigned to deal with major trauma, preparing it for the accident victims they had been warned were on their way. A nurse handed Grace a gown to cover her scrubs and then a face mask that had the plastic eye shield attached.

'Gloves are on the wall there. Choose your size.'

Someone helpfully shone a torch beam over the bench at the side of the area so that Grace could see the 'M' for medium on the front of the box she needed. She also caught a glimpse of an airway cart ready for business, an IV cart, a cardiac monitor, ventilator and portable ultrasound machine.

Okay. She could work with this. Even in semi-darkness she had what she needed to assess an airway, breathing and circulation and to do her best to handle whatever emergencies needed to be treated to stabilise a critically injured patient. And she wasn't alone. As the shadowy figures of paramedics surrounding a gurney came rapidly towards them, Charles was already standing at the head of the bed, ready to take on the most important role of managing an airway.

'Male approximately forty years old,' one of the paramedics told them. He was wearing wet weather gear but his hair was soaked and he had to wipe away the water that was still trickling into his eyes. 'Hit by a truck and thrown about thirty feet to land on the hood of an approaching car. GCS of twelve, blood pressure ninety on palp, tachycardic at one-thirty. Major trauma to left arm and leg.'

The man was semi-conscious and clearly in pain. Despite wearing a neck collar and being strapped to a back board, he was trying to move and groaning loudly.

'On my count,' Charles directed. 'One, two…*three*…'

The patient was smoothly transferred to the bed.

'I need light here, please,' Charles said. He leaned close to their patient's head as someone shone a beam of light in his direction. 'Can you hear me?' He seemed to understand the muffled change to the groan coming from beneath an oxygen mask. 'You're in hospital, buddy. We're going to take care of you.'

A nurse was cutting away clothing. Another was wrapping a blood pressure cuff around an arm and a young, resident doctor was swapping the leads from an ambulance monitor to their own. Grace was watching, assessing the injuries that were becoming apparent. A mangled right arm and a huge wound on the left thigh where a snapped femur had probably gone through the skin and then been pulled back again. The heavy blood loss was an immediate priority. She grabbed a wad of dressing material and put it on the wound to apply direct pressure.

'We need to get back out there,' the lead paramedic told them. 'It's gone crazy. Raining cats and dogs and visibility is almost zero.'

'How widespread is the power cut?'

'At least sixteen blocks from what we've heard.

Lightning strike on a power station, apparently. No-body knows how long it's gonna be before it's back on.'

Charles nodded. 'Thanks, guys.' But his attention was on assessing his patient's breathing. He had crouched to put his line of sight just over head level and Grace knew he was watching the rise and fall of the man's chest to see whether it was symmetrical. If it wasn't, it could indicate a collapsed lung or another problem affecting his breathing.

She was also in a direct line for the steady glance and she saw the shift, when Charles was satisfied with chest movement and had taken on board what she was doing to control haemorrhage and his gaze flicked up to meet her own. For a split second, he held the eye contact and there was something in his gaze that made her feel... what? That he had confidence in her abilities? That she was already a part of the team?

That he was pleased to see her again?

Behind that emotional frisson, there was something else, too. An awareness of how different Charles looked. It shouldn't be a surprise. Thirteen years was a very long time and, even then, they had been young people who were products of their very different backgrounds. But everyone had known that Charles Davenport had the perfect life mapped out for him so why did Grace get the fleeting impression that he looked older than she would have expected? That he had lines in his face that suggested a profound weariness. Sadness, even...

'Blood pressure eighty on forty.' The resident looked up at the overhead monitor. 'And heart rate is one-thirty. Oxygen saturation ninety-four percent.'

'Is that bleeding under control, Grace?'

'Almost. I'd like to get a traction splint on asap for definitive control. It's a mid-shaft femoral fracture.'

Another nod from Charles. 'As soon as you've done that, we need a second line in and more fluids running. And I want an abdominal ultrasound as soon as I've intubated. Can someone ring through to Theatre and see what the situation is up there?'

The buzz of activity around the patient picked up pace and the noise level rose so much that Grace barely noticed the arrival of more paramedics and another patient being delivered to the adjoining trauma room, separated only by curtains. Working conditions were difficult, especially when some of the staff members were directed to the new arrival, but they were by no means impossible. Even with the murky half-light when a torch wasn't being directed at the arm she was working on, Grace managed to get a wide-bore IV line inserted and secured, attaching more fluids to try and stabilise this patient's blood pressure.

With the airway and breathing secured by intubation and ventilation, Charles was able to step back and oversee everything else being done here. He could also watch what was happening on the neighbouring bed, as the curtain had been pulled halfway open. As Grace picked up the ultrasound transducer and squeezed some jelly onto her patient's abdomen, she got a glimpse of what was happening next door.

Judging by the spinal board and the neck collar immobilising the Spanish-looking woman, this was the 'fall down stairs' patient they had been alerted to. What was more of a surprise was that Charles was already in position at the head of this new patient. And he looked... fresher, somehow. Younger...?

No... Grace blinked. It wasn't Charles.

And then she remembered. He'd had a twin brother who'd gone to a different medical school. Elijah? And hadn't their father been the chief of emergency services at a prestigious New York hospital?

This hospital. Of course it was.

Waiting for the image to become readable on her screen as she angled the transducer, Grace allowed herself a moment to think about that. The dynasty was clearly continuing with the Davenport family front and centre in Manhattan Mercy's ER. Hadn't there been a younger sister who was expected to go into medicine as well? It wouldn't surprise her if there was yet another Davenport on the staff here. That was how rich and powerful families worked, wasn't it—sticking together to become even more powerful?

A beat of something like resentment appeared. Or was it an old disappointment that she'd been so insignificant compared to the importance of family for Charles? That she'd become instantly invisible the moment that scandal had erupted?

Whatever. It was easy to push aside. Part of a past that had absolutely nothing to do with the present. Or the future.

'We've got free fluid in the abdomen and pelvis,' she announced. 'Looks like it's coming from the spleen.'

'Let's get him to Theatre,' Charles ordered. 'They've got power and they've been cleared to only take emergencies. He's stable enough for transfer but he needs a medical escort. Grace, can you go with him, please?'

The metallic sounds of brakes being released and sidebars being raised and locked were almost instant. Grace only had time to ensure that IV lines were safe from snagging before the bed began moving. This was an efficient team who were well used to working together and following the directions of their chief. Even in the thick of what had to be an unusually stressful shift for this department, Grace could feel the respect with which Charles was regarded.

Behind her, as she stayed close to the head of the bed to monitor her patient's airway and breathing en route to Theatre, Grace could hear Charles moving onto a new task without missing a beat.

'Any signs of spinal injury, Elijah? Want me to see if the CT lab is clear?'

And then she heard his voice change. 'Oh, my God… *Maria?*'

He must know this patient, she realised. And he was clearly horrified. She could still hear him even though she was some distance on the other side of the curtain now.

'What happened? Where are the boys?'

A break from the barely controlled chaos in a badly lit emergency department was exactly what Grace needed to catch her breath but it was a worry how crowded the corridors were. And a glimpse into the main waiting area as they rushed past on their way to the only elevators being run on a generator suggested that the workload wasn't going to diminish any time soon.

This was a different planet from the kind of environment Grace had been working in for the last few years and the overall impression was initially overwhelming. Why on earth had she thought she could thrive with a volume of work that was so fast-paced? In a totally new place and in a huge city that was at the opposite end of the spectrum from where she'd chosen to be for such a long time.

Because her friend Helena had convinced her that it was time to reconnect with the real world? Because she had become exhausted by relying solely on personal resources to fight every battle that presented itself? Because the isolation of the places she had chosen to practise medicine had finally tipped the balance from being a welcome escape to a bone-deep loneliness that couldn't be ignored for ever?

Like another omen, lights flickered overhead as neon strips came alive with a renewed supply of power. Everybody, including the porters and nurses guiding this bed towards Theatre, looked up and Grace could hear a collective sigh of relief. Normal life would be resumed as soon as the aftermath of this unexpected challenge was dealt with.

And she could cope, too. Possibly even thrive, which had been the plan when she'd signed the contract to begin work in Manhattan Mercy's ER. This was a new beginning and Grace knew better than most that to get the best out of new beginnings you had to draw a line under the past and move on. And yes...some things needed more time to heal but she had taken that time. A lot more time than she had anticipated needing, in fact.

She was ready.

Having stayed longer than the rest of the transfer team so that she could give the anaesthetist and surgeons a comprehensive handover, Grace found that she needed to find her own way back to the ER and it turned out to be a slightly more circuitous route than before. Instead of passing the main reception area, she went past an orthopaedic room where casts were being applied, what looked like a small operating theatre that was labelled for minor surgery and seemed to have someone having a major laceration stitched and then a couple of smaller rooms that looked as if they had been designed for privacy. Were these rooms used for family consultations, perhaps? Or a space where people could be with a loved one who was dying?

A nurse was peering out of one of the doors.

'Oh, thank goodness,' she said, when she saw Grace approaching. 'I'm about to *burst*… Could you please, please stay with the boys in here for two minutes while I dash to the bathroom?'

The young nurse, whose name badge introduced her as 'Jackie', certainly looked desperate. Having had to grab a bathroom stop herself on her way back from Theatre, Grace could sympathise with the urgency. She was probably already later in her return to the ER than might have been expected so another minute or two wouldn't make any difference, would it?

'Sure,' she said. 'But be as quick as you can?'

Jackie sped off with a grateful smile and vigorous nod without giving Grace the chance to ask anything else— like why these 'boys' were in a side room and whether they needed any medical management.

She turned to go through the door and then froze.

Two small faces were filling the space. Identical faces.

These two children had to be the most adorable little boys she had ever seen. They were about three years old, with tousled mops of dark hair, huge curious eyes and small button noses.

There was something about twins…

For someone who'd had to let go of the dream of even

having a single baby, the magic of twins could pack a punch that left a very physical ache somewhere deep inside Grace.

Maybe she wasn't as ready as she'd thought she was to step back into the real world and a new future...

CHAPTER TWO

'WHO ARE YOU?'

'I'm Grace. I'm one of the doctors here.'

It wasn't as hard as she'd expected to find a smile. Who wouldn't smile at this pair? 'Who are *you*?'

'I'm Cameron,' one of the boys told her. 'And he's Max.'

'Hello, Max,' Grace said. 'Hello, Cameron. Can I come into your room?'

'Why?' Cameron seemed to be the spokesman for the pair. 'Where's Jackie gone?'

'Just to the bathroom. She'll be back in a minute. She asked me to look after you.'

'Oh… 'Kay…'

Grace stepped into the room as the children turned. There was a couch and two armchairs in here, some magazines on a low table and a box of toys that had been emptied.

'Are you waiting for somebody?' Grace asked, perching on the arm of the couch.

'Yes. Daddy.' Cameron dropped to his knees and picked up a toy. His brother sat on the floor beside him. 'Here…you can have the fire truck, Max. I'm going to have the p'lice car, 'kay?'

Max nodded. But as he took hold of the plastic fire truck that had been generously gifted with both hands, the back wheels came off.

'Oh…no…' Cameron sounded horrified. 'You *broke* it.'

Max's bottom lip quivered. Grace slid off the arm of the couch and crouched down beside him.

'Let me have a look. I don't think it's very broken. See…?' She clipped the axle of the wheels back into place. 'All fixed.'

She handed the truck back with a smile and, unexpectedly, received a smile back. A delicious curve of a wide little mouth that curled itself instantly right around her heart.

Wow…

'Fank you,' Max said gravely.

'You're so welcome.' Grace's response came out in no more than a whisper.

Love at first sight could catch you unawares in all sorts of different ways, couldn't it? It could be a potential partner for life, or a gorgeous place like a peaceful forest, or a special house or cute puppy. Or it could be a small boy with a heartbreaking smile.

Cameron was pushing his police car across the top of the coffee table and making muted siren noises but Max stayed where he was, with the mended fire truck in his arms. Or not quite where he was. He leaned, so that his head and shoulder were pressed against Grace's arm. It was impossible not to return this gesture of acceptance and it was purely instinctive to shift her arm so that it slid around the small body and let him snuggle more comfortably.

It would only be for a moment because Nurse Jackie

would be back any second. Grace could hear people in the corridor outside. She could feel the draught of air as the door was pushed open behind her so she closed her eyes for a heartbeat to help her lock this exquisite fraction of time into her memory banks. This feeling of connection with a precious small person…

'Daddy…' Cameron's face split into a huge grin.

Max wriggled out from under Grace's arm, dropping the fire truck in his haste to get to his feet, but Grace was still sitting on the floor as she turned her head. And then astonishment stopped her moving at all.

'Charles?'

'Grace…' He sounded as surprised as she had. 'What on earth are you doing in here?'

She felt as guilty as a child caught with her hand in a forbidden cookie jar. 'It was only for a minute. To help out…'

'Jackie had to go to the bathroom.' Cameron had hold of one of his father's hands and he was bouncing up and down.

'She fixed the truck,' Max added, clearly impressed with the skills Grace had demonstrated. 'The wheels came off.'

'Oh…' Charles scooped Cameron up with one arm. Max was next and the ease with which two small boys were positioned on each hip with their arms wrapped around their father's neck suggested that this was a very well-practised manoeuvre. 'That's all right, then…'

Charles was smiling, first at one twin and then the other, and Grace felt her heart melt a little more.

She could feel the intense bond between this man and his children. The power of an infinite amount of love.

She'd been wrong about that moment of doubt earlier, hadn't she? Charles *did* have the perfect life.

'Can we go home now? Is Maria all better?'

Grace was on her feet now. She should excuse herself and get back to where she was supposed to be but something made her hesitate. To stand there and stare at Charles as she remembered hearing the concern in his voice when he'd recognised the new patient in ER.

He was shaking his head now. 'Maria's got a sore back after falling down the stairs. She's going to be fine but she needs to have a rest for a few days.'

He looked up, as if he could feel the questions buzzing in Grace's head.

'Maria is the boys' nanny,' he said. 'I'll be taking a few days' leave to look after them until she's back on her feet. Fortunately, it was only a sprain and not a fracture.'

That didn't stop the questions but Grace couldn't ask why the head of her new department would automatically take time away to care for his children. Where was their mother? Maybe she was another high-achieving medic who was away—presenting at some international conference or something?

Whatever. It was none of her business. And anyway, Jackie the nurse had come back and there was no reason for her to take any more time away from the job she was employed to be doing.

'I'd better get back,' she said. 'Do you still want me to cover Trauma One?'

'Thanks.' Charles nodded. 'I'll come with you. Jackie, I just came to give you some money. The cafeteria should be up and running again now and I thought you could take the boys up for some lunch.'

Planting a kiss on each small, dark head, he deposited the twins back on the floor.

'Be good,' he instructed. 'And if it's not still raining when we go home, we'll stop in the park for a swing.'

He led Grace back towards the main area of the ER.

'It's still crazy in here,' he said. 'But we've got extra staff and it's under control now that we've got power back on.'

'I'm sorry I took so long. I probably shouldn't have stopped to help Jackie out.'

'It's not a problem.'

'They're gorgeous children,' Grace added. 'You're a very lucky man, Charles.'

The look he gave her was almost astonished. Then a wash of something poignant crossed his face and he smiled.

A slow kind of smile that took her back through time instantly. To when the brilliant young man who'd been like royalty in their year at med school had suddenly been interested in her as more than the only barrier he had to be a star academically and not just socially. He had cared about what she had to say. About who she was...

'Yes,' he said slowly. 'I am.'

He held open one of the double doors in front of them. 'How 'bout you, Grace? You got kids?'

She shook her head.

'Too busy with that exciting career I was reading about in your CV? Working with the flying doctors in the remotest parts of the outback?'

Her throat felt tight. 'Something like that.'

She could feel his gaze on her back. A beat of silence—curiosity, even, as if he knew there was a lot being left unspoken.

And then he caught up with her in a single, long stride. Turned his head and, yes…she could see the flicker of curiosity.

'It's been a long time, Grace.'

'It has.'

'Be nice to catch up sometime…'

People were coming towards them. There were obviously matters that required the attention of the chief and Grace had her own work to do. She could see paramedics and junior staff clustered around a new gurney in Trauma One but she took a moment before she broke that eye contact.

A moment when she remembered that smile from a few moments ago. And so much more, from a very long time ago.

'Yes,' she said quietly. 'It would…'

The rest of that first shift in Manhattan Mercy's emergency department passed in something of a blur for Grace. Trauma related to the storm and power outage continued to roll in. A kitchen worker had been badly burned when a huge pot of soup had been tipped over in the confusion of a crowded restaurant kitchen plunged into darkness. A man had suffered a heart attack while trapped in an elevator and had been close to the end of the time window for curtailing the damage to his cardiac muscle by the time he'd been rescued. A pedestrian had been badly injured when they'd made a dash to get across a busy road in the pouring rain and a woman who relied on her home oxygen supply had been brought to the ER in severe respiratory distress after it had been cut off.

Grace was completely focused on each patient that spent time in Trauma One but Charles seemed to be everywhere, suddenly appearing where and when he was most needed. How did he do that?

Sometimes it had to be obvious, of course. Like when the young kitchen worker arrived and his screams from the pain of his severe burns would have been heard all over the department and the general level of tension rocketed skywards. He was so distressed he was in danger of injuring himself further by fighting off staff as they attempted to restrain him enough to gain IV access and administer adequate pain relief and Grace was almost knocked off her feet by a flying fist that caught her hip.

It was Charles who was suddenly there to steady her before she fell. Charles who positioned security personnel to restrain their patient safely. And it was Charles who spoke calmly enough to capture a terrified youth's attention and stop the agonised cries for long enough for him to hear what was being said.

'We're going to help you,' he said. 'Try and hold still for just a minute. It will stop hurting very soon...'

He stayed where he was and took over the task of sedating and intubating the young man. Like everyone else in the department, Grace breathed a sigh of relief as the terrible sounds of agony were silenced. She could assess this patient properly now, start dressing the burns that covered the lower half of his body and arrange his transfer to the specialist unit that could take over his care.

She heard Charles on the phone as she passed the unit desk later, clearly making arrangements for a patient who'd been under someone else's initial care.

'It's a full thickness inferior infarct. He's been trapped

in an elevator for at least four hours. I'm sending him up to the catheter laboratory, stat.'

The hours passed swiftly and it was Charles who reminded Grace that it was time she went home.

'We're under control and the new shift is taking over. Go home and have a well-deserved rest, Grace. And thanks,' he added, as he turned away. 'I knew you would be an asset to this department.'

The smile was a reward for an extraordinarily testing first day and the words of praise stayed with Grace as she made her way to the locker room to find her coat to throw on over her scrubs.

There were new arrivals in the space, locking away their personal belongings before they started their shift. And one of them was a familiar face.

Helena Tate was scraping auburn curls back from her face to restrain with a scrunchie but she abandoned the task as she caught sight of Grace.

'I hear you've had quite a day.'

Grace simply nodded.

'Do you hate me—for persuading you to come back?'

She shook her head now. 'It's been full on,' she said, 'but you know what?'

'What?'

Grace felt her mouth curving into a grin. 'I loved it.'

It was true, she realised. The pace of the work had left no time for first day nerves. She had done her job well enough to earn praise from the chief and, best of all, the moment she'd been dreading—seeing Charles again—had somehow morphed into something that had nothing to do with heartbreak or embarrassment or even resentment. It almost felt like a reconnection with an old friend. With a part of her life that had been so full of promise because she'd had no idea of just how tough life could become.

'Really?' Helena let out a huff of relief. 'Oh, I'm so happy to hear that.' She was smiling now. 'So it wasn't weird, finding that someone you went to med school with is your boss now?'

Grace had never confessed the real reason it was going to be awkward seeing Charles Davenport again. She had never told anybody about that night, not even her best friend. And certainly not the man she had married. It had been a secret—a shameful one when it had become apparent that Charles had no desire to remember it.

But today it seemed that she had finally been able to move past something that had been a mere blip of time in a now distant past life.

'Not really,' she told Helena. 'Not that we had time to chat. I did meet his little boys, though.'

'The twins? Aren't they cute? Such a tragic story.' Helena lowered her voice. 'Nina was the absolute love of Charles's life and she died minutes after they were born. Amniotic embolism. He'll never get over it…'

Shock made Grace speechless but Helena didn't seem to notice. The hum of voices around them was increasing as more people came in and out of the locker room. Helena glanced up, clearly refocusing on what was around her. She pulled her hair back again and wound the elastic band around her short ponytail. 'I'd better get in there. You can tell me all about it in the morning.'

The door of her locker shut with a metallic clang to reveal the figure arriving beside her to open another locker. Charles Davenport glanced sideways as Helena kept talking.

'Have my bed tonight,' she told Grace. 'I'll be home

so late, a couple of hours on that awful couch won't make any difference.'

And then she was gone. Grace immediately turned to look for her own locker because she didn't want to catch Charles's gaze and possibly reveal that she had just learned something very personal about his life. She turned back just as swiftly, however, as she heard him speak.

'You're sleeping on a couch?'

'Only until I find my own place.' Grace could see those new lines on his face in a different light now and it made something tighten in her chest. He'd suffered, hadn't he?

She knew what that was like...

'It's a bit of a squash,' she added hurriedly. 'But Helena's an old friend. Do you remember her from Harvard?'

Charles shook his head and Grace nodded a beat later. Why would he remember someone who was not only several years younger but, like her, had not been anywhere near the kind of elite social circles the Davenports belonged to? Her own close friendship with Helena had only come about because they'd lived in the same student accommodation block.

'She was a few years behind us. We've kept in touch, though. It was Helena who persuaded me to apply for the job here.'

Charles took a warm coat from its hanger and draped it over his arm. 'I'll have to remember to thank her for that.' He pulled a worn-looking leather satchel from his locker before pushing the door shut. He looked like a man in a hurry. 'I'd better go and rescue my boys. Good luck with the apartment hunting.'

'Thanks. I might need it. From what I've heard, it's a bit of a mission to find something affordable within easy commuting of Central Manhattan.'

'Hmm.' Charles turned away, the sound no more than a sympathetic grunt. But then his head turned swiftly, his eyes narrowed, as if he'd just thought of something important. 'Do you like dogs?'

The random question took Grace by surprise. She blinked at Charles.

'Sorry?'

He shook his head. 'It's just a thought. Might come to nothing but...' He was pulling a mobile phone from the pocket of his scrubs and then tapping on the screen. 'Give me your phone number,' he said. 'Just in case...'

What had he been thinking?

Was he really intending to follow through with that crazy idea that had occurred to him when he'd heard that the newest member of his department was camping in another colleague's apartment and sleeping on an apparently uncomfortable couch?

Why would he do that when his life had suddenly become even more complicated than it already was?

'It's not raining, Daddy.' Zipped up inside his bright red puffer jacket, with a matching woolly hat covering his curls, Cameron tugged on his father's hand. 'Swing?'

Max's tired little face lit up at the reminder and he nodded with enthusiasm. 'I want a swing, too.'

'But it's pouring, guys.' Charles had to smile down at his sons. 'See? You're just dry because you're under my umbrella.'

A huge, black umbrella. Big enough for all of them to be sheltered as they walked beneath dripping branches of the massive trees lining this edge of Central Park, the pavement plastered with the evidence of the autumnal leaf fall. Past one of the more than twenty playgrounds for children that this amazing space boasted, currently empty of any nannies or parents trying to entertain their young people.

'Aww...'

The weight of two tired small boys suddenly increased as their steps dragged.

'And it's too dark now, anyway,' Charles pointed out. 'We'll go tomorrow. In the daytime. We can do that because it's Sunday and there's no nursery school. And I'm going to be at home to look after you.'

'Why?'

'Because Maria's got a sore back.'

'Because she fell down the stairs?'

'That's right, buddy.'

'It went dark,' Cameron said.

'I was scared,' Max added. 'Maria was *crying*...'

'Horse was barking and barking.'

'Was he?'

'I told Max to sit on the stair,' Cameron said proudly. 'And Mr Jack came to help.'

Jack was the elderly concierge for their apartment block and he'd been there for many years before Charles had bought the penthouse floor. He was almost part of the family now.

And probably more willing to help than his real family would be if he told them about the latest complication in his home life.

No, that wasn't fair. His siblings would do whatever they could but they were all so busy with their own lives and careers. Elijah would have to step up to take his place as Chief of Emergency in the next few days. His sister Penelope was on a much-needed break, although she was probably on some adrenaline-filled adventure that involved climbing a mountain or extreme skiing. The youngest Davenport, Zachary, was back from his latest tour of duty and working at the Navy Academy in Annapolis and his half-sister, Miranda, would try *too* hard, even if it was too much. Protecting his siblings had become second nature to Charles ever since the Davenports' sheltered world had imploded all those years ago.

And his parents? Hugo Davenport had retired as Chief of Emergency to allow Charles to take the position but he'd barely had time for his own children as they were growing up and he would be at a complete loss if he was left with the sole responsibility of boisterous twin almost three-year-olds. It would be sole responsibility, too, because Vanessa had led an almost completely separate life ever since the scandal, and playing happy grandparents together would never be added to her agenda.

His mother would rush to help, of course, and put out the word that she urgently needed the services of the best nanny available in New York but Charles didn't want that. He didn't want a stranger suddenly appearing in his home. His boys had to feel loved and totally secure at all times. He'd promised them that much when they were only an hour old—in those terrible first minutes after their mother's death.

His grip tightened on the hand of each twin.

'You were both very brave in the dark,' he told them. 'And you've both been a big help by being so good when you had to stay at Daddy's work all day. I'm very, very proud of you both.'

'So we can go to the park?'

'Tomorrow,' he promised. 'We'll go to the park even if it's still raining. You can put your rubber boots on and jump in all the puddles.'

They could take some time out and make the outside world unimportant for an hour or two. Maybe he would be able to put aside the guilt that he was taking emergency leave from his work and stop fretting that he was creating extra pressure for Elijah or that his other siblings would worry about him when they heard that he was struggling as a single parent—yet again. Maybe he could even forget about the background tension of being part of a family that was a far cry from the united presence they could still display for the sake of a gala fundraising event or any other glittering, high-society occasion. A family whose motto of 'What happens in the family stays in the family' had been sorely tested but had, in recent years, regained its former strength.

A yellow taxi swooped into the kerb, sending a spray of water onto the pavement. Charles hurried the twins past a taco restaurant, souvenir shop, a hot dog stand and the twenty-four-seven deli to turn into the tree-lined avenue that was the prestigious address for the brownstone apartment block they called home.

And it was then that Charles recognised why he'd felt the urge to reach out and try to help Grace Forbes.

Like taking the boys to the park, it felt like he had the opportunity to shut the rest of the world out to some extent.

Grace was part of a world that had ceased to exist when the trauma of the family trouble had threatened everything the Davenport family held dear. It had been the happiest time of Charles's life. He had been achieving his dream of following in his father's footsteps and becoming a doctor who could one day be in charge of the most challenging and exciting place he had ever known—Manhattan Mercy's ER. The biggest problem he'd had was how to balance a demanding social life with the drive to achieve the honour of topping his class, and the only real barrier to that position had been Grace.

He'd managed to succeed, despite the appalling pressure that had exploded around him in the run-up to final exams, by focusing only on the things that mattered the most—supporting his mother and protecting his siblings from the fallout of scandal and passing those exams with the best possible results. He had been forced to dismiss Grace, along with every other social aspect of his life. And he'd learned to dismiss any emotion that could threaten his goals.

But he had never forgotten how simple and happy his life at medical school had been up until that point.

And, if he was honest, he'd never forgotten that night with Grace...

He could never go back, of course, but the pull of even connecting with it from a distance was surprisingly compelling. And what harm could it do? His life wasn't about to change. He had his boys and he had his job and that was all he needed. All he could ever hope for.

But Grace had been special. And there was something about her that made him think that, perhaps—like him—life hadn't quite turned out the way she'd planned. Or deserved?

'Shall we stop and say hello to Horse before we go upstairs?'

'*Yes...*' The tug on his hands was in a forward direction now, instead of a reluctant weight he was encouraging to follow him. 'Let's *go*, Daddy...'

CHAPTER THREE

'SO HERE'S THE THING…'

'Mmm?' Grace was still trying to get her head around hearing Charles Davenport's voice on a phone for the first time ever.

The twang of a New York accent had probably been mellowed by so many years at exclusive, private schools but his enunciation was crisp. Decisive, even. It made her think of someone in a suit. Presenting a killer summary in a courtroom, perhaps. Or detailing a take-over bid in the boardroom of a global company.

She was sitting cross-legged on the couch in Helena's apartment, a take-out container of pad Thai on her lap and a pair of chopsticks now idle in her hands. She was in her pyjamas already, thanks to getting soaked in the tail end of the storm during her long walk home from the nearest subway station.

Was her attire partly responsible for hearing that slightly gravelly edge to Charles's voice that made her think that he would sound just like that if his head was on a pillow, very close to her own?

'Sorry…did you say your neighbour's name was *Houston*? As in "Houston, we have a problem"?'

The chuckle of laughter came out of the phone and

went straight for somewhere deep in Grace's chest. Or maybe her belly. It created a warmth that brought a smile to her face.

'Exactly. It's their dog that's called Houston and they chose the name on the first day they brought him home as a puppy when they found what he'd left in the middle of their white carpet.'

The bubble of her own laughter took Grace by surprise. Because it felt like the kind of easy laughter that she hadn't experienced in such a long time? The kind that made her think of a first date? Or worse, made her remember *that* night. When Charles had found her, so stressed before the start of their final exams that she was in pieces and he'd tried to reassure her. To distract her, by talking to her rather like this. By making her laugh through her tears and then...

And then there'd been that astonishing moment when they couldn't break the eye contact between them and the kiss that had started everything had been as inevitable as the sun rising the next morning.

It was an effort to force herself to focus on what Charles was actually saying as he kept talking.

'The boys call him Horse, because they weren't even two when he arrived and they couldn't pronounce Houston but he's quite big so that seemed to work, too.'

Grace cleared her throat, hoping her voice would come out sounding normal. How embarrassing would it be if it was kind of husky and betrayed those memories that refused to stay where they should be. Buried.

'What sort of dog is he?'

'A retro doodle. Half poodle, half golden retriever. One of those designer, hypo-allergenic kind of dogs, you know? But he's lovely. Very well behaved and gentle.'

Grace closed her eyes for a moment. This was *so* weird. She hadn't seen Charles Davenport in more than a decade but here they were chatting about something completely random as if they were friends who caught up every other week. And they'd never been *friends*, exactly. Friend*ly*, certainly—with a lot of respect for each other's abilities. And they'd been passionate—so briefly it had always seemed like nothing more than a fantasy that had unexpectedly achieved reality. But this?

Thanks to the memories it was stirring up, this was doing Grace's head in.

On top of that, her noodles were getting cold and probably wouldn't appreciate another spin in the microwave.

The beat of an awkward silence made her wonder if this apparently easy chatting was actually just as weird for Charles.

'Anyway…I'm sorry to disturb your evening but it occurred to me that it could be a win-win situation.'

'Oh?'

'Houston's parents are my neighbours on the ground floor of this block—which, I should mention, is about two minutes' walk to Central Park and ten at the most to Manhattan Mercy.'

'Oh…' How good would that be, not to have to battle crowds in the subway and a long walk at the end of the commute?

'Stefan's an interior designer and his husband, Jerome, is an artist. They're heading off tomorrow for a belated honeymoon in Europe and they'll be gone for about six weeks. They're both fretting about Houston having to go into kennels. I suggested they get a dog-sitter to live in but…' Charles cleared his throat as if he was slightly embarrassed. 'Apparently Houston is their fur child and they couldn't find someone trustworthy enough. When I got home this evening, I told them about you and they seem to be very impressed with the recommendation I gave them.'

'Oh...?' Good grief, she was beginning to sound like a broken record. 'But...I work long hours. I couldn't look after a dog...'

'Houston has a puppy walker that he loves who would come twice a day on the days that you're working. That's another part of his routine that Stefan and Jerome are worried about disrupting because he gets to play with his dog friends who get taken out at the same time. Even more importantly, if he was still in his own home, he wouldn't miss his dads so much. And I thought that it could give you a bit of breathing space, you know? To find your feet in a new city and where you want to be.'

Not just breathing space. Living space. Sharing a tiny apartment, even with a good friend, was a shock to the system for someone who had guarded their privacy so well for so long.

'I know it's all very last minute with them being due to drop Houston at the kennels in the morning but they're home this evening and they'd love to meet you and have a chat about it. Stefan said he'd be delighted to cover your taxi fares if you were at all interested.' Charles paused and Grace could hear something that sounded like a weary sigh. 'Anyway...I've only just got the boys to bed and I need to have a hunt in the fridge and see if I can find something to eat that isn't the boys' favourite packet mac and cheese.'

Again, Grace was aware of that tightness in her chest. Empathy? Charles might have the blessing of having two gorgeous children but he had lost something huge as well. Something that had changed his future for ever—the loss of a complete family.

They had a lot more than he realised in common.

Her new boss had also had a very difficult day, coping with a crisis in his department and the added blow of having to deal with a personal crisis with his nanny being put out of action. And yet he'd found the time to think about her and a way to possibly help her adjust to a dauntingly huge change in her life?

How astonishing was that?

'Thank you so much, Charles.' Grace dropped the chopsticks into the plastic bowl and put it onto the coffee table as she unfurled her legs. It didn't matter that she would have to get dressed again and then head out into this huge city that never slept. Despite so much going on in his own life, Charles had made a very thoughtful effort on her behalf and she knew exactly how she needed to show her appreciation.

There was something else prompting her, too. A niggle that was purely instinctive that was telling her not to miss this unexpected opportunity. That it might, somehow, be a signpost to the new path in life that she was seeking. The kind of niggle that had persuaded her, in the end, to come to New York in the first place.

'Let me grab a pen. Give me the address and I'll get there as soon as I can.'

'Morning, Doc.'

'Morning, Jack. How's the weather looking out there?' Not that Charles needed to ask. The view from his penthouse apartment over Central Park and the Manhattan skyline had shown him that any residual cloudiness from the storm of a few days ago had been blown well clear of the city. It was a perfect October day. But discussing the weather was a ritual. And it gave him the chance to make sure that the twins were well protected from the chill, with their jackets fastened, ears covered by their hats and twenty little fingers encased in warm mittens.

'It's a day for the park, that's fo' sure.' Jack had a passion for following meteorology and spent any free time on door duty surfing weather channels. 'High of sixteen degrees, thirty-two percent clear skies and twenty-one percent chance of light rain but that won't happen until after two p.m.'

'Perfect. Nice change, isn't it?' As usual, Cameron's mittens were hanging by the strings that attached them to his jacket sleeves. Charles pulled them over the small hands. 'That was some storm we had the other day.'

'Sure was. Won't forget that in a hurry. Not with poor Maria crashing down the stairs like that.' Jack shook his head. 'How's she doin'?'

'Good, but I don't want her coming back to work too soon. She won't be up to lifting small boys out of trouble for a while.' Charles tugged Max's hat down over his ears. 'You guys ready?'

'Can we say "hi" to Horse?'

Charles glanced behind the boys, to the door that led to one of the two ground-floor apartments. He'd been tempted to knock on that door more than once in the last few days—ever since he'd heard the news that Grace had taken on the dog-sitting gig—but something had held him back.

Something odd that felt almost like shyness, which was ridiculous because hanging back had never been an attribute that anyone would associate with the Davenport family.

Maybe he was just waiting for it to happen naturally so that it didn't seem like he was being pushy? He was her boss, after all. Or he would be, as soon as he got back to work properly. There were boundaries here and maybe Grace didn't want to cross them, either. That might explain why she hadn't knocked on *his* door.

He turned, holding out his hands. 'Let's go. Or you'll be wanting a hotdog before we even get to the playground.'

Jack was holding open the front door, letting sunlight stream in to brighten the mosaic tiles of the entrance foyer, but the boys weren't moving to take their father's hands. They were going in the opposite direction, as the door behind Charles swung open.

'Horse...'

The big woolly dog looked as pleased to see the twins as they were to see him. He stood there with what looked like a grin on his face, the long plume of his tail waving, as Cameron and Max wrapped their arms around his neck and buried their faces in his curls.

Grace was grinning as well, as she looked down at the reunion.

'Oh, yeah...cuddles are the best way to start the day, aren't they, Houston?'

She was still smiling as she looked up. The black woollen hat she was wearing made a frame that seemed to accentuate the brightness of that smile. A smile that went all the way to her eyes and made them sparkle.

'We're off to the park,' she said. 'It's my first day off so I'm on dog-walking duty today.'

'We're going to the park, too,' Cameron shouted. 'You can come with us.'

'I want to throw the ball for Horse.' Max nodded.

'I think he has to stay on his lead,' Grace said. 'I've been reading the rules this morning.'

Charles nodded. 'And he's not allowed in the playgrounds. But we can walk with him for a while.'

Grace's smile seemed to wobble, as if a shadow was crossing her face, and Charles had the impression that this was a bigger deal than he would have expected.

'If Grace doesn't mind the extra company, that is,' he added.

'I'd love it,' Grace said firmly. She was clipping the dog's lead onto his harness so Charles couldn't see if she really meant that but then she straightened and caught his gaze.

'You can show me the best places to walk. I don't know anything about Central Park.'

Her smile was strong again and he could see a gleam in her eyes that he remembered very well. He'd seen it often enough in the past, usually when they were both heading in to the same examination.

Determination, that was what it was.

But why did she need to tap into that kind of reserve for something that should be no problem? A pleasure, even...

It was puzzling.

'Have you never been to New York before?' Juggling two small children and a dog on the busy pavement meant that Charles had to wait until they were almost at the gates of the park to say anything more to Grace.

'Never. I was born in Australia and then my family moved to Florida when my dad got a job with NASA.'

She was smiling again. 'He thinks it's hilarious that I've got a job looking after a dog called Houston. Anyway... coming here was always a plan once I got to medical school in Boston but there never seemed to be enough time. I was too busy studying...' The glance Charles received was mischievous. 'Trying to keep up with you.'

'I think it was the other way round.' Charles kept a firm grip on small mittened hands, as he paused to wait until a horse-drawn carriage rolled past, carrying tourists on a relaxed tour of the park, but he was holding Grace's gaze as well. They would have to part company very soon and it felt...disappointing?

'Okay...we have two favourite playgrounds close to here but...'

'But dogs aren't allowed, I know. When I looked on the map, there was a track called the Bridle Path? That sounds like a nice place to walk.'

'It is. Come with us as far as the playground and I'll show you which direction to take to find it. Next time, I'll bring the boys' bikes and we can all go on the Bridle Path.'

The way Grace's eyes widened revealed her surprise, which was quite understandable because Charles was a little surprised himself that the suggestion had emerged so casually. As if this was already a thing—this walking in the park together like a...like a *family*? A whole family, with two parents and even a dog.

And her surprise quickly morphed into something else. Something softer that hadn't been fuelled by determination. Pleasure, even? Was she enjoying their company as much as he was enjoying hers?

Charles was silent the rest of the way to the playground. Not that anybody seemed to notice because

Cameron and Max were making sure that Grace didn't miss any of the important attractions.

'Look, Gace…it's a *sk-wirrel*…'

'Oh, yes…I *love* squirrels.'

'Look at all the leafs. Why are they all on the ground?'

'Because it's autumn. The trees get undressed for winter. Like you do when you're getting ready for bed. Aren't they pretty?'

Why had it felt so natural up until now, Charles wondered, to add feminine and canine company to his little troupe when it could be seen as potentially disturbing? He and his boys didn't need extra people in their lives. Against quite a few odds, he had managed perfectly well up until now and his children were happy and healthy and safe…

At least things would go back to normal any second now. Grace would continue her dog walk and he'd stand around with the other parents, watching the children run and climb and shout, until he was summoned to push the swings.

But when they got to the wrought-iron fence surrounding the playground, it seemed that his boys wanted a larger audience for their exploits.

'I want Horse to watch me on the slide,' Cameron said.

'And Gace,' Max added. His face was serious enough to let them know that this was important. 'Gace can push me on the swing.'

'Um…' Grace hadn't missed the slightly awkward edge to the atmosphere in the last minute or two because it had left her feeling just a bit confused.

She'd been happy to have company on her first walk

to Central Park because it was always so much easier to go somewhere new with somebody who knew the way. And because it had been so good to see the twins again. Especially Max. Cameron's smile was identical, of course, but there was something a little more serious about Max that pulled her heartstrings so hard it was too close to pain to be comfortable. That was why, for a heartbeat back at the apartment block, she had wondered if it wasn't a good idea to share even a part of this walk. But she'd pushed aside any deeply personal misgivings. Maybe it did still hurt that she would never be part of her own family group like this, but surely she could embrace this moment for what it was? Being included, instead of watching from a distance?

Having Houston walking by her side helped a lot. In fact, the last few days had been a revelation. Due to her work hours and never settling in one place for very long, Grace had never considered adopting a dog and getting to know Houston had been a joy. She wished she'd learned years ago that a companion like this could make you feel so much less alone in the world.

Charles's company was surprisingly good, too. When she'd told him of her father's amusement about the dog's name, the appreciative glint in his eyes made her remember how easy that telephone conversation the other night had been. How close to the surface laughter had felt. He'd caught her memory of how focused life had been back in medical school, too, but twisted it slightly, to make it sound as if he'd been a lot more aware of her than she had realised.

And then he'd made that comment about them all coming to the park again together, as if this was the start of something that he'd expected to happen all along? That was when the awkwardness had sprouted.

Had he somehow heard the alarm bells sounding in her own head or did he have a warning system of his own?

Maybe she should just say goodbye and head off with Houston to explore the park and leave Charles to have time with his boys.

Except…it felt like it would suddenly be less interesting. A bit lonely, even?

And the way Max was looking up at her, with those big, blue eyes, as if her being here was the most important thing in the world to him. He had eyes just like his father, she realised. That amazingly bright blue, made even more striking by the darker rim around the irises.

'I have to stay here, on this side of the fence. To look after Horse.' She smiled at Max. 'But I could watch Daddy push you?'

Houston seemed perfectly happy to sit by her side and Grace was grateful for the dog's warmth as he leaned against her leg. She watched Charles lift the little boys into the bucket seats of the swings, side by side, and then position himself between them so that he could push a swing with each hand. She could see the huge grins on the children's faces and hear the peals of their laughter as the arc of movement got steadily higher. And Charles finally looked exactly as she'd remembered him. Happy. Carefree. Enjoying all the best things in life that automatically came his way because he was one of life's golden people that always had the best available.

Except she knew better now. Charles might have had a very different upbringing from her solid, middle-class existence, but he hadn't been protected from the hard things in life any more than she had. His world had been shattered, maybe as much as hers had been, but he was making the best of it and clearly fatherhood was just as important to him as his work. More important, perhaps. He hadn't hesitated in taking time off when his children needed him.

That said a lot about who he was, didn't it? About his ability to cherish the things that were most important in life?

A beat of something very poignant washed through Grace as she remembered those whispered words in the locker room.

'Nina was the absolute love of his life...he'll never get over it...'

The death of his wife was utterly tragic but how lucky had they both been to find a love like that? She certainly hadn't been lucky enough to find it in her marriage and she wasn't about to stumble across it any time soon.

Grace closed her eyes for a heartbeat as she let her breath escape in a sigh. How good was this kind of weather, when she could snuggle beneath layers of warm clothes and a lovely, puffy jacket? Nobody would ever guess what she was hiding.

Charles was smiling again as he came back towards her. He hadn't bothered with a hat or gloves and he was rubbing his hands together against the chill of the late autumn air. The breeze was ruffling his hair, which looked longer and more tousled than Grace remembered. Maybe he didn't get much time for haircuts these days. Or maybe how he looked wasn't a priority. It would be ironic if that was the reason, because the tousled look, along with that designer stubble, actually made him look way more attractive.

'That's my duty done. Now I get to watch them run around and climb things until they either get hungry or need to go to the toilet. Probably both at the same time.'

'I should get going. Horse isn't getting the exercise I promised him.'

'Wait a bit? The boys won't forgive me if you disappear before they've had a chance to show off a bit.'

'Sure.'

With the bars of the fence between them and Charles's attention back on his children, it felt curiously safe to be standing this close to him. It was safe anyway, Grace reminded herself. The last thing Charles Davenport would want would be another complication in his life and nobody could take the place of the twins' mother, anyway. With another wash of that empathy, the words came out before Grace thought to filter them.

'You must miss their mom so much...'

The beat of silence between them was surprisingly loud against the backdrop of happy shrieks and laughter from the small crowd of children swarming over the playground attractions. She couldn't miss the way Charles swallowed so carefully.

'So much,' he agreed. 'I can only be thankful that the boys will never feel that loss.'

Grace was silent but she could feel her brow furrowing as Charles slid a brief glance back in her direction.

'Oh, they'll know that something's missing from their life as they get older and notice that all the other kids have moms but they never knew Nina. She didn't even get to hold them.'

'I'm so sorry, Charles,' Grace said quietly. 'I had no idea until Helena mentioned it the other day. I can't even imagine how awful that must have been.'

'We had no warning.' His voice sounded raw. 'The pregnancy had gone so well and we were both so excited about welcoming the twins. Twins run in the family, you know. My brother Elijah is my twin. And we knew they were boys.'

Grace was listening but didn't say anything. She couldn't say anything because her treacherous mind was racing down its own, private track. Picking the scab off an old, emotional wound. Imagining what it would be like to have an enormous belly sheltering not one but *two* babies. She could actually feel a wash of that excitement of waiting for the birth.

'The birth was textbook perfect, too. Cameron arrived and then five minutes later Max did. They were a few weeks early but healthy enough not to need any intervention. I had just cut Max's umbilical cord and was lifting him up to put him in Nina's arms when it happened. She suddenly started gasping for breath and her blood pressure crashed. She was unconscious even before the massive haemorrhage started.'

'Oh... *God*...' Grace wasn't distracted by any personal baggage now. She was in that room with Charles and his two newborn sons. Watching his wife die right in front of his eyes. Her own eyes filled with tears.

'Sorry...' Charles sucked in a deep breath. 'It's not something I ever talk about. I feel...guilty, you know?'

'What? How could you possibly feel *guilty*? There was nothing you could have done.'

'There *should* have been.' There was an intensity to his voice that made the weight of the burden Charles carried very clear. 'It was my job to protect her. I was a doctor, for God's sake. I should have seen something.

Some warning. She could have had a medically controlled birth. A Caesarean.'

'It could still have happened.' Grace could hear an odd intensity in her own voice now. Why did it seem so important to try and convince Charles that he had nothing to feel guilty about? 'A C-section might not have made any difference. These things are rare but they happen—with no warning. Sometimes, you lose the babies as well.' She glanced away from Charles, her gaze drawn to the two happy, healthy little boys running around in the playground. 'Look at them,' she said softly. 'Feel blessed…not guilty…'

Charles nodded. 'I do. Those boys are the most important thing in my life. They *are* my life. It's just that it gets harder at this time of year. It sucks that the anniversary of losing Nina is also the twins' birthday. They're old enough to know about birthdays now and that they're supposed to be happy. And it's Halloween, for heaven's sake. Every kid in the country is getting dressed up and having fun.'

'That's next week.'

'Yeah.' Charles pushed his fingers through his hair as he watched Max follow Cameron through a tunnel at the base of the wooden fort. 'And, thanks to their little friends at nursery school, they're determined to go trick or treating for the first time. And they all wear their costumes to school that day.'

Clearly, it was the last thing Charles wanted to think about. The urge to offer help of some kind was powerful but that might not be something Charles wanted, either. But, he'd opened up to her about the tragedy, hadn't he? And he'd said that he never talked about it but he'd told her. Oddly, that felt remarkably special.

Grace bit her lip, absently scratching Houston's ear as he leaned his head against her leg.

'I wonder if they do Halloween costumes for dogs,' she murmured.

Clearly, Charles picked up on this subtle offer to help make this time of year more fun. More of a celebration than a source of painful memories. His startled glance reminded her of the one she'd received the other day when she'd told him what a lucky man he was to have such gorgeous children. As if he was unexpectedly looking at something from a very different perspective.

If so, he obviously needed time to think about it and that was fine by Grace. Maybe she did, too. Offering to help—to become more involved in this little family— might very well be a mistake. So why did it feel so much like the right thing to do?

Charles was watching the boys again as they emerged from the other end of the tunnel and immediately ran back to do it all over again.

'Enough about me,' he said. 'I was trying to remember the last time I heard about you and it was at a conference about ten years ago. I'm sure someone told me that you'd got married.'

'Mmm.'

Charles was leaning against the wrought-iron rails between them, so that when he turned his head, he seemed very close. 'But you're not married now?'

'No.'

He held her gaze. He'd just told her about the huge thing that had changed his life for ever. He wasn't going to ask any more questions but he wanted to know her story, didn't he?

He'd just told her about his personal catastrophe that

he never normally told anyone. She *wanted* to tell him about hers. To tell him everything. To reveal that they had a connection in grief that others could never understand completely.

But it was the recognition of that connection that prevented her saying anything. Because it was a time warp. She was suddenly back in that blip of time that had connected them that first time. Outside, on a night that had been almost cold enough to freeze her tears.

She could hear his voice.

'Grace? Oh, my God...are you crying? What's wrong?'

He hadn't asked any more questions then, either. He'd known that it didn't actually matter what had gone wrong, it was comfort that she'd needed. Reassurance.

'Come with me. It's far too cold to be out here...'

He could see that there was something huge that had gone wrong now, too. And maybe she wouldn't need to say anything. If that rail wasn't between them, maybe Charles would take her in his arms again.

The way he had that night, before he'd led her away to a warm place.

His room.

His bed.

It was a very good thing that that strong rail was there. That Charles couldn't come through the gate when he had to be in that playground to supervise his children.

Even though she knew it couldn't happen, Grace still pulled her layers of protective clothing a little more tightly around her body. She still found herself stepping back from the fence.

'I really should go,' she said. 'It's not fair to make Houston wait any longer for his walk.'

Charles nodded slowly. His smile said it was fine.

But his eyes told her that he knew she was running away. That he could see a lot more than she wanted him to.

He couldn't see the physical scars, of course. Nobody got to see those.

Grace had been confident that nobody could see the emotional scars, either.

Until now...

CHAPTER FOUR

I<small>T MIGHT WELL</small> have been the two cops standing outside a curtained cubicle that attracted his attention as he walked past.

If he'd had any inclination to analyse it, though, Charles would probably have realised that it was the voice on the other side of the curtain that made him slow down.

Grace's voice.

'Looks like we've got an entrance wound here. And… an exit wound here. But it's possible that they're two entrance wounds. We need an X-ray.'

One of the cops caught his gaze and responded to the raised eyebrow.

'Drive-by shooting,' he said. 'He's lucky. It was his arm and not his head.'

With a nod, Charles moved on. Grace clearly had things under control. She always did, whenever he noticed her in the department and that was almost every day now that he had adjusted his hours to fit around nursery school for the twins. More than once a day, too. Not that he went out of his way to make their paths cross or anything. It just seemed to happen.

Okay, maybe he was choosing to do some necessary

paperwork at one side of the unit desk instead of tucked away in his office but that was because he liked to keep half an eye on how the whole department was functioning. He could see the steady movement of people and equipment and hear phone calls being made and the radio link to the ambulance service. If anybody needed urgent assistance, he could be on his feet and moving in an instant.

It had nothing to do with the fact that Grace would be in this area before too long, checking the X-rays that would arrive digitally on one of the bank of departmental computer screens beside him.

He had a sheaf of statistics that he needed to review, like the numbers and types of patients that were coming through his department and it was important to see how they stacked up and whether trends were changing. Level one patients were the critical cases that took the most in the way of personnel and resources, but too many level four or five patients could create barriers to meeting target times for treatment and patient flow.

Grace Forbes certainly wasn't wasting time with her patients. It was only minutes later that she was logging in to a computer nearby, flanked by two medical students and a junior doctor. As they waited to upload files, she glanced sideways and acknowledged Charles with a smile but then she peered intently at the screen. Her colleagues leaned in as she used the cursor to highlight what she was looking at.

'There… Can you see that?'

'Is it a bone fragment?'

'No. Look how smooth the edges of the humerus are. And this is well away from it.'

'So it's a bullet fragment?'

'Yes. A very small one.'

'Do we need to get it out?'

'No. It's not clinically significant. And we were right that it's only one entrance and an exit wound but it was also right to check.'

'Want me to clean and dress it, then?' The junior doctor was keen to take over the case. 'Let the cops take him in to talk to him?'

'Yes. We'll put him on a broad-spectrum antibiotic as well. And make sure he gets a tetanus shot. Thanks, Danny. You're in charge now.' Grace's attention was swiftly diverted as she saw an incoming stretcher and she straightened and moved smoothly towards the new arrival as if she'd been ready and waiting all along.

'Hi, honey.' The girl on the stretcher looked very young, very pale and very frightened. 'My name's Grace and I'm going to be looking after you.'

Charles could hear one of the paramedics talking to Grace as they moved past to a vacant cubicle.

'Looks like gastro. Fever of thirty-nine point five and history of vomiting and diarrhoea. Mom called us when she fainted.'

'BP?'

'Eighty systolic. Couldn't get a diastolic.'

'I'm not surprised she fainted, then...'

The voices faded but Charles found himself still watching, even after the curtain had twitched into place to protect the new patient's privacy.

His attention was well and truly caught this time.

Because he was puzzled.

At moments like this, Grace was exactly the person he would have predicted that she would become. Totally on top of her work. Clever, competent and confident.

She got along well with all her colleagues, too. Charles had heard more than one report of how great she was to work with and how generous she was with her time for staff members who were here to learn.

Thanks to the challenge that had been thrown at her within the first minutes of her coming to work here, Charles already knew how good Grace was at her job and how well she coped with difficult circumstances. That ability to think on her feet and adapt was a huge advantage for someone who worked in Emergency and she demonstrated the same kind of attitude in her private life, too, didn't she—in the way she had jumped on board, under pressure, to take on the dog-sitting offer.

But…and this was what was puzzling Charles so much…there was something very different about her personality away from work.

Something that felt off-key.

A timidity, almost. Lack of confidence, anyway.

Vulnerability? The way she'd shrunk away from him at the park yesterday. When he'd ventured onto personal ground by asking her about her marriage. He'd been puzzled then and he hadn't been able to shake it off.

He didn't want to shake it off, in fact. It was quite nice having this distraction because it meant he could ignore the background tension he always had at this time of year when he was walking an emotional tightrope between celebrating the joy of the twins' birth and being swamped by the grief of losing Nina, which was a can of mental worms that included so many other things he felt he should have done better—like protecting his family during the time of that scandal.

A nurse appeared from behind the curtain, with a handful of glass tubes full of blood that were clearly being rushed off for testing. He caught a glimpse of Grace bent over her patient, with her stethoscope in her ears and a frown of concentration on her face.

Grace had understood that grief so easily. He could still see those tears shimmering in her eyes when she'd been listening to him. Perhaps he'd known that she would understand on a different level from anybody else and that was why he had chosen to say more to her than he would have even to members of his own family.

But how had he known that?

And why was it that she did understand so clearly?

Who had she lost? Her husband, obviously, but the tone of her limited response to his queries had made him think that it was a marriage that simply hadn't worked out, not one that had been blown apart by tragedy, as his had been.

He wanted to know, dammit.

More than that, and he knew that it was ridiculous, but he was a bit hurt by being shut out.

Why?

Because—once upon a time—she had fallen into his arms and told him everything she was so worried about? That the pressure of those final exams was doing her head in? That it was times like this that she felt so lonely because it made her miss the mother she'd lost more than ever?

He'd had no intention of revisiting the memories of that night but they were creeping back now. The events that threatened to derail his life that had crashed around him so soon after that night had made it inevitable that it had to be dismissed but there was one aspect he'd never completely buried.

That sense of connection with another person.

He'd never felt it before that night.

He'd been lucky enough to find it again—with Nina—but he'd known that any chance of a third strike was out of the question. He wasn't looking because he didn't want to find it.

But it was already there with Grace, wasn't it? It had been, from the moment he'd taken her into his arms that night to comfort her.

And he'd felt it again at the park, when he'd seen her crying for his loss.

She'd been crying that night, too…

'You okay?'

'Huh?' Charles blinked as he heard the voice beside him. 'I'm fine, thanks, Miranda.'

'Okay…' But his half-sister was frowning at him. 'It's not like you to be sitting staring into space.'

Her frown advertised concern. A closeness that gave Charles a beat of something warm. Something good. Because it had been hard won? Miranda had come into their family as a penniless, lonely and frightened six-teen-year-old who was desperately missing her mother who had just died. It had been Charles who'd taken on the responsibility of trying to make her feel wanted. A little less lonely. Trying to persuade her that the scandal hadn't been *her* fault.

'I was just thinking.' About Grace. And he needed to stop because he was still aware of that warmth of something that felt good but now it was coming from remembering something Grace had said. The way she had tried to convince him that he had no valid reason to feel guilty over Nina's death—as if she really cared about how he felt.

Charles tapped the pile of papers in front of him. 'I'm up to my eyeballs in statistics. What are you up to?'

'I need a portable ultrasound to check a stab wound for underlying damage. It looks superficial but I want to make absolutely sure.' Miranda looked around. 'They seem to have gone walkabout.'

Charles glanced towards the glass board where patient details were constantly updated to keep track of where people were and what was going on. Who could be currently using ultrasound to help a diagnosis?

'It could be in with the abdo pain in Curtain Two.'

'Thanks. I'll check.' Miranda turned her head as she moved away. 'How are the party plans going? Do we get an invitation this year?'

Charles shook his head but offered an apologetic smile. 'I'm keeping it low-key. I'm taking them to visit the grandparents the next day for afternoon tea and I'm sure you'll be invited as well, but my neighbours have said they'd be delighted to have an in-house trick or treat happen on the actual birthday and that's probably as much excitement as two three-year-olds can handle.'

Miranda's nod conveyed understanding of the need to keep the celebration private. She'd seen photographs of the Davenport extravaganzas of years past, before she'd become a part of the family—when there had been bouncy castles, magicians and even ponies or small zoos involved.

Buying into Halloween was a big step forward this year but there was going to be a nursery school parade so the costumes were essential. Charles found himself staring again at the curtain that Grace was behind. Hadn't she said something about finding a costume for Houston? Maybe she'd found a good costume shop.

And maybe Houston could join in the fun? The boys loved that dog and he could be an addition to the private party that would delight them rather than overwhelm them, like a full-on Davenport gathering had the potential to do.

Grace would have to be invited, too, of course, but that wasn't a big deal. Somehow, the intrigue about what had happened to change her had overridden any internal warning about spending time with her. He wanted an answer to the puzzle and getting a little closer was the only way he was going to solve the mystery. Close enough to be friends—like he and Miranda had become all those years ago—but nothing more. And that wouldn't be a problem. The barrier to anything more was so solid he wouldn't have the first idea how to get past it.

And he didn't want to. Even the reminder that that barrier was there was enough to send him back to safe territory and Charles spent the next fifteen minutes focused on the graphs he needed to analyse.

But then Grace appeared from the cubicle and headed straight to the computer closest to where he was sitting. It was tempting to say something totally inappropriate, like asking her whether she might be available for a while in two days' time, to go trick or treating but this wasn't the time or place. It was a bit of a shock, in fact, that the urge was even there. So out of character that it wasn't at all difficult to squash.

'Looking for results?'

'Yep. White blood count and creatinine should be available by now. I've got cultures, throat swabs and urine pending.'

'More than a viral illness, then?'

Grace didn't seem surprised that he was aware of which patient she was dealing with.

'I think she's got staphylococcal toxic shock syndrome. Sixteen years old.'

Charles blinked. It was a rare thing to see these days, which meant that it could be missed until it was late enough for the condition to be extremely serious.

'Signs and symptoms?'

'High fever, vomiting and diarrhoea, muscle aches, a widespread rash that looks like sunburn. She's also hypotensive. Seventy-five over thirty and she's onto her second litre of fluid resus.' Grace flicked him a glance. 'She also finished her period two days ago and likes to leave her tampons in overnight.'

Charles could feel his mouth twisting into a lopsided smile. An impressed one. That was the key question that needed to be asked and could be missed. But not by Grace Forbes, apparently.

'Any foreign material left? Had she forgotten to take a tampon out?'

'No, but I still think I'm right.' Grace clicked a key. 'Yes… Her white count's sky high. So's her creatinine, which means she's got renal involvement. Could be septic shock from another cause but that won't change the initial management.'

'Plan?'

'More fluids, vasopressor support to try and get her BP up. And antibiotics, of course.'

'Flucloxacillin?'

'Yes. And I'll add in clindamycin. There's good evidence that it's effective in decreasing toxin production.' Grace looked past Charles to catch the attention of one of the nursing staff. 'Amy, could you see if there's a bed available in ICU, please? I've got a patient that's going to need intensive monitoring for a while.'

'On it, Dr Forbes.' The nurse reached for the phone.

Grace was gone, too, back to her patient. Charles gave up on the statistics. He would take them home and do his work later tonight, in those quiet hours after the boys were asleep. He was due to go and collect them soon, anyway.

Maybe he should give up on the idea of inviting Grace and Houston to join their party, too. He could give his boys everything they needed. He could take them out later today and let them choose the costumes they wanted themselves.

A sideways glance showed that Amy had finished her urgent arrangements for Grace's patient. She noticed his glance.

'Anything you need, Dr Davenport?'

He smiled at her. 'Not unless you happen to know of a good costume shop in this part of town?'

It seemed like every shop between Manhattan Mercy and home had decorated their windows for Halloween and it made Grace smile, despite her weariness after a couple of such busy days at work, to see the jack-o'-lanterns and ghosts and plastic spiders hanging on fluffy webs.

She'd missed this celebration in Australia.

As she turned towards the more residential area, there were groups of children already out, too, off to do their trick or treating in the late afternoon. So many excited little faces peeping out from beneath witches' hats or lions' ears, dancing along in pretty dresses with fairy wings on their backs or proudly being miniature superheroes.

What a shame that Charles hadn't taken her up on her subtle offer to share Halloween with him and his boys. She'd been thinking about him all day, and wondering just how difficult it had been for him when he had to be reliving every moment of this day three years ago when the twins had been born and he'd lost the love of his life.

Her heart was aching for Charles all over again, as she let herself into the apartment building, so it came as a surprise to hear a peal of laughter echoing down the tiled stairway with its wrought-iron bannisters.

The laughter of small people. And a deeper rumble of an adult male.

Grace paused in the foyer, looking upwards, and was rewarded by a small face she recognised instantly, peering down through the rails. His head was covered by a brown hood that had small round ears.

'*Gace*… Look at *us*…'

'I can't see you properly, Max.'

The face disappeared but she could still hear him.

'Daddy… *Daddy*…we have to visit Gace now…'

And there they were, coming down the stairs. Charles had hold of each twin's hand to keep them steady. In their other hands, the boys clutched a small, orange, plastic bucket shaped like a pumpkin. She could see plenty of candy in each bucket.

The brown hoods were part of a costume that covered them from head to toe.

'You're monkeys.' Grace grinned. 'But…where are your tails?'

The twins gave her a very patient look.

Charles gave her a shadow of a wink. 'Curious George doesn't have a tail,' he explained.

'Oh…'

'Trick or treat!' Cameron shouted. He bounced up and down on small padded feet. 'We want *candy...*'

'Please,' Charles admonished. 'Where are your manners, buddy?'

'Please!' It was Max who was first to comply.

'Grace might not have any candy. Maybe we could just say "hi" to Horse?'

'Actually, I *do* have some candy.' Grace smiled at Charles. 'I have a personal weakness for M&M'S. Would they be suitable?'

'A very small packet?' Charles was smiling back at her but looking slightly haunted. 'We already have enough candy to last till Christmas.'

'They're tiny boxes.' Grace pulled her keys from her bag. 'Come on in. Horse will be so happy to see you.'

Charles had probably been in this apartment before, visiting Stefan and Jerome, but he hadn't come in since Grace had taken over and it felt like a huge step forward somehow. The huge, modern spaces had felt rather empty and totally not her style, although she was slowly getting used to them. With two small boys rolling around on the floor with Houston and Charles following her into the kitchen, it suddenly felt far more like a home.

'Let me open the French doors so that Houston can get out into the garden. It's been an hour or two since Kylie took him out for his last walk.' Grace headed for the pantry next, where she knew the big bag still had plenty of the small boxes of candy-covered chocolate she kept for an after-dinner treat.

She had a bottle of wine in the fridge, too. Would it be a step too far to offer one to Charles? She wanted to ask how the day had gone because she knew that she would be able to see past any cheerful accounts and know how hard it had really been. But she could see that anyway. Charles was looking tired and his smile didn't reach his eyes.

And she wasn't about to get the chance to say anything, because his phone was ringing. He took the call, keeping an eye on the children, who were now racing around the garden with the dog, as he listened and then started firing questions.

'Who's there? How long ago did you activate Code Red?'

Grace caught her breath. 'Code Red' was a term used in Manhattan Mercy's ER to indicate that the level of patient numbers was exceeding the resources the department had to deal with them. Like a traffic light that was not functioning correctly, a traffic jam could ensue and, with patients, it meant that urgent treatment could be delayed and fatalities could result.

He listened a moment longer. 'I'll be there as soon as I can.'

'I can go back,' Grace offered as he ended the call. She could get there in less than ten minutes and she was still in her scrubs—she wouldn't even need to get changed.

But Charles shook his head. 'It's the administrative side that needs management. I'll have to go in.' He looked out at the garden. 'I can take the boys.'

This time, it was Grace who shook her head. 'Don't be daft. I'll look after them.'

Charles looked stunned by the offer. 'But…'

'But, nothing. I'll take them back up to your apartment. That way I can feed them. Or get them to bed if you end up being late. Is it okay if I take Houston up, too?'

'Of course…but…are you sure, Grace? They're going to get tired and cranky after the day they've had.'

Grace held his gaze. 'Go,' she said quietly. 'And don't worry about them. They'll be safe.'

For a heartbeat, she saw the shadows on his face lift as his smile very definitely reached his eyes.

'Thank you,' was all Charles said but it felt like she was the one who was being given something very special.

Trust?

CHAPTER FIVE

IF IT HADN'T been for her small entourage of two little boys and one large, fluffy dog, Grace might have felt like she was doing something wrong, stepping into Charles Davenport's private life like this.

How weird was it that just a few hours of one's lifetime, over a decade ago, could have had such an impact that it could make her feel like…like some kind of *stalker*?

It was her own fault. She had allowed herself to remember those hours. Enshrine them, almost, so that they had become a comfort zone that she had relied on, especially in the early days of coming to terms with what had felt like a broken and very lonely life. In those sleepless hours when things always seemed so much worse, she had imagined herself back in Charles's arms. Being held as though she was something precious.

Being made love to, as if she was the only woman in the world that Charles had wanted to be with.

She could have had a faceless fantasy to tap into but it had seemed perfectly safe to use Charles because she had never expected to see him again. And it had made it all seem so much more believable, because it *had* happened.

Once…

And, somewhere along the way, she had allowed herself to wonder about all the things she didn't know about him. What kind of house he lived in, for example. What his favourite food was. Whether he was married now and had a bunch of gorgeous kids.

She probably could have found out with a quick internet search but she never allowed those secret thoughts any head space in daylight hours. And, as soon as she'd started considering working at Manhattan Mercy, she had shut down even the familiar fantasy. It was no more than a very personal secret—a rather embarrassing one now.

But…entering his private domain like this was…

Satisfying?

Exciting?

Astonishing, certainly.

For some reason, she had expected it to be like the apartment she was living in on the ground floor of this wonderful, old building with its high ceilings and period features like original fireplaces and polished wooden floors. She had also expected the slightly overwhelming aura of wealth and style that Stefan and Jerome had created with their bespoke furniture and expertly displayed artworks.

The framework of the apartment with the floors and ceilings was no surprise but Grace's breath was taken away the moment she stepped through the door to face floor-to-ceiling windows that opened onto a terrace looking directly over Central Park. The polished floors didn't have huge Persian rugs like hers and the furniture looked like it had once been in a house out in the country somewhere. A big, old rambling farmhouse, maybe.

The couch was enormous and so well used that the

leather looked crinkled and soft. There were picture books scattered over the rustic coffee table, along with crayons and paper and even the curling crust of an abandoned sandwich. There were toys all over the place, too—building bricks and brightly coloured cars, soft toy animals and half-done jigsaw puzzles.

It looked like...*home*...

The kind of home that was as much of a fantasy for Grace as being held—and loved—by someone totally genuine.

She had to swallow a huge lump in her throat.

And then she had to laugh, because Houston made a beeline for the coffee table and scoffed the old sandwich crust.

'I'm hungry,' Cameron announced, as he spotted the dog licking its lips.

'Me, too.' Max nodded.

Cameron upended his pumpkin bucket of candy onto the coffee table. Grace gave Houston a stern look that warned him to keep his nose out. Then she extracted the handfuls of candy from Cameron's fists.

'You can choose *one* thing,' she told him. 'But you can't eat it until after your dinner, okay?'

Cameron scowled at her. 'But I'm *hungry.*'

'I know.' Grace was putting the candy back into the bucket. 'Show me where the kitchen is and I'll make you some dinner. You'd better show me where the bathroom is, too.'

The twins led her into a spacious kitchen with a walk-in pantry.

'I'll show you,' Max offered.

He climbed onto a small step and wobbled precariously as he reached for something on a shelf. Grace caught him as he, and the packet he had triumphantly caught the edge of, fell off the step. For a moment, she stood there with the small, warm body in its fluffy monkey suit in her arms. She could smell the soft scent of something that was distinctly child-like. Baby shampoo, maybe?

Max giggled at the pleasure of being caught and, without thinking, Grace planted a kiss on his forehead.

'Down you go,' she said. 'And keep those monkey paws on the floor, where they're safe.'

She stooped to pick up the packet as she set him down.

'Mac and cheese? Is that what you guys want to eat?'

'Yes…*yes*…mac and cheese. For Horse, too…'

Houston waved his plume of a tail, clearly in agreement with the plan, but Grace was more dubious. She eyed the fruit bowl on the table in the kitchen and then the big fridge freezer. Could she tempt them to something healthier first—like an apple or a carrot? Were there some vegetables they might like in the freezer to go with the cheese and pasta? And packet pasta? *Really?* If she could find the ingredients, it wouldn't be hard to throw a fresh version in the oven. Cooking—and baking—were splinter skills she had enjoyed honing over the years.

The twins—and Horse—crowded around as she checked out what she might have to work with. There wasn't much in the way of fresh vegetables but the freezer looked well stocked.

'What's this?' The long cylindrical object was unfamiliar.

'Cookie dough,' Cameron told her. 'Maria makes us cookies.'

'Can you make cookies, Gace?' Max leaned forward so that he could turn his head to look up at her as she crouched. 'I *like* cookies.' Again, she had to catch him before he lost his balance and toppled into the freezer drawer.

'I don't see why not,' she decided. 'You can help. But only if you both eat an apple while I'm getting things ready. And we won't use the frozen sort. If there's some flour in the pantry and butter in the fridge, we'll make our own. From scratch.'

Over an hour later, Grace realised that the grand plan might have been ill-advised. This huge kitchen with its granite and stainless-steel work surfaces looked like a food bomb had been detonated and the sink was stacked with dirty pots and bowls. A fine snowstorm of flour had settled everywhere along with shreds of grated cheese and dribbles of chocolate icing. Houston had done his best to help and there wasn't a single crumb to be found on the floor, but he wasn't so keen on raw flour.

Whose idea had it been to make Halloween spider cookies?

The boys were sitting on the bench right now, on either side of the tray of cookies that had come out of the oven a short time ago. They had to be so tired by now, but they both had their hands clasped firmly in front of them, their eyes huge with excitement as they waited patiently for Grace to tell them it was safe to touch the hot cookies. It was so cute, she had to get her phone out and take a photo. Then she took a close-up of the cookies. The pale dough had made a perfect canvas for the iced chocolate spiders that had M&M eyes. She'd used a plastic bag to make a piping tool and had done her best to guide three-year-old hands to position spider legs but the results were haphazard. One spider appeared to be holding its eyes on the ends of a very fat leg.

Should she send one of the photos to Charles?

A closer glance at the image of his sons made her decide not to. Still in their monkey suits, the boys now had chocolate smears on their faces and the curls of Max's hair that had escaped his hood had something that looked like cheese sauce in it. Her own hair had somehow escaped its fastenings recently and she was fairly sure that she would find a surprise or two when she tried to brush it later.

Hopefully, she would have time to clean up before their father got home but the children and the kitchen would have to take priority. Not wanting to look a wreck in front of Charles was no excuse to worry about her own appearance. She was still in her work scrubs, for heaven's sake—what did it matter?

She prodded one of the cookies.

'Still too hot, guys,' she said. 'But our mac and cheese has cooled down. You can have some of that and then the cookies will be ready for dessert.'

She lifted one twin and then the other off the bench. 'Do you want to take your monkey suits off now?'

'No. We want to be George.'

'And *watch* George,' Max added, nodding his agreement.

'Okay. Do you eat your dinner at the table?'

'Our table,' Cameron told her. 'With TV.'

'Hmm. Let's wash those monkey paws.'

Grace wasn't sure that eating in front of the television was really the norm but, hey…they were all tired now and it was a birthday, after all. She served bowls of the homemade pasta bake on the top of a small, bright

yellow table that Cameron and Max dragged to be right
in front of the widescreen television. The chairs were different primary shades and had the boys' names painted
on the back. Fortunately, it was easy to see how to use
the DVD player and an episode of *Curious George* was
already loaded.

The smell of the mac and cheese made Grace realise how hungry she was herself. She knew she should
tackle the mess in the kitchen but it wouldn't hurt to
curl up on the couch with a bowl of food for a few minutes, would it?

The yellow table, and the bowls, were suspiciously
clean when Grace came in later with the platter of cookies and Houston had an innocent air that looked well
practised. She had to press her lips together not to laugh
out loud. She needed some practice of her own, perhaps,
in good parenting?

The thought caught her unawares. She'd been enjoying this time so much it hadn't occurred to her to realise
that she was living a fantasy. But that was good, wasn't
it? That day at the park, she had wanted to able to embrace a special moment for what it was and not ruin it
by remembering old pain. She had done that with bells
on with this unexpected babysitting job.

The laughter had evaporated, though. And her smile
felt distinctly wobbly. It was just as well that Cameron
turned his head to notice what she was carrying.

'*Cookies...*'

Max's chair fell over backwards in his haste to get
up and Houston barked his approval of the new game
as they all rushed at Grace. She sat on the couch with a
bump and held the platter too high to be reached by all
those small fingers.

'One each,' she commanded. 'And none for Horse, okay?'

They ended up having two each but they weren't overly big cookies. And the crumbs didn't really matter because a leather couch would be easy enough to clean. Not that Grace wanted to move just yet. She had two small boys nestled on either side of her and they were all mesmerised by what Curious George was up to on the screen.

'He's a very naughty monkey, isn't he? Look at all that paint he's spilling everywhere!'

The boys thought it was hilarious but she could feel their warm bodies getting heavier and heavier against her own. Houston was sound asleep with his head pillowed on her feet and Grace could feel her own eyes drooping. Full of comfort food and suddenly exhausted by throwing herself so enthusiastically into what would undoubtedly become an emotionally charged memory, it was impossible not to let herself slip into a moment of putting off the inevitable return to reality.

She wouldn't let herself fall asleep, of course. She would just close her eyes and sink into this group cuddle for a minute or two longer...

It was the last thing Charles had expected to see when he let himself quietly into his apartment late that evening.

He knew his boys would have crashed hours ago and he had assumed they would be tucked up in their shared bedroom, in the racing car beds that had been last year's extravagant gift from their grandparents.

They were, indeed, fast asleep when he arrived home after his hectic troubleshooting in a stretched emergency department, but they weren't in their own beds. Or even in their pyjamas. Still encased in their little monkey suits, Cameron and Max were curled up like puppies on either side of Grace, who was also apparently sound asleep on the couch. Houston had woken at the scratch of the key in the lock, of course, but he wasn't about to abandon the humans he was protecting. He didn't budge from where he was lying across Grace's feet but he seemed to be smiling up at Charles and his tail was twitching in a muted wag.

It might have been a totally unexpected sight, but it was also the cutest thing Charles had ever seen. He gazed at the angelic, sleeping faces of his sons and could feel his heart expanding with love so much it felt like it was in danger of bursting. They were both tucked under a protective arm. Grace had managed to stay sitting upright in her sleep but her head was tilted to one side. He had never seen her face in slumber and she looked far younger than the thirty-six years he knew she shared with him. Far more vulnerable than she ever looked when she was awake.

Maybe it was because she was a single unit with his boys at the moment that she was automatically included in this soft wash of feeling so protective.

So…blessed?

But then Charles stepped closer. What was that in Grace's hair? And smeared on her cheek?

Chocolate?

A closer glance at the twins revealed unexplained substances in odd places as well. Charles could feel his face crease into a deep frown. What on earth had been going on here? Walking quietly, he went through the sitting room towards the kitchen and it wasn't long before he stopped in his tracks, utterly stunned.

He'd never seen a mess like this.

Ever...

His feet were leaving prints in the layer of flour on the floor. The sink was overflowing with dirty dishes. There was a deep dish half-full of what looked like mac and cheese and a wire rack that was covered with cookies. Cookies that were decorated with...good grief...what were those strange blobs and squiggles with chocolate candies poked amongst them?

Ah...there was one with a recognisable shape.

A spider...

And then it hit Charles. Grace had been making Halloween cookies with the boys and clearly she had let them do most of the decorating themselves.

Suddenly, the appalling mess in the kitchen ceased to matter because Charles had glimpsed a much bigger picture. One that caught his heart in a very different way to seeing his boys sleeping so contentedly.

This was a kind of scene that he had never envisaged in the lives of his precious little family. Because it was a dimension that only a woman would think of including?

A *mother*?

Somehow, it wrapped itself into the whole idea of a home. Of a kitchen being the heart of the house. Of putting up with unnecessary mess because that was how children learned important things. Not just about how to make cookies but about...about *home*.

About being safe. And loved.

For a moment, the feeling was overwhelming enough to bring a lump to his throat and a prickle to the back of his eyes that brought all sorts of other sensations in their wake.

Feelings of loss.

And longing...

He had to cradle his forehead between his thumb and finger and rub hard at his temples to stop himself falling into a complete wreck.

It was too much. On top of such an emotionally charged day riding that roller-coaster between remembered grief and the very real celebration of his boys' lives, topped off with an exhausting few hours of high-powered management of a potentially dangerous situation, it was no wonder this was overwhelming.

It was too much.

But it was also kind of perfect.

It was the gentle extraction of a small body from beneath her arm that woke Grace.

For a moment, she blinked sleepily up at Charles, thinking that she was dreaming.

That *smile*...

She had never seen anything quite so tender.

He was smiling at her as if he loved her as much as she knew he loved his children.

Yep. Definitely a dream.

But then Max gave a tiny whimper in his sleep as he was lifted. And the warm weight on her feet shifted as Houston got up and then it all came rushing back to Grace.

'Oh, my God...' she whispered. 'I fell asleep. Oh, Charles, I'm *so* sorry...'

'Don't be.'

'But the *mess*. I was going to clean it all up before you got home.'

'Shh...' Charles was turning away, a still sleeping Max cradled in his arms. 'I'll put Max down and then come back for Cameron. Don't move, or you might wake him up.'

That gave Grace all the time she needed to remember exactly what state she'd left this beautiful apartment in. It was bad enough in here, with the television still going, scattered toys and dinner dishes where they'd been left, but the kitchen...

Oh, help... She'd been given total responsibility and she had created a complete disaster.

But Charles didn't seem to mind. He lifted Cameron with a gentleness that took her breath away. Maybe because his hands brushed her own body as he slid them into place and she could feel just how much care he was taking not to wake his son. His gaze caught hers as she lifted her arm to make his task easier and, amazingly, he was still smiling.

As if he didn't actually care about the mess.

Grace cared. She got to her feet and any residual fuzziness from being woken from a deep sleep evaporated instantly as she went back to the kitchen.

It was even worse than she'd remembered.

Should she start with that pile of unwashed dishes or find a broom and start sweeping the floor?

Reaching out, she touched a puddle of chocolate icing on the granite surface of the work bench. It had hardened enough that it would need a lot more than a cloth to wipe it clean. Where were the cleaning supplies kept? Grace pushed her hair back from her face as she looked around and, to her horror, she found a hard lump that had glued a large clump of hair together. Hard enough to suggest it was more chocolate icing.

She was still standing there, mortified, when Charles came to find her.

For a long moment, she couldn't think of anything to say that could encompass how embarrassed she was. Finally, she had to risk making eye contact. He had to be furious, surely, even if he'd been doing a superb job of hiding it so far.

He caught her gaze and held it firmly. Grace couldn't look away.

Yes...there was something stern enough there to let her know he knew exactly how major the clean-up job would be. That he knew how carried away she'd been in her attempt to keep the twins entertained. That she'd surprised him, to say the very least.

But there was something else there as well.

A...twinkle...

Of amusement, laced with something else.

Appreciation maybe.

No...it was deeper than that. Something she couldn't identify.

'What?' she heard herself whisper. 'What are you thinking? That you'll never leave me in charge of your kids again?'

One corner of his mouth lifted into a smile that could only be described as poignant.

'I'm thinking,' he said quietly. 'That I've spent the last three years trying to be both a father and a mother to my kids and keep their lives as predictable and safe as I can and then someone comes in and, in the space of a few hours, wrecks my house and shows me exactly what I didn't realise was missing.'

Grace's brain had fixed on the comment about wrecking his house.

'I'm sorry,' she murmured.

Charles's gaze shifted a fraction. Oh, help…was he staring at the lump of chocolate icing in her hair?

'I've never even thought of making cookies with the boys,' he said. 'I wouldn't know where to start. I know Maria makes them sometimes, but all that's involved there is slicing up a frozen roll and sticking them in the oven. I'm surprised you even found a bag of flour in the pantry. Not only that, you let them draw spiders on the top.'

'Oh…' Grace could feel her lips curve with pleasure. 'You could tell what they were, then?'

'Only after I spotted one that you probably did. Some of them seem to have eyes on their legs.'

'Helps to see round corners,' Grace suggested. Her smile widened.

Charles was smiling back at her and that twinkle in his eyes had changed into something else.

Something that was giving her a very distinctive shaft of sensation deep in her belly.

Attraction, that's what it was.

A very physical and very definite attraction.

Maybe Charles was feeling it, too. Maybe that was why he lifted his hand to touch her hair.

'Chocolate,' he told her.

'I know…' Grace made a face. 'You might find you need to wash the boys' hair in the morning as well.'

'It's not a problem.' Charles was touching her cheek now, his finger feather-light. 'You've got some here, too.'

Grace couldn't say anything. She was shocked by the touch and the electricity of the current it was producing that flashed through her body like a lightning bolt to join the pool of sensation lower down.

The smile on Charles's face was fading fast. For another one of those endless moments, they stared at each other again.

Fragments of unformed thoughts bombarded Grace. Memories of another time when they'd looked at each other just like this. Before Charles had kissed her for the very first time. Snatches of the conversation they'd just had. What had he meant when he'd said that she'd shown him what he hadn't realised was missing in his life?

Surely he didn't mean *her*?

Part of her really wanted that to have been the meaning.

The part that held his gaze, willing him to make the first move...

He was still touching her cheek but his finger moved past any smear of chocolate, tracing the edge of her nose and then out to the corner of her mouth and along her bottom lip.

And then he shut his eyes as he bent his head, taking his finger away just before his lips took its place.

Another shock wave of unbearably exquisite pleasure shot through Grace's body and she had to close her own eyes as she fell into it.

Dear Lord...she had relived a kiss from this man so many times in her imagination but somehow the reality had been muted over the years.

Nobody else had ever kissed her like this.

Ever...

It was impossible not to respond. To welcome the deepening of that kiss. To press herself closer to the re-membered planes of that hard, lean body. It wasn't until his hand shifted from her back to slide under her ribs and up onto her breast that Grace was suddenly blind-sided by reality.

By what Charles was about to touch.

She could feel the adrenaline flood her body now, her muscles tensing instantly in a classic fight-or-flight reflex, in the same moment that she jerked herself back.

Charles dropped his hand instantly. Stepped back from the kiss just as swiftly.

And this time there was a note of bewilderment in his eyes. Of horror, even...

They both looked away.

'Um...' Grace struggled to find her voice. And a reason to escape. 'I...I really need to take Houston downstairs. He must be a bit desperate to get out by now.'

'Of course.' Was it her imagination or did Charles seem grateful for an excuse to ignore what had just happened? 'He needs his garden.'

'I can't leave you with this mess, though.'

'My cleaner's due in the morning. It really isn't a problem.'

No. Grace swallowed hard. They had another problem now, though, didn't they?

But she could feel the distance between them accelerating. She wasn't the only one who needed to escape, was she?

They hadn't just crossed a barrier here. They had smashed through it with no consideration of any repercussions.

And maybe they were just as big for Charles as they were for herself.

But Grace couldn't afford to feel any empathy right now. The need to protect herself was too overwhelming.

With no more than a nod to acknowledge her being excused from cleaning up the mess she had created, Grace took her leave and fled downstairs with Houston.

She had no mental space to feel guilty about escaping.

Besides, Charles had created a bit of a mess himself, hadn't he? By kissing her like that.

That was more than enough to deal with for the moment.

CHAPTER SIX

'OH, MY...' VANESSA DAVENPORT looked slightly appalled as she peered more closely at what was being held up for her admiration. 'What *are* they?'

'Cookies, Grandma.' Cameron was using that patient tone that told adults they were being deliberately obtuse. 'We *made* them.'

'And Gace,' Max added.

'Gace?' Vanessa was looking bewildered now but Charles didn't offer an explanation.

He was kicking himself inwardly. He should have known exactly what his mother's reaction would be to the less than perfect cookies, but he couldn't forgive the slap to his boys' pride that had prompted them to insist on bringing their creations to the family afternoon tea.

It was the complete opposite end to the spectrum that Grace was also on. She'd been just as proud of the boys at the results of their efforts. This morning, she'd sent him the photo she'd taken of them sitting on the bench, their hands clasped and eyes shining with the tray of cookies between them. It even had Horse's nose photo-bombing the bottom of the image and Charles had been so taken with it, he'd thought of using it for his Christmas cards this year.

Maybe not, if his mother was going to look like this.

'Let's give them to Alice.' Vanessa was an expert in ignoring anything that she didn't approve of. 'She can put them in the kitchen.'

Alice was hovering in the background, ready to help with hanging coats up in the cloakroom, but she moved swiftly when there was another knock on the massive front door of the Davenport mansion. His father, Hugo, was coming into the foyer at the same time and the twins' faces brightened.

'Look, Grandpa...look what we made.'

'Wow...cookies...they look delicious.'

'Did I hear someone mention cookies?'

Charles turned towards the door. 'Miranda. Hey... I'm glad you could make it.'

His half-sister had two brightly wrapped parcels under her arm and the twins' eyes got very round.

'Presents, Daddy. For us?'

But Charles had been distracted by someone who had followed Miranda into the house. He hadn't seen his youngest brother, Zachary, for such a long time.

'*Zac*... What are you doing here?'

'I heard there was a birthday celebration happening.'

'But I thought you were in Annapolis.'

'I was. I am. I'm just in town for the day—you should know why...'

Charles had to shake his head but there was no time to ask. The shriek of excitement behind him had to mean that Miranda had handed over the parcels and, turning his head, he could see his mother already moving towards the main reception lounge.

'For goodness' sake,' she said. 'Let's go somewhere a little more civilised than the doorstep, shall we?'

Charles saw the glance that flashed between Zac and Miranda. Would there ever come a day when Vanessa actually welcomed Miranda into this house, instead of barely tolerating her?

His father was now holding the platter of cookies.

'Shall I take those to the kitchen, sir?' Alice asked.

'No…no…they have to go on the table with all the other treats.'

Charles felt a wash of relief. Families were always complicated and this one a lot more than most but there was still a thread of something good to be found. Something worth celebrating.

He scooped up Cameron, who was already ripping the paper off his gift. 'Hang on, buddy. Let's do that in the big room.'

Zac had parcels in his hands, too. And when the door swung open behind him to reveal Elijah with a single, impressively large box in his arms, Charles could only hope that this gathering wasn't going to be too overwhelming for small boys. He thought wistfully of the relatively calm oasis of their own apartment and, unbidden, an image of the ultimately peaceful scene he'd come home to last night filled his mind.

The one of Grace, asleep on the couch, cuddled up with the boys and with a dog asleep on her feet.

So peaceful. So…perfect…?

'I can't stay,' Elijah said, as they all started moving to the lounge. 'I got someone to cover me for an hour at work. I'll be getting a taxi back in half an hour.'

'Oh…' Miranda was beside him. 'Could I share? My shift starts at five but it takes so long on the Tube I'd have to leave about then, anyway.'

'Flying visit,' Zac murmured. 'It's always the way

with us Davenports, isn't it? Do your duty but preferably with an excuse to escape before things get awkward?'

'Mmm.' The sound was noncommittal but Charles put Cameron down with an inward sigh. This vast room, with a feature fireplace and enough seating for forty people, had obviously been professionally decorated. Huge, helium balloons were tethered everywhere and there were streamers looping between the chandeliers and a banner covering the wall behind the mahogany dining table that had been shifted in here from the adjoining dining room. A table that was laden with perfectly decorated cakes and cookies and any number of other delicious treats that had been provided by professional caterers.

Cameron, with his half-unwrapped parcel in his arms, ran towards the pile of other gifts near the table, Max hot on his heels. A maid he didn't recognise came towards the adults with a silver tray laden with flutes of champagne.

'Orange juice for me, thanks,' Elijah said. Miranda just shook her head politely and went after the twins to help them with the unwrapping.

'So what's with your flying visit?' he asked Zac. 'And why should I know about it?'

'Because I'm here for an interview. I've applied for a job at Manhattan Mercy that starts next month.'

'Really? Wow…' Charles took a sip of his champagne. 'That's great, man. And there I was thinking you were going to be a navy medic for the rest of your life.'

Zac shrugged. 'Maybe I'm thinking that life's short, you know? If I don't get around to building some bridges soon, it's never going to happen.'

Charles could only nod. He knew better than anyone

how short life could be, didn't he? About the kind of jagged hole that could be left when someone you loved got ripped from it.

But that hole had been covered last night, hadn't it? Just for a moment or two, he had stepped far enough away from it for it to have become invisible. And it had been that perfect family scene that had led him away. His two boys, under the sheltering arms of someone who had looked, for all the world, like their mother. With a loyal family pet at their feet, even.

But now Zac had shown him the signpost that led straight back to the gaping hole in his life.

And Elijah was shaking his head. 'I hope you're not harbouring any hope of this lot playing happy families any time soon.'

They all turned their gazes on their parents. Hugo and Miranda were both down on the floor with the twins. Miranda's gifts of a new toy car for Cameron and a tractor for Max had been opened and set aside and now the first of the many parcels from the grandparents were being opened. It looked like it was a very large train set, judging by the lengths of wooden rails that were appearing. The level of excitement was increasing and Charles needed to go and share it. Maybe that way, the twins wouldn't notice the way their grandmother was perched on a sofa at some distance, merely watching the spectacle.

'Anyone else coming?' Zac asked. 'Where's Penny?'

'Still on holiday. Skiing, I think. Or was it sky-diving?'

'Sounds like her. And Jude? I'd love to catch up with him.'

'Are you kidding?' Elijah's eyebrows rose. 'Being a

cousin is a perfect "get out of jail" card for most of our family get-togethers.'

Charles moved away from his brothers. It was always like this. Yes, there were moments of joy to be found in his family but the undercurrents were strong enough to mean that there was always tension. And most of that tension came from Vanessa and Elijah.

You had to make allowances, of course. It was his mother who'd been hardest hit by the scandal of learning that her husband had been having an affair that had resulted in a child—Miranda. That knowledge would have been hard enough, but to find out because Miranda's mother had died and her father had insisted on acknowledging her and bringing her into the family home had been unbearable for Vanessa.

Unbearable for everyone. The difference in age between himself and his twin might have been insignificant but Charles had always known that he was the oldest child. The firstborn. And that came with a responsibility that he took very seriously. That turbulent period of the scandal had been his first real test and he'd done everything he could to comfort his siblings—especially Elijah, who'd been so angry and bitter. To protect the frightened teenager who had suddenly become one of their number as well. And to support his devastated mother, who was being forced to start an unexpected chapter in her life.

Like the authors of many of the gossip columns, he'd expected his mother would walk away from her marriage but Vanessa had chosen not to take that option. She'd claimed that she didn't want to bring more shame on the Davenport family but they all knew that what scared her more would have been walking away from her own exalted position in New York society and the fundraising efforts that had become her passion.

To outward appearances, the shocking changes had been tolerated with extraordinary grace. Behind closed doors, however, it had been a rather different story. There were no-go areas that Vanessa had constructed for her own protection and nobody, including her husband, would dream of intruding on them uninvited.

Charles had always wondered if he could have done more, especially for Elijah, who had ended up so bitter about marriage and what he sarcastically referred to as 'happy families'. If he could have done a better job as the firstborn, maybe he could have protected his family more successfully, perhaps by somehow diverting the destructive force of the scandal breaking. It hadn't been his fault, of course, any more than Nina's death had been. Why didn't that lessen the burden that a sense of responsibility created?

But surely enough time had passed to let them all move on?

Charles felt tired of it all suddenly. The effort it had taken to try and keep his shattered family together would have been all-consuming at any time. To have had it happen in the run-up to his final exams had been unbelievably difficult. Life-changing.

If it hadn't happened, right after that night he'd shared with Grace, how different might his life have been?

Would he have shut her out so completely? Pretended that night had never happened because that was a factor he had absolutely no head space to even consider?

To his shame, Charles had been so successful in shutting it out in that overwhelmingly stressful period, he had never thought of how it might have hurt Grace.

Was *that* why she'd pretty much flinched during that kiss last night? Why she'd practically run away from him as hard and fast as she could politely manage?

Receiving that photo this morning had felt kind of like Grace was sending an olive branch. An apology for running, perhaps. Or at least an indication that they could still be friends?

The effect was a swirl of confusion. He had glimpsed something huge that was missing from his life, along with the impression that Grace was possibly the only person who could fill that gap. The very edges of that notion should be stirring his usual reaction of disloyalty to Nina that thoughts of including any other woman in his life usually engendered.

But it wasn't happening…

Because there was a part of his brain that was standing back and providing a rather different perspective? Would Nina have wanted her babies to grow up without a mom?

Would *he* have wanted them to grow up without a dad, if he'd been the one to die too soon?

Of course not.

He had experienced the first real surge of physical desire in three long years, too. That should be sparking the guilt but it didn't seem to be. Not in the way he'd become so accustomed to, anyway.

He wouldn't have inflicted a life of celibacy on Nina, either.

Maybe the guilt was muted by something more than a different perspective. Because, after the way she had reacted last night, it seemed that going any further down that path was very unlikely?

The more he thought about it, the more his curiosity about Grace was intensifying.

She had felt the same level of need, he knew she had. She had responded to that kiss in a way that had inflamed that desire to a mind-blowing height.

And then she'd flinched as though he had caused her physical pain.

Why?

It wasn't really any of his business but curiosity was becoming a need to know.

Because, as unlikely as it was, could the small part he had played in Grace's life in the past somehow have contributed to whatever it was?

A ridiculous notion but, if nothing else, it seemed like a legitimate reason to try and find out the truth. Not that it was going to be easy, mind you. Some people were very good at building walls to keep their pain private. Like his mother. Thanks to that enormous effort he'd made to try and keep his family together during the worst time of that scandal breaking, however, he had learned more than anyone about exactly what was behind Vanessa Davenport's walls. Because he'd respected that pain and had had a base of complete trust to work from.

He could hardly expect Grace to trust him that much. Not when he looked back over the years and could see the way he'd treated her from her point of view.

But there was something there.

And, oddly, it did *feel* a bit like trust.

Stepping over train tracks that his father was slotting together, smiling at the delight on his sons' faces as they unwrapped a bright blue steam engine with a happy face on the front, Charles moved towards the couch and bent to kiss Vanessa's cheek.

'Awesome present, Mom,' he said with a smile. 'Clever of you to know how much the boys love Thomas the Tank Engine.'

That kiss had changed everything.

Only a few, short weeks ago Grace had been so nervous about meeting Charles Davenport again that she had almost decided against applying for the job at Manhattan Mercy.

What had she been so afraid of? That old feelings might resurface and she'd have to suffer the humiliation of being dismissed so completely again?

To find that the opposite had happened was even scarier. That old connection was still there and could clearly be tapped into but... Grace didn't want that.

Well...she *did*...but she wasn't ready.

She might never be ready.

Charles must think she was crazy. He must have sensed the connection at the same moment she had, when they'd shared their amusement about the spiders that had eyes on their legs, otherwise he wouldn't have touched her like that.

And he must have seen that fierce shaft of desire because she had felt it throughout her entire body so why wouldn't it have shown in her eyes?

Just for those few, deliciously long moments she had been unaware of anything but that desire when he'd kissed her. That spiralling need for more.

And then his hand had—almost—touched her breast and she'd reacted as if he'd pulled a knife on her or something.

It had been purely instinctive and Grace knew how over the top it must have seemed. She was embarrassed.

A bit ashamed of herself, to be honest, but there it was. A trigger that had been too deeply set to be disabled.

The net effect was to make her feel even more nervous about her next meeting with Charles than she had been about the first one and he hadn't been at work the next day so her anxiety kept growing.

She had sent out mixed messages and he had every right to be annoyed with her. How awkward would it be to work together from now on? Did she really want to live with a resurrection of all the reasons why she'd taken herself off to work in the remotest places she could find?

No. What she wanted was to wind back the clock just a little. To the time before that kiss, when it had felt like an important friendship was being cemented. When she had discovered a totally unexpected dimension in her life by embracing a sense of family in her time with Charles and his sons and Houston.

So she had sent through that photo she had taken of Max and Cameron waiting for the cookies to cool. Along with another apology for the mess they had all created. Maybe she wanted to test the waters and see just how annoyed he might be.

He had texted back to thank her, and say that it was one of the best photos of the boys he'd ever seen. He also said that they were going to a family birthday celebration that afternoon and surprised her by saying he didn't think it would be nearly as much fun as baking Halloween cookies.

A friendly message—as if nothing had changed.

The relief was welcome.

But confusing.

Unless Charles was just as keen as she was to turn the clock back?

Of course he was, she decided by the end of that day, as she took Houston for a long, solitary walk in the park. He had as big a reason as she did not to want to get that close to someone. He had lost the absolute love of his life under horrifically traumatic circumstances. Part of him had to want to keep on living—as she did—and not to be deprived of the best things that life had to offer.

But maybe he wasn't ready yet, either.

Maybe he never would be.

And that was okay—because maybe they could still be friends and that was something that could be treasured.

Evidence that Charles wanted to push the 'reset' button on their friendship came at increasingly frequent intervals over the next week or two. Now that his nanny, Maria, had recovered from her back injury enough to work during week days, he was in the emergency room every day that Grace was working.

He gave her a printed copy of the photograph, during a quiet moment when they both happened to be near the unit desk on one occasion.

'Did you see that Horse photobombed it?'

Grace laughed. 'No…I thought I'd had my thumb on the lens or something. I was going to edit it out.'

She wouldn't now. She would tuck this small picture into her wallet and she knew that sometimes she would take it out and look at it. A part of her would melt with love every time. And part of her would splinter into little pieces and cry?

She avoided looking directly at Charles as she slipped the image carefully into her pocket.

'Did your cleaning lady resign the next day?'

'No. She wants the recipe for your homemade mac and cheese.'

It was unfortunate that Grace glanced at Charles as he stopped speaking to lick his lips. That punch of sensation in her belly was a warning that friendship with this man would never be simple. Or easy. That it could become even worse, in fact, because there might come a time when she was ready to take that enormous step into a new life only to find that Charles would never feel the same way.

'I'd like it, too.' He didn't seem to have noticed that she was edging away. 'I had some later that night and it was the most delicious thing ever. It had *bacon* in it.'

'Mmm… It's not hard.'

'Maybe you could show me. Sometime…'

The suggestion was casual but Grace had to push an image from her mind of standing beside Charles as she taught him how to make a cheese sauce. Of being close enough to touch him whilst wrapped in the warmth and smells of a kitchen—the heart of a home. She could even feel a beat of the fear that being so close would bring and she had to swallow hard.

'I'll write down how to do it for you.'

Charles smiled and nodded but seemed distracted now. He was staring at the patient details board. 'What's going on with that patient in Curtain Six? She's been here for a long time.'

'We're waiting for a paediatric psyche consult. This is her third admission in a week. Looks like a self-inflicted

injury and I think there's something going on at home
that she's trying to escape from.'

'Oh...' His breath was a sigh. 'Who brought her in?'

'Her stepfather. And he's very reluctant to leave her
alone with staff.'

'Need any help?'

'I think we're getting there. I've told him that we
need to run more tests. Might even have to keep her in
overnight for observation. I know we've blocked up a
bed for too long, but...'

'Don't worry about it.' The glance Grace received
was direct. Warm. 'Do whatever you need to do. I trust
you. Just let me know if you need backup.'

Feeling trusted was a powerful thing.

Knowing that you had the kind of backup that could
also be trusted was even better and Grace was particularly grateful for that a couple of mornings later with
the first case that arrived on her shift.

A thirteen-month-old boy, who had somehow managed to crawl out of the house at some point during the
night and had been found, virtually frozen solid, in the
back yard.

'VF arrest,' the paramedics had radioed in. 'CPR
under way. We can't intubate—his mouth's frozen.
We've just got an OPA in.'

Grace had the team ready in their resuscitation area.

'We need warmed blankets and heat packs. Warmed
IV fluids. We'll be looking at thoracic lavage or even
ECMO. Have we heard back from the cardiac surgical
team yet?'

'Someone's on their way.'

'ECMO?' she heard a nurse whisper. 'What's that?'

'Extra corporeal membrane oxygenation,' she told

them. 'It's a form of cardiopulmonary bypass and we can warm the blood at the same time. Because, like we've all been taught, you're not—'

'—dead until you're warm and dead.'

It was Charles who finished her sentence for her, as he appeared beside her, pushing his arms through the sleeves of a gown. He didn't smile at her, but there was a crinkle at the corners of his eyes that gave her a boost of confidence.

'Thought you might like a hand,' he murmured. 'We've done this before, remember?'

Grace tilted her head in a single nod of acknowledgement. She was focused on the gurney being wheeled rapidly towards them through the doors. Of course she remembered. It had been the only time she and Charles had worked so closely together during those long years of training. They had been left to deal with a case of severe hypothermia in an overstretched emergency department when they had been no more than senior medical students. Their patient had been an older homeless woman that nobody had seemed to want to bother with.

They had looked at each other and quietly chanted their new mantra in unison.

'You're not dead until you're warm and dead.'

And they'd stayed with her, taking turns to change heat packs and blankets while keeping up continuous CPR for more than ninety minutes. Until her body temperature was high enough for defibrillation to be an effective option.

Nobody ever forgot the first time they defibrillated somebody.

Especially when it was successful.

But this was very different. This wasn't an elderly

woman who might not have even been missed if she had succumbed to her hypothermia. This was a precious child who had distraught members of his family watching their every move. A tiny body that looked, and felt, as if it was made of chilled wax as he was gently transferred to the heated mattress, where his soaked, frozen nappy was removed and heat packs were nestled under his arms and in his groin.

'Pupils?'

'Fixed and dilated.'

Grace caught Charles's gaze as she answered his query and it was no surprise that she couldn't see any hint of a suggestion that it might be too late to help this child. It was more an acknowledgement that the battle had just begun. That they'd done this before and they could do it again. And they might be surrounded by other staff members but it almost felt like it was just them again. A tight team, bonded by an enormous challenge and the determination to succeed.

Finding a vein to start infusing warmed IV fluids presented a challenge they didn't have time for so Grace used an intraosseous needle to place a catheter inside the tibia where the bone marrow provided a reliable connection to the central circulation. It was Charles who took over the chest compressions from the paramedics and initiated the start of warmed oxygen for ventilation and then it was Elijah who stepped in to continue while Charles and Grace worked together to intubate and hook the baby up to the ventilator.

The cardiac surgical team arrived soon after that, along with the equipment that could be used for more aggressive internal warming, by direct cannulation of major veins and arteries to both warm the blood and take over the work of the heart and lungs or the procedure of infusing the chest cavity with warmed fluids and then draining it off again. If ECMO or bypass was going to be used, the decision had to be made whether to do it here in the department or move their small patient to Theatre.

'How long has CPR been going?'

'Seventy-five minutes.'

'Body temperature?'

'Twenty-two degrees Celsius. Up from twenty-one on arrival. It was under twenty on scene.'

'Rhythm?'

'Still ventricular fibrillation.'

'Has he been shocked?'

'Once. On scene.' Again, it was Charles's gaze that Grace sought. 'We were waiting to get his temperature up a bit more before we tried again but maybe...'

'It's worth a try,' one of the cardiac team said. 'Before we start cannulation.'

But it was the nod from Charles that Grace really wanted to see before she pushed the charge button on the defibrillator.

'Stand clear,' she warned as crescendo of sound switched to a loud beeping. 'Shocking now.'

It was very unlikely that one shock would convert the fatal rhythm into one that was capable of pumping blood but, to everyone's astonishment, that was exactly what it did. Charles had his fingers resting gently near a tiny elbow.

'I've got a pulse.'

'Might not last,' the surgeon warned. 'He's still cold enough for it to deteriorate back into VF at any time, especially if he's moved.'

Grace nodded. 'We won't move him. Let's keep on

with what we're doing with active external rewarming and ventilation. We'll add in some inotropes as well.'

'It could take hours.' The surgeon looked at his watch. 'I can't stay, I'm afraid. I've got a theatre list I'm already late for but page me if you run into trouble.'

Charles nodded but the glance he gave Grace echoed what she was thinking herself. They had won the first round of this battle and, together, they would win the next.

There wasn't much that they could do, other than keep up an intensive monitoring that meant not stepping away from this bedside. Heat packs were refreshed and body temperature crept up, half a degree at a time. There were blood tests to run and drugs to be cautiously administered. They could let the parents come in for a short time to see what was happening and to reassure them that everything possible was being done but they couldn't be allowed to touch their son yet. The situation was still fragile and only time would give them the answers they all needed.

His name, they learned, was Toby.

It wasn't necessary to have two senior doctors present the whole time but neither Charles nor Grace gave any hint of wanting to be anywhere else and, fortunately, there were enough staff to cover everything else that was happening in the department.

More than once, they were the only people in the room with Toby. Their conversation was quiet and professional, focused solely on the challenge they were dealing with and, at first, any eye contact was that of colleagues. Encouraging. Appreciative. Hopeful...

It was an odd bubble to be in, at the centre of a busy department but isolated at the same time. And when it was just the two of them, when a nurse left to deliver blood samples or collect new heat packs, there was an atmosphere that Grace could only describe as...peaceful?

No. That wasn't the right word. It felt as though she was a piece of a puzzle that was complete enough to see what the whole picture was going to be. There were only a few pieces still to fit into the puzzle and they were lying close by, waiting to be picked up. It was a feeling of trust that went a step beyond hope. It was simply a matter of time.

So perhaps that was why those moments of eye contact changed as one hour morphed into the next. Why it was so hard to look away, because that was when she could feel it the most—that feeling that the puzzle was going to be completed and that it was a picture she had been waiting her whole life to see.

It felt like...happiness.

Nearly three hours later, Toby was declared stable enough to move to the paediatric intensive care unit. He was still unconscious but his heart and other organs were functioning normally again. Whether he had suffered any brain damage would not be able to be assessed until he woke up.

If he woke up?

Was that why Grace was left with the feeling that she hadn't quite been able to reach those last puzzle pieces? Why the picture she wanted to see so badly was still a little blurred?

No. The way Charles was looking at her as Toby's bed disappeared through the internal doors of the ER assured Grace that she had done the best job she could and, for now, the outcome was the best it could possibly be. That he was proud of her. Proud of his department.

And then he turned to start catching up with the multitude of tasks that had accumulated and needed his attention. Grace watched him walking away from her and that was when instinct kicked in.

That puzzle wasn't really about a patient at all, was it?

It was about herself.

And Charles.

'BIT COLD FOR the park today, isn't it, Doc? They're sayin'
it could snow.'

CHAPTER SEVEN

'BIT COLD FOR the park today, isn't it, Doc? They're sayin'
it could snow.'

'I know, but the boys are desperate for a bike ride.
We haven't been able to get outside to play for days.'

Jack brightened at the prospect of leaving the tiny
space that was his office by the front door of this apartment block.

'Stay here. I'll fetch those bikes from the basement.
Could do with checkin' that the rubbish has been collected.'

'Oh, thanks, Jack.' It was always a mission managing two small boys and their bikes in the elevator. This
way, he could get their coats and helmets securely fastened without them trying to climb on board their beloved bikes.

As always, he cast more than one glance towards
the door at the back of the foyer as he got ready to head
outside. He remembered wanting to knock on it when
Grace had first moved in and that he'd been held back
by some nebulous idea of boundaries. He didn't have
any problems with it now.

They'd come a long way since then. Too far, perhaps,
but they'd obviously both decided to put that ill-advised

kiss behind them and focus on a friendship that was growing steadily stronger.

And Charles had news that he really wanted to share.

So he knocked on Grace's door. He knew she had a day off today because he'd started taking more notice of her name on the weekly rosters.

'Charles... Hi...' Was it his imagination or was there a glow of real pleasure amidst the surprise of a morning caller?

He could certainly feel that glow but maybe it was coming from his own pleasure at seeing *her*. Especially away from work, when she wasn't wearing her scrubs, with her hair scraped back from her face in her usual ponytail. Today, she was in jeans tucked into sheepskin-lined boots and she had a bright red sweater and her hair was falling around her face in messy waves—a bit like it had been when he'd come home to find her sound asleep on his couch.

Horse sneaked past her legs and made a beeline for the boys, who shrieked with glee and fell on their furry friend for cuddles.

'I have something I have to tell you,' Charles said.

Her eyes widened. 'Oh, no...is it Miranda? Helena texted me to say she was involved in that subway tunnel collapse—that she'd been trapped under rubble or something.'

Charles shook his head. 'She's fine. She didn't even need to come into the ER. A paramedic took care of her, apparently. No, it's about Toby. I just had a call from PICU.'

He could hear the gasp as Grace sucked in her breath. 'Toby?'

'Yes. He woke up this morning.'

'Oh...it's been forty-eight hours. I was starting to think the worst... Is he...? Has he...?'

'As far as they can tell, he's neurologically intact. They're going to run more tests but he recognises his parents and he's said the few words he knows. And he's smiling...'

Grace was smiling, too. Beaming, in fact. And then she noticed Jack as the elevator doors opened and he stepped out with a small bike under each arm.

'Morning, Jack.'

'Morning, Miss Forbes.' His face broke into a wide grin. 'Yo' sure look happy today.'

'I am...' There was a sparkle in her eyes that looked like unshed tears as she met Charles's gaze again. 'So happy. Thanks so much for coming to tell me.'

'Can Horse come to the park?' Max was beside his father's legs. 'Can he watch us ride our bikes?'

The glance from Grace held a query now. Did Charles want their company?

He smiled. Of course he did.

'Wrap up warm,' Jack warned. 'It's only about five degrees out there. It might snow.'

'Really?' Grace sounded excited. 'I can't wait for it to snow. And I'm really, really hoping for a white Christmas this year.'

'Could happen.' Jack nodded. 'They're predicting some big storms for December and that's not far off. It'll be Christmas before we know it.'

Charles groaned. 'Let's get Thanksgiving out of the way before we start talking Christmas. We've only just finished Halloween!'

Except Halloween felt like a long way in the past now,

didn't it? Long enough for this friendship to feel like it was becoming something much more solid.

Real.

'Give me two minutes,' Grace said. 'I need to find my hat and scarf. Horse? Come and get your harness on.'

The boys had trainer wheels on their small bikes and needed constant reminding not to get too far ahead of the adults. Pedestrians on the busy pavement had to jump out of the way as the boys powered towards the park but most of them smiled at the two identical little faces with their proud smiles. Charles kept a firm hand on each set of handlebars as they crossed the main road at the lights but once they were through the gates of Central Park, he let them go as fast as they wanted.

'Phew…I think we're safe now. I'm pretty sure the tourist carriages don't use this path.'

'Do they do sleigh rides here when it snows?'

'I don't know. I've seen carriages that look like sleighs but I think they have wheels rather than runners. Why?'

Grace's breath came out in a huff of white as she sighed. 'It's always been my dream for Christmas. A sleigh ride in a snowy park. At night, when there's sparkly lights everywhere and there are bells on the horses and you have to be all wrapped up in soft blankets.'

Charles smiled but he felt a squeeze of something poignant catch his heart. The picture she was painting was ultimately romantic but did she see herself alone in that sleigh?

He couldn't ask. They might have reached new ground with their friendship, especially after that oddly intimate case of working to save little Toby, but asking such a personal question seemed premature. Risky.

Besides, Grace was still talking.

'Christmas in Australia was so weird. Too hot to do anything but head for the nearest beach or pool but lots of people still want to do the whole roast turkey thing. Or dress up in Santa suits.' She rubbed at her nose, which was already red from the cold. 'It feels much more like a proper Christmas when it snows.'

The boys were turning their bikes in a circle ahead of them, which seemed to be a complicated procedure. And then they were pedalling furiously back towards them.

'Look at us, Gace! Look how fast we can go.'

Grace leapt out of Cameron's way, pulling Houston to safety as Cameron tried, and failed, to slow down. The bike tilted sideways and then toppled.

'Whoops...' Charles scooped up his son. 'Okay, buddy?'

Cameron's face crumpled but then he sniffed hard and nodded.

'Is it time for a hotdog?'

'Soon.' He was climbing back onto his bike. 'I have to ride some more first.'

'He's determined,' Grace said, watching him pedal after his brother. 'Like his daddy.'

'Oh? You think I'm determined?'

'Absolutely. You don't give up easily, even if you have a challenge that would defeat a lot of people.'

'You mean Toby? You were just as determined as I was to save him.'

'Mmm. But I'd seen that look in your eyes before, remember? I'm not sure if I would have had the confidence to try that hard when I had absolutely no experience, like you did back when we were students.' She shook her head. 'I still don't have that much experience of arrest from hypothermia. That old woman that we worked on is the only other case I've ever had. Bit of a coincidence, isn't it?'

'Meant to be,' Charles suggested lightly. 'We're a good team.'

'It's easier to be determined when you're part of a team,' Grace said quietly. 'I think you've coped amazingly with challenges you've had to face alone. Your boys are a credit to you.'

He might not know her story yet but he knew that Grace had been through her own share of tough challenges.

He spoke quietly as well. 'I have a feeling you've done that, too.'

The glance they shared acknowledged the truth. And their connection. A mutual appreciation of another person's strength of character, perhaps?

And Charles was quite sure that Grace was almost ready to tell him what he wanted to know. That all it would take was the right question. But he had no idea what that question might be and this was hardly the best place to start a conversation that needed care. He could feel the cold seeping through his shoes and gloves and he would need to take the boys home soon.

'Come and visit later, if you're not busy,' he found himself suggesting. 'The boys got a train set from my parents for their birthday and they'd love to show it to you.'

The twins were on the return leg of one of the loops that took them away from their father and then back again.

'What do you think, Max?' he called out. 'Is it a good idea for Grace to come and see your new train?'

Later, Charles knew he would feel a little guilty about

enlisting his sons' backup like this but right then, he just wanted to know that he was going to get to spend some more time with Grace.

Soon.

It seemed important.

'*Yes*,' Max shouted obligingly, his instant grin an irresistible invitation. 'And Horse.'

'And mac and cheese,' Cameron added.

But Max shook his head. 'Not Daddy's,' he said sadly. 'It comes in a box. I don't like it…'

Charles raised an eyebrow. 'This is your fault, Grace. I have at least half a dozen boxes of Easy Mac 'n' Cheese in my pantry—my go-to quick favourite dinner for the boys—and they're useless. Even when I try adding bacon.'

'Oh, dear…' Grace was smiling. 'Guess I'd better teach you how to make cheese sauce, then?'

His nod was solemn. 'I think so. You did promise.'

Her cheeks were already pink from the cold but Charles had the impression that the colour had deepened even more suddenly.

'I think I promised to write it down for you.'

'Ah…but I learn so much better by doing something. Do you remember that class we did on suturing once? When we had that pig skin to practise on?'

'Yes… It was fun.'

'Tricky, though. I'd stayed up the night before, reading all about exactly where to grasp a needle with the needle driver and wrapping the suture around it and then switching hand positions to make the knots. I even watched a whole bunch of videos.'

'Ha! I knew you always stayed up all night studying. It was why I had so much trouble keeping up with you.'

'My point is, actually doing it was a completely different story. I felt like I had two left hands. You were way better at it.'

'Not by the end of the class. You aced it.'

'Because I was doing it. Not reading about it, or watching it.'

Why was he working so hard to persuade her to do something that she might not be comfortable with? Because it felt important—just like the idea of spending more time with her?

There was something about the way her gaze slid away from his that made him want to touch her arm. To tell her that this was okay. That she could trust him.

But maybe he managed to communicate that, anyway, in the briefest glance she returned to, because her breath came out in a cloudy puff again—the way it had when she'd sighed after confessing her dream of having a Christmas sleigh ride in the snow. Her chin bobbed in a single nod.

'I'll pick up some ingredients on my way home.'

'We don't want to go home, Daddy,' Cameron said. 'We want to go to the playground.'

With their determined pedalling efforts, their feet probably weren't as cold as his, Charles decided. And with some running and climbing added in, they were going to be very tired by this evening. They'd probably fall asleep as soon as they'd had their dinner and…and that would be the perfect opportunity to talk to Grace, wouldn't it?

Really talk to Grace.

He smiled at his boys. 'Okay. Let's head for the playground.'

'And Gace,' Max added.

But she shook her head. 'I can't, sorry, sweetheart. I have to take Horse home now.'

'Why?'

'Because Stefan and Jerome are going to Skype us and talk to him, like they do every Sunday. And he needs his hair brushed first. Oh... I've just had an idea.' She held the dog's lead out to Charles. 'Can you stand with the boys? I'll take a photo I can send them, so they can see that he's been having fun in the park today.'

It took a moment or two to get two small boys, two bikes, a large fluffy dog and a tall man into a cohesive enough group to photograph. And then a passer-by stopped and insisted on taking the phone from Grace's hands.

'You need one of the whole family,' he said firmly.

Grace looked startled. And then embarrassed as she caught Charles's gaze.

It reminded him of Davenport family photos. Where everyone had to look as though they were a happy family and hide the undercurrents and secret emotions that were too private to share. The kind of image that would be taken very soon for their annual Thanksgiving gathering?

Charles was good at this. He'd been doing it for a very long time. And he knew it was far easier to just get it over with than try and explain why it wasn't a good idea.

So he smiled at Grace and pulled Houston a bit closer to make a space for her to stand beside him, behind the boys on their bikes.

'Come on,' he encouraged. 'Before we all freeze to death here.'

Strangely, when Grace was in place a moment later, with Charles's arm draped over her shoulders, it didn't feel at all like the uncomfortable publicity shots of the New York Davenports destined to appear in some glossy magazine.

It was, in fact, surprisingly easy to find the 'big smile' that the stranger requested.

It wasn't a case of her heart conflicting with her head, which would have been far simpler to deal with.

This was more like her heart arranging itself into two separate divisions on either side of what was more like a solid wall than a battle line.

There were moments when Grace could even believe there was a door hidden in that wall, somewhere, and time with Charles felt like she was moving along, tapping on that solid surface, waiting for the change in sound that would tell her she was close.

Moments like this, as she stood beside Charles in his kitchen, supervising his first attempt at making a cheese sauce.

'Add the milk gradually and just keep stirring.'

'It's all lumpy.'

'It'll be fine. Stir a bit faster. And have faith.'

'Hmm…okay…' Charles peered into the pot, frowning. 'How did your Skype session go?'

'Houston wasn't terribly co-operative. He didn't want to wake up. I showed them the photo from the park, though, and they said to say "hi" and wish you a happy Thanksgiving.'

'That's nice.' Charles added some more milk to his sauce. 'Where are they going to be celebrating? Still in Italy?'

'Yes. They're fallen head over heels in love with the Amalfi coast. They've bought a house there.'

'What? How's that going to work?'

'They've got this idea that they could spend six months in Europe and six months here every year and never have winters.'

'But what about Houston?'

'I guess he'll have to get used to travelling.' Grace pointed at the pot. 'Keep stirring or lumps will sneak in. You can add the grated cheese now, too.'

Charles was shaking his head. 'I don't think Houston would like summers in Italy. It'd be too hot for a big, fluffy dog.'

'Mmm…' Grace looked over her shoulder. Not that she could see into the living area from here but she could imagine that Houston hadn't moved from where the boys had commanded him to stay—a canine mountain that they were constructing a new train line around. From the happy tooting noises she could hear, it seemed like the line was up and running now.

'I'd adopt him,' Charles said. 'Max and Cameron think he's another brother.'

'I would, too.' Grace smiled. 'I love that dog. I don't think you ever feel truly lonely when you're sharing your life with a dog.'

The glance from Charles was quick enough to be sharp. A flash of surprise followed by something very warm, like sympathy. Concern…

She was stepping onto dangerous territory here, inadvertently admitting that she was often lonely.

'Right…let's drain that pasta, mix in the bacon and you can pour the sauce over the top. All we need is the breadcrumbs on top with a bit more cheese and it can go in the oven for half an hour.'

The distraction seemed to have been successful and

Grace relaxed again, helping herself to a glass of wine when Charles chased the boys into the bathroom to get clean. She had to abandon her drink before their dinner was ready to come out of the oven, though, in order to answer the summons to the bathroom where she found Charles kneeling beside a huge tub that contained two small boys, a flotilla of plastic toys and a ridiculous amount of bubbles.

'Look, Gace. A snowman!'

'Could be a snow woman,' Charles suggested. 'Or possibly a snow dog.'

He had taken off the ribbed, navy pullover he'd been wearing and his T-shirt had large, damp patches on the front. There were clumps of bubbles on his bare arms and another one on the top of his head and the grin on his face told her that, in this moment, Charles Davenport was possibly the happiest man on earth.

Tap, tap, tap...

Would she be brave enough to go through that door if she *did* find it?

What if she opened her heart to this little family and then found they didn't actually want her?

'Nobody's ever going to want you again... Not now...'

That ugly voice from the past should have lost its power long ago but there were still moments. Like this one, when she was smiling down at two, perfect, beautiful children and a man that she knew was even more gorgeous without those designer jeans and shirt.

Even as her smile began to wobble, though, she was saved by the bell of the oven timer.

'I'll take that out,' she excused herself. 'Dinner will be ready by the time you guys have got your jimjams on.'

The twins were just as cute in their pyjamas as they

had been in their monkey suits for Halloween but another glass of wine had made it easier for Grace. The pleasant fuzziness reminded her that it was possible to embrace the moment and enjoy this for simply what it was—spending time with a friend and being included in his family.

Because they were real friends now, with a shared history of good times in the past and an understanding of how hard it could be to move on from tougher aspects in life. Maybe that kiss had let them both know that anything other than friendship would be a mistake. It was weeks ago and there had been no hint of anything more than a growing trust.

Look at them…having a relaxed dinner in front of a fire, with an episode of *Curious George* on the television and a contented dog stretched out on the mat, and the might-have-beens weren't trying to break her heart. Grace was loving every minute of it.

Okay, it was a bit harder when she got the sleepy cuddles and kisses from the boys before Charles carried them off to bed but even then she wasn't in any hurry to escape. This time, she wasn't going to go home until she had cleaned up the kitchen. She wasn't even going to get off this couch until she had finished this particularly delicious glass of wine.

And then Charles came back and sat on the couch beside her and everything suddenly seemed even more delicious.

Tap, tap, tap…

For a heartbeat, Grace could actually hear the sound. Because the expression on Charles's face made her wonder if he was tapping at a wall of his own?

Maybe it was her own heartbeat she could hear as it picked up its pace.

He hadn't forgotten that comment about being lonely at all, had he?

'Have you got any plans for Thanksgiving tomorrow, Grace? You'd be welcome to join us, although a full-on Davenport occasion might be a bit...' He made a face that suggested he wasn't particularly looking forward to it himself. 'Sorry, I shouldn't make assumptions. You've probably got your own family to think about.'

Her own family. A separate family. That wall had just got a lot more solid.

Grace didn't protest when Charles refilled her glass.

'I had thought of going to visit my dad but I would have had to find someone to care for Houston and I didn't have enough of a gap in my roster. It's a long way to go just for a night or two. He might come to New York for Christmas, though.'

'And you lost your mum, didn't you? I remember you telling me how much you missed her.'

Good grief...he actually remembered what she'd said that night when she'd been crying on his shoulder as a result of her stress about her final exams?

'She died a couple of years before I went to med school. Ovarian cancer.'

'Oh...that must have been tough.'

'Yeah...it was. Dad's never got over it.' Grace fell silent. Had she just reminded Charles of his own loss. That he would never get over it?

The silence stretched long enough for Charles to finish his glass of wine and refill it.

'There's something else I should apologise for, too.'

'What?' Grace tried to lighten what felt like an oddly

serious vibe. Was he going to apologise for that kiss? Explain why it had been such a mistake? 'You're going to send me into the kitchen to do the dishes?'

He wasn't smiling.

'I treated you badly,' he said quietly. 'Back in med school. After…that night…'

Oh, help… This was breaking the first rule in the new book. The one that made that night a taboo subject.

'I don't know how much you knew of what hit the fan the next day regarding the Davenport scandal…'

'Not much,' Grace confessed. 'I heard about it, of course, but I was a bit preoccupied. With, you know… finals coming up.'

And dealing with the rejection…

He nodded. 'The pressure was intense, wasn't it? And I was trying to stop my family completely disintegrating. The intrusion of the media was unbelievable. They ripped my father to shreds, which only made us all more aware of how damaged our own relationship with him was. It tarnished all the good memories we had as a family. It nearly destroyed us.

'We'd always been in the limelight as one of the most important families in New York,' he continued quietly. 'A perfect family. And then it turns out that my father had been living a lie. That he'd had an affair. That there was a half-sister none of us knew about.'

He cleared his throat. 'I was the oldest and it was down to me to handle the media and focus on what mattered and the only way I could do that was to ignore how *I* felt. My only job was to protect the people that mattered most to me and, at that time, it had to be my family. It hit my mother hardest, as you can probably imagine, but they went to town on Miranda's mother, too. Describing her as worthless was one of the kinder labels. I didn't know her and I probably wouldn't have wanted to but I did know that my new half-sister was just a scared kid who had nobody to protect her. She was as vulnerable as you could get...'

Grace bit her lip. Charles couldn't help himself, could he? He had to protect the vulnerable. It had been the reason why they'd been together that night—he'd felt the need to protect *her*. To comfort her. To make her feel strong enough to cope with the world.

That ability to care for others more than himself was a huge part of what made him such an amazing person.

And, yes...she could understand why his attention had been so convincingly distracted.

Could forgive it, even?

'By the time things settled down, you were gone.'

Grace shrugged. Of course she had gone. There had been nothing to stay for. Would it have changed things if she'd known how difficult life was for Charles at that time?

Maybe.

Or maybe not. It was more likely that she would have been made much more aware of how different his world was and how unlikely it would have been that she could have been a part of it.

'I can't imagine what it must have been like. Life can be difficult enough without having your privacy invaded like that. I couldn't think of anything worse...' Grace shook her head. 'I get that a one-night stand would have fallen off your radar. You don't need to apologise.'

But it was nice that he had.

'It was a lot more than a one-night stand, Grace.' The words were quiet. Convincing. 'You need to know that.

And I asked about you, later—every time I came across someone from school at a conference or something. That was how I found out you'd got married.'

Grace was silent. He'd been asking about her? Looking for her, even? If she had known that, would she have taken her relationship with Mike as far as marrying him?

Possibly not. She had thought she'd found love but she'd always known the connection hadn't been as fierce as the one she'd found with Charles that night.

'It was just after that that I met Nina,' he continued. There was a hint of a smile tugging at his lips. 'Even then, I thought, well…if you could get married and live happily ever after, I'd better make sure I didn't get left behind.'

The silence was very poignant this time.

'I'm sorry,' Grace whispered. 'Everybody knows how much you loved her. I'm so sorry you didn't get your happily ever after.'

'I got some wonderful memories. And two amazing children. You reminded me just how lucky I am, on your first day at work.' Charles drew in a deep breath and let it out slowly. 'I hope you have things to feel lucky about, too.'

'Of course I do.'

'Like?'

Grace swallowed hard. She was leaning against that wall in her heart now, as if she needed support to stay upright.

But maybe she needed more than that. To hear someone agree that she was lucky?

'I'm alive,' she whispered.

She could feel his shock. Did he think she was making

a reference to Nina? Grace closed her eyes. She hadn't intended saying more but she couldn't leave it like that.

'I found a lump in my breast,' she said slowly, into the silence. 'I'd been married for about a year by then and Mike was keen to start a family. The lump turned out to be only a cyst but, because of my mother, they ran a lot of tests and one of them was for the genetic markers that let you know how much risk you have of getting ovarian or breast cancer. Mine was as high as it gets. And some people think that pregnancy can make that worse.'

'So you decided not to have kids?'

Grace shook her head, glancing up. 'No. I decided I'd have them as quickly as possible and then have a hysterectomy and mastectomy. Only…it didn't work out that way because they found another lump and that one wasn't a cyst. So… I decided to get the surgery and give up any dreams of having kids.'

She had to close her eyes again. 'Mike couldn't handle that. And he couldn't handle the treatment—especially the chemo and living with someone who was sick all the time. And later, my scars were just a reminder of what I'd taken away from him. A mother for his children. A woman he could look at without being…' her next word came out like a tiny sob '…disgusted…'

Maybe she had known how Charles would react.

Maybe she had wanted, more than anything, to feel his arms around her, like this.

To hear his voice, soft against her ear.

'You're gorgeous, Grace. There are no scars that could ever take that away.'

She could hear the steady thump of his heart and feel the solid comfort of the band of his arms around her.

'You're strong, too. I fought external things and I'm

not sure that I did such a great job but you...you fought a battle that you could never step away from, even for a moment. And you won.'

Grace's breath caught in a hitch. She *had* won. She would never forget any one of those steps towards hearing those magic words...

Cancer-free...

'Your courage blows me away,' Charles continued. 'You not only got through that battle with the kind of obstacles that your jerk of a husband added but you took yourself off to work in places that are as tough as they get. You didn't let it dent your sense of adventure or the amazing ability you have to care for others.' His arms tightened around her. 'You should be so proud of yourself. Don't ever let anything that he said or did take any of that away from you.'

Grace had to look up. To make sure that his eyes were telling her the same thing that his words were. To see if what she was feeling right now was something real. That she could be proud of everything she'd been through. That she could, finally, dismiss the legacy that Mike's rejection had engraved on her soul. That she was so much stronger now...

How amazing was this that Charles could make her feel as if she'd just taken the biggest step ever into a bright, new future?

That she'd found someone who made it possible to take the kind of risk that she'd never believed she would be strong enough to take again?

And maybe she had known what would happen when they fell into each other's eyes again like this.

As the distance between them slowly disappeared and their lips touched.

That door in the wall in her heart had been so well hidden she hadn't even realised she was leaning right against it until it fell open with their combined weight.

And the other side was a magic place where scars didn't matter.

Where they could be touched by someone else. Kissed, even, and it wasn't shameful. Or terrifying.

It was real. Raw. And heartbreakingly beautiful.

No. It wasn't 'someone else' who could have done this.

It could only have been Charles.

CHAPTER EIGHT

THE SOFT TRILL advertising an incoming text message on his phone woke Charles.

It could have been from anyone. One of his siblings, perhaps. Or a message from work to warn him that there was a situation requiring his input.

But he knew it was from Grace.

He just *knew*...

And, in that moment of knowing, there was a profound pleasure. Excitement, even. An instant pull back into the astonishing connection they had rediscovered last night that was still hovering at the edges of his consciousness as he reached sleepily for the phone on his bedside table.

Okay, he'd broken rule number one, not only by allowing female companionship to progress to this level but by allowing it to happen under his own roof and not keeping it totally separate from his home life—and his children.

And he'd broken an even bigger, albeit undefined, rule, by doing it with someone that he had a potentially important emotional connection to.

Had he been blindsided, because that connection had already been there and only waiting to be uncovered and that meant he hadn't been able to make a conscious choice to back off before it was even a possibility?

Maybe his undoing had been the way her story had touched his heart. That someone as clever and warm and beautiful as Grace could have been made to believe that she didn't deserve to be loved.

Whatever had pushed him past his boundaries, it had felt inevitable by the time he'd led Grace to his bed. And everything that had happened after that was a blurred mix of sensation and emotion that was overwhelming, even now.

Physically, it had been as astonishing as that first time. Exquisite. But there had been more to it this time. So much more. The gift of trust that she'd given him. The feeling that the dark place in his soul had been flooded with a light he'd never expected to experience again after Nina had died. Had never wanted to experience again because he knew what it was like when it got turned off?

It was early, with only the faintest suggestion of the approaching day between the gap of curtains that had been hastily pulled. Grace would be at work already, though. Her early shift had been the reason she hadn't stayed all night and Charles hadn't tried to persuade her. The twins might be far too young to read anything into finding Grace and Horse in their apartment first thing in the morning but what if they dropped an innocent bombshell in front of their grandparents, for instance, during the family's Thanksgiving dinner tonight?

He wasn't ready to share any of this.

It was too new—this feeling of an intimate connection, when you could get a burst of pleasure from even the prospect of communication via text.

He wasn't exactly sure how he felt about it himself yet, so he certainly didn't want the opinions of anyone else—like his parents or his siblings. This was very private.

There was only one other person on the planet who could share this.

Can't believe I left without doing the dishes again. I owe you one. xx

For a moment Charles let his head sink into his pillow again, a smile spreading over his face. He loved Grace's humour. And how powerful two little letters could be at the end of a message. Not one kiss, but two…

Powerful letters.

Even more powerful feelings.

They reminded him of the heady days of falling in love with Nina, when they couldn't bear to be apart. When they were the only two people in the world that mattered.

Was that what was happening here?

Was he falling in *love* with Grace?

His smile faded. The swirling potentially humorous responses to her text message vanished. He'd known that he would never fall in love again. He'd known that from the moment Nina's life had ebbed away that terrible day and he hadn't given it a second thought since. That part of his life had simply been dismissed as he'd coped with what had been important. His babies. And his work.

It had been a very long time before his body reminded him that there were other needs that could be deemed of importance. That was when rule number one had been considered and then put into place.

And he'd broken it.

Without giving any thought to any implications.

The jarring sound of his phone starting to ring cut through the heavy thoughts pressing down and suffocating the pleasure of any memories of last night. His heart skipped a beat with what felt like alarm as he glanced at the screen.

But it wasn't Grace calling. It was his mother.

At this time of the day?

'Mom…what's up? Is everything all right?'

'Maybe you can tell me, Charles. Who is she?'

'Sorry?'

'I'm reading the *New York Post*. Page six…'

Of course she was. Anyone who was anyone in New York turned to page six first, either to read about someone they knew or about themselves. It was a prime example of the gossip columns that Charles hated above everything else. The kind that had almost destroyed his family once as people fed on every juicy detail that the Davenport scandal had offered. The kind that had made getting through the tragedy of losing his wife just that much harder as the details of their fairy-tale romance and wedding were pored over again. The kind that had made him keep his own life as private as possible ever since in his determination to protect his sons.

'Why now?' Vanessa continued. 'Really, Charles. We could do without another airing of the family's dirty laundry. Especially today, with it being Thanksgiving.'

He was out of bed now, clad only in his pyjama pants as he headed into the living area. His laptop was on the dining table, already open. It took only a couple of clicks to find what his mother was referring to.

The photograph was a shock. How on earth had a

journalist got hold of it when it had been taken only yesterday—on Grace's phone?

But there it was. The boys on their bikes on either side of Houston. Himself with his arm slung over Grace's shoulders. And they were all grinning like the archetypal happy family.

His brain was working overtime. Had that friendly stranger actually been a journalist? Or had Grace shared the photograph on social media? No... But she had shared it with Stefan and Jerome and they had many friends who were the kind of celebrities that often graced page six. Easy pickings for anyone who contributed to this gossip column, thanks to a thoughtless moment on his behalf.

'She's a friend, Mom. Someone I went to med school with, who happens to be living downstairs at the moment. Dog-sitting.'

'That's not what's getting assumed.'

'Of course it isn't. Why do you even read this stuff?' He scanned the headline.

Who is the mystery woman in Charles Davenport's life?

'And why are they raking over old news? It's too much. Really, Charles. Can't you be more careful?'

Speed-reading was a skill he had mastered a long time ago.

It's been a while since we caught up with the New York Davenports. Who could forget the scandal of the love child that almost blew this famous family apart? Where is she now, you might be asking? Where are any of them, in fact?

Moving on with their lives, apparently. Dr Charles Davenport is retired, with his notoriously private firstborn son taking over as chief of the ER at Manhattan Mercy in the manner of the best dynasties. He's become something of a recluse since the tragic death of his wife but it looks as though he's finally moving on. And isn't it a treat to get a peek at his adorable twin sons?

We see his own twin brother Elijah more than any of the family members, with his penchant for attending every important party, and with a different woman on his arm every time. Their sister Penelope is a celebrated daredevil and the youngest brother, Zachary, is reportedly returning to the family fold very soon, in more ways than one. He has resigned from the Navy and will be adding his medical skills to the Davenport team at Manhattan Mercy. Watch this space for more news later.

And the love child, Miranda? Well...she's so much a part of the family now she's also a doctor and it's no surprise that she's working in exactly the same place.

Are the New York Davenports an example of what doesn't kill you makes you stronger? Or is it just window dressing...?

Charles stopped reading as the article went on to focus on Vanessa Davenport's recent philanthropic endeavours. His mother was still talking—about a fundraising luncheon she was supposed to be attending in a matter of hours.

'How can I go? There'll be reporters everywhere and intrusive questions. But, if I don't go, it'll just fuel speculation. *Everybody* will be talking about it.'

'Just ignore it,' Charles advised. 'Keep your head high, smile and say "No comment". It'll die down. It always does.'

He could hear the weary sigh on the other end of the line.

'I'm so sick of it. We've all been through enough. Haven't we?'

'Mmm.' Charles rubbed his forehead with his fingers. 'I have to go, Mom. The boys are waking up and we need to get ready. It's the Macy's Thanksgiving parade today and we'll have to get there early to find a good place to watch. I'll see you tonight.'

It should have been such a happy day.

Some of Charles's earliest memories were of the sheer wonder of this famous parade. Of being in a privileged viewing position with his siblings, bundled up against the cold, jumping up and down with the amazement of every new sight and adding his own contribution to the cacophony of sound—the music and cheers and squeals of excitement—that built and built until the finale they were all waiting for when Santa Claus in his sleigh being pulled by reindeer with spectacular gilded antlers would let them know that the excitement wasn't over. Christmas was coming...

This was the first year that Cameron and Max were old enough to appreciate the spectacle and not be frightened by the crowds and noise. They were well bundled up in their coats and mittens and hats and their little faces were shining with excitement. They found a spot on Central Park West, not far from one of their favourite playgrounds, and Charles held a twin on each hip, giving them a clear view over the older children in front of them.

The towering balloons sailed past. Superman and Spiderman and Muppets and Disney characters. There was a brass band with its members dressed like tin soldiers and people on stilts that looked like enormous candy canes with their striped costumes and the handles on their tall hats. There were clowns and jugglers and dancers and they kept coming. Charles's arms began to ache with the weight of the twins and their joyous wriggling.

He wasn't going to put them down. This was his job. Supporting his boys. Protecting them. And he could cope. The three of them would always cope. The happiness that today should have provided was clouded for Charles, though. He could feel an echo that reminded him of his mother's heavy sigh earlier this morning.

That it was starting again. The media interest that could become like a searchlight, illuminating so many things that were best left in the shade now. Things that were nobody else's business. Putting them out there for others to speculate on only made things so much harder to deal with.

He could still feel the pain of photographs that had been put on public display in the aftermath of the family scandal breaking. Of the snippets of gossip, whether true or not, that had been raked over. The fresh wave of interest in the days after Nina's death had been even worse as he'd struggled to deal with his own grief. Seeing that photograph that had been taken at their engagement party, with Nina looking so stunning in her white designer gown, proudly showing off the famed Davenport, pink diamond ring, had been like a kick in the guts.

What if that photograph surfaced again now, with gossip mills cranking up at the notion that he'd found a new partner? Grace was nothing like Nina, who'd been part of the kind of society he'd grown up in. Nina had been well used to being in the public eye. Grace was someone who kept herself in the background, working as part of a team in her job where the centre stage was always taken by the person needing her help.

Or making two small boys happy by baking cookies and trashing his kitchen...

She would be appalled at any media interest. She'd as much as told him how she wouldn't be able to cope.

'I can't imagine what it must have been like. Life can be difficult enough without having your privacy invaded like that. I couldn't think of anything worse...'

The cloud settled even more heavily over Charles as the real implications hit him.

He knew her story now. That she had been broken by the reaction of the man who had been her husband to the battle she'd had to fight. That she'd actually hidden herself from the world to come to terms with being made to feel less than loveable. Ugly, even...

He hadn't even noticed her scars last night. Not as anything that detracted from her beauty, anyway. If anything, they added to it because they were a mark of her astonishing courage and strength.

But he knew exactly how vulnerable she could still be, despite that strength.

As vulnerable as his younger siblings had been when the 'love child' scandal had broken. He'd learned how to shut things down then, in order to protect them.

Maybe he needed to call on those skills again now.

To protect Grace. He could imagine the devastating effect if the spotlight was turned on her. If someone thought to find images of what mastectomy scars looked like, perhaps, and coupled it with headline bait like *Is this why her husband left her?*

He couldn't let that happen.

He *wouldn't* let that happen.

He had to protect his boys, too.

They weren't just old enough to appreciate this parade now. They knew—and loved—the new person who had come into their lives. Someone who was as happy as he was to stand in the cold and watch them run and climb in a playground. Who baked cookies with them and fell asleep on the couch with them cuddled beside her.

He wouldn't be the only one to be left with a dark place if she vanished from their lives.

What about that different perspective he'd found the day after the twins' birthday, when he'd known that he wouldn't want his boys growing up without a dad, if the tragedy had been reversed? That he wouldn't have wanted Nina to have a restricted, celibate life?

It was all spiralling out of control. His feelings for Grace. How close they had suddenly become. The threat of having his private life picked over by emotional vultures, thanks to media interest and having important things damaged beyond repair.

Yes. He needed to remember lessons learned. That control could be regained eventually if things could be ignored. He had done this before but this time he could do it better. He was responsible and he was old enough and wise enough this time around not to make the same mistakes.

He had to choose each step with great care. And the first step was to narrow his focus to what was most important.

And he was holding that in his arms.

'Show's almost over, guys. Want to go to the playground on the way home?'

'There's something different about you today.' Helena looked up as she finished scribbling a note in a patient file on the main desk in the ER. 'You look…happy.'

Grace's huff was indignant. 'Are you trying to tell me I usually look miserable?'

'No…' Helena was smiling but she still had a puzzled frown. 'You never look *miserable*. You just don't usually look…I don't know…*this* happy. Not at this time of the morning, anyway.'

Grace shrugged but found herself averting her gaze in case her friend might actually see more than she was ready to share.

She'd already seen too much.

This happiness was seeping out of every cell in her body and it was no surprise it was visible to someone who knew her well. It felt like she was glowing. As if she could still feel the touch of Charles's hands—and lips—on her body.

On more than her body, in fact. It felt like her soul was glowing this morning.

Reborn.

Oh, help… She wasn't going to be as focused on her work today as she needed to be if she let herself get pulled back into memories of last night. That was a pleasure that needed to wait until later. With a huge effort, Grace closed the mental door on that compelling space.

'I have a clown in Curtain Three,' she told Helena.

Helena shook her head with a grimace. 'We get a lot of clowns in here. They're usually drunk.'

'No…this is a real clown. He was trying to do a cartwheel and I've just finished relocating his shoulder that couldn't cope. I want to check his X-ray before I discharge him. He has a clown friend with him, too. Didn't you see them come in? Spotty suits, squeaky horns, bright red wigs—the whole works.'

But Helena didn't seem to be listening. She was staring at an ambulance gurney that was being wheeled past the desk. The person lying on the gurney seemed to be a life-sized tin soldier.

'Oh…of course…' she sighed. 'It's the Macy's Thanksgiving parade today, isn't it?'

'Chest pain,' one of the paramedics announced. 'Query ST elevation in the inferior leads.'

'Straight into Resus, thanks.' Grace shared a glance with Helena. This tin soldier was probably having a heart attack. 'I can take this.'

Helena nodded. 'I'll follow up on your clown, if you like.' She glanced over her shoulder as if she was expecting more gurneys to be rolling up. 'We're in for a crazy day,' she murmured. 'It always is, with the parade.'

Crazy was probably good, Grace decided as she followed her tin soldier into Resus.

'Let's get him onto the bed. On my count. One, two… *three*.' She smiled at the middle-aged man. 'My name's Grace and I'm one of the doctors here at Manhattan Mercy. Don't worry, we're going to take good care of you. What's your name?'

'Tom.'

'How old are you, Tom?'

'Fifty-three.'

'Do you have any medical history of heart problems? Hypertension? Diabetes?'

Tom was shaking his head to every query.

'Have you ever had chest pain like this before?'

Another shake. 'I get a bit out of puff sometimes. But playing the trumpet is hard, you know?'

'And you got out of breath this morning?'

'Yeah. And then I felt sick and got real sweaty. And the pain...'

'He's had six milligrams of morphine.' A paramedic was busy helping the nursing staff to change the leads that clipped to the electrodes dotting Tom's chest so that he was attached to the hospital's monitor. His oxygen tubing came off the portable cylinder to be linked to the overhead supply and a different blood pressure cuff was being wrapped around his arm.

'How's the pain now, Tom?' Grace asked. 'On a scale of zero to ten, with ten being the worst?'

'About six, I guess.'

'It was ten when we got to him.'

'Let's give you a bit more pain relief, then,' Grace said. 'And I want some bloods off for cardiac enzymes, please. I want a twelve-lead ECG, stat. And can someone call the cath lab and check availability?'

Yes. Crazy was definitely good. From the moment Tom had arrived in her care to nearly an hour later, when she accompanied him to the cardiac catheter laboratory so that he could receive angioplasty to open his blocked artery, she didn't have a spare second where her thoughts could travel to where they wanted to go so much.

Heading back to the ER was a different matter.

Her route that took her back to bypass the main waiting area was familiar now. The medical staff all used it because if you went through the waiting area at busy times, you ran the risk of being confronted by angry people who didn't like the fact that they had to wait while more urgent cases were prioritised. If Helena was right, this was going to be a very busy day. Which made sense, because they were the closest hospital to where the parade was happening and the participants and spectators would number in the tens of thousands.

Had Charles taken the boys to see the parade?

Was that why he hadn't had the time to answer her text message yet?

Grace's hand touched the phone that was clipped to the waistband of her scrub trousers but she resisted the urge to bring the screen to life and check that she hadn't missed a message.

She wasn't some love-crazed teenager who was holding her breath to hear from a boy.

She'd never been that girl. Had never dated a boy that had had that much of an impact on her. She'd been confident in her life choices and her focus on her study and the career she wanted more than anything.

But she'd turned into that girl, hadn't she? After that first night with Charles Davenport. The waiting for that message or call. The excitement that had morphed into anxiety and then crushing disappointment and heartbreak.

And humiliation…

Grace dropped her hand. They were a long way from being teenagers now. Charles was a busy man. Quite apart from his job, he was a hands-on father with two small boys. History was not about to repeat itself. Charles understood how badly he had treated her by ignoring her last time. He had apologised for it, even. There was no way he would do that again.

And she was stronger. He'd told her that. He'd made her believe it was true.

Walking past the cast room, Grace could see an elderly woman having a broken wrist plastered. There were people in the minor surgery area, too, with another elderly patient who looked like he was having a skin flap replaced. And then she was walking past the small rooms, their doors open and the interiors empty, but that couldn't stop a memory of the first time she had walked past one of them. When she'd seen those two small faces peering out and she had met Cameron and Max.

It couldn't stop the tight squeeze on her heart as she remembered falling in love with Max when he'd smiled at her and thanked her for fixing his truck and then cuddled up against her. He was more cuddly than his brother but she loved Cameron just as much now.

And their father?

Oh… Grace paused for a moment to grab a cup of water from the cooler before she pushed through the double doors into the coal face of the ER.

It hadn't been love at first sight with Charles.

But it had been love at first *night*.

That was why she'd been so nervous about working with him again. He'd surprised her by calling her that night about the dog-sitting possibility by revealing that he'd been thinking about her.

And he'd made her laugh. Made her drop her guard a little?

She'd realised soon after that that the connection was still there. The way he'd looked at her that day at the park—as if he really wanted to hear her story.

As if he really cared.

Oh, and that *kiss*. In that wreck of a kitchen still redolent with the smells of grilled cheese and freshly baked cookies. Even now, Grace could remember the fear that had stepped in when he'd been about to touch her breast. As though the lumpy scars beneath her clothing had suddenly been flashing like neon signs.

Crumpling the empty polystyrene cup, she dropped it into the bin beside the cooler, catching her bottom lip between her teeth as if she wanted to hide a smile.

They hadn't mattered last night, those scars. She'd barely been aware of them herself...

She was back in the department now and she could see a new patient being wheeled into Resus.

So many patients came and went from that intensive diagnostic and treatment area but some were so much more memorable than others.

Like the first patient she had ever dealt with here. That badly injured cyclist who'd been a casualty of the power cut when the traffic lights had gone out. And the frozen baby that she and Charles had miraculously brought back to life. Yep... Grace would never forget that one.

That time with just the two of them when it had seemed as if time had been somehow rewound and that there was nothing standing between herself and Charles. No social differences that had put them on separate planets all those years ago. No past history of partners who had been loved and lost. No barriers apart from the defensive walls they had both constructed and maybe that had been the moment when Grace had believed there might be a way through those barriers.

She'd been right. And Helena had been right in noticing that there was something different about her today.

The only thing that could have made her even happier would be to feel the vibration against her waistband that would advertise an incoming text message.

But it didn't happen. Case after case took her attention during the next few hours. An asthmatic child who had forgotten his inhaler in the excitement of heading to watch the parade and suffered an attack that meant an urgent trip to the nearest ER. A man who'd had his foot stepped on by a horse. A woman who'd been caught up in the crowd when the first pains of her miscarriage had struck.

Case after case and the time flew by and Grace focused on each and every case as if it was the only thing that mattered. To stop herself checking her phone? It was well past lunchtime when she finally took a break in a deserted staffroom and sat down with a cup of coffee and could no longer ignore the weight and shape of her phone. No way to avoid glancing at it. At a blank screen that had no new messages or missed calls flagged.

Anxiety crept in as she stared at that blank screen. Was Charles sick or injured or had something happened to one of the twins? She could forgive this silence if that was the case but it would have to be something major like that because to treat her like this again when he knew how it would make her feel was…well, it was unforgiveable. All he'd had to do was send a simple message. A stupid smiley face would have been enough. Surely he would understand that every minute of continuing silence would feel like hours? That hours would actually start to feel like days?

But if something major like that had happened, she

would have heard about it. Like she'd heard about Miranda being caught up in that tunnel collapse. A thread of anger took over from anxiety. How could she have allowed herself to get into a position where everything she had worked so hard for was under threat? She had come to New York to start a new life. To move on from so much loss. The loss of her marriage. The loss of the family she'd dreamed of having. The loss of feeling desirable, even.

Charles had given her a glimpse of a future that could have filled all those empty places in her soul.

This silence felt like a warning shot that it was no more than an illusion.

That the extraordinary happiness she had brought to work with her was no more than a puff of breath on an icy morning. The kind she had been making as she'd walked to Manhattan Mercy this morning in a haze of happiness after last night.

Last night?

It was beginning to feel like a lifetime ago. A lifetime in which this scenario had already played out to a miserable ending.

Anxiety and anger both gave way to doubt.

Had she really thought that history couldn't repeat itself? This was certainly beginning to feel like a re-run.

Maybe it had only been in her imagination that her scars didn't matter.

Maybe having a woman in his bed had opened old wounds for Charles and he was realising how much he missed Nina and that no one could ever take her place.

Maybe it had been too much, too soon and everything had been ruined.

For a moment, Grace considered sending another

message. Just something casual, like asking whether they'd been to the parade this morning or saying that she hoped they were all having a good day.

But this new doubt was strong enough to make her hesitate and, in that moment of hesitation, she knew she couldn't do it.

Her confidence was starting to ebb away just as quickly as that happiness.

CHAPTER NINE

ANOTHER HOUR WENT past and then another…and still nothing.

Nothing…

No call. No text. No serendipitous meeting as their paths crossed in the ER, which was such a normal thing to happen that its absence was starting to feel deliberate.

Grace knew Charles had finally come to work this afternoon because the door to his office was open and she'd seen his leather laptop bag on his desk when she'd gone past a while back. She'd heard someone say he was in a meeting, which wasn't unusual for the chief of emergency services, but surely there weren't administrative issues that would take hours and hours to discuss? Maybe it hadn't actually been that long but it was certainly beginning to feel like it.

She thought she saw him heading for the unit desk when she slipped through a curtain, intending to chase up the first test results on one of her patients.

Her heart skipped a beat and started racing.

She'd know, wouldn't she? In that first instant of eye contact, she'd know exactly what was going on. She'd know whether it had been a huge mistake to get this close to Charles Davenport again. To be so completely in love and have so many shiny hopes for a new future that were floating around her like fragile, newly blown bubbles.

She'd know whether she was going to find herself right back at Square One in rebuilding her life.

Almost in the same instant, however, and even though she couldn't see his face properly, she knew it wasn't Charles, it was his twin, Elijah. And she knew this because the air she was sucking into her lungs felt completely normal. There was none of that indefinable extra energy that permeated the atmosphere when she was in the same space as Charles. The energy that made those bubbles shine with iridescent colours and change their shape as if they were dancing in response to the sizzle of hope.

'Dr Forbes?'

The tone in her migraine patient's voice made her swing back, letting the curtain fall into place behind her.

'I'm going to be sick…'

Grace grabbed a vomit container but she was too late. A nurse responded swiftly to her call for assistance and her gaze was sympathetic.

'I'll clean up in here,' she said. 'You'd better go and find some clean scrubs.' Pulling on gloves, she added a murmur that their patient couldn't overhear. 'It's been one of *those* days, hasn't it?'

Helena was in the linen supply room.

'Oh, no…' She wrinkled her nose. 'You poor thing…'

'Do we have any plastic bags in here? For super-soiled laundry?'

'Over there. Want me to guard the door for a minute so you can strip that lot off?'

'Please. I'm starting to feel a bit queasy myself.'

'Do you need a shower?'

'No. It's just on my scrubs.' Grace unhooked her stethoscope and then unclipped her phone and pager from her waistband. She put them onto a stainless-steel trolley and then peeled off her tunic. 'What are you doing in here, anyway?'

'We were low on blankets in the warmer and everyone was busy. I'm due for a break.' Helena was leaning against the closed door, blocking the small window. 'Past due to go home, in fact. We both are.' Her smile was rueful. 'How come we were among the ones to offer to stay on?'

'We were short-staffed and overloaded. It was lucky Sarah Grayson could stay on as well.'

'I know. Well, I've hardly seen you since this morning. You okay?' She wrinkled her nose. 'Sorry—silly question. Crazy day, huh?'

'Mmm.' Grace was folding the tunic carefully so she could put it into the bag without touching the worst stains. 'I certainly wouldn't want another one like this in a hurry.'

Not that staying on past her rostered hours had bothered her, mind you. Or the patient load. She loved a professional challenge. It was the personal challenge she was in the middle of that was a lot less welcome.

'What are you doing after work? There's a group going out for Thanksgiving dinner at a local restaurant that sounds like it might be fun. I know you'd be more than welcome.'

But, again, Grace shook her head. 'I can't abandon my dog after being at work so much longer than expected. And I need to Skype my dad. I haven't spoken to him for a while and it's Thanksgiving. Family time.'

'Ah…' Helena's gaze was mischievous. 'And there

was me thinking you might be going to some glitzy Davenport occasion.'

Pulling on her clean scrub trousers, Grace let the elastic waist band go with more force than necessary. 'What?'

'You and Charles…?' Helena was smiling now. 'Is *that* why you were looking so happy first thing this morning? Everybody's wondering…'

A heavy knot formed in Grace's gut. People were gossiping about her? And Charles? Had he said something to someone else when he hadn't bothered talking to her? Or had someone seen something or said something to remind Charles that he would never be able to replace his beloved wife? Maybe *that* was why he was ignoring her.

'I have no idea what you're talking about,' she said. 'We're just friends.'

'That's what he said, too.'

'What?' Grace fought the shock wave that made it difficult to move. *'When?'*

'There was someone here earlier this afternoon. A journalist pretending to be a patient and she was asking for you. You'd taken a patient off for an MRI, I think. Or maybe you were finally having a late lunch. Anyway… Charles told her she was wasting her time. That you were nothing more than a colleague and friend. And never would be.'

Was it simply the waft of soiled laundry that was making Grace feel a little faint? She secured the top of the plastic bag and shoved it into the contaminated linen sack.

So she didn't need to make eye contact with Charles

to know that the truth was every bit as gut wrenching as she had suspected it would be.

'I don't understand,' she murmured. 'Why was he even saying anything?'

'It's because of the gossip column. That photo. Any Davenport news is going to be jumped on around here. They're like New York royalty.'

'What gossip column? What *photo*?'

'You don't know?' Helena's eyes widened. 'Look. I can show you on my phone. I have to admit, you do look like a really happy little family…'

Focus, Charles reminded himself. Shut out anything irrelevant that's only going to make everything worse.

He had responsibilities that took priority over any personal discomfort.

His boys came first. He'd been a little later for work this afternoon, after getting home from the parade, because he'd needed to brief Maria about the renewed media interest in his life and warn her not to say anything about his private life if she was approached by a journalist. He was going to keep the boys away from nursery school for a day or two, as well, for the same reason.

He'd assumed that he'd see Grace at work and be able to have a quiet word and warn her that she might be faced with some unwelcome attention but she hadn't been in the department when he'd arrived. Instead, he'd been confronted with the reality that interest in the Davenport family's private lives was never going to vanish. How had someone found out that Grace worked here? Had it helped to deal so brusquely with that journalist who had been masquerading as a patient or had he protested too much?

At least Grace hadn't been there to hear him dismissing her as someone who would never be anything more significant than a friend but the echo of his own words was haunting him now.

It wasn't true. He might have no idea how to handle these unexpected emotions that were undermining everything in his personal life that he'd believed would never change but the thing he could be certain of was that his own feelings were irrelevant right now.

He was in a meeting, for heaven's sake, where his push for additional resources in his department was dependent on being able to defend the statistics of patient outcomes and being able to explain anomalies in terms of scientific reasoning that was balanced by morality and the mission statements of Manhattan Mercy's emergency room.

He had to focus.

One meeting merged into the next until it was late in the day and he was still caught up in a boardroom. The detailed report of how his department and others had coped in the power cut last month was up for discussion with the purpose of making sure that they would be better prepared if it should ever happen again.

It was hard to focus in this meeting as well. The day of the power cut had been the day that Grace Forbes had walked back into his life in more than a professional sense. It seemed like fate had been determined to bring her close as quickly as possible. How else could he explain the series of events that had led her to meet his sons and remind him of how lucky he actually was? That had been when his barriers had been weakened, he realised.

When that curiosity about Grace had put her into a different space than any other woman could have reached.

The kind of determination to focus that was needed here was reminiscent of one of the most difficult times of his life—when he'd had to try and pass his final exams in medicine while the fallout of the Davenport scandal had been exploding around him. How hard that had been had been eclipsed by the tragedy of Nina's death, of course, but he'd somehow coped then as well.

And he could cope now.

'We can't base future plans on the normal throughput of the department,' he reminded the people gathered in this boardroom. 'What we have to factor in is that this kind of widespread disruption causes a huge spike in admissions due to the accidents directly caused by it. Fortunately, it's a rare event so we can't resource the department to be ready at all times. What we can do is have a management plan in place that will put us in the best position to deal with whatever disaster we find on our doorstep. And haven't there been predictions already for severe snow storms in December? If it's correct, that could also impact our power supply and patient numbers.'

By the time his meeting finished, a new shift was staffing the department and Grace was nowhere to be seen.

He could knock on her door when he got home, Charles decided, but a glance at his watch told him that he'd have to be quick. He was due to take the boys to their grandparents' house for Thanksgiving dinner tonight and he was already running late.

Was she even at home? He'd heard about the staff dinner at a restaurant being planned and, when there was no response to his knock other than a warning bark from Houston, he hoped that was exactly where she was.

Out having fun.

More fun than he was likely to have tonight, with his mother still stressed about renewed media interest in the family and the necessity of trying to keep two three-year-old boys behaving themselves at a very formal dining table.

Maria had got the boys dressed and said she didn't mind waiting while he got changed himself. A quick shower was needed and then Charles found his dinner jacket and bow tie. The formality was a family tradition, like getting the annual Davenport photograph that would be made available to the media to remind them that this family was still together. Still strong enough to survive anything.

Charles rummaged in the top drawer of his dresser, to find the box that contained his silver cufflinks. He didn't know how many of the family members would be there tonight but hopefully the table would be full. Elijah would definitely be there. And Zac, who was about to start his new job at Manhattan Mercy.

His fingers closed around a velvet box and he opened it, only to have his breath catch in his throat.

This wasn't the box that contained his cufflinks. It was the box that contained the Davenport ring. The astonishing pink diamond that Nina had accepted when she had accepted his proposal of marriage. A symbol of the continuation of the Davenport name. A symbol of their position in New York society, even, given the value and rarity of this famous stone.

As the oldest son, it had been given to Charles for his

wife-to-be and there was only one person in the world who could have worn it.

Nina.

Shadows of old grief enclosed Charles as he stared at the ring. He could never give it to anyone else.

It wouldn't even suit Grace…

Oh, help…where had *that* come from?

Memories of how he'd felt waking up this morning came back to him in a rush. That excitement. The pleasure.

The…longing…

And right now, those feelings were at war with remnants of grief. With the weight of all the responsibilities he had been trying so hard to focus on.

The battle was leaving him even more confused.

Drained, even.

He left the ring in its opened box on top of the dresser as he found and inserted his cufflinks and then slipped on his silk-lined jacket.

He closed the box on the ring then, and was about to put it back where he'd found it but his hand stopped in mid-air.

He had no right to keep this ring shut away in a drawer when he had no intention of ever using it again himself. It could be hidden for decades if he waited to hand it on to his firstborn, Cameron.

He should give it to the next Davenport in line. Elijah.

Charles let his breath out in a sigh. He knew perfectly well how his twin felt about marriage. With his bitterness about the marriage of their parents and scepticism about its value in general, he wouldn't want anything to do with the Davenport ring.

He couldn't give it to Penelope, because it was traditional for it to go to a son who would be carrying on the family name. Miranda was out of the question, even if she hadn't been another female, because of the distress that could cause to his mother, given her reluctance to absorb his half-sister into the family.

Zac. Was that his answer? The youngest Davenport male in his own generation. Okay, Zac had always had a tendency to rebel against Davenport traditions but he was making an effort now, wasn't he? Coming back into the fold. Trying to rebuild bridges? Was it possible that could even extend to taking an interest in Dr Ella Lockwood, the daughter of family friends and the woman who everyone had once expected Zac to marry? Though he'd noticed Ella hadn't seemed too pleased to learn that Zac was joining the team, so maybe not. But whatever happened, he hoped his youngest brother would find the happiness he deserved.

Yes. Charles slipped the ring box into his pocket. Even if Zac wasn't ready to accept it yet, he would know that it would be waiting for him.

He'd have a word with Elijah, first, of course. And then Zac. Maybe with his parents as well. If he could handle it all diplomatically, it could actually be a focus for this evening that would bring them all a little closer together and distract them from directing any attention on his own life. It would also be a symbol that he was moving on from his past, too. For himself as much as his family.

Yes. This felt like the next step in dealing with this unexpected intrusion into their lives. And maybe it would help settle the confusing boundaries between his responsibilities and his desires. Between the determination to protect everyone he had cared about in his life so far and the longing to just be somewhere alone with the new person in his life that he also wanted to protect?

Grace heard the knock on her door.

But what could she do? Her father had just answered her Skype call and he was so delighted to see her.

If there'd been a second knock, she might have excused herself for a moment but, after a single bark, Houston came and settled himself with his head on her feet. There was obviously no one on the other side of the door now. Maybe it had been someone else who lived in this apartment block. After all, Charles had had an entire day in which he could have called or texted her. Or he could have found her at work this afternoon because she'd certainly hung around long enough.

And he hadn't.

History was clearly repeating itself.

She had offered him everything she had to give and he had accepted it and then simply walked away without a backward glance.

'Sorry—what was that, Dad?'

'Just saying we hit the national high again today. Blue skies and sunshine here in Florida. How's it looking in the big smoke?'

'Grey. And freezing. They're predicting snow tomorrow. It could be heavy.'

Her father laughed. 'We have hospitals in this neck of the woods, you know. You don't have to suffer!'

'Maybe I'll see what's being advertised.'

The comment was light-hearted but, as they chatted about other things, the thought stayed in the back of her mind.

She could walk away from New York, couldn't she? She didn't *have* to stay here and feel...rejected...

Grace had to swallow a sudden lump in her throat. 'I feel a long way away at the moment. I miss you, Dad.'

'Miss you, too, honey.' Her father's smile wobbled a bit. 'So tell me, what are you doing for Thanksgiving dinner? Have you got yourself some turkey?'

'No. Work's been really busy and, anyway, it seemed a bit silly buying a turkey for one person.'

'I'll bet that dog you're living with could have helped you out there.'

Grace laughed but her brain was racing down another track. It couldn't have been Charles knocking at her door because wasn't he going to some big Davenport family dinner tonight? A dinner that he had suggested she could also go to but then he'd made a face as if the idea was distasteful.

Why? Did he not enjoy the family gathering himself or was it more the idea that she would hate it because she wouldn't fit in?

Of course she wouldn't. As Helena had reminded her so recently, the Davenports were New York royalty and she wasn't even American by birth. She was a foreigner. A divorced foreigner. A divorced foreigner with a scarred body who wasn't even capable of becoming a mother.

Oh, help... Going down this track any further when she had a night alone stretching out in front of her was a very bad idea.

'Have you got some wine to go with your turkey, Dad?'

'Of course. A very nice Australian chardonnay.'

'Well... I've got something in the fridge. Prosecco, I

think. Why don't we both have a glass together and we can tap the screen and say cheers.' It was hard to summon up a cheerful smile but Grace gave it her best shot.

She could deal with this.

She had, in fact, just had a very good idea of exactly how she could deal with it. When she had finished this call with her dad, and had had a glass or two of wine, she was going to do something very proactive.

It was ironic that it had been Charles who'd pointed out how far she had come from being someone vulnerable enough to be easily crushed. How strong she was now.

Ironic because she was going to write her resignation letter from Manhattan Mercy. And, tomorrow, as soon as she started her shift, it would be Charles Davenport's desk that she would put that letter on.

CHAPTER TEN

'THANKS EVER SO much for coming home, Dr Davenport.'

'It's no problem, Maria. You need to get to this appointment for the final check on that back of yours. I hope you won't need the brace any more after this.'

'I shouldn't be more than a couple of hours. I'll text you if there's any hold-up.'

'Don't worry about it. I've got more than enough work that I can do from home.'

His nanny nodded, wrapping a thick scarf around her neck. 'The boys are happy. They're busy drawing pictures at the moment.'

A glance into the living area showed a coffee table covered with sheets of paper and scattered crayons. Two tousled heads were bent as the twins focused on their masterpieces. Charles stayed where he was for a moment, pulling his phone from his pocket and hitting a rapid-dial key.

'Emergency Room.'

Charles recognised the voice of one of the staff members who managed the phone system and incoming radio calls.

'Hi, Sharon. Charles Davenport here. I'm working from home for a few hours.'

'Yes, we're aware of that, Dr Davenport. Did you want to speak to the other Dr Davenport?'

'No. I actually wanted to speak to Dr Forbes. Is she available at the moment?'

'Hang on, I'll check.'

Charles could hear the busy sounds of the department through the line but it sounded a little calmer than it had been earlier today. When he'd gone to his office to collect his briefcase after the latest meeting, there'd been security personnel and police officers there but Elijah had assured him that everything was under control and he was free to take the time he needed away.

Right now, the voices close by were probably doctors checking lab results or X-rays on the computers. Would one of them be Grace, by any chance?

He hadn't seen her when he'd been in at work earlier and this was getting ridiculous. It was well into the second day after their night together and they hadn't even spoken. His intention to protect everyone he cared about by ignoring the potential for public scrutiny on his private life had been so strong, it was only now that it was beginning to feel like something was very wrong.

No. Make that more than 'feel'. He knew that he was in trouble.

He'd met the Australian dog walker, Kylie, in the foyer on his way in, minutes ago. The one that looked after Houston when Grace was at work.

She'd introduced herself. Because, she explained, she might be in residence for a while—if Grace left before Houston's owners were due to return.

But Stefan and Jerome had been planning to come back in less than a couple of weeks as far as Charles was aware.

Why would Grace be thinking of leaving before then?

It had only been just over a day since he'd seen her. How could something that huge have changed so much in such a short space of time?

He needed to speak to her. To apologise for not having spoken to her yesterday. At the very least, he had to arrange a time when they could talk. To find out what was going on.

To repair any damage he had the horrible feeling he might be responsible for? He'd tried so hard to do things perfectly this time—to think through each step logically so that he could avoid making a mistake.

But he'd missed something. Something that was seeming increasingly important.

Sharon was back on the line.

'Sorry, Dr Davenport. Dr Forbes is in CT at the moment. We had a head injury patient earlier who was extremely combative. We had to call Security in to help restrain him while he got sedated and intubated.'

'Yes, I saw them there when I was leaving.'

'He was Dr Forbes's patient. She's gone with him to CT and may have to stay with him if he needs to go to Theatre so I have no idea how long she'll be. Do you want me to page her to call you back when she can?'

'Daddy... *Daddy*...' Cameron was tugging on his arm, a sheet of paper in his other hand. 'Look at *this*.'

'No, thanks, Sharon. She's busy enough, by the sound of things. I'll catch up with her later.'

He ended the call. Was he kidding himself? He'd been trying to 'catch up' with her from the moment he'd arrived at work yesterday and it hadn't happened. And suddenly he felt like he was chasing something that was rapidly disappearing into the distance.

'Daddy? What's the matter?'

The concern in Max's voice snapped Charles back to where he was. He crouched down as Max joined his brother.

'Nothing's the matter, buddy.'

'But you look sad.'

'No-o-o…' Charles ruffled the heads of both his boys. 'How could I be sad when I get to spend some extra time with you guys? Hey…did you really draw that picture all by yourself?' He reached out for the paper to admire the artwork more closely but, to his surprise, Max shook his head and stepped back.

'It's for Gace,' he said solemnly.

'So's mine,' Cameron said. 'But you can look.'

The colourful scribbles were getting more recognisable these days. A stick figure person with a huge, crooked smile. And another one with too many legs.

'It's Gace. And Horse.'

'Aww…she'll love them. You know what?'

'What?'

'I'll bet she puts them in a frame and puts them on her wall.'

The boys beamed at him but then Max's smile wobbled.

'And then she'll come back?'

Why hadn't it occurred to him how much the twins were already missing Grace? How much they loved her as well as Horse. He hadn't factored that in when he'd chosen to distance himself enough to keep his family temporarily out of the spotlight, had he? When he'd left her text unanswered and had told that journalist that they were nothing more than friends.

And never would be.

How many people had overheard that comment? Passed it on, even?

Could *that* have been enough to persuade Grace that she didn't want to be in New York any more?

The sinking sensation that had begun with that chance meeting with Kylie gained momentum and crashed into the pit of Charles's stomach but he smiled reassuringly and nodded.

It was tantamount to a promise, that smile and nod. A promise that Grace would be back. Now he just had to find a way to make sure he didn't let his boys down.

'You guys hungry? Want some cookies and milk? And *Curious George* on TV?'

'Yes!'

At least three-year-old boys were easily distracted.

Or maybe not.

'*Spider* cookies,' Cameron shouted. 'They're the best-est.'

'I think we've run out of spider cookies,' he apologised.

'That's okay, Daddy.' Max patted his arm. 'I'll tell Gace and we'll help her make some more.'

He had to sit down with the boys and supervise the milk drinking but Charles wasn't taking any notice of the monkey's antics on the screen that were sending the twins into fits of giggles.

His mind was somewhere else entirely, carried away by the echo of his son's words. The tone of his voice.

That confidence that everything would be put to rights when he'd had the chance to explain what was wrong to Grace.

It hadn't even occurred to either of his boys to suggest that *he* make them some more homemade cookies. It might be only a superficial example but it symbolised all those things a mother could do that perhaps he couldn't even recognise as being missing from their lives.

And that longing in Max's voice.

And then she'll come back?

It touched something very deep inside Charles. Opened the door he'd shut in his head and heart that was a space that was filled with the same longing. Not just for a woman in his life or for sex. That need was there, of course, but this longing—it was for Grace.

He had to do a whole lot more than simply apologise for leaving her text unanswered when he spoke to her. He had to make her understand how important she'd become to his boys. How much they loved her.

And...and he had to tell her that he felt the same way. That *he* loved her.

That the idea of life without her had become something unthinkable.

There was a painful lump in his throat that he tried to clear away but that only made Max look up at him with those big, blue eyes that could often see so much more than you'd expect a small boy to see.

'You happy, Daddy?'

'Sure am, buddy.' Man, it was hard work to sound as though he meant it. 'You finished with that milk?'

He took the empty cups back to the kitchen. He glanced at his phone lying on the table beside his laptop on his return.

Was it worth trying to find out if Grace was available?

There was a sense of urgency about this now. What if she really was planning to leave? What if she was actually planning to leave New York? Surely she wouldn't do that without telling him?

But why would she?

He hadn't spoken to her since they'd spent the night together. He hadn't even answered her text message.

Okay, stuff had happened and events had conspired to prevent him seeing her the way he'd assumed he'd be able to, but the truth was there was no excuse for what the combination of things had produced. Without any intention of doing so, he had allowed history to repeat itself. He'd made love to Grace and then seemingly ignored her. Pushed her out of his life because something else had seemed more important.

So why wouldn't she just walk away?

He'd thought he was protecting her by not giving any journalists a reason to pry into her life when there were things that he knew she would prefer to keep very private.

Those same things that had made her so vulnerable to allowing herself to get close to another man.

Why had he assumed that she needed his protection anyway? As he'd reminded her himself, she was a strong, courageous woman and she had dealt with far worse things in her life than the threat of having her privacy invaded.

She had been courageous enough to take the risk of letting *him* that close.

And somehow—albeit unintentionally—he'd repeated the same mistake he'd made the first time.

He'd made everything worse.

He hadn't even been protecting his boys in one sense, either. He'd created the risk of them losing someone they loved. Someone they needed in their lives.

Charles rubbed the back of his neck, lifting his gaze as he tried to fight his way through this mess in his head. The view from the massive windows caught his attention for a blessed moment of distraction. It was beginning to snow heavily. Huge, fat flakes were drifting down, misting the view of the Manhattan skyline and Central Park.

Charles loved snow. He'd never quite lost that childish excitement of seeing it fall or waking up to find his world transformed by the soft, white blanket of a thick covering. But there wasn't even a spark of that excitement right now. All he could feel was that lump-inducing longing. A bone-deep need to be close to Grace.

He'd never thought he'd ever feel like this again. He'd never wanted to after Nina had died because the grief had been crippling and he never wanted to face another loss like that. He didn't want his boys to have to face that kind of loss, either.

But it had happened. He had fallen in love. Maybe it had always been there, in an enforced hibernation after that first night they'd been together, thanks to the life events that had happened afterwards.

And here he was, possibly facing the loss of this love and, in a way, it would be worse than losing Nina because Grace would still be alive. If she wasn't actually planning on leaving Manhattan Mercy, and was only thinking of finding a new place to live, he'd see her at work and see that smile and hear her voice and know that being together could have been possible if he'd done things differently.

There had to be some way he could fix this.

If Grace had feelings for him that were anything like as powerful as the ones he had finally recognised, surely there was a way to put things right.

But how?

A phone call couldn't do it.

Even a conversation might not be enough.

Charles took a deep inward breath and then let it out very slowly as he watched the flakes continuing to fall. This was no passing shower. This snow would settle. Maybe not for long. It would probably be slush by the morning if the temperature lifted but for the next few hours at least it would look like a different world out there.

A world that Grace had been so eager to see.

An echo of her voice whispered in his mind.

'It's always been my dream for Christmas. A sleigh ride in a snowy park. At night, when there's sparkly lights everywhere and there are bells on the horses and you have to be all wrapped up in soft blankets.'

He could have given her that. But how likely was it to be possible now? Christmas was weeks away and maybe she wouldn't even be here.

He needed a small miracle.

And as he stood there, watching the snow fall, Charles became aware of the spark that had been missing. Excitement about the snow?

Maybe.

Or maybe it was just hope.

The letter was still in her pocket.

Grace could feel it crinkle as she sat down on the chair beside her elderly patient's bed.

She could have gone in and put it on Charles Davenport's desk first thing this morning but she hadn't.

Because he'd been in the office. Sitting at his desk, his head bent, clearly focused on the paperwork in front of him. And it had been just too hard to know what it would be like to meet his eyes. To explain what was in the sealed envelope in her hands. To have the conversation that might have suggested they were both adults and surely they could continue working together. To be friends, even?

Nope. She didn't think she could do that. Okay, maybe it was cowardly to leave a letter and run away. She was going to have to work out her notice and that meant that they would be working in the same space for the next couple of weeks but she would cope with that the same way she was going to cope today. By immersing herself in her work to the exclusion of absolutely everything else.

And fate seemed set to help her do exactly that, by providing an endless stream of patients that needed her complete focus.

Like the guy this morning. A victim of assault but it was highly likely he'd started the fight himself. The huge and very aggressive man had presented a danger to all staff involved with his care, despite the presence of the police escort who'd brought him in. Security had had to be called and it had been a real challenge to sedate this patient and get him on a ventilator. Due to his size, the drugs needed to keep him sedated were at a high level and Grace had needed to monitor their effects very closely. Knowing what could happen if his levels dropped meant that she'd had to stay with him while he went to CT and then to Theatre so the case had taken up a good part of her morning.

Charles was nowhere to be seen when she was back in the ER but, even if he had been there, she could have kept herself almost invisible behind the curtains of various cubicles or the resuscitation areas. Patient after patient came under her care. A man with a broken finger who'd needed a nerve block before it could be realigned and splinted. A stroke victim. Two heart attacks. A woman who'd slipped on the snow that was apparently starting to fall outside and had a compound tib and fib fracture and no circulation in her foot.

And now she was in a side room with a very elderly woman called Mary who had been brought in a couple of hours ago in severe respiratory distress from an advanced case of pneumonia. Mary was eighty-six years old and had adamantly refused to have any treatment other than something to make her more comfortable.

'It's my time,' she'd told Grace quietly. 'I don't want to fight any more.'

Grace had called up her patient's notes. Mary had had a double mastectomy for breast cancer more than thirty years ago and only a few weeks back she had been diagnosed with ovarian cancer. She had refused treatment then as well. While it was difficult, as a doctor, to stand by and not provide treatment that could help, like antibiotics, it was Mary's right to make this decision and her reasoning was understandable. Very much of sound mind, she had smiled very sweetly at Grace and squeezed her hand.

'You're a darling to be so concerned but please don't worry. I'm not afraid.'

'Do you have any family we can call? Or close friends?'

'There was only ever my Billy. And he's waiting for me. He's been waiting a long time now...'

Helena had been concerned that Grace was caring for this patient.

'I can take her,' she said. 'I know how hard this must be for you. Your mum died of ovarian cancer, didn't she?'

Grace nodded, swallowing past the constriction in

her throat. 'I sat with her at the end, too. Right now it feels like it was yesterday.'

'Which is why you should step back, maybe. We'll make her as comfortable as possible in one of the private rooms out the back. It could take a while, you know. I'll find a nurse to sit with her so she won't be alone.'

'She knows me now. And I don't care how long it takes, as long as you can cope without me in here?'

'Of course. But—'

'It's because of my mum that I'm the right person to do this,' Grace said softly. 'Because of how real it feels for me. I want to do this for Mary. I want her to know that she's with someone who really cares.'

So, here they were. In one of the rooms she had noticed on her very first day here when she had wondered what they might be used for. It might even be the room next door to the one that she had stayed in with the twins and fixed Max's fire truck but this one had a bed with a comfortable air mattress. It was warm and softly lit. There was an oxygen port that was providing a little comfort to ease how difficult it was for Mary to breathe and there was a trolley that contained the drugs Grace might need to keep her from any undue distress. The morphine had taken away her pain and made her drowsy but they had talked off and on for the last hour and Grace knew that her husband Billy had died suddenly ten years ago.

'I'm so glad he didn't know about this new cancer,' Mary whispered. 'He would have been so upset. He was so good to me the first time...'

She knew that they had met seventy years ago at a summer event in Central Park.

'People say that there's no such thing as true love at first sight. But we knew different, Billy and me...'

She knew that they'd never had children.

'We never got blessed like that. It wasn't so hard... we had each other and that was enough...'

In the last half an hour Mary had stopped talking and her breathing had become shallow and rapid. Grace knew that she was still aware of her surroundings, however, because every so often she would feel a gentle squeeze from the hand her own fingers were curled around.

And finally that laboured breathing hitched and then stopped and Mary slipped away so quietly and peacefully that Grace simply sat there, still holding her hand, for the longest time.

It didn't matter now that she had tears rolling down her cheeks. She wasn't sad, exactly. Mary had believed that she was about to be reunited with her love and she had welcomed the release from any more suffering. She hadn't died alone, either. She had been grateful for Grace's company. For a hand to hold.

And she'd been lucky, hadn't she?

She had known true love. Had loved and been loved in equal measure.

Or maybe she *was* sad.

Not for Mary, but for herself.

Grace had come so close to finding that sort of love for herself—or she'd thought she had. But now, it seemed as far away as ever. As if she was standing on the other side of a plate-glass window, looking in at a scene that she couldn't be a part of.

A perfect scene.

A Christmas one, perhaps. With pretty lights on a tree

and parcels tied up with bows underneath. A fire in a grate beneath a mantelpiece that had colourful stockings hanging from it. There were people in that scene, too. A tall man with dark hair and piercing blue eyes. Two little mop-topped, happy boys. And a big, curly, adorable dog.

It took a while to get those overwhelming emotions under control but the company of this brave old woman who had unexpectedly appeared in her life helped, so by the time Grace alerted others of Mary's death, nobody would have guessed how much it had affected her. They probably just thought she looked very tired and who wouldn't, after such a long day?

It took a while after that to do what was necessary after a death of a patient and it was past time for Grace's shift to finish by the time she bundled herself up in her warm coat and scarf and gloves, ready for her walk home.

She walked out of the ER via the ambulance bay and found that it had been snowing far more than she'd been told about. A soft blanket of whiteness had cloaked everything and the world had that muted sound that came with snow when even the traffic was almost silent. And it was cold. Despite her gloves, Grace could feel her fingers tingling so she shoved her hands in her pockets and that was when she felt the crinkle of that envelope again.

Thanks to her time with Mary, she had completely forgotten to put it on Charles's desk.

Perhaps that was a good thing?

Running away from something because it was difficult wasn't the kind of person she was now.

Charles had told her how courageous she was. He had made her believe it and that belief had been enough to push her into risking her heart again.

And that had to be a good thing, too.

Even if it didn't feel like it right now.

She had almost reached the street now where the lamps were casting a circle of light amidst a swirl of snowflakes but she turned back, hesitating.

She hadn't even looked in the direction of Charles's office when she'd left. Maybe he was still there?

Maybe the kind of person she was now would actually go back and talk about this. Take the risk of making herself even more vulnerable?

And that was when she heard it.

Someone calling her name.

No. It was a jingle of bells. She had just imagined hearing her name.

She turned back to the road and any need to make a decision on what direction she was about to take evaporated.

There was a sleigh just outside the ambulance entrance to Manhattan Mercy.

A bright red sleigh, with swirling gold patterns on its sides and a canopy that was rimmed with fairy lights. A single white horse was in front, its red harness covered with small bells and, on its head—instead of the usual feathery plume—it had a set of reindeer antlers.

A driver sat in the front, a dark shape in a heavy black coat and scarf and top hat. But, in the back, there was someone else.

Charles…

'Grace…?'

Her legs were taking her forward without any instruction from her brain.

She was too stunned to be thinking of anything, in fact. Other than that Charles was here.

In a *sleigh*?

Maybe she'd got that image behind the plate-glass window a little wrong earlier.

Maybe *this* was the magic place she hadn't been able to reach.

Just Charles. In a sleigh. In the snow.

And he was holding out his hand now, to invite her to join him under the canopy at the back. Waiting to help her reach that place.

Grace was still too stunned to be aware of any coherent thoughts but her body seemed to know what to do and she found herself reaching up to take that hand.

She had been on the point of summoning the courage to go and find Charles even if it meant stepping into the most vulnerable space she could imagine.

Here she was, literally stepping into that space.

And it hadn't taken as much courage as she'd expected.

Because it felt…right…

Because it was Charles who was reaching out to her and there was no way on earth she could have turned away.

CHAPTER ELEVEN

HEART-WRENCHING...

That look on Grace's face when she'd seen him waiting for her in the sleigh.

He'd expected her to be surprised, of course. The sleigh might not be genuine but the sides had been cleverly designed to cover most of the wheels so it not only looked the part but was a pretty unusual sight on a New York street. Along with the bells and fairy lights and the reindeer antlers on the horse, he had already been a target for every phone or camera that people had been able to produce.

For once, he didn't mind the attention. Bundled up in his thick coat and scarf, with a hat pulled well down over his head, Charles Davenport was unrecognisable but the worry about publicity was a million miles from his mind, anyway. The sight of this spectacle—that had taken him most of the day to organise—didn't just make people want to capture the image. It was delighting them, making them point and wave. To smile and laugh.

But Grace hadn't smiled when she saw him.

She'd looked shocked.

Scared, almost?

So, so vulnerable that Charles knew in that instant just how much damage his silence had caused.

And how vital it was to fix it.

The sheer relief when Grace had accepted his hand to climb up into the carriage had been so overwhelming that perhaps he couldn't blame the biting cold for making his eyes water. Or for making it too hard to say anything just yet. How much courage had it taken for her to accept his hand?

He loved her for that courage. And for everything else he knew to be true about her.

And nothing needed to be said just yet. For now, it was too important to make sure that Grace was going to be warm enough. To pull one faux fur blanket after another from the pile at his feet, to wrap them both in a soft cocoon. A single cocoon, so that as soon as he was satisfied there was no danger of hypothermia, he could wrap his arms around Grace beneath these blankets and simply hold her close.

Extra protection from the cold?

No. This was about protecting what he knew was the most important thing in his life at this moment. Grace. So important in his boys' lives as well. The only thing he wasn't sure of yet was how important it might be in her life.

The steady, rocking motion of the carriage was like a slow heartbeat that made him acutely aware of every curve in the body of the woman he was holding and, as the driver finished negotiating traffic and turned into the lamplit, almost deserted paths of Central Park, he could feel the tension in Grace's body begin to lessen. It was under the halo of one of those antique streetlamps that Grace finally raised her head to meet his gaze and he could see that the shock had worn off.

There was something else in her gaze now.

Hope?

That wouldn't be there, would it? Unless this was just as important to her as it was to him?

Again, the rush of emotion made it impossible to find any words.

Instead, Charles bent his head and touched Grace's lips gently with his own. Her lips parted beneath his and he felt the astonishing warmth of her mouth. Of her breath.

A breath of life...

Maybe he still didn't need to say anything yet. Or maybe he could say it another way...

For the longest time, Grace's brain had been stunned into immobility. She was aware of what was around her but couldn't begin to understand what any of it meant.

Her senses were oddly heightened. The softness of the furry blankets felt like she was being wrapped inside a cloud. The motion of the carriage was like being rocked in someone's arms. And then she *was* in someone's arms. Charles's. Grace didn't want to think about what this meant. She just wanted to feel it. This sense of being in the one place in the world she most wanted to be. This feeling of being protected.

Precious...

Finally, she had to raise her head. To check whether this was real. Had she slipped in the snow and knocked herself out cold, perhaps? Was this dream-come-to-life no more than an elaborate creation of her subconscious?

If it was, it couldn't have conjured up a more compelling expression in the eyes of the man she loved.

It was a gaze that told her she was the only thing in the world that mattered right now.

That she was loved…

And then his lips touched her own and Grace could feel how cold they were, which only intensified the heat that was coming from inside his body. From his breath. From the touch of his tongue.

She wasn't unconscious.

Grace had never felt more alive in her life.

It was the longest, most tender kiss she had ever experienced. A whole conversation in itself.

An apology from Charles, definitely. A declaration of love, even.

And on her part? A statement that the agony of his silence and distance since they'd last been together didn't matter, perhaps. That she forgave him. That nothing mattered other than being together, like this.

They had to come up for air eventually, however, and the magic of the kiss retreated.

Actions might speak a whole lot louder than words, but words were important, too.

Charles was the first to use some.

'I'm so sorry,' he said. 'It's been crazy…but when Kylie told me this morning that you were thinking of leaving, I got enough of a shock to realise just how much I'd messed this up.'

'You didn't even answer my text message,' Grace whispered, her voice cracking. 'The morning after we'd…we'd…'

'I know. I'm sorry. I woke up that morning and realised how I felt about you and…and it was huge. My head was all over the place and then my mother rang. She'd seen something in the paper that suggested we were a couple. That photo of us all in the park.'

Grace nodded. 'Helena showed it to me. She said that there'd been a reporter in the department pretending to be a patient. That you'd told her we were just colleagues. Friends. That it would never be anything more than that.'

She looked away from Charles. A long, pristine stretch of the wide pathway lay ahead of them, the string of lamps shining to illuminate the bare, snow-laden branches of the huge, old trees guarding this passage. The snow was still falling but it was gentle now. Slow enough to be seen as separate stars beneath the glow of the lamps.

'I'd thought I would be able to find you as soon as I got to work. That I could warn you of the media interest. I thought…that I was protecting you from having your privacy invaded by putting them off the scent. And… and it didn't seem that long. It was only a day…'

Grace squeezed her eyes shut. 'It felt like a month…'

'I'm sorry…'

The silence continued on and then she heard Charles take a deep breath.

'I can't believe I made the same mistake. For the same reasons.'

'It's who you are, Charles.' Grace opened her eyes but she didn't turn to meet his gaze. 'You're always going to try and protect your family above everything else.'

She was looking at the fountain they were approaching. She'd seen it in the daytime—an angel with one hand held out over a pond. The angel looked weighed down now, her wings encrusted with a thick layer of snow.

Their carriage driver was doing a slow circuit around

the fountain. Grace felt Charles shift slightly and looked up to see him staring at the angel.

'She's the Angel of the Waters, did you know that?'

'No.'

'The statue was commissioned to commemorate the first fresh water system for New York. It came after a cholera outbreak. She's blessing the water, to give it healing powers.'

He turned to meet her gaze directly and there was something very serious in his own. A plea, almost.

For healing?

'I do understand,' Grace said softly. 'And I don't blame you for ignoring me that first time. But it hurt, you know? I really didn't think you would do it again...'

'I didn't realise I was. I went into the pattern that I'd learned back then, to focus on protecting the people that mattered. My mother was upset. It was Thanksgiving and the family was gathering. The worst thing that could happen was to have everything out there and being raked up all over again.'

Grace was silent. Confused. He had gone to goodness only knew how much trouble to create this dream sleigh ride for her and he'd kissed her as if she was the only person who mattered. And yet he had made that same mistake. Maybe it hadn't seemed like very much time to him but it had felt like an eternity to her.

'What I said to that reporter was intended to protect you, Grace, as much as to try and keep the spotlight off my family. I had the feeling that you never talk about what you've been through. That maybe I was the only person who knew your story. I didn't want someone digging through your past and making something private public. You'd told me that that was the worst thing you could imagine happening. Especially something that was perhaps private between just *us*—that made it even more important to protect.'

He sighed as the carriage turned away from the fountain and continued its journey.

'I needed to talk to you somewhere private and it just wasn't happening. I couldn't get near you at work. There was the family Thanksgiving dinner and I was running late. I knocked on your door but you weren't home.'

'I was Skyping my dad. I couldn't answer the door.' And she could have made it easier for him, couldn't she? If she'd only had a little more confidence. She could have texted him again. Or made an effort to find him at work instead of waiting for him to come and find her.

He hadn't been put off by her scarred body. He'd been trying to protect her from others finding out about it. It made it a secret. One that didn't matter but was just between them. A private bond.

'I know that you don't actually need my protection,' Charles said slowly. 'That you're strong enough to survive anything on your own, but there's a part of me that would like you to need it, I guess. Because I want to be able to give it to you.'

They were passing the carousel now, the brightly coloured horses rising and falling under bright lights. There were children riding the horses and they could hear shrieks of glee.

'The boys are missing you,' Charles added quietly. 'They were drawing pictures for you this morning and I said that you'd love them and probably put them in a frame and Max said...he asked if you'd come back then.'

'Oh...' Grace had a huge lump in her throat.

'We need you, Grace. The boys need you. *I* need you.'

He took his hands from beneath the warmth of the blankets to cradle her face between them.

'I love you, Grace Forbes. I think I always have…

The lump was painful to swallow. It was too hard to find more than a single word.

'Same…'

'You were right in what you said—I will always protect my family above everything else. But you're part of my family now. The part we need the most.'

They didn't notice they had left the carousel behind them as they sank into another slow, heartbreakingly tender kiss.

When Grace opened her eyes again, she found they were going past the Wollman skating rink. Dozens of people were on the ice, with the lights of the Manhattan skyline a dramatic backdrop.

'I thought I had to ignore how I felt in order to protect the people around me,' Charles told her. 'But now I know how wrong I was.'

He kissed her again.

'I want everybody to know how much I love you. And I'm going to protect that love before everything else because that's what's going to keep us all safe. You. Me. The boys…' He caught Grace's hand in his own and brought it up to his lips. 'I can't go down on one knee, and I don't have a ring because I'd want you to choose what's perfect just for you, but…will you let me love you and protect you for the rest of our lives—even if you don't need it and even if I don't get it quite right sometimes? Will you…will you marry me, Grace?

'Yes…' The word came out in no more than a whisper but it felt like the loudest thing Grace had ever said in her life.

This sleigh ride might have been a dream come true but it was nothing more than a stage set for her *real* dream. One that she'd thought she'd lost for ever. To love and be loved in equal measure.

To have her own family…

She had to blink back the sudden tears that filled her eyes. Had to clear away the lump in her throat so that she could be sure that Charles could hear her.

'Yes,' she said firmly, a huge smile starting to spread over her face. 'Yes and yes and *yes*…'

EPILOGUE

IT WAS A twenty-minute walk from the apartment block to the Rockefeller Center but the two small boys weren't complaining about the distance. It was too exciting to be walking through the park in the dark of the evening and besides, if they weren't having a turn riding on Daddy's shoulders, they got to hold hands with Grace.

'Look, Daddy...look, Gace...' It was Max's turn to be carried high on his father's shoulders. 'What are they doing?'

'Ice skating,' Charles told him. 'Would you like to try it one day soon?'

'Is Gace coming, too?'

'Yes.' Grace grinned up at the little boy, her heart swelling with love. One day maybe he would call her 'Mummy' but it really didn't matter.

'Of course she is,' Charles said. 'Remember what we talked about? Grace and I are going to be married. Very soon. Before Christmas, even. We're a family now.'

'And Gace is going to be our *mummy*,' Cameron shouted.

Max bounced on Charles's shoulders as a signal to be put down. 'I want to hold my mummy's hand,' he said.

'She's *my* mummy, too.' Cameron glared at his brother.

'Hey…I've got two hands. One each.' Grace caught Charles's gaze over the heads of the boys and the look in his eyes melted her heart.

Mummy.

It *did* matter.

Not the name. The feeling. Feeling like the bond between all of them was unbreakable.

Family.

A branch of the Davenport family of New York—something which she still hadn't got used to—but their own unique unit within that dynasty.

Charles had shown her the Davenport ring last week, after that magical sleigh ride in the park.

'I've told Zac it's waiting for him, if he ever gets round to needing it. It belongs to the past and, even before you agreed to marry me, I knew it wouldn't suit you.'

'Because it's so flashy?'

'Because it represents everything that is window dressing in life, not the really important stuff.'

'Like love?'

'Like love. Like what's beneath any kind of window dressing.'

He'd touched her body then. A gentle reminder that what her clothes covered was real. Not something to be ashamed of but a symbol of struggle and triumph. Something to be proud of.

So she had chosen a ring that could have also made its way through struggle and triumph already. An antique ring with a simple, small diamond.

'We're almost there, guys.' Charles was leading them through the increasingly dense crowds on the Manhattan streets. 'Let's find somewhere we'll be able to see.'

Grace could hear the music now. And smell hotdogs

and popcorn from street stalls. People around them were wearing Santa hats with flashing stars and reindeer antlers that made her remember the horse that had pulled her sleigh so recently on the night that had changed her life for ever.

They couldn't get very close to the Rockefeller Center in midtown Manhattan but it didn't matter because the huge tree towered above the crowds and the live music was loud enough to be heard for miles. Charles lifted Cameron to his shoulders and Grace picked up Max to rest him on her hip. He wrapped his arms around her neck and planted a kiss on her cheek.

'I love you, Mummy.'

'I love you, too, Max,' she whispered back.

A new performance was starting. If it wasn't Mariah Carey singing, it was someone who sounded exactly like her. And it was *her* song: 'All I Want for Christmas Is You'.

Grace leaned back against the man standing protectively so close behind her. She turned her head and smiled up at him.

'That's so true,' she told him. 'It's now officially my favourite Christmas song, ever.'

'Mine, too.'

When the song finished, the countdown started and when the countdown finished, the magnificent tree with its gorgeous crystal star on the top blazed into life.

The Christmas season had officially begun.

And Grace had all she had ever wanted. All she would ever want.

The tender kiss that Charles bent to place on her lips right then made it clear that they both did.

* * * * *

SURGEON IN A
WEDDING DRESS

SUE MacKAY

To Tania

For all the moments we have shared, and the moments to come.

And

Kate David: the newest, and very supportive, member of the Blenheim Writers' Group.

CHAPTER ONE

NEW YEAR'S DAY. Resolutions and new beginnings.

'Huh.' Sarah Livingston scowled. As if anything new, or interesting, was likely to be found down here in the South Island, so far from the cities. Thanks to her fiancé—very *ex*-fiancé—coming to this godforsaken place had more to do with excising the pain and hurt he'd caused, and nothing at all to do with anything new.

But there was a resolution hiding somewhere in her thinking. It went something like '*Get a new life*'. One that didn't involve getting serious with a man and being expected to trust him. Surely that was possible. There had to be plenty of men out there willing to date a well-groomed surgeon with a penchant for fine dining; who didn't want anything other than a good time with no strings.

So why couldn't she raise some enthusiasm for that idea? Because she hadn't got over her last debacle yet. Six months since she'd been dumped, let down badly by the one man who'd told her repeatedly he'd loved and cherished her. Her heart still hadn't recovered from those lies. Or from the humiliation that rankled every time someone at work spoke of how sorry they were to hear about her broken engagement. Of course they were. Sorry they'd missed out on going to her big, fancy wedding, more like.

After learning of the baby *her* fiancé was expecting

with that sweet little nurse working in Recovery, Sarah had started putting in horrendous hours at the private hospital where she was a partner. It had been a useless attempt to numb the agony his infidelity caused her. Not to mention how she'd exhausted herself so she fell into bed at the end of each day instead of drumming up painful and nasty things to do to the man she'd loved.

And it was that man's fault her father had decided, actually insisted, she get away for a few months. What had really tipped the scales for her in favour of time away from Auckland was that her ex was due back shortly from his honeymoon in Paris.

Swiping at the annoying moisture in her eyes, Sarah pushed aside the image of *her* beautiful French-styled wedding gown still hanging in its cover in the wardrobe of her spare bedroom.

Why couldn't she forget those damning words her fiancé had uttered as he'd left her apartment for the last time. *You should never have children. You'd be taking a risk of screwing up their lives for ever.*

It had been depressingly easy to replace her at work with an eager young surgeon thrilled to get an opportunity to work in the prestigious surgical hospital her father had created. And who could blame the guy? Not her. Even being a little jaded with the endless parade of patients she saw daily, she still fully understood the power of her father's reputation.

'So here I am.' She sighed. 'Stuck on a narrow strip of sodden grass beside the coastal highway that leads from nowhere to nowhere.'

Her Jaguar was copping a pounding from a deluge so heavy the metalwork would probably be dented when the rain stopped. If it ever stopped.

Using her forearm to wipe the condensation from the

inside of her window, she peered through the murk. The end of the Jag's bonnet was barely visible, let alone the road she'd crept off to park on the verge. Following the tortuous route along the coast where numerous cliffs fell away to the wild ocean, she'd been terrified of driving over the edge to a watery grave. But staying on the road when she couldn't see a thing had been equally dangerous.

So much for new beginnings. A totally inauspicious start to the year. And she still had to front up to the surgical job she'd agreed to take. Sarah's hands clenched, as they were prone to do these days whenever she wondered what her future held for her. These coming months in Port Weston were an interim measure. This wasn't a place she'd be stopping in for long. Fancy leaving a balmy Auckland to come and spend the summer in one of New Zealand's wettest regions. Yep. A really clever move.

Her father's none-too-gentle arguments aside, the CEO of Port Weston Hospital had been very persuasive, if not a little desperate. He'd needed a general surgeon so that Dr Daniel Reilly could take a long overdue break. A *forced* break, apparently. What sort of man did that make this Reilly character? A workaholic? She shuddered. She knew what they were like, having grown up with one. Or was she an arrogant surgeon who believed no one could replace him? Her ex-fiancé came to mind.

Sharp wind gusts buffeted the heavy car, shaking it alarmingly. Was she destined to spend her three-month contract perched on the top of a cliff face? On the passenger seat lay one half-full bottle of glacial water, a mottled banana and two day-old fruit muffins that had looked dubious when she'd bought them back at some one-store town with a forgettable name. Not a lot of food to survive on if this storm didn't hurry up and pass through.

Sarah returned to staring out the window. Was it raining

in Paris? She hoped so. Then she blinked. And craned her neck forward. There was the road she'd abandoned half an hour ago. And the edge of the precipice she'd parked on— less than two metres from the nose of her car. A chill slid down her spine, her mouth dried. Her eyes bulged in disbelief at how close she'd come to plummeting down to the sea.

With the rain easing, she could hear the wild crash of waves on the rocks below. Reaching for the ignition, she suddenly hesitated. It might be wise to check her situation before backing onto the road.

Outside the car she shivered and tugged her jacket closer to her body. A quick lap around the vehicle showed no difficulties with returning to the road. Then voices reached her. Shouts, cries, words—snatched away by the wind.

Pushing one foot forward cautiously, then the other, she moved ever closer to the cliff edge. As she slowly leaned forward and peered gingerly over the side, her heart thumped against her ribs. The bank dropped directly down to the ocean-licked rocks.

More shouts. From the left. Sarah steeled herself for another look. Fifty metres away, on a rock-strewn beach, people clustered at the water's edge, dicing with the treacherous waves crashing around their feet and tugging them off balance. Her survey of the scene stopped at one dark-haired man standing further into the sea, hands on hips. From this angle it was impossible to guess his height, but his shoulders were impressive. Her interest quickened. He seemed focused on one particular spot in the water.

Trying to follow the direction of his gaze, she saw a boat bouncing against the waves as it pushed out to sea at an achingly slow pace. She gasped. Beyond the waves floated a person—face down.

Happy New Year.

* * *

Daniel Reilly stood knee-deep in the roiling water, his heart in his throat as the rescuers tried to navigate the charging waves. Aboard their boat lay an injured person. Alive or dead, Dan didn't know, but *he'd* have a cardiac arrest soon if these incredibly brave—and foolhardy— men didn't get back on land before someone else was lost.

The whole situation infuriated him. If only people would read the wretched signs and take heed. They weren't put there for fun. It was bad enough having two people missing in the sea, a father and son according to the police. It would be totally stupid if one of the volunteer rescuers drowned while searching for them.

'Doc, get back up the beach. We'll bring him to you,' a rescuer yelled at him. 'It's the lad, Anders Starne.'

'He doesn't look too good,' Pat O'Connor, the local constable, called over the din.

Like the middle-aged cop, Dan had seen similar tragedies all too often around here. It wasn't known as a wild, unforgiving coastline for nothing. But most calamities could be avoided if people used their brains. His hands gripped his hips as he cursed under his breath.

The kid had better be alive. Though Dan didn't like the chances, it was inherent in him to believe there was life still beating in a body until proven otherwise.

Waterlogged men laid Anders on the sand, a teenager with his life ahead of him. Dan's gut clenched as he thought of his own daughter. Even at four she pushed all the boundaries, and Dan couldn't begin to imagine how he'd cope with a scenario like this. He totally understood why the father had leapt off the rocks in a vain attempt to save his son. *He* would do anything if Leah's life was in jeopardy.

'Except take a long break to spend time with her.' The annoying voice of one of his closest friends, and boss, resonated in his head.

Yeah, well, he was doing his best. And because of interference from the board's chairman, Charlie Drummond, he *was* taking time off, starting tomorrow. Pity Charlie couldn't tell him how he was supposed to entertain his daughter, because he sure didn't have a clue. Hopscotch and finger puppets were all very well, but for twelve weeks? What if he got it all wrong again? He'd be back at the beginning with Leah an emotional mess and he distraught from not knowing how to look after his girl. That scared him witless. He focused on the boy lying on the beach. Far easier.

Dropping to his knees, he tore at the boy's clothing, his fingers touching cold skin in their search for a carotid pulse. A light, yet steady, throbbing under his fingers lifted his mood. He smiled up at the silent crowd of locals surrounding him. 'He's alive.'

'Excuse me. Let me through. I'm a doctor.' A lilting, female voice intruded on Dan's concentration.

Annoyed at the disturbance, he flicked a look up at the interloper. 'That makes two of us,' he snapped, and returned his attention to his patient. But not before he saw a vision of a shapely female frame looming over him. *Very* shapely.

'Where'd you come from?' he demanded as he explored Anders's head with his fingers.

'Does that matter at this moment?' she retorted.

'Not really.' He was local and therefore in charge.

'What have you found so far?' She, whoever she was, knelt on the other side of the boy.

He was aware of her scrutinising him. 'His pulse is steady.' He was abrupt with her as he straightened and looked her in the eye. Her gaze slammed into him, shocking the air out of his lungs. Eyes as green as the bush-clad hills behind them. And as compelling.

'Then he's one very lucky boy.' Her tone so reasonable it was irritating.

And intriguing. Who was she? He'd never seen her before, and she wasn't someone he'd easily forget with that elegant stance and striking face. He shook his head. Right now he didn't need to know anything about her.

Jerking his gaze away, he spoke to the crowd again, 'Someone get my bag from my truck. Fast.' To the doctor—how did she distract him so easily?—he said, 'I'll wrap him in a survival blanket to prevent any more loss of body heat.'

The kid coughed. Spewed salt water. Together they rolled him onto his side, water oozing out the corner of his mouth as he continued coughing. His eyelids dragged open, then drooped shut.

'Here, Dan.' Malcolm, his brother and the head of the local search and rescue crew, pushed through the crowd to drop a bag in the sand. Dan snapped open the catches and delved into the bag for tissues and the foil blanket.

'Thanks.' The other doctor flicked the tissues from his grasp. Dan squashed his admiration for her efficiency watching her cleaning the boy's mouth and chin as she tenderly checked his bruised face simultaneously. Her long, slim fingers tipped with pale rose-coloured polish were thorough in their survey.

'I don't think the cheek bones are fractured.' Her face tilted up, and her eyes met his.

Again her gaze slammed into him, taking his breath away. The same relief he felt for the boy was reflected in her eyes. Facial bones were delicate and required the kind of surgical procedures he wasn't trained to perform. He gave her a thumbs-up. 'Thank goodness.'

The rain returned, adding to the boy's discomfort. Dan began rolling Anders gently one way, then the other, tucking him into the blanket, at the same time checking for injuries. He found deep gashes on Anders's back and one arm lay at an odd angle, undoubtedly fractured. For now the wounds weren't bleeding, no doubt due to the low body temperature, but as that rose the haemorrhaging would start. The deep gash above one eyebrow would be the worst.

'Where's the ambulance?' Dan asked Pat.

'On its way. About three minutes out. It was held up by a slip at Black's Corner.'

Anger shook Dan once more. This boy's life could've indirectly been jeopardised because of some officious idiot's unsound reasoning. For years now the locals had been petitioning to get Black's Corner straightened and the unstable hillside bulldozed away, but the council didn't have a lot of funds and small towns like Port Weston missed out all the time. He'd be making a phone call to the mayor later.

Looking down at the boy, Dan asked, 'Anders, can you hear me?' Eyelids flickered, which Dan took for a yes. 'You've been in an accident. A wave swept you off the rocks. I'm checking for broken bones. Okay?'

Dan didn't expect an answer. He didn't get one. He wasn't sure if the boy could hear clearly or was just responding to any vocal sounds, so he kept talking. It must be hellishly frightening for Anders to be surrounded by strangers while in pain and freezing cold.

Beneath the thermal blanket Dan felt the boy's abdomen. No hard swelling to indicate internal bleeding. The spleen felt normal. So far so good. But the sooner this boy was in hospital the better.

'That left arm doesn't look right,' a knowledgeable, and sensual, feminine voice spoke across the boy.

Dan's fingers worked at the point where the arm twisted

under Anders's body. His nod was terse. 'Compound fracture, and dislocated shoulder.'

'Are we going to pop that shoulder back in place now?'

'We should. Otherwise the time frame will be too long and he might require surgery.'

'I'll hold him for you.' No questions, no time wasting. She trusted him to get on with it.

Daniel appreciated anyone who trusted his judgement, or anything about him, come to that. His mouth twisted sideways as he slid the boy's tattered shirt away from his shoulder. 'A shot of morphine will make him more comfortable.'

The drug quickly took effect. Dan raised the arm and, using all his strength, rotated the head of the humerus, popping the ball joint back into its socket. Sweat beaded on his forehead.

The woman lifted Anders's upper body while Dan wound a crepe bandage around the shoulder to hold it in place temporarily. As they worked, a whiff of her exotic perfume tantalised him, brought memories of another fragrance, another woman. His wife. She'd always worn perfume, even when mucking out the horses.

'Where's that ambulance?' He was brusque, annoyed at the painful images conjured up in his mind by a darned scent.

Warmth touched his face, and so distracted had he been that it took a moment to realise that it was the sun. A quick look around showed the clouds had rolled back and once again the beach was sparkling as it bathed in the yellow light. Things were looking up.

As though reading his mind, Pat said, 'Now that the rain has moved up the coast, the helicopter will be on its way. That'll make our search a little easier.'

The boy's father. Dan's stomach clenched as he looked

up at Pat, saw the imperceptible shake of the cop's head in answer to his unspoken question. Deep sadness gripped him. Time was running out to find the man alive.

'It was sheer chance the men found the lad when they did.' Even as Pat talked they heard the deep sound of rotors beating in the air.

'Hey, Daniel,' a familiar voice called. Kerry was a local volunteer ambulance officer. 'What've we got?'

Dan quickly filled him in and within moments Anders was being ferried on a stretcher to the ambulance. There went one very lucky boy. Dan watched the vehicle pull away, thinking about the waves throwing a body onto the sharp jags of the rocks. He shivered abruptly.

'What happened out there?' The woman stood beside him, nodding towards the sea.

Dan shook the image from his head and turned to face this other distraction. His world tilted as he once more looked into those fathomless eyes. It was hard to focus on answering her question. 'Anders and his father were fishing off the rocks—'

'In this weather? That's crazy,' she interrupted.

'Of course it's crazy.' His jaw tightened. 'But it happens. Anders slipped and his father leapt in after him.'

'And the father's still missing.' It was a soft statement of fact. Her eyes were directed to the sea, scanning the horizon.

'I'm afraid so.' He lightened his tone. 'Thank you for your help. You happened along at exactly the right moment.' He wouldn't thank her for the unwelcome hollow feeling in his gut that had started when this perturbing woman had arrived. Or the sensation of something missing from his life that he hadn't been aware of until now. Soon she'd be on her way and then he'd forget this silly, unwelcome impression she'd made.

'You can thank the appalling weather for that. I'd pulled off the road, and when the rain cleared I saw you all down here.'

His eyes scanned the close horizon. Already the sun was disappearing behind a veil of clouds. 'Looks like we're in for more.'

'When doesn't it rain?' Exasperation tightened her face.

'If it's not raining around here that's because it either just stopped or is about to start.' In reality it wasn't all that bad, but why destroy the coast's reputation for bad weather? Especially with someone just passing through. Weird how that notion suddenly saddened him. Odd that a complete stranger had rocked him, reminding him of things he'd deliberately forgotten for years.

A sudden, unexpected thought slammed into his brain. Maybe it was time to start dating again. Like when? If he didn't have time for his daughter, how would he manage fitting another person into his life? He couldn't. End of story. End of stupid ideas.

The woman's tight smile was still in place as her hands wiped at her damp jacket. 'Guess we just had a fine spell, then.'

'At least you got to see it.' He mustered a joke, and was rewarded with a light laugh. A carefree tinkle that hovered in the air between them, drew him closer to her, wound an invisible thread around them both.

Then she glanced down at her feet and grimaced with disgust as she noticed the sloppy, glue-like mud that coated her pretty sandals. He'd swear she shuddered. Definitely a city dweller. Nothing like the women he knew and loved: wholesome, country women like his sisters and his late wife.

Trying to sound sympathetic, he said, 'You should've worn gumboots.'

'Gumboots?' Those carefully crafted eyebrows rose with indignation.

'Yes. Rubber boots that reach the tops of your shins.'

'I know what gumboots are.'

Bet she'd never worn them. 'Sure you do.'

'Do you suppose I might be able to get a designer pair?'

'Possum fur around the tops?' Keep it light, then send her on her way before he did something dumb, like offer her coffee.

She tilted her head to one side. 'How about crochet daisies? Yellow, to contrast with the black rubber.'

'Hey, Dan, you heading to the hospital?' Pat called across the sand.

Thankful for the interruption, Dan shook his head. 'No, Alison can take care of the lad. I'll hang around in case the guys find Starne senior.' He patted his belt, checking for his pager.

'Who's Alison?' the woman beside him asked.

'She's in charge of the emergency department and has a surgical background. She'd call if she needs me.' *What does this have to do with you? You're an outsider.*

'Do you mind if I wait a while with you?'

Yes, I do. Inexplicably he wanted her gone. As though a safety mechanism was warning him to get away from her before it was too late.

Yet he couldn't prevent his head turning towards her. Blonde strands of hair whipped across her cheeks in the skittish wind. He let his gaze wander over her. She was designer from head to foot. Her jacket was soft suede. Her well-fitted trousers had not come off a rack, at least not any ordinary shop rack. But what really caught his interest were the long, shapely legs those wet trousers clung to. They went on for ever.

'Pardon? Oh, sorry. You want to stay? It's not necessary.' Flustered at having been sidetracked, he tripped over his words. First she had him joking with her, then she addled his brain. He struggled to focus on the important issues, not her. 'If the searchers find anything now, it's more likely to be a body. No one can survive in that icy water for very long.'

'True, but it's hard to give up hope, isn't it?' Her eyes were enormous in her pale face.

'Very hard.' His stomach tightened, because of the sad and pointless waste of a life. Not because of the empathy in her eyes.

'I'd still like to wait.' She wasn't asking him, she was telling him, quietly but firmly.

Then from left field he felt a stirring in a region of his body he'd thought long dead. For two despair-filled years, he'd been unintentionally celibate. Now he couldn't help himself—he glanced down at his groin. Relief poured through him. His reaction had been small. Tipping his head back, he laughed. Another long-forgotten act.

Definitely time to get out and about. That new nurse in the neonatal unit had dropped enough hints, and she obviously liked babies if she worked with them, which had to be a plus. Leah needed siblings. He'd never wanted her to be an only child.

He rubbed his arms. Wanting more children had led to a load of stress and difficulties in his otherwise wonderful marriage. Family was so important. Look how his sisters and brother had rallied round when Celine had died. But Leah would miss out on so much if he didn't rectify the situation soon. Dating meant getting involved with another person. Was he ready? Would he ever be ready? Not while his guilt over letting down Celine hung over him like a dirty cloud.

Their marriage had been cut short by an aneurysm.

Cut short before they could resolve their problems. The shock of finding Celine's lifeless body in the bathroom, with Leah sitting beside her singing as though nothing was wrong, still rocked Dan when he thought about it.

Which was why he didn't think about it.

That's also why dating was a bad idea. The whole concept of having someone else he might care about taken away from him so abruptly sent him into a cold sweat.

Suddenly the unknown woman thrust a hand out. 'By the way, I'm Sarah Livingston, your replacement surgeon.'

'Stone the crows.' Shock barrelled through him.

It hadn't occurred to him she might be the locum they expected to arrive tomorrow. The idea was absurd. She was too citified to be stopping here. Too...different. She wouldn't fit in at all. His stomach tightened another notch. So she wasn't passing through.

She was moving in.

Into his hospital, his clinic. Into his house.

Sarah tensed. What did the guy mean? *Stone the crows.* Hadn't she just performed in a capable and professional manner? 'You've got a problem with me?'

'Ahh, no.' The man sounded flummoxed. 'Not at all.'

'I didn't try to take control of your accident scene.' Which was unusual. She hated playing second fiddle to anyone. But in this circumstance she'd gone along with him without any concerns. Odd. Was she coming down with something?

So far her impressions of him were straightforward. Strong hands. Sopping-wet, longish hair that appeared black. Eyes that held a load of caution and a quick anger. Then there were those wide shoulders that V'd down to narrow hips. He totally lacked style—his jeans and the baggy, woollen overshirt under his jacket were way past their use-by date. On a professional note, which was far more important, he'd performed very competently with the boy.

'You certainly made things easier for me.' His voice was deep, gruff, reminding her of a thistle—rough and prickly exterior, soft inside.

'You are Dr Daniel Reilly? I heard someone call you Dan so I presumed so. If I'm mistaken, I'm sorry.'

His handshake was firm but brief, as though glad to get the niceties over. But not so fast that she didn't notice the electricity flaring between them at his touch. Heat sizzled across her palm. Deep in her tummy warmth unfurled, reached throughout her body, reddened her cheeks.

'It's my practice you'll be looking after.' His tone hardened.

So that was it. He wasn't happy about leaving his practice in someone else's hands. The reluctance came through loud and clear. So why had he been told to take a break?

'I thought you'd be pleased to see me, eager to get on with your holiday.' She swallowed her disappointment at his lack of welcome. At least with him going on leave she mightn't see much of him. She hoped.

Really? Truly? You don't want to follow up on this attraction for him that's gripping you? Absolutely not. Too soon after Oliver's betrayal. Who said anything about getting close? What about a fling? A sigh slipped across her bottom lip as she studied Dr Reilly. She doubted her ability to have an affair and not get a little bit close to him. What a shame.

He ignored her jibe, instead turning his back to the pounding surf and nodding at an old, weatherboard building on the other side of the road. 'We'll wait in the Gold Miners' Pub. Can't have you catching a chill.'

As if. Sarah looked around at the sodden beach, the

black, churning waters of the Tasman Sea, the heavy, leaden clouds racing in. Everything was wet, wet, wet. How could she have thought leaving home would help put the last few months behind her? She could've decided about her future in an environment she was used to, not on an alien planet.

How stupid to think doing a complete flip-over of her life would change anything. She shoved her fists into her jacket pockets, already knowing she should've stayed at home for these months, should've told her father no. Right now she'd be in her gorgeous apartment overlooking Auckland's inner harbour, the vibrant City of Sails, where money talked. Where gorgeous, chic sandals stayed gorgeous, not getting ruined the moment she hopped out of her car.

The months in Port Weston stretched out before her like an endless road. But she wasn't quitting. Port Weston might be like nothing she was used to, but she had to stay. She'd given her word.

Then her eyes focused on Daniel Reilly, and for some unknown reason she wondered if she'd be wise to leave right away, while she still could.

CHAPTER TWO

DR REILLY made Sarah, at five feet six, feel almost short.
Following him into the dark, wood-panelled interior of the
Gold Miners' Pub, she admired his easy, smooth gait, his
natural grace that belied his big build. The latent strength
she'd glimpsed when he'd popped Anders's joint back was
evident in the set of his shoulders, in the loose swing of his
hands. Her tongue licked her lips. Gorgeous.

He turned to her. 'A shot of something strong will warm
you through and stop your teeth chattering.'

'I'd prefer Earl Grey tea.'

He winced. 'Earl Grey? On the Coast?' His eyes rolled.
'That fancy city stuff won't win you many friends around
here.'

'As that's not why I'm here, it doesn't matter.'

'I'd like a practice to return to.'

'Not a problem.' The man's looks might take her breath
away but his prickly disposition annoyed her. Was she the
only one he treated that way? Probably not, if he had to be
forced to take leave. The intensity with which he studied
her sent a blush right down to her toes. Did he like what he
saw? Did she care? Uh, hello? Unbelievable how quickly
her awareness of him had reached the point where she
wondered how his touch on her skin would affect her. It
would burn her up, she suspected. Her overreaction must

be due to the contrast between the overly hot room and the chilly dampness outside. What else could it be?

Try lust or physical attraction; forget the weather. Really? Then her stomach growled. That's what this was all about. Lack of food. Not Dr Yummy.

'I heard that grumbling,' the man dominating her thoughts said, amusement briefly lightening those cool, assessing eyes.

'I'm starving.' Hardly surprising. Unable to bring herself to eat those woeful muffins, her last meal had been breakfast. A glance at her watch showed it was now after five.

Behind the long bar a pretty woman with wild red hair called across the room. 'Dan, the hospital phoned to say everything's under control.' The woman looked pointedly at Sarah. 'Can I get you both a drink? I'm sure your friend might like something.'

Shock registered on Dan's face. 'This is Sarah Livingston. My locum.'

Not his friend. Probably never would be. What a pity.

'Are you really?' the woman asked Sarah, her face lighting up with a speculative gleam as her gaze moved to Dan and back. 'Wonderful.'

Sarah gulped. Don't get any bright ideas about matchmaking. If Oliver's defection had taught her anything it was not to trust as easily as she had last time. Besides, Dan Reilly was far too unsophisticated for her liking. Except that sculpted body did fascinate her. Maybe she could cope with unsophisticated—as an interlude. Hadn't she thought about having fun with men who didn't want anything more demanding? But an affair with this man? Not likely. That could complicate things when she had to step into his shoes at the local hospital.

Dan continued the introductions. 'Jill's our head theatre nurse, and a barmaid in her spare time. She'll get you whatever you want, though a slug of brandy would do you a sight more good than tea.'

Sarah retorted, 'Suggestion noted.' Forget the interlude. If she ever progressed to having an affair it would be with someone personable and fun, not grumpy and domineering.

Jill leaned across the counter. 'Welcome to Port Weston. Since we'll be working together, give me a call if you have any questions about work or anything else. Or if you're ever hankering for a coffee, I'm available.'

'Thanks for that.' At least someone was pleased to see her here. 'You must be busy, with two jobs.'

'Malcolm, my husband and Dan's brother, runs the pub except when he's out rescuing fools who don't read warning signs.' Jill banged two glasses on the counter. 'What'll it be?'

'Two brandies.' Dan didn't consult Sarah, instead told her, 'Malcolm's the search and rescue coordinator.'

'He was one of the men who'd carried Anders in?' No wonder Jill looked worried.

'Yep.' Dan sipped his drink appreciatively.

'I'll bet he went straight back out to sea after handing his charge over to you.' Jill glared at Dan.

'Hey, steady up. You know there's no way I could've stopped him. A team of Clydesdale horses couldn't have.' Dan reached across and covered Jill's hand with his.

There were tears in the other woman's eyes. 'I know, but he worries me silly. One day he won't come back from a rescue mission.'

Sarah found herself wanting to hug Jill. And she didn't do hugs. Not very often anyway. Certainly not with people she'd only just met. But, then, she wasn't normally rattled by a man like Dan either. Or any man, come to think of it. Must be something in the West Coast air.

Dan said to Jill, 'Don't think like that. You know you wouldn't change him for anything.' Then he turned his attention back to Sarah. 'We'd better get out of our wet clothes. You're shivering non-stop.'

'I'll get some dry things from my car in a moment.' Sarah took a large swallow of brandy, gasping as it burned a track down her throat. 'Wow.'

'Wait till the warmth spreads through you, then you won't be twisting your nose sideways like that.' Dan actually smiled. A long, slow smile that at last went all the way to his eyes.

Blue eyes. So what? It was a common colour. But other blue eyes didn't remind her of hot, lazy days at the beach. Or make her toes curl up in anticipation of exciting things to come. Like what? Who cared? Anything with this man would be exhilarating. Was it possible to become drunk in thirty seconds? Because that's how she felt.

'Where're your keys? I'll get your bag, save you getting another drenching.'

So he could do 'nice'. She dug into her jacket pocket, handed her keyring to him. 'My car's out the front.'

His fingers were warm against hers as he took the keys. 'I know. It's the odd one out amongst the dirty four–wheel-drives and family wagons.'

'It fits in where I come from.'

'I'm sure it does.' Dan hauled the heavy front door open with a jerk. 'Malcolm still hasn't shaved this blasted door, Jill.'

'Tell him, not me.' Jill topped up Sarah's glass even though it wasn't empty. 'Here, a bit more won't hurt you. There's no colour in your cheeks.'

'Thanks, but I'd better go easy on it.' What she really needed was food.

'A hot shower will do you wonders. You can use our bathroom.'

A blast of cold air hit her as Dan poked his head around the door, looking bemused. 'Which bag?'

'The small one.' Hopefully that contained everything she needed.

'You didn't bring a small one,' Dan retorted. 'Why do some women have to cart their whole wardrobe everywhere they go?'

'Guess that's a rhetorical question.' Sarah stared at the closing door.

'Guess he's exaggerating?' Jill's smile warmed her.

'Definitely not *all* my clothes.' Already she liked Jill enough to relax with her. Could she be making a new friend? What was the point? She'd be gone in three months. There again, a friend would be good. She missed the three women she'd known since high school and done all her growing up with.

They'd gone to university together, coming out well versed in life and clutching degrees to their proud chests. Two doctors, one architect and an advertising guru. Three marriages, three mothers; and then there was her. Sometimes she knew she didn't quite belong to the quartet any more. Conversations over dinners and coffee seemed to revolve around children and school timetables, husbands and schedules—things Sarah didn't have a clue about.

Jill was still talking. 'Dan's okay behind that rugged exterior. A pussy cat really. You'll get along fine.'

Sarah knew pussycats, even those in disguise. Dan didn't fit the bill. Tiger was a more apt description. Stealthy when he had to be. Fast when he went for the kill. There was a mix of strength and stubbornness in the set of his chin. His classic handsome features were made interesting by a too-wide mouth and a ragged scar on the point of his chin.

'Here you go, the small one,' Dan said from behind her, causing her to jump. Definitely stealthy.

Jill asked Dan, 'Can you show Sarah to my bedroom? The rescue crew can't be far away and they'll be wanting food.'

At the mention of food Sarah's stomach turned over. 'I'll be as quick as I can, and then I'll give you a hand,' she told Jill. Whoa, back up. She'd help? In a pub? She'd get messy and greasy.

New year, new life, remember?

'Along here.' Dan led the way out to the back and into the private quarters. He opened a door and let her precede him into a double bedroom. 'The bathroom's through there.'

He smelt of damp wool and warm male as she brushed past him. No trace of expensive aftershave or hair product. A clean, uninhibited masculine scent. Sarah hesitated, looked back over her shoulder at him, a sudden longing for something she couldn't put her finger on gripping her.

'What about you?' She was suddenly, oddly, nervous.

Placing her case in the middle of the floor, he turned to leave. His look was cool, his mouth a straight line. 'There's another bathroom next door.'

As she poked through her case for suitable clothes she could hear Dan moving about in that other bathroom, presumably preparing for his shower. An image of a well-muscled body filled her mind. And of a rare but endearing, smile tinged with sadness. What caused that sadness? Of course, she could be wrong about the muscles. She hoped not. A thrill of pleasure warmed her body—and shook her carefully formulated concept of her time in Port Weston.

The jets of water were piping hot against her skin and she gave herself up to them, putting aside thoughts of Daniel Reilly, good and otherwise. Especially those about his body. But how could a bad-tempered man wearing such shapeless clothes ooze so much sex appeal?

The bar was crowded and the mood sombre when Sarah returned. Dan was perched on a stool at the end of the long counter. He waved her over. 'Do you want another drink?'

Schooling her face into a smile, Sarah looked him over as she replied, 'No, thanks.'

His clean shirt fitted snugly across his chest while his dry, worn jeans were tight. Her mouth dried. Beneath the faded denim his thighs were every bit as muscular as she'd imagined.

'Anders's father still hasn't been found.'

'That's not good.' She pulled her shoulders back, focusing on what Dan said, not what he wore.

'That lad needs his father alive and well, not dead and washed up on a beach,' Dan snapped.

'Some people will always take chances.' But not her. She'd focused on her career, foregoing a relationship until she'd specialised, at the same time working on making her father proud.

'They shouldn't, not when they've got a family to consider.'

Sarah totally agreed with him, but diplomatically changed the subject. 'Does Port Weston have a GP? I didn't see one on the beach.'

'Tony Blowers. He's up a valley, delivering a baby, at the moment.'

'Lucky for Anders you were here, then.' She looked around, spied Jill busy pulling beers, and remembered her promise. 'I said I'd help with the food so I'd better find out what's to be done.'

'You did?' He didn't bother disguising his surprise. Those intense cobalt eyes measured her up and down, making her very aware of the snug black slacks and black figure-hugging cotton sweater she'd pulled on.

Dan drawled, 'You might just fit in here yet.'

Pity he didn't sound like he meant it. 'You don't want me here, do you?'

'No, I don't.'

'Thank you for your honesty.' *That* she could deal with. It was a little harder to ignore the fact he wouldn't give her a chance.

'It's nothing personal,' Dan added quietly.

'That's a relief,' she muttered, hoping he meant it and wasn't trying to placate her.

The door crashed back against the wall and drenched men, carrying a stretcher, pressed into the pub. Pat told Dan, 'We've found Starne. He washed up further along and tried to climb the cliff. Fell, and broke his arm, by the look of it.'

'Put him on the couch. It's warmer in here than in a bedroom.' Dan removed cushions and the men lowered the stretcher.

Kneeling down beside the man, Sarah told him, 'I'm Sarah Livingston, a doctor. Can you hear me?'

The man's eyes flew open. 'Where's my son? Is he all right?' He tried sitting up, pushing on his elbows, only to flop back down, groaning with pain.

Dan laid a hand on the man's chest. 'Take it easy.'

Starne tried to knock Dan's hand away with his good arm. 'Is my boy all right? Tell me what happened to him.' The distressed man looked ready to leap up off the couch.

'I'm Dan Reilly, a surgeon. I saw Anders when the rescuers brought him onto the beach.' Dan continued giving Starne the details about his boy, finishing with, 'He's in hospital and doing well.'

Jill helped Sarah tuck blankets around the man. 'I'll have hot-water bottles ready very soon.'

Tears streamed down the man's face. 'The waves banged Anders against the rocks so many times. I couldn't reach him. I thought he was gone.'

'You're both very lucky.' Sarah noted his pulse rate as she talked.

Dan nudged her, spoke softly. 'You're doing great with him, calming him down better than I managed. I'll do the secondary survey.'

She nodded, pleased with the compliment, however small, and silently counted the rise and fall of their patient's chest. 'I'm onto the resps.'

As his fingers felt for contusions Dan told their patient, 'I'll check you over, starting with your head.'

Those firm, gently probing fingers on Starnes's scalp tantalised her. What would they be like on her skin, stroking, teasing, racking up the tension? 'Damn.' She started counting again.

Dan glanced at Sarah as he worked. 'The sooner we get this man to hospital where he can see his boy, the better. I know that's what I'd want if I'd been thinking the worst.'

Sarah's heart squeezed. No parent wanted to outlive their child. As hers had done. 'The downside of being a parent.'

She hadn't realised she'd spoken aloud until Dan said, 'Children cause a lot of worry and heartache, that's for sure. Have you got any?'

'No.'

'I guess now's not the time to ask why not.'

There'd never be a right time. 'Resps slightly slow.'

'Temperature?' Dan asked. At least he could take a hint.

Sarah looked around for Jill. 'You wouldn't have a thermometer?'

'Coming up.' Jill was already halfway out the room.

'Finding anything?' Dan asked Sarah as she palpated Starnes's stomach and liver.

She shook her head. 'These two should buy a lottery ticket.'

'We're certainly not giving you time to settle in quietly, are we?' Dan looked at her for a moment.

No, and being so close to him, breathing his very maleness, added to the sense of walking a swaying tightrope. 'Guess I'll manage,' she muttered, not sure whether she meant the patients or Dan.

Someone handed them hot-water bottles, Sarah reaching for them at the same moment as Dan. Their hands touched, fingers curled around each other's before they could untwine themselves. 'S-sorry.' Sarah snatched her hand back.

'No problem,' snapped Dan, his eyes wide and his face still.

Sarah cringed. Did he think she'd done that on purpose? Surely not? She couldn't deny her attraction for him, but to deliberately grab his hand when she hardly knew him was not her style. Knowing that to say anything in her defence would only make the situation worse, she kept quiet, and again reached for the bottles, making sure to keep well away from Dan.

She placed the bottles in Starnes's armpits and around his groin to maximise his potential for absorbing the warmth.

'The left ankle is swollen, possibly sprained,' Sarah pointed.

'My thoughts exactly.'

'Will we—I—be required to go into theatre if surgery's needed?' Sarah almost hoped not. She was tired and hungry, not in good shape to be operating.

Dan sat back on his haunches and those piercing eyes clashed with hers. 'You don't officially start until tomorrow so if someone's needed I'll do it.'

Why? She'd come for one reason only, and he was holding her back. As her blood started heating up and her tongue forming a sharp reply, he continued, 'You'll want to unpack and settle in at the house. Alison should manage unless she's got another emergency.'

Sarah eased off on her annoyance. How could she stay mad when those eyes bored into her like hot summer rays? 'As long as you know I'm happy to assist if needed.'

A blast of cold air announced the arrival of the ambulance crew. 'Hi, there, again.' Kerry hunkered down beside Dan. 'What've we got this time?'

While Dan relayed the details Sarah stood and stretched her calf muscles, arching her back and pulling her shoulders taut. Dan's gaze followed her movements as he talked to the paramedic, sending a thrill through her. Those eyes seemed to cruise over her, as though they could see right through her to things she never told anyone. Which was plain crazy. How could this man, a stranger really, see through her façade? See beyond the clothes to her soul? He couldn't. Could he?

'Here...' Jill waved across the punters' heads. 'Sandwiches and a coffee. Or would you like something stronger?'

'Coffee's fine.' Grateful for the food, Sarah swallowed her disappointment at the mug of murky instant coffee being slid across the counter towards her. 'Do you still need a hand in the kitchen?'

'I've got it covered. Bea arrived while you were in the

shower, and she's happy as a kid in a sandpit out there cooking up fries.'

'Bea?'

'Dan's sister.'

'Is everyone around here related to him?' Biting into a thick sandwich filled with ham and tomato, Sarah told her stomach to be patient, sustenance was on the way down.

'Not quite.' Dan sent Jill a silent message before turning to Sarah. 'You want to share those?' He nodded at the sandwiches.

Not really. She could eat the lot. 'Sure.' Sarah prodded the plate along the counter towards him, wondering what he hadn't wanted Jill to mention in front of her. 'So you come from a big family.'

'Yep, and they're quite useful at times.'

'What he means is we all run round after him most of the time.' Jill winked at Sarah.

They needn't think she'd play that game. She'd come to run his clinic, nothing else. 'How far from here is the house I'm staying in? I've got some directions but it's probably quicker if you tell me.'

Wariness filtered into Dan's eyes. 'You can follow me shortly.'

'I'd really like to go now.'

'Soon.' Then suddenly his eyes twinkled and he waved at someone behind her. 'Sweetheart, there you are.'

Disappointment jolted Sarah. Of course Dan would have a wife. No man as good looking as this one would be single. Turning to see who he was smiling at, her heart slowed and a lump blocked her throat. The most gorgeous little girl bounded past her, her arms flung high and wide as she reached Dan.

'Daddy, there you are. Auntie Bea brought me here. She made me some fries.'

'Hi, sweetheart. Guess you won't be needing dinner now.' Dan scooped the pink and yellow bundle up and sat her on his knee.

'You're late, Daddy.'

'Sorry, sweetheart.' The man looked unhappy, as though he'd slipped up somehow. 'I had to help Uncle Malcolm.'

Sarah stared at father and daughter. Their eyes were the same shade of blue. They had identical wide, full mouths, the only difference being the little girl's was one big smile while Dan's rarely got past a scowl. Except now, with his daughter in his arms. The lump blocking Sarah's throat slowly evaporated, her heart resumed its normal rhythm. But she melted inside, watching the child.

Since when did children do that to her? Since her wrecked marriage plans had stolen her dream of having a family. Why hadn't Oliver taken that test for the cystic fibrosis gene as he'd promised to do when she'd first told him she was a carrier? Had he been afraid he might find he was imperfect? Did the idea that they might have to decide whether to have children or not if he'd tested positive prove too hard to face? Whatever the answers, he could've talked to her, not gone off and played around behind her back.

'Hello.'

Sarah blinked, looked around, caught the eye of Dan, and, remembering where she was, immediately shoved the past aside. 'Hi.'

The child wriggled around on Dan's knee until she was staring at Sarah. 'Are you the lady who's coming to stay with us?'

Definitely not. 'No, I'm Sarah, a doctor like your father.'

'Sarah…' Dan eased a breath through his teeth. 'Leah's right. You are staying with us.'

'What?' Absolutely not. No one had ever mentioned such a notion. Perspiration broke out on her forehead. Had she missed something? No, she couldn't have. Staying with the local surgeon would've been one detail she'd definitely not overlook. 'The board arranged a hospital house for me.'

'That's right. The one and only hospital house. Where I live with my daughter.'

Her shoulders sagged. He meant it. She was staying at Dan's house. With Dan. And his daughter. 'Your wife?'

'There's just the two of us.' His mouth tightened. 'You'll be comfortable enough.'

No way. She couldn't, wouldn't. What about her un-precedented attraction to him? How could she handle that when they were squeezed into the same place? Then there was the job. He'd always be asking how she was doing. Who had she seen? How was she treating them? Her voice sounded shrill even to her. 'There must be somewhere else. I don't mind a small flat or apartment.'

'This is Port Weston, not Auckland. Rental properties are few and far between. When I say there's nothing else then there's nothing. Believe me, I've checked.' Dan stood up. 'I'm not happy about it either. Unfortunately we're going to have to bump along together—somehow.'

Of course Dan didn't want her staying with him. He didn't want her here, full stop. Tiredness dragged her shoulders down as she stood up from the stool she'd been perched on. 'I'll get my case.'

Bump along together, indeed. Her eyes widened and her face heated up. In a fantasy world, bumping up against Dan might be a whole heap of fun. There were definitely some very intriguing ways. But not in the ho-hum kind of way he was suggesting. Right now she wanted to bang him over the head for letting this happen.

* * *

Swinging Leah down to the floor, Dan watched Sarah striding across the room in a second, clean pair of silly sandals. Her cheeks had coloured up, and her shoulders were stiff. Those amazing eyes were giving off sparks. Passion ran through her veins, he'd bet his job on it.

'Sarah's unhappy, Daddy.' Leah wriggled down to the floor and grabbed his hand.

So was he. He didn't need a sex siren in his home. Not when his body suddenly seemed to be waking up. But he couldn't be blamed for the board crying off outlaying money for separate accommodation for her. It was part of his tenancy agreement that visiting doctors stayed with him. Of course, none of them came for more than a week at a time.

Charlie had also stressed the importance of keeping Dr Livingston happy during her time here. *And then they put her in with me?* Dan bit off an expletive.

Everyone in the district knew that Dr Livingston had to be looked out for. There'd be a concerted effort to make sure she wanted for nothing. The board had a plan. One where the locum would fall in love with Port Weston and its hospital and want to stay on when the contract was up. The plan was doomed from the start. By all appearances Sarah would not stay one minute longer than her contract stated. But the relief that knowledge should engender within him wasn't forthcoming.

Did he want her to stay? No.

Did he want to cut back his working hours permanently? Maybe. If it all worked out with Leah. If he learned how to give her what she needed and didn't fail her like he had last time he'd tried to be a hands-on solo dad. If. If. If.

Then he had to think about those little mistakes he'd begun making at work because he'd become exhausted. Thankfully none of them had been serious. Yet. He'd been doing horrendously long hours and Charlie had been right to start looking for another surgeon to share the load. Those long days had been an excuse to avoid going home and facing the truth that Celine was never coming back. He'd worked until he was so tired he could fall into bed and sleep.

He should be grateful to Sarah. She hadn't forced this holiday on him, he had. By all accounts, she appeared to be the perfect locum, despite being an arrogant 'suit' from Auckland. Okay, not totally arrogant, but she was going to have difficulty fitting in here with those city mannerisms.

His eyes were riveted on the way her legs moved as she negotiated the crowd. Long, long legs that he imagined going— *Get a grip.* She was a colleague, not some female to be drooled over as though he was a sex-starved teenager. He winced. He *was* sex-starved. And only now beginning to notice. It had been so long he could barely remember what making love was like.

Now was not the time to find out. Which was another reason to wish Sarah on the other side of the planet.

Reaching her, he leaned down for her case at the same moment that she grabbed the handle.

'Let me,' he said quietly. And tried to breathe normally. The skin on the back on her hand was soft, smooth. Strands of blonde hair settled on her cheek. His heart stuttered. Such a mundane and delightful thing.

'I can manage,' she retorted.

'I know, but let me.'

Her mouth fashioned a fleeting smile. 'Thank you.'

This close he could see the dark shadows staining her upper cheeks. 'Do you feel up to driving, or would you rather come back for your car in the morning?'

'What, and have you hauling all those cases between

vehicles?' She managed another almost-smile. 'I'll follow you. Is it far?'

'About five kilometres, on the other side of town.' Thinking of the short street of shops, mostly farming and fishing suppliers, he knew Sarah would be shocked. There was one, surprisingly good, café run by a couple who'd opted for the quiet life after many years of running a business in Christchurch. Hopefully their coffee would be up to this woman's expectations.

Sarah pulled the outside door open. 'Allow me.'

'Oh, no. After you.' Dan gripped the edge of the door above her head.

She shrugged and ducked under his arm, out the doorway, bang into a throng of people crowding the steps. Leah danced along behind her. Fishermen crowded the porch, gathering to celebrate the rescue operation's success.

'Careful, lady!' someone exclaimed. 'Those steps are slippery.'

Sarah teetered at the edge of the top step. She put a hand out for balance but there was no railing to grab. Tripping, she made a desperate attempt to regain her footing. The heel of her sandal twisted, tipped her sideways and she went down hard, crying out as she thumped onto the concrete.

'Sarah.' Dan dropped her case, pushed through the men to crouch down beside her. 'Don't move. Let me look.'

She was on her backside, one leg twisted under her. 'I'm fine. Just help me up, please.' She put a hand out to him.

'Wait until I've checked your leg.'

'There's nothing wrong with it. It's my foot that hurts. Probably bruised.' Putting her hands down on either side of her hips, she tried to stand, but couldn't. 'Are you going to give me a hand, or do I ask someone else?'

'Sit still.' Those sandals weren't helping. 'How do you

expect to be able to stand up on that narrow spike you call a heel?'

'Typical male. Women are born to walk on heels,' she retorted through clenched teeth. Leaning to one side, she straightened her leg out from under her bottom, and bit down on her lip.

He gently felt her ankle, then her foot. The tissue was soft, already swelling, and her sharp intake of breath confirmed his suspicions. 'I think you've broken at least one bone. An X-ray will verify that.'

He'd call the radiology technician on the way to A and E. Technically a fracture in the foot could wait until the morning, but he didn't want this particular patient finding their small hospital lacking.

'That easily? That's crazy.' Sarah shook her head at her foot as though it was responsible for her predicament, and not those ridiculous shoes.

So much for Sarah taking over his practice this week. He should be pleased he'd be going to work. But even he understood his promise to Leah was meant to be kept. It didn't matter he was terrified he wouldn't measure up as a full-time dad for three months, and that Leah might revert to the disconsolate little girl he'd finally handed over to his family to help. He'd promised to try. Now, before he'd even started, their time together had to be postponed. He might've resented Sarah coming here, but right now he'd give anything to have her back on both feet and eager to get started.

CHAPTER THREE

SARAH hobbled after Dan as he carried a sleepy bundle of arms and legs into the weatherboard house. Leah had been tucked up in Jill's bed when Dan had finally had time to pick up his little girl on the way home from hospital.

Guilt for keeping this tot out late swamped Sarah. Due to her clumsiness Leah hadn't been with her dad when she should've been.

'Make yourself comfortable while I tuck Leah into bed,' Dan snapped over his shoulder, not easing Sarah's heavy heart.

He had every right to be annoyed with her. As had the other people whose time she'd intruded upon. Jill had driven her car here and someone had followed to pick her up. The radiology technician had gone into the hospital especially for her. And then there was Dan, who hadn't bothered to hide how he felt about this development.

Injuring her foot was a pain in the butt for her, too. If she hadn't been so intent on putting some space between her and Dan, it wouldn't have happened. The X-ray showed two broken bones. Her foot was twice its normal size and hurt like crazy. Thank goodness for painkillers.

Ignoring his order, Sarah followed Dan down the hall. Was he a good dad? Inexplicably she wanted to watch him tuck the child into bed, wanted another peep of Leah looking so cute with a blanket hitched under her chin and a bedraggled teddy bear squashed against her face. 'She's gorgeous,' she whispered, afraid of waking the girl, worried Dan might tell her to go away.

'Especially when she's asleep.' Dan's soft smile made Sarah's heart lurch. His big hand smoothed dark curls away from Leah's forehead. 'Actually, she's gorgeous all the time but, then, I'm biased.'

'So you should be.'

Dan placed feather-light kisses on his daughter's cheeks and forehead. 'Goodnight, sweetheart.'

From deep inside, in the place she hid unwanted emotions, something tugged at Sarah. A reminder of how much she'd been looking forward to having a family of her own when she and Oliver were married. That man had taken a lot from her.

'Are you all right?' Dan stood in front of her.

'Yes, of course.' Or could these emotions come from something else? An image of her own father tucking her into bed floated across her mind. As if. That was a fantasy. Dad had always been at work at her bedtime. No, she was overtired and getting confused.

'Your room is at the end of the hall. You've got an en suite bathroom so you won't have plastic toys to trip over.' Dan turned back towards the kitchen. 'I'll bring your cases in.'

'Thank you. I'll put the kettle on. Do you want a hot drink?'

'If you wait a few minutes, I'll get that. Go and put your foot up.'

'Dan, I am not incapable of boiling water.'

Loud knocking prevented Dan from answering, which by the tightening of his mouth and the narrowing of his eyes had saved her a blasting. Sarah trudged after him, her gait awkward because of the clunky moonboot clipped around her injured foot.

Dan growled at the visitor, 'Charlie, come in. I take it you've heard the news.'

'Three times since I got home from the river.' A dapper man in his sixties stepped into the kitchen. 'How is Dr Livingston?'

'I'm fine.' Sarah made it through the kitchen door and went towards the visitor with her hand out. 'Sarah Livingston.'

'Charlie Drummond. I'm sorry about your accident, lass.' Warmth emanated from his twinkling eyes.

She shrugged. 'Bit of a nuisance but nothing I can't deal with.'

'It changes everything.' Dan frowned. 'I've already told the nanny I'll need her for at least a week.'

Charlie shook his head. 'Oh, no, you don't. You're on leave. That's non-negotiable.'

'For goodness' sake, Charlie. There is no one else.' Dan's voice rose a few decibels. 'Until Sarah's back on her feet I'm your surgeon.'

'I'll ring around, see who I can find. Might don some scrubs myself.'

'It took months to find Sarah. You haven't got a chance in Hades of finding someone quickly, if at all.'

Sarah winced. 'Excuse me, but there's nothing wrong with my hearing.' She'd made a mess of things so she'd sort it. 'Or my brain. I'll be at work tomorrow.'

'Don't be ridiculous,' Dan snapped.

No one talked to her like that. 'Maybe late in the morning but I will be there. Trust me.' Sarah braced as a glare sliced at her, but when Dan said nothing she turned to the other man. 'I'm really sorry this has happened but it won't affect the board's plans too much.'

'Sarah, get real.' Dan dragged a hand through his damp

hair, making the thick curls stand up. Cute. Mouthwatering. Totally out of bounds.

Parking her bottom against the edge of the table, Sarah repeated, 'I'll be at work tomorrow.' She had to take control of the situation before Dan took over completely. 'Is there any surgery scheduled?'

Charlie smiled. 'It's a public holiday, remember? You've got a light week, emergencies not withstanding.'

'I'd planned on taking you in to meet any staff on duty, check out the theatre, and go over patient notes.' Dan shook his head in despair.

'Then there's no problem. We'll decide how to deal with emergencies if and when they arise.' Dan would be the last person she'd call for help. Having caused him enough trouble already, she was unusually contrite. 'If I have to, I can operate sitting down. It won't be easy but it's possible. Let's leave tomorrow's plans as they stand.'

And she could spend the night hoping she'd be fighting fit in the morning.

There was a speculative look in Dan's eyes as he regarded her, his arms folded over his thought-diverting chest.

'What?' How would it feel to curl up with him, her head lying against that chest? Protected and comforted? Huh! The last thing Dan Reilly was was comforting.

He shrugged. 'We'll see.'

'Sarah, I appreciate you coming down here at such short notice. I'm sure we can make this work until you're fully recovered,' Charlie said.

Dan grunted.

Sarah gripped the edge of the table tight as she sucked back a sharp retort. No need to aggravate Dan more than she already had. But hell if it wasn't tempting.

* * *

Dan was dog-tired. Every muscle ached. His head throbbed. He'd performed urgent surgery for a punctured lung following a car-versus-tree accident at three that morning. When he'd crawled into bed afterwards Leah had been grizzly so he'd had a squirming child to keep him awake for the remainder of the night. Then the nanny had been grumpy when he'd woken her for breakfast. Throw in a near-drowning, Sarah's arrival and accident, and he was almost comatose.

He peeped in on Leah. Lucky kid, dead to the world, unaware of the drama that had been going on and how it would affect the holiday he'd promised her.

Sarah's assumption that she'd be able to take over tomorrow wouldn't work, but he was fed up with arguing. Women. When they were in the mood they knew how to be difficult. It came naturally, like curves and bumps.

He sucked a breath. What was happening to him? He didn't usually give women more than cursory glances. Truth, with most of them he wouldn't even notice that they were female. But Sarah had woken him up in a hurry. He didn't know how. He just knew she had. Why her, of all people? Because she was one damned desirable lady.

She was one pain in the neck.

They were opposites: syrup and vinegar.

Opposites attracted.

He shouldn't be thinking about her except in her professional role. Not possible when they were going to be sharing such close living quarters. So how was a man to cope? How could he ignore what was right in front of him? Even with one foot strapped in that ugly moon boot she was more distracting than was good for him.

'Daddy?' Leah murmured in her sleep.

Gorgeous, that's what Sarah had called his little girl, and she was right. Beautiful, innocent, and in need of a

mother figure. Someone special she could call hers; not all
the aunts and cousins who were there for her. Someone to
call Mummy. Someone he wasn't ready to bring into their
lives.

'Go back to sleep, little one.' He tucked the blanket
over her tiny shoulder. When she was like this he believed
himself capable of being a good dad. It was the bad times
when she hurt or cried that undermined his confidence.
He loved how Leah trusted and loved him without question. He certainly didn't deserve it. Not when she spent
most of her time in day care or with various other people
while he ran around being busy and avoiding the issues
that threatened to swamp him.

'You're so beautiful, my girl. Just like your mother.
She'd be proud of you just for being so special and funny
and adorable.' *But would Celine be pleased with the way
her sister and mine are bringing you up for me? More like
she'd be disappointed in the way I've ducked for cover
every time the going's got tough.* He kissed Leah's soft
cheek, his throat tightening at the feel of her soft skin. 'I
love you.'

He stood gazing down at his child, the most important
person in the world, and his heart swelled to the point it
hurt. He mightn't have done much of a job of it yet but
being a dad was so different from anything else he'd ever
tried. Now he had to work hard to make up for lost time,
learn to be there for Leah all the time. Where to start?
What to do? Ask Bea and Jill. They wouldn't hold back in
telling him, or coming to his rescue. He shuddered. No, it
was time to stand on his own two feet.

Back in the lounge he dropped into a large armchair
and studied the other female in his house. The enigmatic
one. The more he saw of Sarah, the more she piqued his
curiosity. Why had she been available to come here at such

short notice? He'd read her CV, knew she held a partnership in some fancy, private surgical hospital with her father and some other dude. So why'd she been available?

'Does Leah sleep right through the night?' Sarah spoke in her lilting voice, now tinged with exhaustion.

'Like a log.' Usually. When she wasn't crying for Mummy. Which happened less and less these days, he realised with a start.

Sarah didn't have children and her résumé hadn't mentioned a husband. Why, considering she was thirty-five? Divorced? What if she hated kids? His heart thumped. He wouldn't accept that. 'Are you used to being around children?'

'Not a lot.'

'Got any nieces or nephews?' This wasn't looking good. How would she cope with Leah?

'No.'

'Siblings?'

'My brother died when he was eighteen. I was sixteen at the time.' Her voice was flat, but there was pain in her eyes, in her fists on her knees.

Her words sent shivers down his spine, made him gasp. 'Sarah, I'm truly sorry. I can be too nosey at times.' There'd been a stoplight in her eyes, but he'd pressed on with his questions regardless, too concerned about his own problems.

What to say now? A tragedy like that stayed with a person for ever. What had happened to her brother? Was there more to her story? For sure he wasn't about to ask. Not with that massive chunk of hurt radiating out from those eyes. But he understood firsthand how death changed things. Everything crashed to a halt. You didn't even notice life was still going on around you. Only after months of agony did you slowly begin to move again, begin to func-

tion semi-normally. It took even longer to recover from
the guilt. 'How awful.' How inadequate.

She jerked her head affirmatively. 'It certainly is.'

Is. Not was. Hadn't she got over it a tiny bit? Her fingers
were twisted and interlaced in her lap, her eyes downcast.
Dan fought the impulse to reach for her, hold her safe. A
friendly gesture that she definitely wouldn't appreciate.
When she finally raised her head he saw sadness and loneliness lurking in those compelling eyes.

Then he surprised himself. 'Leah was two when her
mother died.' Which was too much information. He didn't
want to share personal details with Sarah, not even one.
It was enough that they were sharing his practice, and his
home.

Celine slipped into his mind again. For the past two
years he'd taken the approach of ignoring the gaping hole
left by her passing, hoping that one day he'd find it filled
in with life's trivia. In reality he should've been facing up
to things, like looking after his daughter instead of leaving that to everyone else. Like accepting he couldn't wind
back the clock and pack Celine up to take her home to the
city she'd loved and missed. Back to her interfering mother
who'd put those ideas of distrust in Celine's head.

'That's really tough. For both of you.' Sarah's tone was
compassionate. 'How does Leah cope?'

'She's very resilient.' More so than him. 'Most of the
time. She has her moments. We manage.' Sort of. With a
lot of help. 'I hope you'll get on with her.'

'I doubt I'll see much of her.' Then she changed the
subject. 'Tell me how your local health board operates. It
seems to be very successful when others in remote areas
have failed.'

'It wasn't always like this but with a bit of lateral thinking the board members came up with a scheme to employ

a full-time surgeon. Instead of sending patients out of the area, they contracted for the overflow from Christchurch public hospitals. It was a perfect solution for my wife and me as we wanted to be near my family once Leah was born.' Yes, *we* wanted to make the move. Celine had been as much for it as he had. She'd loved her horses; enjoyed getting to know Jill, the sister she hadn't grown up with. When had he forgotten that? Had he been so immersed in self-pity that he hadn't looked at all sides of the problem? Celine had had a part to play in her welfare too. Because the other side of the story was that he fitted in here, loved giving back to his community through his work.

'So you grew up in Port Weston?' An alien female voice intruded.

He blinked. Sarah sat opposite him, an expression of polite interest on her beautiful face. 'Yes, I did.' What had they been talking about? Of course, the hospital. What else? That's all Sarah would be interested in. 'There's been a flow-on effect for the town from having the surgical unit here. Most patients coming for elective surgery bring friends or relatives with them. Those people need entertaining, feeding, housing.'

'So you've got a lively metropolis out there somewhere?' Her sweet, tired smile pulled at his heart.

How could that be when he'd known her less than twelve hours? Something to think about—later.

Back to her question. 'Not quite what you're used to.' The understatement of the year. 'But the shops are improving, and you'll be glad to know our café is first rate.'

'Can't go past a great coffee shop.'

He saw her stifled yawn in her tightened mouth and clenched jaw, and leapt up. 'Here I am blathering on and you're half-asleep. I'll help you get ready for bed.' And gain some freedom from those all-seeing eyes.

Taking her elbow, he helped her up onto her good foot, then without warning swung her into his arms and carried her down to her room. She felt wonderful. Soft. Warm. Desirable.

He croaked, 'Stop wriggling. You're making it difficult for me to hold you.' *And causing certain soft feminine parts of your anatomy to rub against my chest. Very nice.* Shocked described how he felt. And hot. Hard. Stunned.

'Then put me down,' she responded, instantly tense and remaining that way until he sat her on the bed and bent down to remove the moon boot.

'I'll do that.' She yanked her leg away from him, groaning when pain jagged her.

'Let's be reasonable about this. You're all-out tired and with my help you'll be in bed a lot quicker. Probably with much less pain. I am a doctor, remember?' Great logic that.

'I'm sure you're right, but I'll manage,' she wheezed through gritted teeth. 'I have to get used to this boot as soon as possible.'

So she was concerned she wouldn't be functioning properly tomorrow.

'Take it easy and leave worrying about how you're going to get around till the morning.' He stared at the three cases he'd hauled in earlier. Gucci, of course. 'Which bag has your night things?'

Sarah took the negligee he finally found and pointed to the door. 'I'll do this.'

Plastering his best bedside manner on his face, he put a hand under her arm and, trying to ignore his increasing pulse, said, 'There's the easy way, and the hard way. Let's go for easy.'

She tipped her head back to stare up at him and he saw the exhaustion in her eyes, in her loose shoulders, in the slack hands lying in her lap.

'You're right.' And then she lifted her top up over her head.

Dan's mouth dried, and it was a lifetime before he moved to help her. Her creamy skin was like warm satin. The swell of her breasts in their frothy, black lace cups caused him to bite painfully into his bottom lip. His hands shook when he took the garment from her and tossed it onto a chair in the corner. It missed.

Her fingers fumbled at the button on her waistband. He tried to help but she pushed his hands away. Lifting his eyes to her face, he saw the faint pink colour rising in her cheeks. Had he embarrassed her with his quickening interest? *Daniel Reilly, you need your head read. You have to live with this woman for twelve whole weeks. Keep everything above board.*

'Here, I'll lift you so you can slide your trousers down,' he muttered, and placing his hands on her elbows focused on being practical. As if. But he tried.

Next he knelt to remove the moon boot, taking care not to jar her foot. Under his fingers her satin skin reminded him of sultry summer nights. He ached to caress it. Common sense prevailed. Just.

'Thanks.' Sarah flopped back against the pillow, pulling the covers over herself. Then she closed her eyes. The determination and fierce independence she'd displayed all evening disappeared, leaving her looking defenceless. Any pain from her foot was hidden behind her eyelids.

Without thinking, he reached out to brush a strand of hair off her cheek, hesitated, withdrew. How would he explain such impulsiveness? She was one tough lady, and he suspected that sassy attitude hid a lot of things from the world. Things he'd like to learn more about. But right now it was way past time to get out of her room. 'See you in the morning.'

He'd made her door when he heard her whisper. 'Is it safe to open a window? It's very stuffy in here.'

'That's because we're between rain spells again.' He crossed to the windows. 'And of course it's safe. You're not in the city now.'

'I suppose you leave your doors unlocked.' She rolled onto her side and the covers slid off her shoulders.

Again Dan's gaze was drawn to her flawless skin and her negligee highlighting the swell of her breasts. He mightn't have had a sex life for a very long time but suddenly that didn't seem to mean a thing. It was as though he'd—she'd—flicked a switch and, whammo!

'Just one window open?' he said breathlessly, his throat as tight as a clamped artery.

'I think so. Is that the surf I can hear?'

'Yes. We're quite close to the sea.' He made for the door again, this time with no intention of stopping, regardless of what she said. *Keep talking so she can't get a word in.* 'The high fence surrounding the property is to stop Leah from wandering down to the water. Even with the main road and a stretch of grassed land between us, I don't take any chances.'

Of course he wouldn't. That much Sarah had figured out already. A yawn stretched her mouth. Despite the exhaustion gripping her, she doubted she was about to get much sleep. If the pain didn't keep her awake then a load of other concerns would. For starters, she'd let Dan down big time. He needed her here, whether he accepted it or not.

Already she sensed her time in Port Weston wasn't just about sorting out her own life. She may have come to free up Dan's life, but now she wanted to do more for him. And for his daughter. But what? Her experience of children and happy families was non-existent.

An image of a darling little girl floated across her mind. Leah. How to remain aloof when the child had already touched her heart? She had to. That's all there was to it. Getting attached to Dan's daughter had no place in her life. And she must not listen to the increasingly loud ticking of her biological clock.

What about Dan himself? His wife had died. No wonder he was running solo here with Leah. It wouldn't be easy to put his loss behind him with a child to care for.

So she had to get a grip on her unprecedented attraction to him. But what would his kisses be like? Hungry? Soft? Demanding? *Hello, Sarah, back to earth, please.*

The man crashing through her head placed a glass by her bed. 'Thought you might like some water.'

'Thanks.' She clenched her fists. How long had he been standing there? 'I don't usually make such a hash of things. I'm truly sorry.' But she felt even more regretful she wouldn't taste his kisses. Kisses had to be avoided if she was to keep her relationship with Dan strictly professional.

'It was an accident, okay?'

'You're not putting off doing all those dad things Leah's hankering for.' She pulled the bedcover back up to her neck. He could stop peeking at her negligee. He'd already had more than an eyeful. Admittedly she'd enjoyed the appreciative glint in his eyes. Enjoyed? Get real. When he looked at her so intently she became a very desirable woman. What a salve for her battered self-esteem. By having an affair, Oliver had made her feel unwanted, undesirable.

Dan hesitated, his hand on the light switch. 'Why don't

you wear oversized T-shirts to bed, like most women I know?'

'They didn't have any in my colour.'

How many women did he see in their night attire?

CHAPTER FOUR

'HURRY up, Daddy. We'll be late,' Leah shrieked the next morning, bouncing between Dan's knees as he brushed her hair.

'Stand still, young lady,' Dan answered at a much lower decibel, his eyes narrowed as he fought the hair into submission.

'Flicker's waiting for me.' Leah bit into her bottom lip as she struggled to keep from jiggling.

Sarah grinned at Dan. 'You need to speed up, man.'

'I'm never fast enough for Leah. She was born in a hurry.'

'Flicker doesn't go very fast. Auntie Bea won't let him cos I could fall off.' Leah twisted around to stare at her father. 'You're riding Jumbo.'

'I was afraid of that.' Dan smiled at his daughter, love shining out of his eyes. 'Of course, if you don't stand quietly while I do these ponytails, neither of us will be riding any horse today.'

'Daddy, we must. Flicker will miss me.'

'Is Flicker your horse?' Sarah asked the little girl.

Big blue eyes peeped back at her from under an overlong fringe. 'He's Auntie Bea's but I'm the only person allowed to ride him. Can you ride a horse?'

'Me? No way. I don't like being so far off the ground.' Anything higher than a short stool was too high.

Dan wrapped an elastic tie around a ponytail, his gaze firmly on the wayward curls he was struggling to contain. The part between the ponytails was well to the side of the middle of Leah's head. 'Have you ever tried?'

'Once, when I was about Leah's age. The horse took exception to having me on its back and tossed me off. No amount of bribery got me back on.'

'I haven't been throwed off.' Leah's eyes glowed with pride.

Dan put the brush down and reached for the ribbons lying on the table. 'Nearly there, missy. Flicker will think you're looking cool today.' His mouth curved with a smile just for his daughter. Pride and love mingled across his face, his big hands gentle as he tried to fashion the blue ribbons into bows.

Leah stood absolutely still for the first time, her elbows resting on Dan's thighs, her little freckle-covered face puckered up in thought.

Sarah caught her breath. They belonged together. Father and daughter. If only she had a camera to take a picture showing the love between these two. The air was warm with it. There was a vulnerability in Dan's eyes she'd never expected from the gruff man she'd known so far.

Her stomach tightened. What these two had was special, something she'd like to share. What? She wanted to be with Dan and his daughter? Only for the time she was in Port Weston, of course. Of course. Because she still loved Oliver, hard as that was to admit after everything he'd done to her.

'Sarah, do I look pretty?' Leah bounced in front of her, unwittingly dragging Sarah's attention onto her and away from the desperate thoughts that threatened to ruin her day. Leah had pulled away from Dan's hands, effectively ruining the bow he was working on.

'Very pretty. Now, hand me those bows and I'll help your dad make you even prettier.' Her throat closed over as she quickly tied two big bows, trying hard not to feel as though she was missing out on something very important. She reached over and flicked one of the ponytails, making Leah giggle. 'If he hasn't already, then Flicker's going to fall in love with you.'

Who wouldn't fall in love with the child? Panic seized Sarah. What if she did? She mustn't. There were too many complications for all of them otherwise. And the child must be protected first and foremost.

Dan shook his head in disgust. 'That easy, huh?' He stood and stretched. 'If you're not careful, the job's yours while you're here.'

She might get to like that. 'Guess you've never had long hair.'

'You think I should've put my hair in ponytails? What sort of guys did you mix with as a teenager?' He blinked at her, but she obviously wasn't meant to answer. 'We'd better get going before my sister sends out a search party.' He ran his knuckles over his bristly chin, worry clouding his eyes. 'I hope I survive the morning.'

'You can't keep up with Leah?' Sarah challenged with a laugh, trying to lift his spirits.

'Sometimes I wonder if she's really only four, she's so confident.'

'Four to your, what? Thirty-two,-three?'

'Flattery is supposed to get you everything. Try thirty-five.' His lips widened from tight to relaxed.

The same age as her. 'Where'd you go to med school?' They'd have been training around the same time.

'Dunedin, then Christchurch to specialise. You?'

'Auckland and London.' Where she'd met Oliver. At first they'd been friends. Liar. She'd thought he was hot from the moment she'd set eyes on him, and he'd known it. But she'd finished her specialist training before succumbing to his charm and going out with him.

'Daddy, come on.' Leah grabbed his hand and began tugging him towards the back door.

'Sure you'll be all right? Nothing you need, like a sandwich, another cup of tea?' Reluctance shadowed his voice. Was it the horse riding he worried he couldn't cope with? Or Leah? 'You could come with us.'

'I don't think so. I don't know much about entertaining children.'

'Sure you don't want to start this morning?'

'Stop procrastinating. Apart from getting a sore backside, you'll be fine. Look how excited Leah is about this.'

'Yeah, that's the problem. And the fact I've forgotten which end of a horse is which.'

'You're not expected to be an expert. Dan, go, now.' Sarah deliberately stood up and turned her back on him, reaching for the kettle to show she could manage. She didn't turn around until the door closed quietly behind her.

Then she stared out the window, watching Dan's vehicle bouncing down the drive, rolling along the highway until it disappeared out of sight around a bend. The tightness in her shoulders eased. This was the first time she'd been alone, without Dan in reach, since she'd charged down the beach yesterday. She should be pleased not to have his disturbing eyes watching her, his acerbic tongue ready to refute everything she said.

Instead loneliness threatened to swamp her. In Auckland she never felt lonely, despite not having a wide circle of friends. There were shops or the hospital to keep her occupied. Here—here there wasn't a lot in the way of distractions now that Dan had gone out.

Beyond the road the sea kept rolling onto the shore. Wind whipped spume off the hypnotic wave-tops. A long, wild coastline with no one in sight. 'What a godforsaken place.' She kept staring at it until a kind of peace stole over her. 'But it's sort of beautiful.'

The strident tones of the phone awoke Sarah from a deep sleep. Confused, she stared around at the unfamiliar room. Her vision filled with soft, warm colours: blues, a dash of yellow, a hint of green. A complete contrast to the clean, white walls and terracotta furnishings of her Auckland apartment. Then she remembered. Port Weston. Bad-tempered Dr Reilly. Her broken bones.

Pushing off the couch, she hopped to the table where she'd unwisely left the phone. Her moon boot bumped against a chair. Pain snatched her breath away. Gripping the back of the chair, she fumbled with the phone, anxious not to miss the call and give Dan another reason to believe she was incompetent.

'Hello, Dr Reilly's residence.'

'This is the hospital A and E department. Is Dan there?'

Apprehension made Sarah straighten up. Please, not an emergency. 'Dan's gone horse riding at his sister's.'

'No wonder I can't reach him on his cellphone.' The caller sounded harassed. 'No coverage up there.'

'Can I do anything? I'm Sarah Livingston, a doctor.'

'Thank goodness.' The relief was obvious. 'I'm Alison Fulton, A and E specialist. We've got a six-year-old girl with appendicitis and, if I'm not mistaken, we need to hurry. Apparently the child's been complaining of stomach pains for hours.'

'I'll come straight away.' This wouldn't be so bad. She'd be able to handle an appendectomy sitting down.

'Thank you so much.'

'You're aware I can't drive at the moment?' Sarah knew how well hospital grapevines worked.

'Dan mentioned it. I'll get someone to pick you up.' Then the specialist's voice changed, became concerned. 'You do feel up to this? I don't want you to think you have to come in. I haven't tried Charlie's phone yet. He's my last resort, though I know he's gone after another trout.'

So Dan had been warning people about her situation. Looking out for her? Or indicating he'd prefer he was called in so he had an excuse to return to work? Putting all the confidence she could muster into her voice, Sarah reassured Alison. 'Operating will be fine. Just send that car.'

She crossed her fingers. Just the one op, please.

Wee Emma Duncan's face was contorted with a mix of fear and pain as she lay on the bed, tucked into her father's side. Her eyes were enormous in her pale face. Neither of her parents looked much better.

'Emma, I'm Dr Sarah, and I'm going to make your tummy better.' Sarah winked at the frightened girl. Then she introduced herself to the parents, trying to ignore their obvious glances at her crutches. 'Mr and Mrs Duncan, Theatre's ready so we'll be getting started very shortly.'

'Where's Dan?' Emma's father asked.

'I'm his replacement while he's on leave.' Sarah forced a smile at their obvious distrust of a stranger. 'Please don't be worried about the fact that I've broken a couple of bones in my foot. I assure you my operating skills are still intact.'

'It's just we know Dan,' Mr Duncan explained.

Not used to being questioned about her role, Sarah tried

to imagine what these parents must be going through. They'd be terrified for their beautiful girl. 'I do understand, but the real concern's whether I'm good at what I do. Dan and Charlie must believe I am, or they wouldn't have taken me on.'

'Never mind the fact that there wasn't a queue of applicants for the job,' Sarah muttered to herself. That wasn't the point. She was a good surgeon.

Emma's mother gazed at her daughter with such love Sarah's heart expanded. To be a parent had to be one of the most wondrous privileges on earth. For the second time that day deep regret at her childlessness gripped Sarah. Within twenty-four hours Port Weston had got to her in ways she'd never have expected. Or was it Dr Dan sneaking in under her skin that had her emotions rocking all over the place? Because something sure was.

Back to Emma. 'Do you want to tell me how long you've had this tummyache?' Sarah asked.

'Em started complaining first thing this morning, Doctor.' Her father still looked uncertain but thankfully he answered all Sarah's questions thoroughly and quickly.

Sarah read the lab results and Alison Fulton's notes. Emma's high white-cell count backed the diagnosis of appendicitis. But it worried Sarah that there were indications of a burst appendix.

An orderly appeared at the doorway. 'Hey, Emma. How's my favourite niece? I'm going to take you for a short ride on the bed.'

Was everyone related in this town? How weird was that? Sarah's living relatives numbered two, her mother and father. She couldn't begin to imagine what it would be like to have cousins, uncles, grandparents, all those extra people in her life. Certainly had no idea how different growing up might have been. If she ever fell in love again, maybe she should find a man with relatives she could come to know and love. Her ex had only one sister who lived in London and they weren't close.

Sarah spoke to Emma's mother. 'It's Gayle, isn't it?'

The woman nodded. 'Sorry if we seem silly but—'

'It's okay. I know I'm asking the impossible but please try not to worry too much. I'll come and see you the moment I've finished,' Sarah tried to reassure her.

Then a nurse helped Sarah to scrub up. Surrounded by people she didn't know, about to operate at a hospital she'd never worked in before, it all seemed a little surreal. But theatres were theatres wherever she went. Nurses and anaesthetists did the same job everywhere. She just had to get over herself and concentrate on Emma's operation.

Jill popped her head around the corner. 'Heard you got called in and thought you might like a friendly face.'

'Yes, definitely.' Warmth washed through Sarah as she raised a thumb in acknowledgment, thrilled that Jill had been so considerate.

'We've found you a stool if you need it,' Jill told her.

In Theatre Hamish, the anaesthetist Sarah had met moments earlier, administered the drug that would keep Emma unconscious throughout the operation.

Sarah shuffled awkwardly on her injured foot, trying to find the most comfortable position without having to use the stool. Taking a deep breath, she lifted a scalpel and looked around at the attending staff. 'Ready?'

She concentrated on finding the infected appendix and assessing the situation. 'We're in luck. It hasn't perforated.'

Jill held out a clamp in a gloved hand. 'Poor kid. She still must've been hurting bad.'

Sarah clamped off all circulation to the appendix. 'Wonder what took her family so long to bring her in?'

'They live about a hundred and fifty kilometres from

here, up a valley in very difficult terrain,' Jill explained. 'It's no easy ride out of those hills.'

Sarah moved abruptly to one side to get a better view of the incision. Pain shot through her foot, diverting her attention briefly.

'You okay?' Hamish was watching her closely. 'Use the stool.'

'Thanks, but I prefer standing.' The stool might be too clumsy. Hamish's concern for her was nice. So far, working with this team was going well: no tension, everyone confident in their role yet also believing in each other's competence. Very different from the surgical hospital back home where everyone seemed to be trying to outdo each other on a regular basis. Today, here, she was beginning to understand how jaded she'd become and that her father might've been right to nudge her out of town. Working in this theatre was like a breath of fresh air.

Finally Sarah began tying off internally. The appendix stump. The blood vessels she'd had to cut. Her hands were heavy, like bricks. More thread required. Her back ached from the lopsided stance she'd maintained to counterbalance her boot-encased foot.

There was a soft whooshing sound as the door swung open, then closed. Sarah didn't have to be told Dan had arrived. With every nerve ending in her body she sensed his presence. She tried to concentrate on her work and not glance up, but her eyes lifted anyway. She looked directly at him. Warmth spread through her tired muscles and momentarily she felt recharged and capable of going on for ever.

He was fully scrubbed up, looking at Emma carefully. Checking up on his replacement? Sarah tried to read his eyes, saw a reprimand.

'Want a hand?' His voice was muffled behind his mask,

but there was no mistaking his anger. What exactly had she done wrong?

'I'm perfectly capable of finishing off.' She didn't need his help. Except that moments ago she'd noted how tired she'd become. Emma was her priority, not her pride. 'Could you close up for me?' she asked quietly.

Admiration filtered through his eyes, toning down the anger. Relief relaxed Sarah. She'd done the right thing. Gingerly shuffling sideways, she made room for Dan. Despite his unnecessary disapproval, it felt so right standing beside him here in Theatre, two professionals working to help Emma.

'Alison's message came through as we got to the bottom of the valley so I dropped Leah off at her nanny's and came straight over in case I was required. Obviously I wasn't.' Dan deftly pressed the suture needle through the flesh to pull another section of the wound together. 'You still should've got someone in to assist you, under the circumstances.'

'I'm glad it wasn't anything difficult,' Sarah admitted. But when Dan raised one eyebrow at her in an 'I told you so' fashion she retorted, 'There wasn't anyone else. Alison checked, and she was too busy to help.'

'I can see Emma was in excellent hands.' The grudging admittance in his voice confused her. Why did he find it hard to accept she knew what she was doing?

As Sarah swabbed away a speck of blood Jill reached across from the other side of the operating table to do it. Lifting her gaze to meet the other woman's, Sarah nearly choked. Jill was winking at her, her eyes holding a knowing glint. It could be interpreted in a trillion ways, but Sarah bet Jill still had ideas of matchmaking. A scheme that was doomed to crash and burn. Sarah had to go back to Auckland, if not at the end of her contract then some time in the next six months. Her father didn't mean for her to walk away from her partnership, just recoup her energy. Neither did she want to. She liked her comfortable lifestyle and the predictability of her job in Auckland.

Get real. You were bored. Exhausted. Fed up. Burying yourself in work to get over a broken heart. Why would you want to go back to that? Because it was the only life she knew and understood.

So, learn a new one. This is the perfect opportunity. A trickle of excitement seeped into her veins, lifted her spirits. Could she do that? Did she want to? She grinned. Possibly.

She headed for the scrub room, struggling to remove her gown. Her fingers fumbled with the knots on the ties.

'Let me do that.'

She hadn't heard Dan come in. 'Thanks.'

His fingers covered hers, took the cotton ties and tugged lightly to undo the impossible knots. 'You ready to go home?'

Home? 'Sure.'

Dan's fingers rested on the back of her neck. A simple touch, a very potent touch that made her feel good about herself. At the same time he disturbed her on a deeper level. Right now it was all too much to take in, she needed time to sift through the emotions pinging around her head.

She twisted around. 'I promised Emma's parents I'd see them as soon as I was finished.'

'No one expects you to. You must be exhausted.' His hand didn't shift.

'Maybe, but I do keep my word. And they must be fraught with worry by now.' With effort she shuffled away, forcing his arm to drop. She had no right to continue standing there enjoying his touch, no matter how innocently he gave it. She couldn't afford to surrender to wild needs. But, heaven knew, she wanted to. And, worse, it was hard to ignore those needs. But to give in to them with this man? After knowing him how long? One day. No, she must not. Hadn't she learnt anything from Oliver?

'You're right.' Daniel tugged his gown off. 'I'll come with you.'

All she was going to do was tell Emma's parents that their precious little girl was doing fine, but Dan accompanying her seemed right. Like they were a team. Scary. So she reacted with a verbal swipe. 'You're on holiday.'

'Coming from a large city, you can't be expected to appreciate how our patients are also our families, or our friends and neighbours. We treat the whole picture, not just the immediate illness.'

'I understand.' How mortifying that Dan thought so badly of her. He was totally wrong. She did care for her patients outside the operating theatre. *Huh? How often do you see any of your patients in any other capacity?* They come for consultation, surgery, a follow-up visit, then goodbye. She swallowed her chagrin. Dan had a point. But that didn't mean she wasn't as compassionate as he was. 'What are we waiting for?'

Jill poked her head around the door. 'Since you're both here, Anders and his father would love it if you dropped in on them when you're done with the Duncans.'

'Good idea.' The more time spent at the hospital meant less at home with only Dan and the conflicting emotions he stirred up. Sarah swung awkwardly on her crutches, hoping the ward wasn't too far away.

'Here, park your bottom in this.' Dan spun a wheelchair in her direction.

Great. 'I don't think so.' Where'd he found that so quickly?

'No one's going to think worse of you for conserving

your energy and protecting your foot.' Dan waited to push her. 'Sit,' he growled when she started to protest.

'Oh, all right.' Sarah eased into the wheelchair. Arguing took too much energy.

'Very gracious,' Dan muttered in her ear as he took the crutches from her.

Emma's parents were soon brought up to date and then a nurse took them to see their daughter. Dan whizzed Sarah along to the Starnes men, Jill going with them.

Anders and his father were sitting up in their respective beds, two dark heads turning at the sound of Sarah's chair wheels on the vinyl floor.

'Are you the doctors who saved me?' Anders raised his arm and winced.

'Don't move too much yet,' Dan advised in a friendly tone Sarah hadn't heard before. 'That shoulder will be tender for a while. This is Dr Livingston and I'm Dan Reilly.'

'We're very grateful for all you did for my boy,' the older man said, thrusting out his hand. 'Peter Starne.'

'You're both looking a lot better than the last time I saw you.' Sarah smiled as she took his hand.

'Unlike you, Doctor. What happened?'

'A slippery step got in my way.'

Dan's mood changed and he glared at the father. 'You're very fortunate, the pair of you. That's a wild coast out there.'

Peter looked sheepish. 'I know. I was an idiot to take Anders fishing off those rocks. Won't be doing that again in a hurry.'

'Glad you've learnt your lesson,' Dan snapped. 'A lot of people were involved in your rescue and any one of them could've been hurt. Or worse.'

Jill stepped closer, gripped Dan's elbow in warning. 'Pat

and Malcolm have been in to talk to Peter and Anders this morning. They've got the message loud and clear.'

'They'd...' Dan spluttered to a stop as Jill wrenched him away.

'Come on. You can show Sarah around the medical ward.' Out in the corridor Jill continued talking to Dan. 'Leave it. Pat gave them enough of a talking to about safety to last them a lifetime. They don't need the same lecture from you.'

'Why not? Did you see him? He looked embarrassed, not contrite.' Dan stared at Jill. 'He should be on his knees, thanking every last man who went out in that horrendous sea to save his butt.'

'Keep your voice down. This is a medical ward, not the sideline of a rugby field.' Jill cuffed him lightly. 'I understand how you feel, what with Malcolm being one of those men, but it's not our place to tell Peter Starne.'

Dan jerked a thumb over his shoulder. 'I haven't finished in there.'

Jill looked exasperated. 'Dan, leave it.'

'I need to check the boy's dislocated shoulder.'

Sarah looked up at Dan and asked gently, trying to keep reproof out of her voice so as not to antagonise him any more, 'Today's the first day of your holiday, remember? That means I'll take a look at Anders.'

He frowned. 'Don't you think you're being a little too keen to get off the mark, Doctor?'

'I suppose I could return to the house and put my foot up on pillows, demand pots of tea, and flick through magazines to while away the rest of the day.'

'What a good idea.' His frown lightened and he began pushing her. 'Let's go.'

'Dan.' Jill stepped in front of the wheelchair, effectively

stopping Dan's progress. Her eyes drilled into him. 'You're being obstructive'

'I'm trying to do the right thing for Sarah.' He began pushing the chair around Jill. 'Okay, she can go over next week's surgery schedule while I see to Anders.'

Sarah retorted, 'And then you will hand over the reins and go enjoy yourself.'

When the wheelchair moved off at speed she widened her smile. Men. Obstinate creatures.

'Why are women so difficult?' Dan asked Jill as he leaned against the nurses' station, reading Anders's case notes. 'Why aren't they more like men? What's wrong with accepting your limitations?'

Jill cocked her head on one side and looked at him, her earlier annoyance with him gone. 'You're talking about Sarah, I presume.'

Dan didn't like that all-knowing glimmer in his sister-in-law's eyes. 'Who else?'

'Sarah's being a real champ. She's certainly not bemoaning the fact she's been incapacitated, despite being in some pain. Nothing stopped her coming in when Alison called her for help.'

Dan's gaze rested on Sarah as she studied patient files at a desk at the other end of the ward. A little frown creased her brow as she concentrated. He'd noted that frown in Theatre when she'd focused on Emma, again when she'd explained everything about the operation to Gayle and John. He'd wanted to smooth the crease away then. He wanted to smooth it away now. What a distraction the woman was becoming. A very sexy distraction.

'Tell me.' Jill picked up the conversation again. 'What would you have done in the same circumstances? Stayed at home, grizzling? Or would you've got on with things, taking it on the chin like a man?'

'I am a man.'

'Yeah, and I don't think Sarah's a woman who spends a lot of time feeling sorry for herself.'

'You've got her all figured out already?'

'Call it woman's intuition, but I think our locum is one very self-contained lady who doesn't shirk her duties.'

'Huh,' Dan muttered. He had a sneaking suspicion Jill was right. 'That'll make Leah one happy kid. She's not sure of Sarah yet, gave her the fifth degree about her broken foot over breakfast.' Dan grinned. 'Then told Sarah she was naughty for going too fast and falling over. That child takes after her dad.'

Jill rolled her eyes. 'Poor little tyke.'

'Thanks very much. Glad to know who my friends are.' He covered a yawn. 'Having Sarah in the house might work out after all.' He'd get help with Leah and Sarah would learn to enjoy being around kids.

'Sleepless night?' Jill asked, her eyes widening and her mouth twitching.

'Sort of.' He'd taken hours to fall asleep, only to dream of creamy skin and a black lace bra filled to perfection. Not to mention a beautiful face and endearing smile. 'I think I'm already winding down into holiday mode.'

'Oh, sure. Nothing to do with your house guest, I presume.' Jill elbowed him. 'Go on, get out of here. It's time you had some fun. And I'm not just referring to Leah. Sarah could be the best thing to happen to you in a long time.'

It's time he had some sex, he knew that. But not with Dr Livingston. There again, why not? She was only here for a few months, long enough to have some fun with but not so long as to create problems. Like which side of the wardrobe she could hang her clothes. As if there'd ever be enough wardrobe space for all her outfits.

No, if he was getting back into the man-woman thing then it should be with a woman he could settle down and have more kids with. That job description did not suit Sarah. Except she'd been good with Leah that morning, and Gayle had said Sarah knew how to talk to Emma before her surgery.

On the other hand, she was too upmarket for Port Weston. For him. And he'd learned the hard way what happened when you tried to take the city out of a woman. It didn't work. She'd start blaming him for everything that went wrong, looking for problems that didn't exist.

In his pocket his phone vibrated as a text came through. He sighed as he read the message. Leah needed to change her top and Dan hadn't left the bag of clean clothes with the nanny.

One step forward, one back. Or was it sideways?

CHAPTER FIVE

'CAN we pull over for a moment?' Sarah asked Dan on the way to the hospital and her Saturday-morning patient round three days later.

'Something wrong?' He turned his four-wheel-drive into a lay-by on the ocean side of the road.

'Not at all.' As the vehicle stopped she pushed her door open and began to ease down on her feet, favouring the bad one. 'I want some wind and salt spray on my face.' The huge breakers that continuously rolled in fascinated her, drawing her into their rhythm. They lulled her to sleep at night, lifted her mood during the day. Very different from the sounds of downtown Auckland—dense traffic, sirens, people of every nationality calling out to each other.

'Can I sit in here, Daddy? I'm listening to the Singing Frogs.' Leah was belted into a back seat, twisting the cord of her small CD player.

'Sure can, kiddo.' Dan appeared at Sarah's side in double-quick time. 'This coastline is wild. Crazy and dangerous. It's very much a part of Coasters and who they are.'

'You're so right.' He could be referring to himself. Wild, crazy and dangerous. Definitely dangerous to her equilibrium. She breathed in the vibrant air, smelt salt and wet sand and seagulls. The thudding waves drowned out extraneous sounds except for the screeching gulls rising and falling on the air currents above them.

'Have you been to the Coast before?' Dan's hands rested on his slim hips, which drew her eye.

'Never.' She concentrated on the sea, trying to ignore the man. 'There weren't a lot of holidays when I was growing up, and none to the South Island.' Her brother, Bobby, might have got ill while they were away, which would have thrown her mother into a spin. 'And I confess that as an adult I've tended to head overseas for vacations. Not very patriotic of me, I guess, but the friends I used to go away with are more interested in the exotic and I've always gone along.' Even to her that sounded like a copout. 'Willingly,' she added.

Dan shook his head at her. 'Tourists say this is exotic. They pay to come here.'

'Tourists usually do pay.' Stop being difficult with him. 'You're right. I should've seen my own country by now. Maybe I'll have time to look around a bit while I'm here.' She could take a day trip on her day off. Shifting the conversation away from herself, she asked, 'Did I hear you've got a sister in Australia?'

'Pauline, our adopted sister. I'd like to take Leah over to get to know her extended family some time.'

'Adopted? Older or younger?' Family. Why did everything come back to that? Was she just being over-sensitive since Oliver had left her?

'She comes between Bea and me. Her mother and ours were sisters. Pauline's mother was a single mum and when she died in a house fire our parents naturally took Pauline in. No one ever knew who her father was.'

'What a wonderful thing for your parents to do.' Hers couldn't wait to see the back of each other after her brother had died. The stress and pressure of losing their son had taken a big toll. And no matter how hard she'd tried, she hadn't been able to make them understand she'd needed them to stay together as much as Bobby had.

Dan looked at her in disbelief. 'Not at all. That's what families are all about.'

Really? He didn't get how lucky he was. 'When did you last see Pauline?'

Dan turned to stare out over the waves. 'Two years ago. She came over for Celine's funeral and stayed on for two weeks, helping me get my head around what had happened. She was incredibly patient with me.'

'Had your wife been ill?' All these questions. Any minute he'd tell her to mind her own business, but she wanted to know what made him tick.

'Celine had never been ill in her life. She was struck down by an aneurysm.' His fingers dug into his hips, the knuckles turning white. His gaze went way beyond the waves to some place only he could see.

Wishing she hadn't caused him distress, Sarah said the first thing that came into her head. 'Do you want to take a hobble along the beach? There's time before my first patient.' She glanced down at the moon boot. 'It won't matter if I get this a bit wet.'

'Hang on, there're some plastic grocery bags in the Toyota I can put over it for protection. Sand inside that thing will be a pain.' Dan went to get a bag and Leah clambered out of the vehicle to join him, skipping in circles as Dan slipped the bag over Sarah's foot.

Looking down as he deftly knotted it at the top and tucked the ends inside her boot, the urge to run her fingers through his thick, dark hair was almost uncontainable. Almost. He'd think her whacky if she followed through. *She'd* think she was whacky. Touching another person unasked went totally against who she was. Having never had lots of hugs or kisses, no spontaneous touches, from her parents or Oliver, she usually struggled with reaching out to people like that. And yet right now she had to fight the urge to touch Dan.

She'd seen the bleakness in his eyes and touching him would be a way of saying she was sorry he had been so badly hurt, to show she understood. Instead she shoved her hands deep into her trouser pockets, distorting the perfect line of the soft fabric. And said nothing. What could she say that wouldn't sound trite? Her brother had died, having a terrible effect on her. But to lose the love of your life? The mother of your child? Much worse.

He stood up and his gaze clashed with hers, sending warmth spiralling through her despite her muddled feelings.

'Let's go.' He began striding down the hard sand, leaving her to follow at an uneven, slower pace.

His shoulders were hunched as he studied the ground in front of his feet, his hands clenched at his sides. A man hurting? Or angry at her again for intruding on his privacy? Keep this up and they were going to have many clashes over the coming months.

Then Leah ran up to her, pulled at Sarah's arm to free her hand. Warm, sticky fingers wrapped around Sarah's forefinger and she was tugged along the beach. Suddenly Sarah laughed. A completely unexpected laugh that relaxed the tension that had been dogging her for weeks. What was happening to her?

'Want to share the joke?' Dan stopped to wait for her. 'I could do with a good chuckle.'

'Nothing, really. It's good to be walking on the beach as though I've got nothing to worry about. I haven't done anything like this on a regular basis.' Face it, she didn't go for any sort of exercise, ever.

'Lucky you,' her companion grunted.

'Dan, give it a break.' She wouldn't let him drag her mood down, and as Leah ran off to study a dead gull she asked, 'What are you two doing today?'

'We've got a birthday party at twelve for one of Leah's preschool mates.'

'That sounds like fun.' What did adults do at those things? Play pass-the-parcel with the kids or hide in the kitchen, drinking wine? She knew which she'd be best at and it had nothing to do with parcels.

Dan jerked his head around to glare at her. 'Fun? Fun? Lady, what do you do for entertainment if you think spending hours with a bunch of four-year-olds is fun? Want to swap places?'

They were on the same wavelength—sort of. 'Okay, it's fun for Leah, but I'm sure you'll manage to raise a smile or two of your own.'

'Why would I want to do that?' But his eyes twinkled briefly. If only he knew how gorgeous and sexy and wonderful he looked when that twinkle appeared. 'At least I won't get a sore butt today.' He ran his hands down his thighs. 'Remind me again how great a time I had riding that bolshy horse. I'm sure Bea gave me Jumbo deliberately.'

'You need Deep Heat rubbed into your muscles.' Uh-oh.

The tip of his tongue appeared between his lips. His eyes widened, darkened. 'What are you suggesting? Massaging my thighs?'

She'd prefer his backside. Oh, great. Prize idiot. If he read her mind he'd think she was making a pass at him. Again. Charging along the beach as fast as her foot allowed, she said loudly, 'So no more riding?'

'We're going again tomorrow. I think Bea has a sadistic streak that I'm only just learning about.'

'You could say you're washing your hair.' Sarah grinned, thankful the subject of rubbing his muscles had been got past even if a very definite picture of her hands on that backside remained uppermost in her head.

'Can you see Leah letting me get away with that?' He kicked a small pebble into the froth surging at the water's edge. 'Seriously, do you think you're going to enjoy your time here? Yesterday, on my way to the supermarket, I tried to see Port Weston through your eyes and I must admit the town looks a little scruffy. The tired, weatherboard buildings, the shopfronts that belong to another generation. It's not flash.'

'I wasn't expecting a miniature Auckland. I'd have stayed at home otherwise.'

'So why did you take up the contract? I mean, you're a partner in a big, modern clinic. If you wanted a change, why not cruising somewhere like the Caribbean?'

'My father talked me into taking a break.' The words slipped out without thought.

'This is a break?' He shrugged his shoulders. 'Doing my job is a holiday?'

Damn, did he think she was mocking him? 'Not at all. It's just that it's so different working here. New people, total change of scenery. Hopefully not so competitive.' So much for self-control. Around Dan it was always disappearing. 'I'd been putting in extremely long hours.'

'Why? There must be enough surgeons lining up to work with your father to last his lifetime. His reputation is awesome. You could've backed off the hours.'

And then what would she have done? How would she have filled in the time and blocked out the pain caused by

Oliver? 'I wanted to do the hours. There were things going on in my life I was ignoring.'

'I can certainly sympathise with that sentiment.' Dan sighed. 'The exact same reasons I'm now on leave. I tended to spend time with my patients rather than deal with Leah and all her problems. Because she didn't react well to my way of dealing with her distress, hasn't ever since her mother died. Family kept stepping in and helping out, taking Leah home and making her happy for a while.' He shrugged. 'It all just became so much easier to leave them all to it and I could get on with building up the hospital's surgical unit.'

'Dan, you're great with Leah. She seems so happy and well adjusted.'

'I wish you hadn't said that.' Dan winced.

'Think I'm tempting fate? That now she'll be a little hellion? I can't see it. She's so sweet.'

'You can be quite supportive, did you know that? I could get used to having you around,' he growled, but his mouth lifted at the corners.

She stared at him. 'You'd better not. I don't intend staying on past the end of March.'

He shrugged. 'Fair enough. So what were you working so hard to avoid?'

'Not avoid,' Sarah grumbled, not wanting to go there. But Dan had shared some of his story with her. It seemed natural to return the favour. 'Actually, you're right. That's exactly what I was doing. I should be in Paris right now on my honeymoon.'

Dan's eyes widened. 'Really? It'd be very cold over there at this time of the year.'

Good, a spiteful little voice squeaked in her head. 'I was supposed to get married at the beginning of December but my fiancé called it off six months ago. He was having an affair with one of the clinic's nurses, which resulted in the baby they're expecting.'

'Whoever the guy is, he doesn't deserve you. That's a lousy thing for any man to do. Didn't he have the gumption to come to you from the moment he decided the nurse was the centre of his attention?' Dan looked hurt on her behalf. Which felt good, in an odd way.

'Oliver's also a partner in my father's surgical hospital, which kind of complicates things.' There was an understatement. 'Thankfully the nurse was more than happy to give up work once she learned she was pregnant.'

'Unlike you. You'd want to keep your career on track.' His eyes bored into hers.

'Yes, I would. But I believe I'd have managed to balance a family with work.' She'd have cut back her hours, certainly not spent evenings away lecturing or studying, as her father had done. 'Anyway, it doesn't matter now. I'm single and can remain focused entirely on my career.'

'What about love, Sarah? Surely you haven't cut yourself off from that happening. The kind of love that melts your heart, makes you jump out of burning buildings, brings you home every night? Don't you want to try for that again? And what about kids?'

Of course she wanted all that. Some time in the future. It was still too soon, although she already felt more at ease about her situation than she ever had.

'Time I went to work.' She spun back the way they'd come. Her foot jagged, the pain taking her breath away. What had happened to being careful?

Dan had happened. That's what. So distracting, so annoying, so endearing, that's what. He had her so mixed up emotionally it could take months to get back on an even keel. And now he'd taken her elbow to lead her slowly back to the car, ever mindful of her foot.

Emma was full of beans when Sarah hobbled into the ward, Dan beside her, his hand hovering on her elbow.

'I can manage from here,' Sarah muttered, desperate for a break from those sensual fingers on her skin. The tension she'd hoped to dispel while walking on the beach had increased beyond reason, tightening her tummy further. Instead of pushing Dan away with her revelations, they seemed to have drawn a little closer to each other. She had yet to work out if that was a good thing. 'I could've managed from the car park.'

'I've got half an hour to fill in.' Dan shrugged away her annoyance as if he didn't care what she thought. Which he probably didn't.

'You must have something else to do, something that has nothing to do with the hospital or patients.' She ground out the words through clenched teeth. Why had he come here? To check out her patient skills? Or did he just like being with her? If she had to choose a reason she hoped it was the second. Wishful thinking. Daniel Reilly was a control freak struggling to let go of his practice.

Jerking out of his grasp, Sarah waved to Emma across the room. Dressed in blue shorts and a T-shirt covered in bright pink daisies with flaming red centres, she looked a picture of happiness and health.

'Hi, Dr Sarah. I'm going home today.'

'Emma, sit still for a moment.' Gayle Duncan tried to grab hold of her daughter. Not a chance. 'Sorry, Sarah, but she's so happy to be getting out of here.'

'Who can blame her for that?' Sarah had got to know

Gayle quite well while she'd spent the days since Emma's appendectomy reading or playing games with her daughter.

Just as she would in the same situation. The thought slammed into Sarah's brain. Tick tock went the biological clock. She bit down on her bottom lip, desperately wanting this uncalled-for need to go away. Why now? Why here? Her gaze went straight to Dan standing on the other side of the bed, his thoughtful expression focused directly on her. Uh-oh. Did he have anything to do with this need? No way. He might be very attractive and distracting but what she felt for him was plain old lust. Certainly not grounds for considering having babies with the guy.

'Dr Dan, is your holiday finished?' Emma bobbed up and down before him.

He was slow to look away from Sarah to the girl trying to get his attention, and Sarah worried that she'd given away too much in those brief moments. He seemed able to see past all her defences right to her real wants and needs. Almost as though he knew her better than she did.

Which made him very dangerous to be around.

'Not yet. I brought Dr Livingston in and soon I'm going to pick up Leah from the library reading morning.'

So go. Get out of here. Give me space to gather my thoughts and put my head back in order. Sarah sent silent messages to him but he didn't move. *That's right, be obtuse. You were reading my mind fine before.*

'I'm going to play outside when I get home,' Emma told him.

Gayle asked Sarah, 'Do you want to check Emma before we go?'

Sarah scanned Emma's charts and notes. 'Everything looks absolutely fine. My main concern was Emma's temperature. As that's now completely normal you can take her home and spoil her.'

Sitting on the edge of the bed, Sarah patted the covers beside her. 'Emma, I want you to do something for me. Your tummy has been very sick so you have to look after it for a few more days. You mustn't do rough things that might hurt it. No climbing trees or riding the bike yet.'

Gayle chipped in before Sarah could say any more. 'Careful. This calls for reverse psychology. A certain young lady will immediately do anything you tell her not to.'

'I'll be very, very good. Won't I, Mummy?' Those enormous brown eyes were turned on Gayle.

Sarah chuckled. 'I don't know how you can say no to her.' She'd make a hopeless parent, spoiling any children she had. Children. Plural. Thinking of more than one child now? Unbidden, her longing swamped her, making her powerless to move. Then Emma leaned close to place a damp kiss on her chin, causing Sarah's eyes to mist over. Wordlessly she reached for Emma, gave her a quick hug.

She had to get out of here. She was making an idiot of herself. Getting all teary and giving spontaneous hugs. Next she'd be turning up to work in track pants and a T-shirt. This place sure had a way of playing havoc with everything as she knew it.

'Tell me again how I got to be at a child's birthday party?' Sarah asked Dan as they sat on the lawn, watching Leah leaping along in a sack trying to beat all the other kids to the finish line.

'You had nothing else to do.'

Sure, but a kid's party? 'I'd have found something.'

'Relax. No one's going to bite you.' Dan grinned at her discomfort, reminding her of the first morning when she'd been shocked awake by Leah crawling under the covers with her. Once the surprise had faded Sarah had enjoyed having a warm tot wriggling down beside her under the sheet.

She nudged Dan. 'Think you're needed. Leah's taken a tumble in her sack.'

'The tears will be because she hasn't won, not because she's hurt herself. Let's hope they don't last long.' He was quick to lift Leah up and set her on her feet again. 'Keep going. You've got to finish the race.'

Leah's heart wasn't in it. 'No, I'm going to sit with Sarah.'

'You've got to learn not to quit, my girl.' Dan's hands were on his hips.

'She's only four,' Sarah said. Sounding like a mother? Eek.

'Got to teach her these things right from the start.' Dan reached down to Leah as though to set her in the right direction but she ducked and slid past him, in her hurry tripping over the sack again and skidding on the rough grass.

The ensuing shrieks and cries were ear-piercing. Everyone turned to see what had happened. Two mothers rushed over to check on Leah. Dan scooped her up into his arms, holding her to his chest. 'She's all right,' he told everyone, and kissed Leah's forehead, at which point Leah squealed louder. 'Carry on with the race.'

One of the mothers remained with them while the other returned to the young partygoers and got them racing again. Leah cried louder. 'It hurts, Daddy.' And she snuggled in closer to his chest.

Panic filled Dan's eyes. He sat down on the ground, his big hand on Leah's head. 'Shh, little one. Take it easy. Where does it hurt?'

'Everywhere,' Leah answered between sobs.

Sarah was perplexed. A tumble in a sack shouldn't cause

this amount of distress. Unless… 'Does Leah suffer from
any medical condition that would precipitate this reaction?'

Dan gulped. 'Ah, no. Here, can you hold her while I
look her over?'

About to put her arms out to take the child, Sarah hesitated. Why the panic in Dan's eyes if there wasn't a condition to worry about? What upset him so much? Leah
needed him more than anyone else. Light-bulb moment.
That was the problem. He was afraid he couldn't comfort
her. 'No, Dan, it's you Leah wants.' Sarah knelt down beside them. 'I'll look her over while you hold her.'

Dan's eyes darkened with disappointment and something like fear. He looked around, spied the mother still
standing with them and began to lift Leah towards her.
'Would you?'

Sarah shook her head at the woman, silently asking her
to say no. She sensed Dan had to get through this moment
without letting his daughter go to someone else.

'Sarah's right, Dan. Leah needs her daddy right now.'

'But listen to her. She's not quietening down for me.'

'With some kids it takes a while.' The woman gave
Sarah a knowing smile and strolled away.

'You're doing fine. I think the volume might be lowering a bit.' Sarah's heart squeezed for this big man totally
out of his depth. She gently took one of Leah's arms and
checked it over, then her legs. 'You've scrapped some skin
off your knee, sweetheart.' And she bent to kiss it. 'There
you go, all better.'

Sarah sat down beside Dan to wait while Leah slowly
began to quieten down. The crying became soft sobs, then
hiccups, and finally a large yawn as she settled further
down into the comfort of her father's arms. And slowly
the tension eased in Dan's muscles, relaxing away until

he watched Leah in awe, his chest rising and falling as his breathing became settled.

Sarah swallowed around the lump in her throat. 'See, you're a great dad.'

'That's the first time I've managed to settle her when she gets that worked up.'

Leah's reaction had been out of proportion. 'Does she always do that? Get herself totally wound up?'

'Ever since her mother died and it's been up to me to comfort her.'

'I think there are two issues there, not one. It's not that you can't console her, it's that she just needs to work through her pain about her mum. You've made a habit of handing her over to others to comfort, haven't you?' *Don't do that, Dan. Your daughter loves you more than anyone else. You're her father.* There were a few things she'd like to point out to Dan but didn't want him thinking she was a know-all. And she wasn't about to tell him she had first-hand experience of a father who was never there when she really needed him.

Dan glanced across to Sarah. 'You're the first person to ever refuse to take her for me.' He gulped. 'Thank you. I think.'

Sarah forced a laugh. 'You were trying to palm her off on someone who hasn't a clue how to console an upset child. I had to do something to save her.' She leaned over and kissed the top of Leah's head, got a lungful of the heady male scent of Dan. Her eyes closed for a second before she lifted her head and placed a light kiss on Dan's cheek.

Shock rippled through her as her lips touched his freshly shaven cheek, as she inhaled the scent of him. What had she done? She jerked back, out of reach. She was crazy. Risking a glance, she saw surprise reflected in Dan's eyes.

'Daddy, what's a three-legged race?'

Thank you, Leah, now your father can concentrate on you and forget my little mistake. But Sarah rolled her lips together softly, thinking it didn't really feel like a mistake. If she wound back a few minutes to before she'd brushed her lips over Dan's cheek, would she have done it? Yes.

Dan's gaze dropped to his precious bundle. 'You tie one of your legs to someone else's and run to the finish line.'

'Can we do that? Will you run with me?' Leah asked, her eyes wide and puffy.

'This I can't wait to see.' Sarah tried for a laugh. Five minutes later the laughter was wiped off her face.

'The three-legged race is split between girls with their mothers, and boys with their fathers.' Dan studied Sarah with a big question in his eyes.

'Um, I'm not Leah's mother.' Why had she come to this party? Because Dan had talked her into doing something she didn't want to do. And now he wanted her to take part in a race with his daughter. 'Sorry, got a moon boot, re-member?'

Leah's little face fell. 'We can tie the other leg to me. Please Sarah. There's chocolate for the winner.'

That face got to her. What a sucker she was turning into. How much would it hurt her foot to try? She held her hand up to Dan to be hauled off the ground. 'Go easy on me, okay?' She tickled Leah under the chin and tried to ignore Dan's fingers as they tied the ribbon around her leg.

Together with Leah she hobbled to the start line, Leah tripping over more than once. Gritting her teeth as her fractures protested, Sarah said, 'Okay, we need a plan.' And whispered in Leah's ear.

Leah wrapped her arms around Sarah's waist and put her free foot on top of the one joined to Sarah's leg. And at the blow of the whistle they were racing. Step, thump. Step, thump.

'Daddy, Sarah and me got chocolate,' Leah shrieked a few minutes later.

'Sarah and I,' Dan automatically corrected.

'Cos we were the most un-unusualist.'

'Unusual,' Dan corrected her again, before turning to Sarah. 'Thanks. You've made Leah's day.'

'It was kind of fun.' Despite her foot, and that people were looking at her funny, as though she and Dan were an item, she was enjoying herself. Quite a few women were glancing at Dan and her, questions written all over their faces. So she obviously wasn't his usual type. They needn't worry. He wasn't hers either.

'Looks like lunch is next.' Dan led them to the laden tables. 'Ready for jelly and chicken nuggets?'

'On the same plate?' Sarah shuddered.

'Live dangerously.' Dan winked.

'Sarah, do you like fairy bread?' Leah peered up at her, holding out a plate filled with bread smothered in the tiniest dots of coloured sugar.

Sarah, do you like fairy bread? she could hear her brother asking, pressing a plateful into her hand. Where had that come from? There hadn't been parties like this when she was little. Yes, there had. When she'd been about Leah's age Robbie had had a birthday party and her parents had taken them to the zoo, along with lots of other children. They'd fed the monkeys with leftover food. No way. She was in lala land. That had not happened. She'd never forget a party.

'Sarah? Are you okay?' Dan took her elbow as though he expected her to fall down in a heap.

She shook away the memory, if that's what it was, and said, 'I'm fine. And, yes, I love fairy bread.' She had thirty-something years ago anyway. *See, it's not a dream. It happened.* What else from her childhood had she forgotten? What other good, fun things had been lost in the need to impress her father and gain his attention?

CHAPTER SIX

DAN flicked the vegetable knife into the sink and snapped the cold tap on so fiercely water sprayed over the bench and across the front of his T-shirt. The walls closed in on him as he leaned back against the bench.

At the kitchen table Sarah and Leah were making cookies. Both of them had cute smudges of flour on their cheeks. Leah's eyes were enormous in her face as she followed Sarah's instructions on mixing the chocolate pieces into the dough.

'Oops!' Sarah chuckled and scooped up a handful of creamed mix from the table where it had flicked from the bowl due to Leah's over-enthusiastic stirring. 'Slow down a bit. Here.' She popped a chocolate button into Leah's grinning mouth.

'Look, Daddy, I'm mixing the biscuits.'

'You're doing a great job.' Warmth stole over him. His girl couldn't be happier. Sarah had done that for her. Antsy Sarah, who swore she knew nothing about children's needs. Sarah, who did three-legged races with a moon boot just to give a child a special moment. 'So are you, big girl.'

He got glared at with piercing green eyes. 'Big girl?'

'As in Leah's my little one.' The glare sharpened. 'Can I pour you a wine? It's that time of the day.' He opened the fridge and took out a bottle of white wine, waving it at her. Hopefully diverting her.

The green lightened, her mouth twitched. 'Yes, please.'

'Me too, Daddy.'

Dan shook his head as he poured one wine and a juice. What had happened to his plan to have dinner cooking and Leah bathed and in her PJs by now? Females, young and older, that's what had happened. Both distracting in their own way. Both taking over his kitchen and making the mother of all messes.

'Aren't you having anything?' Sarah asked as he put the bottles back in the fridge.

'Yes, actually, I am.' He'd forgotten to get himself a beer. His nice, orderly world seemed to be going all to hell. How could this woman cause so much mayhem just by being—being there? He was even starting to think that she'd make a good mother for his Leah, and that was a really, stupid idea. It would never work. He wasn't moving to Auckland with all its traffic and no green paddocks. And Sarah? Well, she'd never consider living permanently so far away from those spas and dress designers. Though those trousers she had on now weren't as posh as some of the outfits she'd worn so far. Slumming it? Snapping the tab on a can of lager, he grinned. Sarah was most definitely relaxing a bit.

'Good, I don't like drinking alone.' A smile curved her full lips. 'What are we having for dinner?' she asked.

'You're as bad as Leah. We've got fresh blue cod caught by a local fisherman.'

'Yum. How are you cooking it?'

'In the pan.' This wasn't one of her fancy restaurants where she'd get sauces and fresh herbs and other garnishes.

One corner of Sarah's delectable mouth curled upward before she asked Leah, 'Do you want to stir the nuts in now?'

'I don't like nuts.' Leah stopped poking the buttons into the mixture with her fingers. 'They're yukky.'

'Have you tried them?' Sarah looked a bit stunned.

'Not many kids Leah's age do. Could be because parents don't let them have nuts in case they choke.'

Sarah's face fell. 'I didn't think. How stupid of me. Chocolate hazelnut cookies are a favourite of mine.' She looked at Dan, lifted her shoulders in an eloquent gesture. 'I blew it, didn't I?'

'It's not a biggie, Sarah.'

'Yes, it is. I've gone and spoiled the whole thing of having fun with Leah and being able to eat the cookies together.' She leaned down and hugged Leah to her. 'I'm sorry, sweetheart.'

'Can I eat the rest of the chocolate?'

Dan shook his head at his daughter. 'You're never one to miss an opportunity, are you? I've got a suggestion.' He looked at Sarah. 'How about Leah stirs in the rest of the buttons and makes them double chocolate cookies?'

Gratitude shone back at him. 'Good thinking.'

As the mixing resumed, Dan added for Sarah's benefit, 'You didn't spoil anything. Even if a certain young lady hadn't been able to eat the biscuits, she's still having a blast. I've never cooked with her, but it is something I'd envisaged she'd do with her mother. You've started something that I might have to keep up.' When carefully sculpted eyebrows rose he added, 'Seriously, the fun is in the doing, not just the eating.'

'Thanks.' She took a big gulp of wine. 'I remember making biscuits with Gran when we stayed at her house.'

Why the surprise in her eyes? 'Didn't you enjoy it?'

'I loved it.' Another gulp. 'I'd forgotten we did that.' Then she murmured something like, 'Seems as though I've forgotten a lot of things.'

Dan wanted to ask her what her childhood had been like but twice already he'd put his size-eleven feet in his mouth when asking her personal things so he kept quiet.

Soon the cookies were in the oven and Sarah stared at the messy table. 'Guess I know what I'm doing next.'

'I'll take care of that.' It would keep him busy for half the night. He jerked a thumb at the door. 'Go and put that leg up. I bet it hurts like crazy.'

'That's to be expected.'

'I'll check it for swelling once I've finished here. You did spend a lot of time standing on it today. Not to mention the race.'

'I'm glad I opted for the moon boot. A cast would've been clunky.' She leaned her saucy hip against the kitchen table. A smattering of flour had somehow got onto her trousers, smeared over her butt.

Dan tried desperately to focus on filling a pot with spuds rather than on the mouthwatering sight at his table. The very feminine curves appealed to his male senses. More than that, his hormones were stirring up a storm. Again. Still.

'It isn't necessary for you to check my foot. I'm qualified to do my own check-ups.' Had her voice wobbled?

'Daddy check-ups my hurts.' Leah's eyes sparkled.

Dan smiled over his shoulder at Leah, warmth bubbling through him. He'd do anything to make his girl happy. Even clean up after the sex goddess. Only days into it, he seemed to be getting a handle on this full-time-dad lark. Though he'd nearly blown it when Leah had tripped in that silly sack race. The one scenario he'd been dreading since the day he'd learned he was going on leave had happened, but Sarah had forced him to face up to his insecurities. And, with no alternative, he had. And won.

He owed Sarah big time. For the first time one of Leah's crying episodes hadn't escalated into a full-blown meltdown that he couldn't manage. He'd consoled her, comforted her, and within a short time she'd been happily bouncing all over the place, not refusing to talk, and crying for hours as had happened so often in the past. *He'd* done it. Without Auntie Bea, or Jill, or the nanny. But with Sarah on the sidelines, encouraging him with her sweet smile. What about that sweet kiss she'd dropped on his cheek? It had taken his breath away.

'Daddy, can I take the plaster off my knee now? It's all better.'

'Of course you can.' He looked at his daughter, grateful of the interruption to where his thoughts were heading. 'You're a cracker kid.'

'A Christmas cracker.' Leah put one hand in Sarah's and the other in his. 'Pull me. See what's inside like a real cracker.'

'A paper hat and a plastic toy.' Sarah smiled at Leah before her gaze turned to him.

What was she thinking? She'd appeared to enjoy the baking session until she'd realised her mistake about the nuts. Did she wish she had her own family? Of course she would. Who didn't? Not anyone with a heart. Sarah might think she'd hidden hers but he'd watched her with Emma, with Anders. Sarah gave more of herself than was expected of a surgeon dealing with a young patient. She'd taken some knocks, which could explain why she tried so hard to remain aloof. She certainly coped with Leah's demands like a veteran.

'Pot's boiling over.' Sarah nodded at him.

'What?'

'Daddy, you're dreaming. The pot's too hot.'

He spun around, flicked the gas to low. Goddamn it. He *had* been daydreaming. Why wouldn't he? A beautiful woman stood in his kitchen and he hadn't had sex for a long time. What else would a bloke be doing? It had been for ever since he'd scratched that particular urge.

A town the size of Port Weston made it difficult to have a brief fling. The gossipmongers would have a field day. Mostly when he got randy as hell, he took to digging up the garden. Nothing like hard, physical work to douse the urge. The fact that his garden was extremely overgrown was testimony to how often that happened.

But it would be impossible to find any red-blooded male who wouldn't be interested in the stunning Dr Livingston. Except, maybe, this Oliver character.

He was going to have to take Leah away for some overnight trips. Living under the same roof as Sarah was akin to lighting a fire and leaping into it.

'Thought I'd give you a treat today.' Dan spoke from Sarah's office doorway.

She leaned back in her chair, shaking her head at him. Some time over the week since the baking fiasco Dan had finally managed to stop wanting to read all the patient files and going over cases with her. But occasionally he still turned up unannounced to see if she needed help with anything. 'You're going to whisk me off to a beauty clinic where I'll be pampered for hours on end.'

'I don't think so.' He looked stunned, as if that was an odd suggestion.

'Not my lucky day, then, is it?' She smiled to soften her words.

'What about a real coffee in a real café? If you're not busy, that is? It's time you met George and Robert.'

'Sounds wonderful.' She glanced at her day planner. 'As you know full well, I'm not exactly rushed off my feet.'

'Come Monday you will be. That's a heavy schedule you've got so let's make the most of today's opportunity while we can.' His mouth twisted in a sheepish manner when she raised an eyebrow at him. 'I happened to see the operating list when I stopped to say hello to Jill.'

'Left it lying around, did we?' The list had been in a drawer at Jill's desk half an hour ago.

'I was looking for a pen.' Then he shrugged and gave her a rare grin, one that hit her right in the belly and had her wanting to know more about him. 'All right. I can't help myself. I'm an interfering beaver, I know. But for the record, you're doing a brilliant job and I couldn't have asked for a better replacement.'

About to get out of her chair, Sarah found her arms didn't have the strength to push her up. 'You what?' *Close your mouth, you're looking like a fish out of water. I feel like one.*

Dan jerked a thumb over his shoulder. 'You want that coffee or not?'

'I guess,' she croaked. She'd been paid a compliment. By Daniel Reilly. What had brought that on? Mr Grumpy had more sides to him than a hexagonal block. Or else he wanted something from her.

The ride to Port Weston's main street was a silent one. Sarah dwelt on what Dan might want and as he pulled his Land Cruiser into a park outside the café she decided she'd been a bit harsh. As far as she'd noted, Dan didn't do devious so there probably wasn't any ulterior motive behind that statement. He'd meant it. And he was taking her out. Not on a date, as such, but they were going for coffee where they'd be seen by locals. So when he came around to open her door and help her down she gave him a full-beam smile. Which seemed to fluster him completely.

Inside the café he pulled out a chair for her, then waved to the two men working behind the counter. 'Robert, George, can we have some coffee please? And you'd better meet Sarah.'

Watching the men hurrying to the table, Sarah grinned. 'Seems you're popular.'

Dan twisted his mouth sideways in that wry way of his. 'It's you they want to meet. You're about to get a thorough going over.'

'Like a bag of coffee beans, you mean?'

Dan merely raised his dark eyebrows. 'Something like that.'

The shorter of the two men touched her lightly on the shoulder. 'I'm Robert, and this is my partner, George.'

George held out his hand. 'Pleased to meet you.'

She shook hands with both men.

'Your reputation has gone before you.' Robert took a long look at her.

'What am I reputed to have done?' Sarah asked, intrigued despite herself.

'It's nothing to do with what you've done, apart from falling down the pub's steps. Talk about making a grand entrance to our little community.' Robert paused, then, 'Everyone's talking about the new surgeon and her absolutely fabulous car, not to mention her exquisite clothes.'

Leaning sideways, Robert appraised her stylish mid-calf, café-au-lait-coloured trousers and peach sleeveless shirt. 'I'd have to agree. Very classy.'

Dan leaned back on his chair, arms folded across his chest, a well-worn black T-shirt stretched too tight across his muscular frame. 'Not like me at all.' And the damned man winked at her.

Sarah tried to ignore that wide chest and failed. Miserably. Her mouth dried. She itched to slip her hands between the fabric and his skin. As her stomach did a flip she wondered how she could think like this when the man annoyed the daylights out of her most of the time. Somehow, despite that, contemplating those muscles under his shirt kept her awake most nights until the sound of the sea worked its magic on her.

Wasn't she supposed to be grieving over a broken engagement? Yet here she was, drooling over the first man she'd spent any time with since Oliver. Looking up at his face, she was shocked to see him watching her. Heat pooled in the pit of her stomach as something dark and dangerous glittered back at her.

Finally Dan waved a hand. 'Hey, there, Robert, could we have some coffees? Today would be good.'

Robert rolled his eyes. 'This is what happens when you try keeping Sarah all to yourself. But we can't have her thinking we can't match it with the city types so excellent coffee coming up.'

Keeping her all to himself? Not likely. He'd taken her to that birthday party, hadn't he? Hardly the social event of the year, but there had been lots of mothers there. Not her scene at all and yet she'd had fun.

Sarah leaned her elbows on the table and dropped her chin into her hand. 'How long have George and Robert been living in Port Weston?' she asked, while her mind was still on Dan.

'About five years. Robert's a West Coaster, originally from further south in Hokitika.'

'He limps quite badly, and seems to be in some pain.' Sarah had noted the sideways drag and occasional grimace when he'd approached their table.

'He snapped a tendon and, despite surgery to reattach it,

he's had nothing but trouble since. Don't waste your breath suggesting a second operation. He's adamant he's not having one,' Dan explained. 'I've tried countless times to get him to see an orthopaedic surgeon I can recommend.'

'That's sad when he possibly could be walking around pain free.' Sarah wondered why Robert felt so strongly against a repeat op. 'Did something happen during surgery?'

Leaning his chin on his chest, Dan murmured, 'He's not saying. It was done in Christchurch but without his permission I can't request his file.'

'Has George said anything to you?'

Dan shook his head. 'He's promised Robert he won't, though I think he's bursting to discuss it. See if you can get anything out of him once you've been here a little while.'

If Dan couldn't convince Robert when he knew them so well, she didn't stand a chance. Sarah twisted around to look out the window onto the street and the people wandering past, all dressed very casually. Despite the summer temperature, many of the men wore gumboots or heavy work boots, and some people had caps on to keep the sun off their faces.

She couldn't get much further from the fashionable, bustling crowds of downtown Auckland. But if she'd been back there she'd have been tense, tapping the floor with the toe of her shoe, in a hurry to down her coffee and get back to work. Not a lot of enjoyment in that, while here she was happy to take her time, savouring the company, and hopefully the coffee when it came.

Robert placed their cups on the table, turned to Sarah. 'I hear there's a roster for driving you to the hospital.'

'There is. It astonishes me how total strangers are waiting outside the gate in the morning, ready to drive me to work. The same thing happens when it's time to go home.'

'That's what living on the Coast is all about, helping one another,' Robert said.

Even at three o'clock that morning someone had picked her up when she'd been called in to an emergency. She hoped it wasn't part of their 'keep Dr Sarah here' plan, which she'd heard about through the hospital grapevine.

She'd be disappointing the board about that. Although she'd begun appreciating the friendliness of everyone, and their genuine enquiries about how she was coping, the reality was that this place did frustrate her at times. Yesterday had been a prime example.

Turning to Dan, she said, 'I ordered a book from the local stationery shop, and they told me it would be a week before it arrived. A week!'

'So?' Dan drawled.

'So in Auckland it would arrive overnight. What are they doing? Writing the thing longhand?'

'Get used to it. That's how it is around here.'

'Be glad it's only a book you want.' Robert chuckled from the next table where he was wiping the surface. 'The bench top for our new kitchen took two months.'

Sarah pulled a face. And people seriously thought they could persuade her to stay? Apart from the fact that she had a partnership at the clinic to go back to, one she'd barely given a thought to since she'd arrived, she realised with a start, there was nothing in this sleepy hollow that attracted her. Not even its exceptionally up-to-date surgical unit.

What about a certain surgeon with the gentlest touch whenever he took her elbow to guide her around some obstacle? The man's startling blue eyes seemed to follow her every move. Was Dan a man who could possibly be trusted? Whoa. That was going too far. She didn't know him well enough to make that assumption. She'd known

Oliver a long time and still hadn't seen his infidelity coming.

She tapped her forehead in a feeble attempt to dash Dan from her thoughts. Impossible when he was sitting opposite her, those very blue eyes watching her.

'Sorry to gatecrash this cosy scene.' Jill loomed into Sarah's peripheral vision. 'But I've got to tell Dan my news.' Jill was bobbing up and down on her toes, grinning from ear to ear, her eyes glowing like coals on a fire.

'Jill? What is it?' Sarah looked from her new friend to Dan and saw a surprised kind of excitement lightening his face. 'Someone tell me what's going on.'

'I'm pregnant.'

'I'd say she's pregnant.'

They spoke in unison. Then Dan was out of his chair and swooping his sister-in-law into his arms and swinging her around in a circle, nearly colliding with the next table. 'Aren't you?'

'Yes, yes, yes.' Jill's eyes brimmed and fat tears spilled down her cheeks as Dan gently let her down again. 'Yes.' She squeezed her hands into fists and shook them with glee.

'That's wonderful. I'm thrilled for you.' Sarah got up to hug Jill. Oops, she didn't do hugs. Too late. And it felt good.

'We've been trying for well over a year. Malcolm and I were beginning to think we'd never be parents.' Jill danced on the spot. 'I intended keeping it a secret for a few weeks in case something went wrong.' She faltered for a moment. 'But we couldn't. So here I am, making sure you're one of the first to know, Dan.'

Dan wrapped his arms around her again, rested his chin on her head. 'Thank you, sis. I've been hoping for this news for so long, you've made my day. You really have.

And now I suppose I'd better give that brother of mine a call. He'll be busting a valve with excitement.' He tugged his phone out of his pocket.

'A call?' Jill laughed. 'He'll want a party.'

'That can be arranged.' Dan grinned. 'Yes, that's exactly what I'll do. Leave it all to me.'

Jill dropped into a chair beside Sarah, and a cup of coffee appeared at her elbow.

'Congratulations, Jill.' Robert hugged her too.

Sarah smiled as if it was the most wonderful news she'd ever heard. 'When did you actually find out?'

'First thing this morning I was banging on the door of the pharmacy before they opened. I'm late but at first I was afraid to do the test. I didn't want to find out it was a hiccup with my system. Malcolm and I agreed we'd wait until I was at least two weeks overdue.'

'How did you manage that?'

Jill hugged herself. 'We didn't. That's why I had to go get a test kit. Two weeks aren't up yet.'

Sarah grinned. 'That's better. I'd never be able to wait. I'm thrilled for you.' She really meant it. So why the gloomy sensation seeping through her? Everyone except her was having babies.

Thankfully her pager beeped. 'Guess that's the end of my break.' She read the message. 'Yep, I'm needed in A and E.' She drained her superb coffee and pushed away from the table.

Dan snapped his phone shut after a cheeky quip to Malcolm about being an old father, and said to Sarah, 'I'll drive you back and come in to see what's up. I've still got time to fill in before Leah's library session finishes.'

'Then go and see Malcolm.'

'Can't. He's got a beer tanker being unloaded, and the freight truck's due in any minute.'

There had to be something he could do rather than hang around with her. 'Then go shopping or something.'

His eyes rolled in that annoying manner. 'Shopping? Me? What for?'

'I don't know. How about some new clothes? Or groceries?' Anything, but get out of her hair, give her some breathing space. She was getting too used to him hanging around, found herself looking for him whenever he was away for very long.

Dan was still shaking his head at her suggestion as he pulled away from the café and turned back to the hospital. Then he lightly slapped the steering-wheel. 'Actually, you're right. I'll go to the shops and get something for Jill and Malcolm to celebrate their news.'

'Lovely idea.' Why hadn't she thought of that? She'd arrange for some flowers to be delivered to Jill at the pub. And she must remember to pick up a new platter from the gift shop to replace the chipped one at home.

'Malcolm's stoked.' He slowed for a truck pulling out of a side street. 'It's kind of neat we're having another child in the family. Leah's going to be so excited. A new cousin.'

'Isn't she just?' Sarah tried not to feel like even more of an outsider than she was. But it was hard to deny the twinge of envy. Dan's family had such strong bonds of love tying them all together. Unlike hers.

'I'd have loved more babies but Celine kept miscarrying.' Dan's smile dimmed briefly.

'It's not too late.' She swallowed. 'I mean, you could remarry and before you know it you'll have kids from here to Christmas.'

'Really? Now, there's a thought. Were you thinking of next Christmas?' He recovered quickly. Jill's news had made him happy. She'd have thought it would have made him sad, bringing back all those memories of Celine and the family they'd planned.

'That might take some fast work on your behalf. Unless you've already got a woman in mind.' Did he have a woman friend out there that she knew nothing about? Why wouldn't he? He was a very attractive man with a lot going for him.

'When have I had the time to date?'

'Where there's a will there's a way. Or so they say.' Relief trickled through Sarah, lifting her spirits. Something she shouldn't be feeling. She and Dan were never going to have a relationship, at least not one that led to babies. And if he was intent on having another family, he wouldn't want to be wasting time on a fling with her.

'What about you? You're not going to let that ex-fiancé spoil your chances, are you?' His eyes were fixed on the road ahead.

'Give me time to get over him before suggesting I find another man to have babies with. There's the little matter of falling in love with someone first.' But when had she last thought about Oliver? Certainly not at all today so far. He didn't keep her awake at nights any more either.

Dan did.

Dan said casually as he pulled up outside the hospital's main entrance, 'Don't take too long mending that broken heart of yours. It's holding you back from getting the most out of life.'

Her mouth fell open. 'Like what?' She shoved her door wide and snatched up her handbag. 'I've still got a lot: a fantastic apartment, my partnership in the clinic, a great job. More than enough to fill my days.' Even she found it hard to get excited about that picture.

'By the way,' he called out his window as she headed up the hospital steps, 'you'd make a wonderful mum.'

CHAPTER SEVEN

'I'M OUT in the spa,' Dan called out to Sarah as she came through the front door that evening.

And when she stepped out onto the deck he heard her faint gasp. 'That looks wonderful.'

'Come and join me.' Would she? Suddenly he was silently begging to whatever was out there that made these things happen. *Please make her want to soak in the hot water. Please.* 'The warmth works wonders on tense muscles.'

'I'm not tense.' Her teeth nibbled her lip.

Sure you're not. 'We can have dinner any time. It's all prepared.'

'Maybe I'll take a stroll along the beach instead. I've had a big day.'

Yep. I can see your tight shoulders, your tired eyes.

Just then a gust of wind blew through the trees, filling the air with the sound of rustling leaves. *Thank you.* Dan grinned. 'There's rain coming.'

Her eyebrows rose in that delightful way she had. 'I'll go change into my swimsuit.'

Thank goodness she'd packed a swimsuit. He'd have blown a gasket if she'd told him she was coming in naked. When she wandered out five minutes later he still nearly blew one. Her simple black costume fitted superbly, outlining those full breasts to perfection, accentuating the curves of her hips. Her flat stomach sent his into spasms. He could not take his eyes off her as she climbed into the bubbling water and sat beside him.

Beside him? Being in the spa with Sarah suddenly became a really, really bad idea. His blood pressure started rising. What was wrong with him? Of course. Blame Sarah for being so delectable.

Clearing his throat, he tried to sound nonchalant. 'Would you like a wine?'

She glanced at the low table beside the spa where two glasses and a bottle stood next to a plate of crackers and Brie. Again her eyebrows rose, and her mouth twitched. 'A very small one.'

Stupid, stupid. Dan berated himself as he poured her drink. She must think he was seducing her. That's how it looked from here. He'd wanted everything seeming effortless so she wouldn't think anything of it when he suggested she join him. Went to show how out of practice at entertaining women he'd become. He was more like the new kid at kindergarten with all the unfamiliar toys and too frightened to touch any of them than a confident man and father of one.

Right now he should be leaping out of the spa, putting distance between them. Then she'd think him a really hopeless case. He'd stay put, but for the life of him he didn't know how he was going to keep his hands to himself.

Sarah slid deep into the warm water, letting the bubbles roll up her back, around her neck. Her eyes closed and she smiled. 'This has to be the best invention ever.'

He passed over her glass. 'Keep an ear out for the oven timer. I've got some muffins baking for tomorrow.' Keep the conversation on normal, everyday things and he might survive the next half-hour without making a complete fool of himself.

'You and Leah going somewhere that you need muffins?'

'Depending on the weather we might head to the river for a swim.' Dan studied her over the rim of his glass. Something was bothering her. Occasionally over the last few days he'd seen her wandering along the beach, hands in her pockets, chin on her chest, deep in thought. And when she'd come back those beautiful big eyes had been dark with sadness, and he'd want to haul her into his arms and hug her tight. Like he would for any of his family. That look was there now.

Sarah isn't family. Sarah's a hot woman whom you'd like to bed. There is a difference, man. Couldn't he bed her and help her at the same time?

'You're enjoying your time off now, aren't you?' She sounded wistful. 'Having a great time with Leah.'

'Absolutely. I wish I'd done it ages ago. Who knows what I've missed out on with my girl? If I ever have any more kids, I'll definitely be there all the time, not hiding at work.'

'You said you wanted more children. Got a number in mind?'

He tasted his wine and looked out beyond the end of the lawn to where he could hear the waves pounding their relentless rhythm. 'There was a time I wanted four.'

'Four?' She smiled. 'You're a devil for punishment.'

'I've always been surrounded by people. I can't imagine life without siblings and I want the same for Leah. Celine and I were trying but she kept miscarrying. Five times. The doctors couldn't explain it. We saw everyone, and I mean everyone. Specialists here and in Australia. The more we were told there was no obvious reason, the more

Celine blamed herself. Nothing I said made the slightest bit of difference.'

'That must have been hard for you both.'

'Very.'

'How did Celine cope?'

'At first she was distraught, as any woman would be. I admit, so was I. But after each miscarriage she became moodier, filled with despair, spiralling into a black hole that no one could coax her out of.' He gulped at his drink. He recalled those dark nights and days, trying to make Celine understand that he was happy with their small family; that she and Leah were precious to him. She'd argued she wasn't good enough for him because she couldn't give him what he wanted. That had hurt. Badly. 'Not even me. Heaven knows, I tried.'

Movement in the water and Sarah leaned closer to lay her hand on his arm. She didn't say anything, just touched him.

He took her hand in his and sat there looking at the woman who was changing so much for him. Her determination to carry on even when her foot hurt, her cheerful manner, her sweet smile, the way she was always ready to listen, even her occasional crankiness—all these things and more were helping him get back a life he'd forgotten existed. A life that looked pretty darned good from where he sat. As did his companion. Her cheeks had coloured to a soft pink, and the tiredness staining her face had vanished.

When Sarah turned to place her glass on the table her gaze clashed with his. Without thought he caught her arms and tugged her gently towards him just as she leaned forward. They slid off their seats. Dan instinctively wrapped his arms around her, holding her to his chest, as they bobbed in the bubbling water.

Sarah slid her arms around his waist. Her hands spread out over his back. He could feel each fingertip where they pressed lightly on his skin. The swirling water and her touch were a sensual mix of satin and silk, of soft and firm. He'd arrived in heaven.

His lungs suspended all breathing while his mind assimilated the feel of Sarah's slick, warm skin under his palms. He moved closer, placed his lips on her throat. Her pulse thumped under his mouth, and he could feel her throbbing response in the fingers that were now pushing through his hair, beating a feverish massage on his scalp. Heard it in the hiss of her indrawn breath.

His tongue traced a line under her chin and up to the corner of her mouth, where he teased her lips gently with his teeth, warming the cooler flesh. He lost all sense of time, place, everything—except Sarah, and he couldn't get enough of her. Her mouth, when he tasted it, was sweet with wine. An outpouring of exquisite sensations overtook him.

Then she touched his face, held his head closer, and kissed him back with all the fierceness of a starved woman. He didn't, couldn't, stop to question what was behind her actions. Her need fired his own to an even deeper level and he leaned further into her, his bones melting.

On the periphery he thought he heard something. What? Ignoring it, his mind sank back into the pool of whirling sensations Sarah stirred up.

Beep. Beep. Beep.

He dragged his mouth away from those wondrous lips. Cocked his head to one side. Every swear word he could think of flicked through his mind as he tried to blink his eyes into focus.

'What?' Sarah croaked.

'The goddamned muffins are ready.'

'Let them burn.'

'You want the fire brigade turning up?'

Dan swore under his breath. The kitchen floor was slippery with water that had dripped from his shorts when he'd charged inside to save the wretched muffins. He fetched a mop and began cleaning up, at the same time trying to put that kiss into perspective. Yeah, right. Like how? When his body was in a state of expectation, turned on as quickly as a flick of a switch. Unfortunately it couldn't be turned off as swiftly.

Sarah walked through from outside, quietly, as though hoping he wouldn't notice her. She'd have to be invisible for that to happen. And not wear that special fragrance of hers.

'Sarah?' he couldn't resist calling in a low voice as she passed. He did not want her to ignore what had just happened between them. That kiss had been as real as the waves pounding the beach across the road. And as hard to hold onto. Especially if Sarah decided to pretend it had been a passing clashing of lips with nothing more to it.

'I'm going to have a shower and head to bed. It's been a long day.' The yellow of her towel highlighted the gold flecks in her eyes when she met his gaze.

He couldn't read her. 'You don't want tea and a muffin?' She always had a cup of tea and something sweet to eat before retiring. 'You haven't had dinner.'

'No, thanks.' She was rejecting him—after that heart-stopping kiss.

A chill lifted bumps on his arms. The depth of his yearning shocked him. Whatever they'd started must not stop. He wanted more from her, much more. So he should be grateful this was as far as it was going, should be glad one of them had the sense to put the brakes on before it got out of hand.

But he'd begun to enjoy having Sarah here, in his house, his hospital. In his life. He woke up in the mornings feeling happier than he had in years and he didn't believe that was only because he was on leave with his daughter. He grimaced. Even if making daisy chains had been a novel way of filling in an afternoon. No, he enjoyed having another adult at home to talk with, to share meals with.

Get real. You enjoy having a very hot woman under your roof and you're only biding your time until she's under your sheets.

He managed to say something sane and sensible. 'Goodnight.'

Her relief was almost palpable as she paused. 'Goodnight, Dan.' Her fragrance reminded him of the scent of lavender on a gentle breeze. 'I'm, um, sorry we were interrupted.'

'What?' Talk about mixed messages.

'But I think it's for the best. We've got to live together for quite a while and if we'd carried on it would only have made life very difficult for us.'

Okay, not mixed. Clear as day. He gripped his hips in an attempt to stop reaching out to touch her. To stop from running his fingers behind her ear and down beneath her chin, over the fair skin of her throat. He yearned to kiss away that frown, to make her mouth soft and pliant under his again.

'Yes, you're right.' Damn it. She was. An affair might solve the immediate problem of needing sex, but Sarah was still hurting from what that other character had done to her. She needed time, patience and care before she was ready for something as hot and casual as a fling with him. But now he'd tasted her it had become even harder to ignore the frisson of tension she whipped up in him.

The Jaguar crawled along, the big engine purring. Thankfully Sarah's foot had pretty much returned to normal, allowing her the luxury of driving again. As long as she didn't go jogging or anything equally mad.

What a busy week with long hours, though nothing like the pressure she worked under back home. She hadn't seen a lot of Dan since that kiss. As though he was staying well away from her.

Tonight, knowing she didn't have to be up at the crack of dawn, she'd relax with a glass of wine, cook a meal that did not involve satisfying a four-year-old palate, and watch a good crime programme on TV. Something that didn't involve a red-blooded male's idea of good television, meaning cricket or any other sport.

Turning into the drive, her foot lifted off the accelerator as disappointment enveloped her. Vehicles were parked haphazardly between the gate and the house. Worse, people, lots of them, were gathered on the lawn and the deck.

'There goes the poached salmon.' Sarah eased the Jag between Dan's Land Cruiser and a small truck. Gathering up her groceries, she eased open the door. Laughter and voices carried to her, Leah's shrieks outdoing them all. Reaching back into the car, she lifted up the bunch of roses and the twisted glass vase she'd purchased that afternoon at the florist next to the café. The house needed a sparkle put into it.

'Can I carry those for you?'

She jerked around at Dan's question. 'Sure. Are we having a party?'

Guilt clouded his eyes to almost black. 'Sorry. I

should've warned you.' He waved a hand towards the over-crowded deck.

'So all these people…' she nodded '…just turned up?'

'Not exactly. Remember I told Jill I'd give Malcolm a party to celebrate the pregnancy? Well, she decided tonight was the night.' His hand brushed hers as he took the grocery bags.

The familiar tug of heat stopped whatever she'd been about to say. No matter that they'd managed to avoid each other most of the week, the desire their kiss awakened had only been tamped down, not put out.

Obviously Dan wasn't affected in the same way because he was strolling up the drive, explaining what had happened. 'This is way bigger than I'd intended. Malcolm's to blame. He took it into his head to organise someone to run the pub tonight and then invited half the patrons here.' Dan didn't look at all repentant.

'Right.' With her body shivering and shimmying with desire it was difficult to concentrate on what Dan was saying as she walked beside him. 'You must've spent the whole day preparing food.' There'd been next to nothing in the fridge that morning when she'd got her breakfast and she could see a large table laden with containers of food.

'That's just it. They all know me enough to bring food with them. I've been working on the section all day—mowing, weeding, trimming trees. No time for the supermarket.'

Sarah looked around, for the first time noticing how cared for the property looked. 'You have been busy. The place looks wonderful.'

Dan growled, 'I probably shouldn't have started. Now I'll have to keep it looking like this. I'd forgotten how much effort it takes. It's years since I gave a hoot about gardens and lawns, but when today dawned sunny and calm I made the most of the opportunity to get stuck in.'

'Don't tell me you're a surfer from way back?' She pointed to a surfboard leaning against the shed. Her mouth dried as she pictured Dan in swimming shorts, his legs braced on the board as he rode a wave, balanced by those strong arms.

'Like the horse riding, it's been years. But I'm going to give it a crack over the next few days. More sore muscles coming up.' He smiled at her. 'And there's something else I'd obviously forgotten.'

'What's that?'

'How to have fun. I can thank you for my awakening.'

'How's that?' Leah made better conversation than she did.

He pointed to the flowers. 'You make our house feel like a home again.' Dan flicked out a second finger. 'I'm enjoying cooking for cooking's sake. It's no longer a chore to be done as quickly and effortlessly as possible. And I spend more time on the deck watching sunsets and sunrises than I've ever done. It's great.'

He was crediting her with that? He needed his head read. She'd contributed less than zilch to the way he got on with his life. 'You're on leave and finally relaxing.'

The third finger popped up. 'It dawned on me today when I began poking around in the shed that there's a lot more to do than work, work and work.'

'There's Leah.' Could she learn a thing or two from Dan? Find something else to do other than work? Like what? Sport? Knitting? Flower decorating? Nothing rang any bells of excitement. She'd never spent time playing.

'And there's me.' Dan spun around in front of her. 'No one is going to be me, do my things—except me. So let's get rid of these bags and party.'

Right. Sure. Surely his plans for living didn't include her?

'Sarah, there you are.' Jill approached to give her a hug. 'You're becoming a bit like Dan, all work and no play. Come and meet the rest of the mob.'

'I thought it was a family affair.' Not Dan's comingout party. 'Is there anyone left in town?'

Jill rolled her eyes. 'This is family, sort of. These Reillys are a prolific lot.'

Dan retorted, 'Especially since Malcolm has finally worked out how it's done. I'm looking forward to meeting the newest member of our clan.'

Jill laughed. 'You've got eight months to wait.'

Sarah grinned. 'Eight months. You're obviously counting the minutes.' Did she fear something happening to her as it had to her sister? Did she ever think her child might be left motherless like Leah? If the glow on her face and the happiness in her eyes were pointers then definitely not. Besides, it must be reassuring to know someone in the extended family would look out for the child if the unimaginable happened.

Sarah moved towards the house. 'I'll go and put my bag in my room and change into something more in keeping with a barbecue.'

'No, you don't. You'll hide away and I'll have to drag you out here.' Dan followed her.

She'd been going to sit down, try to pretend that a crowd of strangers weren't outside having a great time, and that she had to meet them all. 'Five minutes?'

'Two.'

Stifling an oath, she stomped through the house, threw her handbag on the bed and quickly divested herself of her suit, replacing it with shorts and a blouse. Port Weston had turned on a superb day, which was continuing into the evening. She could do with some sun on her skin. As long as it didn't bring out the freckles.

What could she talk about to everyone? They had nothing in common with her. Everyone she'd met since arriving here had been very friendly but she stood out like a bean in a fruit salad.

'Time's up.' Dan leaned against her bedroom door.

'You ever heard of knocking?' At least her blouse was buttoned up and her shorts zippered.

'No one's going to eat you, so you can take that worried expression off your face.' So why did he look like he wanted to indulge in a little nibbling? 'And here's a glass of your favourite bubbles.' He offered her the cold glass, and as she gratefully took it, he added, 'Relax, you'll be fine. They're mostly my family.'

Exactly.

Sarah parked herself on the steps leading from the deck to the lawn and very soon a tall, slim woman joined her. 'I'm Bea, Dan's older, and apparently bossier, sister. I hope we're not overwhelming you.'

'There are quite a few of you. Especially when Jill's relatives are added into the mix.' Could she ever get used to having so many people in her life, people who would want to know her business? Want to share the ups and downs of life? Why was she even wondering about it?

'When my brothers married the two sisters, our family seemed to expand rapidly. Jill and Celine have even more family than the Reillys.' Bea glanced across the lawn. 'Speaking of children, here comes Leah, heading directly for you.'

'Me?' Sarah blinked. 'I doubt it. I hardly see her during the week. She's usually in bed by the time I get home, and I'm gone again before anyone's up.' But her heart warmed as she watched Leah racing towards her.

'Yeah, and whenever I have her she talks nonstop about you. Sarah this, Sarah that. She adores you.'

'Sarah, you came home for the party.' A bundle of arms and legs hurtled into her, knocking her glass over and tipping her back against the railing post.

'Hey, kiddo, slow down.' Automatically Sarah wrapped her arms around Leah's body to protect her. And to hug her. She did a lot of hugs these days. Then Leah plonked a sloppy kiss on her chin. Tears threatened, and Sarah blinked rapidly. Leah adored her? Her? Surely not. So why was her heart dancing?

'What did I say?' Bea winked at her. 'Seems like you're having the same effect on our Dan, too.'

'Dan's talking nonstop about me?' Bea was crazy. First Leah adored her and now she was changing Dan too. Did insanity run in the family? She glanced at Leah, a perfectly normal child if ever there was one.

Bea shook her head at Sarah. 'No. He doesn't mention you at all, not a word.'

Now she was really confused. 'I'm not following you.'

'My brother's always talking about people, mostly how useless they are at this, how bad at that. But you, nothing. His lips are sealed. Which says to me you are getting to him.' Bea stood up, and added, 'For the record, I like it. I really do.'

'You don't know me.' With her arms still wound around Leah Sarah stared up at Bea. People didn't love her, not unconditionally as Bea had suggested Leah might. 'For the record, Dan definitely isn't interested in me.'

Bea only laughed. 'I'll get you another drink while you and Leah talk about your respective days.'

'I've been helping Daddy clean the shed.' Leah wriggled around on Sarah's knees. 'We found lots of his toys.' Her little hands picked up one of Sarah's and held it tight.

Warm and sticky hands. A small, bony bottom that bounced on Sarah's thighs. Leah chattered nonstop, her sweet, freckled face lit up with an enormous smile, a smile just like those rare ones of Dan's. A lump closed Sarah's throat. Her arms gently tugged Leah a little closer. Darn, she'd miss Leah when she went away.

'Here.' Dan handed down the refilled glass. An odd look filled his eyes as he looked from his daughter to Sarah and back. 'That was a big welcome home.'

Wasn't he happy Leah had raced to see her? Sarah gulped at the bubbly, studying his face and preparing to put Leah away from her. No, she'd read Dan wrong. He looked more…confused. As though he sensed a bond growing between Leah and herself that he was unsure about. His protective instincts kicking in? Very wise. Someone had to look out for Leah's heart and Dan was the man.

Sarah put down her glass and placed Leah on the step beside her, growing cold when the contact between them broke. *And I'll look after my own heart, keep it intact, avoid too much involvement with this gorgeous man and his child.* The lump in her throat expanded. Could be she was already too late.

Bea's conversation filtered into her mind. So Dan didn't say a word about her to his sister.

She needed to get away from his looming presence to make some sense of what Bea had said. She'd mix and mingle, meet some of these people. Meet the family. Okay, jump back in her car and head somewhere, anywhere. Reaching up to the railing to haul herself onto her feet, her hand encountered Dan's and he helped her up.

'Thanks,' she muttered, and leaned down to retrieve her glass.

'You're very good with Leah. Patient and fun.' Those blue eyes locked with hers. Searching for what?

'Patience is not my strong point.' Certainly not with children. What was with these people? Pushing Leah at her as though it was normal.

Dan ran a thumb across the edge of her chin. 'You underrate yourself.' Then he repeated Bea's words. 'Leah thinks you're the best, and I'm starting to think she may be a good judge of character.'

Before Sarah could think up an answer to that, they were thankfully interrupted.

'Hello, there, Dan. Sorry we're late but Brent's truck got stuck out at the mine.'

'Cathy, you're looking good.' Dan gave the very pregnant woman a hug before introducing her to Sarah. 'And here's Brent and their daughter, Cushla. Hey, cutey-pie.' Dan chucked the girl under her chin and received a shy smile in return.

'Hi.' Sarah shook Brent's hand and smiled at the toddler with the flat facial features suggestive of Down's syndrome. 'Hello, Cushla.'

The child peeked up at her from behind her father's legs. 'Wello.'

Sarah turned back to Cathy. 'When's your baby due?' The woman appeared to be in her late thirties, maybe early forties.

'Five weeks, and counting,' Cathy rubbed her extended tummy. 'Hot days like today are very uncomfortable.'

'And you can't wait for him to arrive so you can do all those things mums do with their newborns,' Brent hugged Cathy around the shoulders. 'Cathy's a wonderful mum.'

'I just love it,' Cathy agreed. 'Now I've got to see Jill. It's so exciting. Two babies being born into our family this year.'

Sarah raised an eyebrow. 'Don't tell me you're related to the Reillys too?'

'Dan and I are cousins.'

Sarah shook her head. This went way past her idea of a big family.

Dan glanced at her. 'Always room for new blood.' His gaze slid over her, hesitating at her mouth, before he turned away.

Surely he wasn't considering her for the role? They'd shared one kiss. That was all. He could not be getting ideas of having all those extra children he wanted with her. Lighten up. That look had been more about sex than babies. Hadn't it?

Did she want Dan's babies? As Dan wandered away she glanced from him to Leah and back, her teeth nibbling her lip. Leah was gorgeous. Dan made beautiful babies. But, then, he was gorgeous too. She smiled, despite herself. This was so out of left field. They'd shared one kiss and she was thinking happy families with him.

She needed to get to know him a whole lot better before she gave in to this need building in her. But already Dan had woven a spell around her, had her looking to the future with more hope than she had been on New Year's Day. Had her father been right, pushing her to come here?

Across the lawn Dan talked with two women who'd just arrived. He was completely at ease with them, and they were laughing at something he'd said.

Dan. A likeable, reliable man. A loveable man. An excellent parent despite the problems he had to sort out with Leah. He wasn't ready for anything more exciting than an affair either. So go for one. Could she? Dared she?

A sobering thought crashed into her head. Was he trustworthy? Women gravitated to him, here, at the hospital, in the street. Could he be trusted not to stray? She thought so, especially for the duration of an affair. But she was afraid to believe so. History had taught her to be very careful about that.

CHAPTER EIGHT

SARAH sat on the deck listening to the waves slapping onto the beach, hearing Dan in the kitchen as he rinsed the remaining few glasses. The last couple had finally left at about one o'clock. Leah had been sound asleep in her bed for hours. Apart from the rattle of the dishwasher being stacked, the quiet she'd been looking forward to all day had finally settled over the house.

Stars twinkled, so much brighter here on the coast without a huge city lighting up the sky. A full moon turned the sky black and made shadows on the lawn. She stretched her legs out and tipped her head back, studying the universe, looking for familiar constellations.

Instead an image of Dan's face floated across her vision. His deep-set eyes were unreadable, his lips inviting. Reminding her of their kiss. The kiss that stole into her dreams every night, that hovered in the air whenever they were in the same room together, that filled every other minute not filled with work.

That kiss had begun undoing all her defences. Dan had kissed her as though she was to be treasured and awakened, like she was hot. Some of her lost self-esteem had begun creeping back, still fragile but there nonetheless. Being desired by a sexy man like Dan did her good. She was coming alive, and suddenly wanted to reach for more.

She'd taken to staying late at the hospital, sometimes eating in the cafeteria, striving for normality. Or calm at least. Keeping her distance from temptation. She might be thinking about wanting to take this further with Dan but she'd never put herself out there, afraid he might turn her down.

'I've made you some tea.'

Sarah jerked her head around. 'Tea?'

When she was thinking about the effects of Dan's kiss, he was making tea. Suddenly she giggled, just like Leah. This whole scene was crazy.

'Earl Grey.' Dan's look was quizzical. 'What's so funny?'

Did he think she was laughing at him? 'Tea's great. Truly.' Then the words just popped out. 'A little tame.'

And was rewarded with the sound of his sharply indrawn breath. 'You don't like tame?'

Now it was her turn to be rendered speechless. She turned back to the stars. She should leave flirting alone. She wasn't up to speed, and now she'd backed herself into a corner. One she had to get out of in a hurry. Before temptation overrode common sense.

Dan would swear Sarah wanted him as much as he wanted her. Her gaze never left him for long. Then there was the way her tongue did that quick little flick at the corner of her mouth whenever he looked at her. So what was she afraid of? Not him, surely? Getting involved? Yeah, well, that scared the hell out of him too. Which was why a fling was the answer. But was Sarah ready for that? Did he nudge her along, or give her space to come to her own conclusion? The right one for him, of course.

His hands clenched at his sides. Go do something practical and get over her. For now, anyway. Nothing was happening tonight. Stomping inside, he headed for the laundry, his brain ignoring his warning, taunting him with sensations her lips had evoked. He wanted her. In his bed.

'You're not having her.' He bit down on an expletive. But... 'But nothing.' It would be the dumbest idea to sleep with her when they had to share his house for many more weeks. Flings were exactly that—flings. Throwaways. They invariably finished. How much more uncomfortable it would be for them then, sharing the same house. Even if she did find somewhere else to stay, it was a small town, and they'd inevitably bump into each other.

The way his relatives had taken to Sarah tonight, she'd be going to every family meal, picnic, celebration for the rest of her time here. There'd be no getting away from her. And now Bea and Jill seemed intent on helping a romance blossom for him with Sarah. As though it was the most natural thing in the whole wide world. Damn their meddling. He'd have to put a stop to that.

Except he kind of liked the idea, when he thought about it. So he shouldn't think about it. But what if he convinced Sarah to stay on come the end of March? They'd be able to pursue this thing going on between them. Because something sure as hell was. He couldn't rid his head of her. Look at the way his hormones ramped up whenever she was around. And sometimes when she wasn't.

The washing-machine lid slammed back against the wall. Dan made to toss in the wet kitchen towels, and noticed Sarah's clean washing still in the bottom of the machine. She must have forgotten it. Or been in such a hurry to get away in the morning that hanging it out was rendered unimportant.

Tugging out her clothes, he tossed them into the washing basket, before putting his wash on. When he had the machine running he took Sarah's clothes and headed out to the back porch, where there was a line under the roof. That was the norm, living on the Coast. Otherwise there'd be weeks when nothing dried.

Bending down for a handful of pegs and clothes, he groaned at the lacy white pieces of fabric in his hand. Bras and a thong. He dropped them. Blew a breath up over his face. She wore thongs. His erection was back with a vengeance.

Cool sand pushed between Sarah's toes, covered her feet, as she strolled along, easily avoiding stones and driftwood in the moonlight. Down here the waves were louder. Foam spread out, pushed towards her, rolling shells over and over. Beautiful. This coastline drew her in, gave her a sense of peace when her mind was flip-flopping all over the place. She wanted Dan. She wasn't going to have him.

'You're restless tonight.' Dan spoke from behind her.

She jerked her head up, dragging her mind with her. The tension she'd been trying to ease cranked tighter. 'Why are you here?'

'I saw you wander down and thought I'd join you.'

'What about Leah? Shouldn't you be with her?'

'She's sound asleep, with Toby guarding her. If she even tries to roll over, that dog will make such a racket I'll hear.'

'Why's Toby at your place?' She still couldn't call it her house. If she did she'd be admitting that she liked sharing a home with Dan and his daughter.

'Sometimes Bea leaves him with us. Leah adores him and wants her own puppy, which I don't have the time for. It would be left on its own too much with me at work and Leah going to kindergarten.' Dan reached for her hand, began walking again.

'Oh.' Why had he taken her hand? *Why* wasn't she tugging it away? 'Dan?' she whispered.

He stopped, turned to her and gently pulled her in against him. His chest was hard and firm under her cheek, his thighs strong against her legs. His hands held her head, each fingertip a touch of magic.

'Sarah.' His voice was low, commanding. Tipping her head back, her breath caught in her throat as Dan's mouth came down to cover hers. Those lips she'd dreamed about for a week now a reality. Only better. Firm, demanding. Was this wise? She pulled away from him. Dan tugged her close again. This time her body folded in against his and she lost herself in the sweet longing his kiss stirred up. His tongue gently probed her mouth, exploring, tasting.

Her arms wound around his back, pulled him even closer. She wanted more of him. She craved all of him.

Lights from a car travelling along the road lit up his face. Toot, toot.

Sarah leapt back, feeling like a guilty schoolgirl. Dan chuckled. 'Takes you back, doesn't it?' He reached for her again. 'But I don't remember kisses being like this.'

Neither did she. Under his mouth her lips curved into a wide smile. Kissing was rapidly becoming her favourite pastime. Her fingers touched the light stubble on his jaw, traced over his bristly cheeks. That quintessential maleness sent shivers of desire down her spine, spreading through her body.

The sea air brushed her arms as Dan's hands slid under her blouse. Goose-bumps lifted on her skin. From the air? Or from the excitement of fingers teasing her nerve endings by tracing circles over her back? Her muscles felt languid. Any moment she'd drop to the sand, her legs unable to hold her up. Dragging her hands down his cheeks, over his chin, throat, she touched his chest, the muscles hard through his shirt.

Dan pulled his mouth from hers, stared into her eyes.

'Sarah Livingston, you're going to the undoing of me.' His voice cracked, his mouth took on a wry expression. 'But I am enjoying the experience.'

'Then hush and kiss me some more.' Sarah took a handful of shirtfront and pulled him closer. Her mouth stifled his laugh.

Hungry lips melded with hungry lips. Hot tongues danced around each other. Dan's hands gripped her buttocks, hugged her against him. Heat roared through her, over her. Desire wound between them, joined them. Sarah had no doubt how this would end if she let it. Which was why she pulled back, tearing her mouth away from Dan's, putting space between their bodies. 'I'm not sure we should be doing this. I'm sorry, I got a bit carried away.'

He didn't say a word, just shoved his hands deep into his jeans pockets, staring at her all the while.

How to tell him she wanted him so much but daren't? Her heart wouldn't take another pounding. *But he's not asking for your heart.* Dan might be thinking about having an affair, and she'd thought that's what she wanted too. But some time over the last week or two, somewhere between the hospital and this house, she'd started feeling strongly for this man. And if she went further then she was going to get very hurt when it all crashed to an end when she headed north again.

Turning back towards the house, she glanced over her shoulder. He was skimming pebbles across the wave tops, his shoulders slouched, his chin on his chest.

Her heart rolled over. She wanted him so much it burned, but she was behaving sensibly by walking away.

Dan heaved another pebble, watched it sink into the cold, black water. Why couldn't he keep his hands to himself? His blasted hormones would be the death of him if he wasn't careful. He should be grateful Sarah had had more self control than him. From the moment her mouth had met his he'd had absolutely none.

The next pebble bit the dust, bouncing along the sand. Sarah had been hurt, was still grappling with getting her life back together. She didn't need to add some randy man with his own problems to the mix. She may have wanted him, and he'd swear she did, but she certainly didn't need him. He was bad for her. She had trust issues.

So did he. He needed to be trusted one hundred and ten per cent. Something Celine had found impossible to do once the miscarriages began taking their toll on her. Being accused of infractions where there hadn't been any had hurt him deep inside. No, Sarah was wise to have walked off.

None of which made him feel any happier with himself. Bending down, he tugged his sandals off his feet, tossed them up the beach. Then he started running along the sand, heading away from the house, going faster and faster, trying to outrun the need for Sarah Livingston that gripped him hard.

'Wake up. Now.' Leah tugged at the pillow, disrupting Sarah's sleep and jerking her head. 'Daddy's taking us to the Pancake Rocks.'

Sarah cracked one eye open. 'Hello, lovely.' Who let little girls out of bed before midday in the weekend?

Leah giggled. 'Hello, sleepy.' Then she began pulling back the sheet. 'Get up. We're having pancakes for breakfast.'

Breakfast? It was far too early. The bedside clock showed eight-thirty. Definitely too early. She tried to retrieve the sheet and a tug of war ensured. Leah won.

'Why pancakes?' Sarah flopped back against her pillow, her stomach groaning at the thought of something so heavy this early.

'Cos we're going to the Pancake Rocks. Get it?'

'Leah, I'm not going there.'

'Daddy said you were.' Leah's bottom lip pushed into a pout, turning Sarah into a spoilsport.

'Sorry, Leah. I'm going to the library today.' She'd decided to join up and get back into reading for pleasure, something she hadn't done for years.

'Daddy will make you come.'

Daddy, whose fault it was she'd been awake for a substantial part of the remainder of the night. 'Your father,' she ground out, 'is making assumptions.'

'Not at all.' A deep, gravelly voice cut across the room from the doorway.

Instinctively Sarah reached for the sheet, pulling it from Leah's grasp, tucking it around her throat. When she looked at Dan he had a glazed look. Because he'd seen her in a negligee? Surely not. Looking around the room, checking out Leah, she couldn't see what else might've put that look on his face.

Dan's tongue slid across his bottom lip. 'Have you ever been to Punakaiki?'

He knew very well she hadn't. 'I must've driven past it on my way here but didn't see anything through the driving rain.'

'Then you're in for an experience.' Dan finally dragged his gaze away from her and looked to his daughter. 'You'd better get dressed, my girl. No one eats pancakes in their pyjamas.'

'Hello? Dan? Which part of "I'm not going" don't you understand? I'm on call, remember? I've also got a patient round to do. There are people expecting to go home today.'

'All taken care of.'

That was it? All taken care of? She rolled one hand through the air, finishing palm up pointing at him. 'How? Who? Since when did you think you can organise my life? My work?'

'By phone, Charlie, this morning.' His smile was slow and cheeky, and devastating to her heart. 'You are entitled to weekends off, you know.'

Dan whisked the pancake batter fast. He wanted sex so badly he hurt. Not just any old sex either. Only the kind that involved Sarah Livingston.

She looked beautiful in that black negligee thing, the front scooping down over the swell of her breasts. He didn't get why she wore those things when she went to bed alone. What a waste. But she had come out of a relationship so maybe she had drawers full of the stuff. His teeth were grinding hard.

'Look, Daddy, Sarah helped me get dressed.'

Dan peered down at his daughter, the familiar tug of love tightening his gut. 'You look pretty, little one.' How had Sarah managed to cajole Leah into wearing that particular T-shirt with those cute shorts? He'd never been able to persuade Leah that the elephant on the shirt was not going to squash the puppies on the shorts. A tick for Sarah.

'Are the pancakes ready?' Leah dragged a chair over to the bench and hopped up to take the bowl from his hands. 'Can I stir them? You didn't put blueberries in them. How many are you making? I don't know if Sarah likes pancakes. She didn't say.' Leah turned towards the door. 'Sarah. Do you like pancakes?' she yelled at the top of her lungs.

Dan covered his ears and grinned at his girl. 'You'll wake the seagulls with that racket.'

Leah giggled. 'Daddy, they are already up. There're lots of them. Look out the window.'

He did, and noted the birds circling a spot on the beach. A dead fish or bird must've washed up on the morning tide. 'We'll go and take a look while we wait for slowcoach.'

'Who's a slowcoach?' Sarah stood in the doorway, dressed in perfectly fitting, white knee-length shorts and a crimson, thin-strapped top that hugged her curves.

And sent his pulse rate into orbit. He turned away to break the connection he felt with her. Otherwise he'd reach out to take her into his arms and kiss her senseless. Despite the talking to he'd given himself on the beach last night. 'Why don't you two go and see what the gulls are squawking about while I make these pancakes? But don't take too long.' Just long enough for him collect his scattered emotions.

Idiot. That would take for ever. He tapped his forehead. You invited, actually insisted, that Sarah come with us today. Now you're going to spend the whole day noticing how sexy she is every time you look at her. Idiot, he repeated.

Through the window he saw Sarah take Leah's hand as they got close to the road. Sarah had the right instincts with his child, for sure. And Leah liked her.

So did he. A lot. This wasn't about lust. Some time while he'd been trying to keep her at bay she'd sneaked in under his skin anyway. Touched his heart and had him wanting to share so much more with her. Truth? From the moment he'd set eyes on her he'd felt a connection that would take more than a tumble in the sheets to fix.

But last night had shown she wasn't ready. And neither was he.

He dropped a large knob of butter into the hot pan and poured in some batter. The smell of melted butter teased his senses, overlaying the scent of Sarah that permeated the house these days. She'd made her presence felt in a lot of little ways. Like those stinky lilies on the dining table. At least the roses she'd bought yesterday smelt sweet. Even if she'd only put something back in its place at a different angle, he felt her aura. In every room except his bedroom.

He hadn't felt this much in need of intimacy in for ever. If this was what stopping work for a while did then he should be getting back to the job. Except that his former life, that one prior to the arrival of Sarah, now seemed dull and uninteresting.

He flipped the first pancake. He needed a hobby. Tomorrow was supposed to be fine. He'd put the surfboard in the water, try riding a wave or two, and likely make a fool of himself. Anything would be better then hanging around Sarah like a lovelorn teen.

'Those pancakes were fabulous.' Sarah stacked dishes in the sink and began wiping down the table. 'Now, off you go and enjoy the rocky version.'

Dan put his hand over hers, effectively stopping the wiping. 'Please come with us. I'd really like you to.'

Spending a day in Dan's company without the benefit of staff or his family to break the friction between them would only increase the tension. 'Leah needs more time with you, just you.'

'She doesn't need my attention every single minute of the day. Now, I...' he tapped his muscular chest '...need some adult company.' His finger under her chin tilted her head back. His eyes met hers, pleading with her. 'Please say you'll come.'

'I shouldn't.'

'Why ever not?' He turned them both to look out the

window. 'How many stunning, clear days like this one have you seen since you arrived?'

'We had one yesterday.' A trip out would be fun, a day away from patients and staff and decisions. She'd been here nearly a month and because of Dan she now had her first full day off. The library was never going to compete.

'I've packed lunch for when we're watching the water spouts and the seals. I used your salmon steak to make a quiche and there're plenty of salads left over from last night.'

'Okay,' she submitted, and felt surprisingly relaxed about it. Suddenly it seemed like time to go and play.

'Daddy, what are those animals? The ones on the pancakes?'

Dan sat Leah on the rail of the safety fence circling the top of the viewing platform and held her firmly. 'Those are seals. They're sunbathing after hunting fish in the sea.'

'I want to pat one.'

'Definitely not, my girl. Seals give big, nasty bites.' Loud grunts could be heard over the waves crashing against the edge of the Punakaiki Rocks. 'Listen to them talking. They sound like you with a tummyache.'

'Do not.'

Sarah studied the cumbersome brown bodies sprawled across the sun-warmed rocks. 'Hard to believe how fast they can move, isn't it?'

'I've seen a grown man running pretty quick with a seal snapping at his heels.' Dan grinned. 'It was funny once the guy made it to safety. We ribbed him about it for weeks.'

'Charming.' Sarah heard the tide roaring in. 'Look at the pancakes, Leah. You might see the water fountain coming out the top.'

'Where? I can't see, Sarah. Show me.'

Sarah leaned on the railing, putting her head close to Leah's, and pointed. 'See that rock that looks a bit like Dad's stack of pancakes? They're a lot bigger than your father's and not as lopsided.' Sweet little-girl smell teased her, made her want to cuddle Leah. 'The rocks on the other side of the seal that's staring at you?'

She stood up straight again. Warm masculine smell tantalised her. Since when did men smell so divine? Or was Dan the only one who did?

'I can't see the fountain.'

'Patience, my girl.' Dan jiggled Leah, smiling over the top of her head at Sarah, sending Sarah's heart rate into overdrive. 'Lopsided, huh?'

'The maple syrup only ran one way.' She grinned at him, her heart turning over. 'Your way.' He looked magnificent in his navy chinos and white shirt so new she'd had to cut the label off the collar as they'd made their way out of the house earlier.

He looked so relaxed and comfortable that Sarah wondered why she'd argued about coming. She couldn't remember the last time she'd enjoyed herself so much. And there wasn't a spa or upmarket wine bar in sight. Three people happy to be together doing something as simple as having a picnic and staring at blowholes in the rocks. Like a real family. Everything seemed easy here with Dan. All the usual worries and fears that haunted her had disappeared in the magic of the day.

She said, 'You never mention your parents.' Neither did she, come to think of it.

Dan looked at her over the top of Leah's head. Sadness tinged the piercing blue of his eyes. 'Mum died of cancer six years ago. Dad missed her so much he died of a broken heart a year later.'

'I'm sorry, that must've hurt.'

'It did. We all felt we might've let Dad down. But at the same time they'd had such a strong marriage I can see why one couldn't live without the other.'

'That's lovely, I think,' Sarah sighed. 'You know, I sometimes wonder about my parents. When Bobby died they separated, but neither of them has remarried, or even had a deep and meaningful relationship.' Her father had found solace in his work.

'You're wondering if they still love each other?'

'I'm being silly. They can't, not after the horrible things they said to each other back then.' But stress did funny things to people. 'I know Dad still supports my mother in a very lavish way, bought her a beautiful house in an up-market suburb, makes sure she has support in anything she does.'

Dan turned to her. 'You always say Dad and my mother, not Mum. Are you not close to your mother?'

Her lips pressed together for a moment. 'I guess not. We never seemed to have anything in common.'

'I'm hungry.' Leah twisted around in her father's arms. 'Can we have our picnic?'

Dan laughed. 'You've only just had breakfast. We'll go for a walk first.'

An hour later Sarah spread a blanket on a patch of grass where they could overlook the rocks and Dan unpacked the lunch he'd put together. Leah sipped a juice and leapt around laughing and talking nonstop.

'I wish I had as much energy.' Sarah leaned on an elbow, her legs stretched out over the grass.

Dan's gaze landed on Sarah. 'Glad you came?'

'Actually, yes. It's ages since I've been on a picnic.' When had the last time been? 'I remember Gran taking my brother and me to the beach once.'

'Only once?' Dan didn't bother to hide his surprise.

'Now I think about it, she took me a few times.' How had she forgotten those happier times? Well, whatever was in the water down here it had given her memory a tickle.

'Did she always take your brother as well?'

Behind her eyes she could see Bobby sitting on the red plaid blanket. She could feel the childish jealousy that used to flare up within her. She'd wanted Gran all to herself. 'Gran was the only adult in our family who gave equal attention to both of us. I latched onto that as my parents were so busy I missed out on a fair bit.'

'Because you were the youngest? Or because they were too busy with their careers?'

'Mum gave up work when she married and had Bobby. Dad was definitely into establishing himself in the surgical field. Add in conferences, studying and teaching. All those things kept him very busy.' But he did come home for Bobby. It wasn't until later that he'd stopped coming home at night.

Dan touched the back of her hand with a finger. 'And you missed him?'

Sarah bit the inside of her cheek. Turned her hand over and wound her fingers through Dan's, drawing warmth from his touch. 'All the time. I tried everything to get his attention, from being super-good to being a teenage brat. I'm not proud of that.' That hadn't got her anywhere either. By then her brother had become severely ill, and he'd got most of their parents' time.

'I imagine you were only doing what any kid would do in the circumstances. I don't know what you did but I'm sure I'd have been ten times worse.' He paused, staring over Punakaiki. 'I wonder.'

'Yes?'

'Is that what I've done to Leah? I know I haven't been

there very much for her, always busy at work. What if she doesn't even know how much I love her?'

'Dan, your love shows in everything you do.' Had her own dad always loved her? Did he now? He'd sent her here, hadn't he? He'd seen she wasn't coping after Oliver had dumped her. Wasn't that love? She wasn't sure. Her father equally could've been putting the clinic first as an overworked surgeon could become a liability.

Beside her Dan said, 'I hope you're right.'

'You've taken three months off for her. I'd have given anything for my father to do that.' She nibbled her lip. 'I followed him into surgery partly so I could work with him.'

'Daddy, I want a biscuit.'

'Can I have a biscuit, please,' Dan gently admonished his daughter. 'And, no, not until you've had a sandwich.' Then he squeezed Sarah's hand and dropped a light kiss on her cheek. 'Ready for some food?'

She stared into his eyes, looking for pity, found only understanding. Her shoulders lifted, her mouth curved into a smile. 'I'm starving.'

Dan drove carefully, his two passengers sound asleep after their day out. They'd all had so much fun. Once Sarah had got over her hesitation about joining them she'd made the day really work, giving a sparkle to everything they'd done.

Leah clearly adored her. Today she'd seemed even happier than usual, getting all the attention she needed from him and Sarah. Like they were a real family. Unlike what Sarah had grown up with. She wouldn't know a lot about children, and yet she always seemed to get it right with Leah. Did Sarah want kids?

His hands tightened on the steering-wheel. Why did any of this concern him? His feelings for Sarah had little to do with families, more to do with raging hormones and hot sex. Didn't it? Even if he had started developing deeper feelings for her he wasn't ready to contemplate going down the relationship track. He'd believed he'd had the perfect marriage with Celine and that had gone pear-shaped when the depression had come into their lives.

'What's that grim look for?' Sarah's voice was sleepy. She stretched her legs as much as the cramped confines of the vehicle allowed. 'I thought you'd enjoyed your day.'

'I've had a wonderful day, thanks to you.' Dan's eyes slid sideways to gawp at her knees. He quickly turned his attention back to the road. But his tongue cleaved to the roof of his mouth. See? This whole Sarah thing was about sex, and only sex. If they didn't make it into bed soon he would explode, and if they did hit the sack they'd open up a whole new can of problems.

And then his mouth got the better of him. 'Since it's your day off, let's make the most of it and go out for dinner tonight. I'm sure Jill or Bea will take Leah for the evening.'

He shot a quick glance over at his disturbing passenger, saw her tongue do a fast circuit of her lips. Should've kept his eyes on the road. Too late. Even now that he'd refocused on the tarmac unfolding before his vehicle he couldn't get the sight of her tongue out of his befuddled brain. What was happening to him? He'd agreed with himself that he had to put space between them, give her time, and then he'd gone and asked her out. On a date. Dinner for two. No child involved.

It's all right. She'll say no, for sure.

'I'd like that.'

So, he knew absolutely nothing about women. Especially this one.

CHAPTER NINE

DAN placed his elbows on the table and laid his chin on his interlaced fingers, his gaze fixed on Sarah. 'How was your venison?'

'Divine.' Instantly she wished she hadn't licked her lips as Dan's eyes followed her tongue. Pushing her plate aside, she struggled to come up with a conversation starter that would divert his attention. 'Leah had a great time today.' How lame was that?

'She'll drive Jill mad talking about it until she goes to bed.'

Bed. Dan. Funny how the two words seemed to combine in her head. She really had it bad for him. 'Today was wonderfully exciting for her.' And me.

Mischief twinkled in Dan's eyes. 'I'm discovering I like doing exciting things. Coming out for dinner falls into that category. It's been so long since I did anything remotely like it.'

Was it the dinner that was exciting? Not her company? She'd had a lot of dinners, and most of them at far more sophisticated restaurants than this one, but she couldn't remember feeling quite so relaxed and tense at the same time in any of them. 'You should make a regular thing of eating out.'

Dan nodded, then asked, 'What's it like, working with

the famous Dr David Livingston? I remember hearing a lot about him when I was training.'

Sarah sank down into her chair. 'He's a hard taskmaster. You give your absolute best and it's never good enough. And that's not just with me, he treats all his staff the same.'

'Bet he gets the results, though.'

'Yes, everyone strives to impress him.' They all wanted his attention in one way or another. That could be hard on her father at times.

'But you haven't followed his penchant for research.'

'I considered it, but no.' Her fingers fidgeted with the dessert spoon lying on the table.

'Not interested?' Dan's question seemed innocuous enough, but would he understand how much pain was behind her reply?

'Not really.'

'I'd have thought that would've been the way to get the attention you craved.' His fingers lightly brushed the back of her hand.

So he did understand. 'So did I, but I quickly found it didn't suit me. I enjoyed fixing people, using tried and true techniques.'

Dan was studying her closely. 'Enjoyed? As in the past? Not any more?' He didn't miss a thing.

'I had begun losing interest in surgery. For every operation we did, two more people popped up on the list and I began to feel I was working by rote.' She glanced into those blue eyes, saw understanding. 'I always did the absolute best I could. But before I came down here I'd reached the stage where there seemed to be so many patients that if one walked up to me in the street the day after I'd operated on them I'd not have known who they were. That doesn't seem right to me, doesn't seem to be the reason I started on this career in the first place. I felt I'd lost my compassion, my need to heal.'

'Sounds familiar,' Dan drawled. 'We have something in common. We were both sent away from our jobs to get some perspective.'

A small smile tugged at her mouth. 'And it is working for both of us. You're getting your life back, discovering the joys of those big toys you'd hidden away in your shed, having fun with your daughter. I'm finding the fun in surgery again. It's great to work with other professionals who are there for the good of the locals and the hospital, not arguing amongst themselves over who's the best. I'm finding I enjoy operating on people that I'm likely to bump into again.' Her smile widened. 'Two days ago I walked into the supermarket and little Emma Duncan came charging down one of the aisles calling out to Dr Sarah and landing a big kiss on my chin. At least it would have been my chin if she'd been a metre taller.' It had felt so good.

Dan laughed. 'There you go. You're fitting right in here.'

Which reminded her... 'Charlie talked to me yesterday. About staying on at the end of my contract.'

Blue eyes bored into hers, the smile hovering on Dan's lips frozen. 'What did you say?'

'That I'd think about it.' Which was a giant step forward considering she'd arrived here intent on getting through the three months and hightailing it back to Auckland quick smart. 'There are a lot of things to consider, not least my father and his clinic.'

'How will he feel if you sell your partnership?'

Once she'd have said he'd be disappointed, angry even, but now she could see how he'd been trying to help her by sending her away. 'Maybe he'd be happy for me.' Sarah leaned forward, watching Dan closely as she asked, 'But how would you feel if I did stay on? It is your clinic. You've built it up from scratch. Do you want someone working alongside you? Specifically, do you want me in that role?'

Caution filtered through the blue, making his eyes dark and brooding. 'If I say I don't know the answer to any of those questions, you've got to understand I'm not trying to hurt you.'

She dipped her head in acknowledgment, hoping he didn't see the spurt of disappointment she'd felt. 'Sure.'

'I'm surprised Charlie has approached you so soon. I thought he'd wait until the end of March, and I admit I was putting off making up my mind about the hours I want to work until then, too. But one thing's certain, I'm not going back to working those long hours I did before I got kicked off the roster. Not when I'm finally straightening out things at home.'

'You were hardly kicked off.'

'Of course I was, and fair enough. I needed to be.' Dan glanced out the window, back to her. 'I guess the only question I can't really give you an answer to is do I want you to stay on? There's a lot more to that question than hospital hours. It's early days to be contemplating that.'

Her stomach tightened uncomfortably. Her heart squeezed and slowed. 'I shouldn't have asked.'

'Always tell me what's on your mind. That's being honest.' His hand touched hers again, covered it, holding her fingers in his. A caress that quickly went from warm to heated.

She certainly wasn't telling him what was on her mind right this instant. It had nothing to do with clinics and hours and staying or going. All to do with desire and hunger and need. All to do with learning more about each other, taking this thing between them to another level, admitting what she'd been denying since the day she'd arrived in town. Daniel Reilly was hot and she wanted him. Come what may.

Tugging her hand away, she swallowed around the heat blocking her throat. 'Can we order some coffee?'

'In a hurry to get home?'

She'd ride a speeding bullet to get there. 'No, definitely not.'

His eyes now sparkling with heat, Dan said, slowly teasing out the words, 'We've got the whole night to enjoy.' Sexual tension ricocheted between them.

Was that a promise? Her blood cranked up its pace, racing through her veins. Was she finally going to touch those muscles, feel all that hard body, kiss that suntanned skin? What had happened to her usual arguments for keeping distant from Dan? He wanted her to be honest with him. Right now she was being honest with herself. She wanted him.

'Let's have dessert.' Dan leaned over the table, his mouth barely moving, the tip of his tongue slipping across his bottom lip.

She'd never manage to swallow a dot. Her stomach was wound so tight it would repel food like a tennis racquet hitting a ball. She squeaked, 'I'll have the cheesecake.'

He smiled, a long, lazy smile that curled her toes and tightened her belly. 'How do you know they've got cheesecake?'

Thankfully their waitress appeared. 'Would you like to see the dessert menu?'

Dan leaned back and looked up at the girl. 'Have you got cheesecake?'

'Boysenberry or lemon,' she replied.

Dan lifted an eyebrow at Sarah in a quirky fashion, making her incapable of deciding which flavour to have. Not that it mattered, if eating was beyond her.

'Lemon,' she croaked.

'Make mine berry,' Dan told the girl as he reached for his glass of water and took a long drink.

The desserts seemed to arrive in super-quick time as though the staff were working at keeping her wound tight.

Dan picked up his spoon and dipped into the cheese-cake. His mouth closed over the spoon, and he slowly slid it out over those lips she ached to kiss. 'Divine,' he whispered. 'You should try it.'

Just like that the delicious tension rippled through her body, sending out tingles of desire so sharp her fingers shook. She pushed her plate aside. Her appetite had totally disappeared. For dessert, that was. Not for Dan. Dan she wanted to kiss and taste and—

He stood up abruptly and came around the table. 'Let's get out of here.'

'Did you pay the bill?' she asked ten minutes later as Dan swung into their drive.

'I think so.' Dan slammed to a stop at the back door. He was out of the Land Cruiser and around at her door so fast he had to be dizzy.

She practically fell out, into his arms. His hands gripping her shoulders were hot on her suddenly hyper-sensitive skin.

His eyes locked with hers. The baby blue caution was gone, replaced with such carnal intensity that she rocked back on her heels. Her lungs stalled. Without any order from her mind her hands gripped the front of his shirt, tugged him closer. Then her lips sought his, found them, covered them. She gave herself up to kissing him. Heady kisses that he returned enthusiastically.

His tongue pushed between her lips, tangled with hers. He tasted wonderful. Hot male. From deep inside a groan crawled up her throat, giving sound to a primitive longing. A need to make love, a hungry urge to be with this man intimately.

Then his hands were pressing her shoulders away from him. 'Sarah, I've wanted to touch you all day.' His voice caught in his throat. 'If we take this any further, I won't guarantee I can stop.'

Leaning back, she looked into those beguiling eyes again. 'I won't ask you to. I don't want you to.'

'You're sure?' His hands held her face, his thumbs rubbing exquisitely tender circles across her cheek bones.

Sarah nodded, unable to speak around the need blocking her throat. She was past being able to hold out. Past rationalising. She wanted him.

'Then why are we standing out here?' Dan took her hand in his and together they raced for the house.

Inside he leaned back against the door and pulled her close again. His mouth found hers, his tongue slid between her lips. Pent-up desire exploded through her taut body. Heat, molten fire, spread through her muscles, her stomach. Her bones liquefied, no longer able to hold her up. Dan alone did that. He wound her tight against him. His response pressed hard against her belly.

Her tongue explored his mouth. Tasted him. She fell against him, needing to touch the whole length of his body with hers. It wasn't enough. Her hands ran over his back, down to his buttocks, over the curves. She was touching those muscles she'd been sneaking looks at for days. Weeks.

Clothing lay between her and his skin. She tried to slide her hands under the waist of his trousers. They were a tight fit. Frustration made her groan, and her mouth temporarily slid away from his.

Dan pulled his mouth well clear. 'This dress...' he slid the thin straps off her shoulders and down to her elbows

'…is stunning but it has to go.' His head ducked and he ran feather-light kisses down her neck, further down between her breasts. His hands gently pushed her dress further and further down, over her breasts, past her stomach, the hemline lowering from mid-thigh to her knees, pooling at her ankles. The silk fabric light and sensual against her skin, Dan's lips hot and demanding as they trailed a line of kisses from her breasts to her stomach. And lower.

She ached to touch him. Everywhere. Her hands touched here, there. Hard to concentrate while he stroked her. Would Dan be shocked if he knew how desperate she was to take him inside her? Her eyes flew open, met his delirious gaze. No, he wouldn't. The bite she gave her bottom lip stung, sharpening all her senses. Who was this woman acting wantonly?

Dan smiled, a quick curling of those full lips that made her heart flip. 'Bedroom. Now.'

She'd never remember how they got from the back door to Dan's bedroom. She only remembered falling onto the soft, cool bed, Dan sprawling on top of her. His tongue traced a hot, slick path over her taut nipple, moving around, over, beneath, until she believed her skin would split wide with desire. He was merciless, and she cried out for more. The only reprieve came when he swapped one nipple for the other and began again. Between her legs the heat built into a hot, moist pool, reaching an intensity she'd never experienced, never believed possible. How much more could she take? How long would this last before she fell apart in his hands?

'Dan, I can't wait. Can we…?' Then she blushed.

He grinned, a wicked, heated grin that did nothing to slow the rapid pounding of her heart. 'We need some protection, if I've got any.' Horror showed in his eyes.

She managed a chuckle. 'All sorted.' Pregnancy was one thing she'd never risk.

'Thank goodness. For a moment there I thought I'd have to do the impossible and stop.'

Her hands hooked at the back of his head, caught at his hair. 'Oh—my—Dan.' She didn't recognise her voice. It was raspy, fragmented.

And then at last they were together as one. Sarah's world exploded into a trillion beautiful fragments as Dan tipped her over the edge into that place where there was no beginning and no end, only pleasure and fulfilment. And so much more.

'You can remove the padding from Toby's throat.' Sarah nodded at Jill over the prostate body of their patient.

Jill used surgical tongs to lift the blood-soaked cotton padding that had been used to prevent blood pouring down the boy's throat during the tonsillectomy. While Sarah waited she arched her back, turned her head left then right, freeing the tight muscles of her neck.

'It's been a long day,' Hamish stood up from his seat at Toby's head, leaned over his monitors to begin bringing his patient round.

Sarah swallowed a yawn. 'It sure has, and we're not finished.' They'd started the day with a breast lumpectomy, followed by a torn Achilles' tendon.

'Anyone for coffee before the next one?' Jill asked.

'Most definitely. An extra-strong one for me.' She needed a caffeine fix. Too much late-night activity at home had left her happily tired. Since dinner on Saturday her relationship with Dan had ramped up big time. It had begun raining on Sunday, continued through Monday, Tuesday, Wednesday, making him restless. Until night-time after

Leah was sound asleep and then he came to life. They'd fall into his bed, making love as though they'd just invented it.

She was astonished at her appetite for Dan. Occasionally she'd lie awake beside his warm body and wonder where they went from there. It frightened her to think that she wanted more, was beginning to seriously considering staying on in Port Weston—if Dan agreed to the idea. During the early evenings when Sarah couldn't go for her usual after-work walk they'd talked and talked about just about everything. But not about what would happen come the end of March.

Neither had Sarah told him about the CF gene she carried. If they were going to take their relationship any further, she had to tell him. The day would arrive when she had to ask him to take the test to see if he was a carrier too. If he was, there'd be some huge decisions to make about taking the chance on having a baby that might have cystic fibrosis. One thing at a time, she told herself.

'What was that noise?' Hamish asked the room in general.

'Sarah's stomach,' Jill replied.

'A chocolate biscuit wouldn't go amiss,' Sarah agreed.

'We didn't have chocolate biscuits until you arrived.' Hamish grinned.

'I'm not that bad.' They didn't have them at the clinic back home either. Everyone there watched waistlines more carefully than the six-o'clock news.

'Yes, you are,' Jill and Hamish answered in unison.

A girl had to keep her energy levels up. Sarah's vinyl gloves snapped as she tugged them off, and she idly wondered what Dan had been doing during the day. He'd hoped to go fishing with mates but while the rain had lightened a strong wind had picked up. Just thinking about the man made her warm.

'What's that smile about?' Jill murmured quietly as she cleared away dirty instruments and blood soaked cotton. 'Or should I say who?'

'Nosey, nosey.' Sarah elbowed her way through the doors and began to change out of her theatre scrubs.

'You've had a permanent grin on your face for the last three days. What have you two been up to?' Jill was right behind her.

'I'm a smiley person.' Especially after mind-blowing sex before coming to work.

Jill rolled her eyes. 'Whatever you say.'

Familiar male laughter came from the other side of the door. Sarah gaped as Dan sauntered through dressed in scrubs and talking with the house surgeon. Her heart rate raced, her fingers itched to touch him.

'Anyone want one?' He said.

'Where's Leah?' Sarah asked.

'Hello to you, too.' Dan shot her a quick, secret look. 'She's gone to the movies with Bea and the girls.'

'But why have you come in here?' She leaned closer and whispered, 'I haven't got time to sneak into the linen cupboard with you.'

A huge sigh crossed his lips. 'Damn. I had such high hopes.' He suddenly looked serious. 'There was an accident on one of the fishing boats a couple of hours ago. A winch handle snapped and smashed into one of the men, rupturing his liver. Since you were already busy with a big schedule, I put my hand up to help out.'

She'd have liked to watch Dan at work. As opposed to watching him in the kitchen, the garden, the bedroom. 'I hope you don't think this excuses you from cooking dinner. It's your turn.'

'On my way to the supermarket as soon as I've finished this.' He waved his mug through the air. 'Bossy woman.'

Sarah chuckled. 'Someone's got to be.'

Jill's jaw dropped, and she looked from Sarah to Dan and back again.

'What?' Sarah asked.

Jill shook her head. 'He's laughing and joking. Whatever you've done to him, keep it up.'

Sarah spluttered into her coffee. 'Time we went back to work. Mabel Carpenter's hernia is next, isn't it?'

Sarah watched Robert closely as he brought across the coffee she'd ordered. His limp was very pronounced, putting his posture out of alignment and no doubt making his hips ache. Fatigue darkened his eyes and lined his mouth. Why did he put up with it?

George caught her eye and shrugged. 'I keep trying,' he said quietly.

But not quietly enough.

'What do you keep trying?' Robert asked, placing the large cups on the table.

'To get you to see another doctor about that leg,' George said.

Robert scowled at him. 'Don't waste your breath. I'm never going through all that again.'

George ignored the outburst, turning instead to Sarah. 'See what I have to put up with, cupcakes?'

Sarah was torn between smiling at her new name and taking Robert's fear seriously. Cupcakes won—for a moment. And then it was too late to talk to Robert as a customer came in, demanding coffee strong enough to take the soles off his shoes.

George raised an eyebrow. 'We sure get them.' Then he leaned closer to Sarah. 'Could you talk to him? He's in a bad way. He thinks I don't know how often he gets up at night because of the pain, but I'm aware the instant he gets out of bed.'

'I'll do my best.' But Sarah knew that would be woefully little unless Robert wanted to talk with her.

Then a familiar voice called across the room, 'Morning, guys. Is that my coffee? Or are you having two, Sarah?'

'I don't want coffee, Daddy.' Leah bounded over to George. 'Can I have a juice?'

'Please,' Dan told her.

'Please, George, can I?'

'Come with me, young lady. I'm sure there's a special treat somewhere for you to go with that juice.'

Watching Leah slip her hand into George's and skip along beside him Sarah felt the now familiar tug at her heart. So much for not getting involved with the child. Or her father. She was more than halfway in love with the guy. Leaving was rapidly becoming the last thing she wanted to do.

'Sarah?' Dan grinned down at her. 'I've bought you a present.'

She studied the large plastic bag with a local farmer's supply shop logo that he placed in front of her. Squinting up at him, she asked, 'What have you done?'

'Just a little number for your shoe collection.'

'Gumboots?' She dug into the bag and pulled out bright red boots painted with sunflowers. 'Heck, I don't think I've seen anything quite like them.' She jumped up and kissed Dan's cheek. 'They're gorgeous.'

He looked smug. 'Thought they'd come in handy now that you've turned into a gardener.'

Sarah slipped her sandals off and slid her feet into the gumboots. They fitted perfectly. When she raised an eyebrow at Dan he told her, 'I borrowed a pair of your shoes to take with me.'

'They are absolutely perfect in all ways.'

'I thought so.' His phone buzzed with an incoming text. 'Excuse me.'

Sarah dropped back onto her chair, staring at the red and yellow creations on her feet. Laughter bubbled up her throat. Laughing at herself. She was changing so much. Gumboots. They'd look way out of place back in her apartment. Face it, there wasn't any gardening to do there either. Over the week she'd started tidying up the vegetable patch that had gone to weeds. She planted seedlings for salads and soups later in the year. Most of them she wouldn't be here to pick unless… She looked at Dan, love pulsing through her. Unless she committed to staying. Her laughter died.

Did she know Dan well enough to take the risk? How would he react if she said yes to Charlie? Did he expect her to consult further with him about that first? When she'd mentioned it the other night he'd said they needed more time. He needed more time. She didn't. She was ready to stay.

But if Dan wasn't ready for that then maybe he wouldn't be ready to face the cystic-fibrosis issue either. And she definitely couldn't cope again with the dillydallying about having that test done. Oliver had become a dab hand at putting it off every time she'd raised the subject. He'd assured her he could deal with the consequences, whatever they were, but as time had gone by and he hadn't spoken to his GP, she'd had to question that. Oliver had blamed her, saying if she left him alone he'd have done it months earlier. Said if she hadn't nagged him he wouldn't have turned to someone else for comfort. Yeah, right.

Now she wondered if he'd been afraid of learning he wasn't perfect. That would rock him, big time. His image was important to him, his ego huge. Something like being a gene carrier would punch a hole in that ego. And a sweet little obliging nurse wouldn't question his perfection.

Dan had intimated he'd had problems with Celine, although he'd never elaborated to her what they had been. Problems he only now seemed to be coming to terms with. Could she ask him to deal with hers so soon? How would he respond if she asked him to take a test for the gene? Probably very well. He was an empathetic man.

Was she willing to test how compassionate Dan really was? There was a risk he'd walk away from the whole issue, walk away from her. She shuddered. Like Oliver had done before him.

CHAPTER TEN

'WE'RE going horse riding,' Dan told Sarah on Saturday morning. 'Bea wants to give the horses a bit of a workout. Want to come with us? We could tell the hospital where you are in case you're needed.'

Sarah glanced out the window. The rain had finally played ball and disappeared, leaving a sparkling day. 'As long as I don't have to mount a horse, I'm all for it.'

Unfortunately Dan appeared to have selective hearing. Bea had three horses waiting when they pulled into the yard.

'Look, Sarah, there's Flicker and Jumbo and Sammy.' Leah's arm shot in front of Sarah's face, her little finger pointing to the massive animals.

Sarah gulped. 'Bea going with you?'

Dan climbed out of the Land Cruiser and slapped a hat on. 'Not that I know of.'

Another gulp. 'You haven't got me out here under false pretences, have you, Daniel Reilly?'

'I never said you wouldn't be riding. You did. It's my job to change your mind.'

'Not this side of Christmas, you're not.' Sarah stayed in the vehicle, staring through the window at the big beasts, their backs a long way from the ground. 'I'll wait here for you. In case the hospital phones.' Her knuckles were white in her lap.

Leah had already climbed the fence and was petting one of the horses. 'I presume that's Flicker.' Leah looked so tiny beside the horse. How could Dan even consider letting the child ride it? 'Don't you worry about Leah getting thrown off?'

'Yes, which is why someone always goes with her.' Dan stood at the door, his hand on her shoulder. 'Sammy's the smallest of the other two, if you change your mind.'

'He's enormous. My feet won't be anywhere near the ground.' Her heart was racing.

'You're confusing this with the merry-go-round.' Dan leaned in to give her a kiss. 'At least come over with me to give Leah a leg up. We can walk around the paddock with her.'

Bea came out from the house, surrounded by children, some of whom Sarah recognised as Dan's nieces and others she'd never seen before. 'Crikey,' Sarah muttered, beginning to feel inundated as they all crowded around.

Dan laughed. 'It's always like this out here. Bea's kids have a lot of friends and half the reason for that is Bea is so good with them.'

'Hi, there.' Bea waved over the many heads. 'What do you think, Sarah? Want to have a go? Sammy's so quiet you'll struggle to get him moving.'

'No, thanks, I'm into spectator sports.' Wimp. Sarah moved closer to Dan. When he took her hand she hoped he wouldn't notice how much she shook. 'I don't mind going up and patting horses, but that's as far I go.'

'Fair enough.' Dan grinned and slapped her bottom lightly. In front of his sister?

Who, when Sarah glanced at her, had definitely noticed the gesture and was smiling at them both. Great. Why were Bea and Jill so keen for Dan to get friendly with her? Hadn't they read the bit in the contract that said she was only here for three months? Did they want to see him get hurt again?

Everyone, including Sarah, climbed the fence to join Leah. Dan hoisted Leah up into the saddle, helped her slide her feet into the stirrups.

Sarah marvelled at Leah's poise. 'Like a pro.'

Bea agreed. 'Born to it, I reckon, same as with all my kids.'

Dan mounted and followed Leah around the paddock. Sarah couldn't take her eyes off him. Sitting straight and tall, his hands firm yet relaxed on the reins, his thighs pressing the horse's flanks, it was a sight she'd never forget. Simply beautiful.

'Have you ever ridden?' Bea's question scratched against the image holding Sarah enthralled.

'Once. The ride lasted all of three minutes before I was unceremoniously tossed off over the horse's head and into a blackberry bush. Definitely not my thing. Trust me on this.'

Bea smiled in sympathy. 'I can see how that could put you off. But who knows, one day we might get you in a saddle again.'

'What is it with the Reillys that none of you will take no for an answer?' Sarah smiled to take the sting out of her words.

'Guess we only see things from our point of view, and because we know how much fun riding is we want to share it with you.'

'How about I take your word for it?'

Dan trotted over to them. 'Want to try?' he asked Sarah. 'Trust me. I won't let anything happen to you.'

'No, thanks.' Why did he look at her as though she'd

hurt him? Of course she trusted him to look out for her, but so what? It wasn't as though riding a horse was the be-all and end-all.

Dan shrugged stiffly. 'Okay.'

She watched him trot back to Leah. They looked good riding together. Family. But it was only half a picture. There should be a wife, a mother, with them. She was sure she could be there, if she learned to trust again. But she'd sensed over the past week there was something Dan was holding back from her and until he told her, how could she trust him?

'Come and have a coffee,' Bea nudged her. 'Dan and Leah will be a while. The rest of the kids are going eeling and I'd love some adult female chat. At the moment all anyone around here wants to talk about is the camping trip we've got planned for next week.'

'I think you're just being kind, but coffee would be great.' Even an instant one. Which went to show how much she'd changed.

The hours flew past. After the horses had been wiped down and put out to graze Bea put on a simple lunch for everyone, including all the extra kids. John arrived home from the mine where he drove a front-end loader, in time to have a beer with Dan before they ate.

Sarah helped set out the food on a huge outdoor table, watching Bea handle the kids with an ease that made her envious.

'Families, eh? Aren't they great?' She hadn't noticed Dan coming up beside her. Her usual radar had failed. Even the scent of his aftershave was absent today, overlaid with the tang of horse smell.

'Yours seems to have it all worked out. Everyone gets along so well.' Even the children helped each other, despite bickering occasionally.

Dan placed his arm around her shoulders. 'You could still have all this. With the right man.'

Turning, she looked up at him. With you? Was he offering her something she daren't hope for? Did she want to spend the rest of her life with him? Yes, darn it, she did. She loved him. Then start by being honest with him. 'There's something I haven't told you.'

His hand traced a line down her cheek, rested on her chin. 'Go ahead. Fill me in on Sarah Livingston and what makes her tick.'

She pulled away from his warm, heavy arm, took a few steps into the paddock. Stopped. Clenched her hands in front of her, and spun around. 'My brother died of cystic fibrosis. I carry the gene too.'

Three long strides and Dan was before her, taking her cold hands in his. 'Sweetheart, I'm so sorry. Now I begin to understand some of the things I felt you left out when talking about your family.'

'You did?' Was there nothing this man couldn't get right with her?

'Yep.' His hand brushed her hair off her face. 'Thank you for telling me.'

Did he get it? Understand he'd have to be tested for the gene if they were taking this relationship to the next stage. He was a doctor, he'd get it. Was she rushing him? But she had to know. 'There's more. I'm not sure what you mean when you say I can have the whole nine yards, husband and family, but if we're heading anywhere together then you'd have to be tested for the CF gene.'

Dan's smile was so tender she nearly cried.

'Sarah, trust me, I understand that.'

Did he understand she'd like him to do it sooner rather than later? That she needed to know the answer before she could make other decisions about their future together?

Because if he had the gene she'd have to walk away and forget about having his babies. That would be doing the right thing by Dan. She could do it. But leaving would be so hard. Dan and Leah had shown her she could love and, more importantly, they loved her back.

Tuesday night and their lovemaking was unhurried, and exquisitely tender. Sarah had never known that desire could uncoil so agonisingly slowly that every cell in her body was dancing as they waited for the promised release.

'Pinch me,' Sarah whispered. 'I'm not sure that wasn't a dream.'

'Oh, it was real, every last bit of it.' Dan wrapped her in his arms and kissed the top of her head.

Every muscle in her body refused to move. Her mind was a cloud of spent desire. How Dan could take her to the edge and hold her there for so long, tantalising her, making her almost beg to be released.

He said into her hair, 'Wish I hadn't agreed to go camping tomorrow.'

'How long will you be away?' Because the trip had been put off for so long she'd begun to believe he wouldn't be going away.

'Four days at the most.'

'What?' she cried. 'You do what you've just done to me and then tell me you're gone for days?' She'd miss him like crazy. 'Where is this camp site?'

A deep chuckle erupted somewhere above her head. 'You're stroking my ego something terrible. Keep going like that and I'll believe anything's possible.'

'Like what?'

Dan slid down the bed until his face was opposite hers. 'Like coming camping with us.'

'Me?' What a ridiculous idea! She had a job to do in

town. 'Do you think the others would appreciate being kept awake by your passionate cries throughout the night?'

'I can do quiet.'

'For sure.' Sarah snuggled closer. 'I am going to miss you, and not just because of the sex.'

Dan stroked her back. 'Do you think you might like to try camping some time? We could go for a night one weekend while you're still here.'

'Me? In a tent? No hot and cold water, no coffee, wearing clothes I wouldn't be seen dead in?' She poked him lightly in the ribs. 'Get real.'

'I was.'

She chuckled. 'I guess anything's possible given enough time. After all, I do wear gumboots these days.' This guy made her do and say things she'd never have believed a few weeks ago. Now caution and excitement mingled in her veins.

'I'd buy you another pair of gumboots, this time with possum fur.'

'Now you're bribing me.'

'That was only an opening bid. You gave up too easily.'

She grinned. 'What else was on offer?'

'My body.'

'Doesn't count. I can get that with one touch.' And she proceeded to show him how easily persuaded he could be.

Further into the night Sarah lay on her side, Dan spooned behind her with his arm over her waist. Despite her languorous body, she was wide awake.

Dan was out of it, so soundly asleep a ten-ton truck driving through the front door wouldn't have woken him. She was storing up all the sensations from his hand splayed across her tummy to his breaths on the back of her neck, from his hard thighs against the back of her legs to the occasional light snore.

She hugged herself. She loved Dan. What more could she ask for?

Dan's love, that's what. And for him to take that gene test. It was starting to burn at her that he hadn't said any more about it since her revelation on Saturday. It had been hard to tell him, then she'd got nothing back since. *Patience*, she warned herself. But she didn't do patience, not when she was desperate to know his take on the situation. Not when this same scenario had backfired on her with Oliver. When would Dan have the test? Would he have it at all?

She tensed. Why should he? They hadn't made a commitment to a joint future. He didn't owe her anything. She was getting way ahead of herself. Comfortable in Port Weston, in love with Dan, desperate to have children.

She rolled over and looked at his sleeping form. Way, way ahead of yourself, Sarah. This is the affair you wanted to have with him. Nothing more, nothing less. Dan may have helped you move on from Oliver, he may have shown you how to love again, but there had never been any promises beyond that. He hadn't even promised that much.

She had less than three weeks left here. Did she spend them in Dan's bed? Or alone in hers?

The sound of a vehicle in the drive woke Dan next morning. The bedside clock read six. 'Who's that at this god-awful hour?'

He rolled over. Where was Sarah? His hand groped across the other side of the bed. The sheets were cold. He sat up. 'Sarah?'

The house was silent, ominously silent. He leapt out of bed and ran, naked, to her bedroom, then the bathroom still warm from the shower having been run on hot, the kitchen where the blinds had been raised and the kettle

was warm to his touch. Sarah was nowhere to be seen.
Outside her car had gone.

'Strange, I didn't hear the phone.' He'd check with the
hospital to see if she'd been called in for an emergency.

'Sarah's not here,' the A and E nurse informed him.
'And we haven't called for her. It's been the quietest night
on record.'

Then where had she gone? Walking the beach had become a regular habit for her now but the sky was buck-
eting down. Not looking good for camping, though John
had assured him it would be fine by midmorning. Dan
banged the phone down. That cold side of his bed bothered
him. Had Sarah gone back to her room after they'd made
love? He shook his head. She never did that. She reckoned
the after-match cuddles were almost as good as the sex.
The lovemaking. Sex sounded too...too impersonal, un-
involved. No, they made love.

Love? Making love didn't mean he was in love. Did it?
Gulp. He'd been thinking it might be time to find a woman
to share his life with but this was for real. He wanted Sarah,
in his bed, in his life, alongside him as he dealt with all
life's vagaries.

But was he ready? What if Sarah wanted to return to
the city? Could he go with her? Leave his family behind?
He sucked air through his teeth. Could he really do that?
He'd hate it, no doubt. But asking Sarah to stay here meant
asking her to leave her family behind. A family who had
let her down big time. But still her family. How did she feel
about leaving Auckland and her dad? If she didn't want to
then he was prepared to give the city a go.

He flicked the kettle on and spooned coffee granules
into a mug. A new mug that matched the other new mugs
and cups in the cupboard. Piece by piece Sarah was making her mark on his home. Which had only been a place

to grab some sleep and feed his daughter until Sarah had come along.

Last night their lovemaking had been even more magical than ever. Sarah had seemed very happy as they'd lain talking afterwards. He'd sensed she didn't want him going away today. So wouldn't that mean she'd be here to say goodbye to him with a few hot kisses to last him until he got back? What about Leah? Surely Sarah would've wanted to give her a hug before they disappeared for a few days?

Now dressed in jeans and nothing else, Dan stood at the window, his coffee growing cold as he watched the rain pelting down on the drive and paths. Had he missed something? Had Sarah gone from the house to get away from him? So she didn't have to see him until he got back from up the valley?

He ran the previous couple of days through his mind, looking for any clues. She'd been a bit preoccupied at times, but he'd put that down to work. She'd had a busy weekend almost from the moment they'd returned from Bea's, with a couple of tricky procedures that had had her phoning specialist surgeons she knew in Auckland.

For the first time in ages Celine popped into his mind. She used to stop talking to him, go out for a day without telling him where she'd gone. His stomach began churning. All the old guilt bubbled up, threatened to overwhelm him. He'd struggled to get through to her when she'd been like that, thinking the depression had had something to do with her reaction to him. What if he was the problem? Sarah was not depressed and yet she'd left the house this morning without a word to him.

No, history could not be repeating itself. Last night Sarah had been so loving, so willing. And afterwards she'd wrapped her body around his, holding him against her like she'd never let go. What had happened, what had entered her mind in the early hours of the morning that had driven her out of his bed?

Cystic fibrosis. The gene she carried. Should he have talked more about that with her? It would be a major issue in any lasting relationship Sarah was involved in. His heart squeezed for her. How hard had it been for her to tell him? Had she told him now in case they took this affair to the next level? Giving him time to digest it, make his mind up on how he felt? Had she been let down in the past? By Oliver? Questions banged around inside his skull, and the lack of answers raised his anxiety level.

When she'd told him he'd filed it away, something to think about in the future if they continued together. There'd be tests for him to have done, decisions to make if the results showed him to be a carrier as well. But Sarah would've wanted to have some indication on how he felt immediately. It would've been hard for her to tell him. Damn it, he hadn't been very understanding. At least he could rectify his blunder, starting this morning, before he headed away.

So where was she?

Sarah pushed her plate aside and reached for the coffee George had just made. 'That was excellent. I should start every day with a cooked breakfast.'

Opposite her Jill finished the last of her scrambled eggs. 'This baby sure gives me an appetite.'

Sarah laughed. 'At how many months?'

'Who's counting?' Jill buttered a slice of toast, smothered it in marmalade. 'Seriously, I'm always hungry at the moment. If that doesn't stop soon, I'll have to start being careful. Don't want to end up looking like the Michelin Man.'

Sarah rolled her eyes. 'No chance.'

'So...' Jill eyed Sarah over her toast. 'How's things going with my brother-in-law?'

'Fine.' Sarah's muttered understatement earned her a wink. 'Truly.'

'We all know that,' Jill drawled.

'All? Who's all?' Did the whole town about their affair?

'Oh, you know, family.' Jill shrugged her shoulders, but as Sarah tried to relax, Jill added, 'And the theatre staff, Charlie, these guys.' She glanced over at George and Robert working behind the counter.

Sarah gulped. Definitely the whole town. 'Tell me you're joking.'

'Everyone cares about you two, wants to see you both happy.'

'They don't know me.'

'They know you've made Dan smile again, that Leah loves you, that you're a superb surgeon who cares about her patients enough to go in before hitting the pillow late at night so she can make them feel better.'

'Like any surgeon would do.' Patients liked reassurance, especially at night when pain kept them awake and the doubts started rolling in. But she hadn't done a lot of that back in Auckland.

Jill's phone gave a muffled ring from the depths of her handbag. 'Odd,' she muttered when she read the incoming number. 'A and E. Why are they calling me before you?'

Because my phone's not switched on in case Dan tries to call. She didn't have an explanation for not being there this morning, not one she was prepared to give him anyway. But her pager should've gone off. Tugging it off her belt, she was surprised there was no message.

'Sarah's with me. We're on our way.' Jill snapped her phone shut. 'That was Tony. You're needed in the delivery suite. Like now.'

'What's up?'

'It's Cathy. She went into labour late yesterday but apparently everything's progressing too slowly. She has a history of pre-eclampsia, and Tony's considering a Caesarean section.'

'That's why he wants me.' She'd done sections, but not recently.

'Let's go, then.'

George stepped in front of her. 'Sarah, would you like to come to dinner tomorrow night? Not in the café but upstairs in our flat. The three of us.'

She blinked. 'I'd love that.' What was that about?

'See you around seven for a drink first.'

Dan's vehicle was in the car park when they pulled up at the hospital. Guilt tugged at Sarah. Would he be angry at her? That was the last thing she wanted, and yet she couldn't blame him if he was. She'd have been hurt if he'd done the same thing to her. But she'd needed to put space between them before she blew up and said things best left alone. Things like he couldn't be trusted to do the one thing that was ultra-important to her, just like her ex hadn't. Never mind that Dan hadn't known about the gene for more than a couple of days, she felt desperate to know that he could be relied on.

But there wasn't time for him right now. Jill had said Tony sounded very worried.

Tony was waiting outside Cathy's room. 'Thanks for coming in so quickly.'

Sarah got straight to the point. 'Details?'

'Cathy's blood pressure is 170 over 120, and rising. She's got excessive fluid retention and protein in her urine.'

Sarah frowned at the abnormal results. 'And the baby?'

'Prolonged tachycardia. Heart rate of 138 beats per minute five minutes ago.'

'Doesn't sound like we've got any choice but to retrieve the baby.' A racing foetal heart rate was serious.

Tony looked behind Sarah. 'Hi, Dan. Have you come in to help with this one?'

Sarah's heart thumped as she turned. 'Morning, Dan.' He looked wary, not angry.

'I'm available if Sarah needs me. I'm not going up the valley until after lunch.' Dan's eyes didn't leave Sarah's face and she could feel her cheeks heating up. 'I missed you this morning. You left very early.'

'I was restless and you were sleeping soundly.' Disbelief gleamed back at her. 'Jill and I went for breakfast at the café.'

'I tried phoning you to say have a good week, but I kept getting voice mail.'

Her tongue licked her dry lips. 'Sorry, I forgot to turn it on.' The lie was rancid in her mouth. 'Did you come to see Cathy?'

'Brent called me so I decided to drop by, offer him some support,' Dan said.

There was a huge question in his eyes, making her feel mean. She turned away, following the GP in to see Cathy. 'Hi, Cathy. Tony has filled me in on your details. He's called me in for your Caesarean.'

Cathy's eyes widened. 'Sarah, thank you for coming in. I'm really pleased you're doing the operation. Hey, hello, Dan.'

'Hey, how's my favourite cousin?' Dan leaned down to kiss her cheek before turning to a very worried-looking Brent and squeezing his shoulder.

'Not so flash right now.' Cathy had indentations in her bottom lip from pressing her teeth down, presumably during contractions. Her face was grey, another indication that things were not right. She looked to Sarah, a plea in her eyes. 'Is my baby going to be all right?'

Sarah winced inwardly. As yet she didn't know all the details so she wasn't about to make a promise she mightn't be able to keep. But she understood Cathy's fear. 'I certainly intend doing all I can to help ensure that it is.' Then she turned to Brent. 'How are you coping?'

'I'm feeling as useless as snow-boots in the desert. If only I could do something for Cathy.' His voice rose, and his Adam's apple bobbed in his throat.

Poor guy. 'It seems harder for the fathers in these situations.'

Cathy's eyes squeezed tight and her hands clenched Brent's. Her knuckles were white as pain racked her body. Beads of sweat popped out across her brow and the midwife sponged her face. Her breast rose and fell rapidly as she struggled to breathe. 'Pain. It's…not…the…contraction.'

'Take your time, breathe through the contraction,' the midwife instructed.

'Not a contraction.' Cathy struggled to speak. 'In my chest. Pain in my chest. I can't get air.'

The midwife glanced at the GP, then Sarah, one eyebrow slightly raised, before she slipped an oxygen mask over her patient's mouth and nose. Cathy's breathing deepened, not back to normal but better than it had been before the intervention of the oxygen supply.

Sarah finished perusing the notes Tony had handed her. 'Let's go. I'll page Hamish now.'

'He's here somewhere. His car's outside,' Dan informed her. Then he leaned close and whispered, 'Do you want me to assist you?'

A wee sigh of relief slid through her lips. Despite everything, having Dan there made operating so much easier. 'Definitely. That chest pain makes me wonder if something else's going on here.'

'I agree, but we'll take it one step at a time.'

Sarah wanted to touch Dan, hug him, but that would be giving him the wrong message after that morning. It was confusing her. How could she stay away from him during her last weeks here? 'Let's go scrub up.'

Everything happened in a rush. Hamish arrived almost before Sarah had finished paging him, and went straight to see Cathy.

Sarah told Dan, 'Antenatal patients are not my forte. They go to the obstetricians and gynaecologists, not to our clinic.'

Dan nodded. 'I guess I do have the upper hand in this case.'

'I'm quite okay about you taking the lead.' She wasn't about to stand on her high horse about his leave when two patients relied on her.

'How about I talk you through the procedure? Then if another case comes your way over the next few weeks, you'll have this one behind you.'

It wasn't likely to happen but Sarah acquiesced. 'Good idea. Let's get moving. Cathy can't afford to wait longer than necessary.'

Standing beside the operating table, Sarah picked up the scalpel and asked everyone, 'Are we ready?' Then she was pushing down into the swollen flesh that protected a little life.

Michael Ross was born with the umbilical cord wound around his neck. Sarah held him while Dan expertly removed the cord. Their reward was a shrieking, ear-piercing squall. A woozy Cathy watched him hungrily through tear-filled eyes. 'He's beautiful.'

By the time Sarah finished repairing the incision she'd made to retrieve the baby Cathy was alert and eager to hold the precious bundle a nurse had wrapped in a tiny cotton blanket. Thankfully nothing had gone wrong and her earlier concerns had disappeared. Sarah watched as the mother held her son for the very first time.

Cathy had eyes only for her son. The world could've imploded right then and she wouldn't have noticed. She certainly wasn't aware of the orderly wheeling her out into Recovery, where Brent waited anxiously.

Sarah followed, and told Brent, 'I don't think I need to say anything. Your wife and son are doing well.'

'He's a noisy little blighter,' Brent said around a face-splitting grin. He leaned over and kissed Cathy on her cheek, then carefully took his son's tiny fist in his.

Sarah watched them, enthralled. Along with Cushla, they made a perfect family. They'd be busy but she didn't doubt they'd cope.

'You okay?' Dan touched her arm lightly.

'Yes. Isn't this the most beautiful sight?' She nodded at Cathy holding her baby. What did it feel like to hold your baby that first time?

Dan nodded. 'It is. I still remember Leah's birth. The moment I saw her, holding her tiny body, so afraid I'd break her, the instant love that overwhelmed me. It's magic.'

The wonder in his voice made Sarah's eyes fill. She'd love to have Dan's child. She'd love to give him that magic moment again. Would he have that test done? Did it matter if he didn't? Ah, hello. Where had *that* weird idea come from?

'We'll call in later,' Dan told the happy couple.

'Thanks.' Both parents barely lifted their heads from their son to acknowledge him.

Dan took Sarah's elbow and led her out of the room.

'I'm heading home to pick up the tent and other things.' He paused. 'Is there anything you need, Sarah?' His thumb traced a line down her cheek, along her jaw. His eyes were dark with confusion.

Yes, a test result. A hug. Some understanding of why I'm so impatient and tense. 'Not at the moment.'

'I guess I'll get going, then.' He stood in front of her, searching her face. Looking for what? An answer to her behaviour?

'Have a good time. Don't let the sand flies bite too often.' She started to lean in to kiss him, thought better of it, and backed away. If she was going to cut the ties then now was the time to start.

Dan watched her stride away. Her shoulders were tugged tight, her back ramrod straight, her steps a little longer and louder than usual. He was definitely on the outer and none the wiser about why. Deep inside a dull ache began to throb. With it came memories of trying to understand Celine, trying to help her when she hadn't wanted to be helped. Was this the same scenario?

Had Sarah come to a decision about returning to Auckland at the end of the month? If she had, could he blame her? He hadn't given her any indications about his feelings. Because he was only beginning to understand them himself. And needed to know exactly how he felt before he made a move.

Jill appeared at his elbow. 'You okay?'

'Yes, of course.' Dan turned to his sister-in-law, saw the concern radiating from her eyes. 'Actually, I haven't got a clue.'

'She needs you as much as you need her. Don't let the past get in the way.' Jill stood on tiptoe and kissed his chin.

And then she was gone, heading for Theatre and the next patient.

'Easy to say,' Dan murmured. But he had a plan. Sarah had been hurt in the past, and so had he. One of them had to make the first move, break the mould that held them both tied to their pasts. So he went to find Tony.

CHAPTER ELEVEN

'SINCE it's such a beautiful evening, we'll sit out on the deck, if that's all right with you.' George told Sarah when she arrived the next night, a huge bunch of summer flowers in her hand.

'Perfect.' Sarah sighed. 'This is heaven.' Well, it would be if Dan were here to share it with her.

'Isn't it? We took a long while to settle here after the pace of Christchurch, but now we'd never leave. This is a little piece of paradise and the locals are delightful.' Robert sat in the chair beside Sarah. 'Port Weston grows on you, if you let it.'

Looking out over the rooftops of the main street shops to the ocean beyond, Sarah was startled to realise she agreed. 'Auckland seems so far away.'

'It is.'

Throughout the meal Sarah found her mind wandering back to that thought. Odd, but she hadn't missed anything or anyone from home. Not the social events, not the restaurants, the shops, or the clinic. She had been born and bred in the city, so when had she shed that persona? Or was it lurking, ready to take up again the moment she pointed the Jag northward?

Robert placed coffee and Cointreau in front of her. 'Port Weston's got under your skin. Already.'

Not Port Weston, but the people living there. Especially one man. Sipping the liqueur, she savoured the heavy orange tang on her tongue, and asked, 'So what do I do now?'

'Stay. It's as simple as that.'

'And as complex.' She couldn't stay if Dan didn't want her.

George leaned across the table and touched the back of her hand. 'Only you make it complicated. It's hard, shedding all those commitments you have in your other life, but if you want to, you'll find a way.'

'Thanks a bundle.' She knew he was right but this feeling of having found her place could be false. It could evaporate as quickly as it had taken her over. And if Dan didn't want her here then she couldn't encroach on his territory.

'We know what we're talking about,' Robert added.

The three of them sat in comfortable silence for a few minutes. Then George drew a deep breath. 'Sarah, we invited you here for a reason. Not that we didn't want to have a meal with you, of course.'

George spoke so quietly Sarah looked at him out of the corner of her eye. He was watching Robert with such tenderness she felt her heart squeeze. They were very lucky to have found each other.

Quietly, in a flat voice, Robert told her, 'George wants me to have my leg operated on. The pain's getting progressively worse and I don't sleep much at nights. I try not to disturb him but I know I do.'

Her heart blocked her throat. Was this what she thought it was? She said nothing, just waited.

'I'm having the operation done.' A quiver rattled his voice and the eyes he raised to her were heavy with fear. 'And I want you to do it.'

'Thank you for your trust in me.' Wow, Dan had said she could get Robert to change his mind, and it seemed she had without saying a single word. She asked softly, 'What went wrong last time?'

'I nearly died. Twice. My heart stopped while I was on the operating table. Then my leg got infected and they couldn't control it.' He reached for her hand, gripped it hard. 'It was terrifying.'

'You're not going to die.' Sarah squeezed his hand in return.

'I hope not.' The smile he gave her was twisted and sad and filled with fear.

'Robert, I'll need your authority to talk to your previous surgeon and to get your files.'

Sarah shivered. Was she up to this? The surgery didn't faze her, but helping these two men worried her. They'd become friends. She closed her eyes and hoped Dan's belief in her was realistic. Then she had an idea.

'George, Robert, of course I'll do the operation unless I find it is beyond me. But how would you feel about Dan assisting me?' She held her breath, not knowing why they'd come to her, a relative newcomer, and not gone to Dan, whom they were very close to.

The men looked at each and nodded. 'We'd be very happy,' George told her. 'You two are a team in everything you do. I'd have been surprised if you hadn't wanted Dan there.'

Some of the tension that had begun tightening her muscles slipped away. She might have personal issues to sort out with Dan but she needed him by her side when she performed this operation. Robert had become a friend and his fear made her nervous.

'Right,' she said. 'Let's talk.' And she spoke quietly, knowledgably, drawing on all her experience with distressed patients.

* * *

Sarah tentatively scheduled Robert's surgery for the evening two days away, worried to leave it any longer in case he changed his mind. Every spare minute of the next day was spent talking to specialists, calling in Robert's medical records to study and discussing with his previous cardiologist what had happened during the first operation. Hamish agreed to be the anaesthetist and she kept him appraised of everything.

She dropped into the café at lunchtime to reassure Robert. Over a double shot, long black, George tried to voice his gratitude for Sarah getting his partner this far already.

'It's unbelievable. I've been hoping and praying he'd have this done for so long now, and here...' He stopped, unable to finish his sentence.

Sarah leaned forward and touched his hand. 'It's not me you have to thank, it's Robert. He's a very brave man.'

It was nearly six that night when she tossed her theatre scrubs into the laundry basket and changed into jeans and a T-shirt. Outside she waved the key at the Jag to unlock it and slid behind the steering-wheel. A dull ache throbbed behind her eyes as she smoothed out the rough map Jill had drawn for her.

Finding the camping site was unbelievably easy, even for a city girl. Six tents were clustered along the flat grassed area above the river. A fire flickered within a circle of rocks. When Sarah pushed her door open, the harsh pitch of crickets filled the air.

'Sarah?' Dan approached the car. 'What brings you out here? Is something wrong?'

Darn, but he looked so good. Big and strong, his hair a riot of curls, his shorts revealing those muscular thighs she loved to run her hands down. How could she even think about heading north? Leaving Dan?

'Sarah?' Fingers caught her shoulders and his large hands shook her gently. 'What brings you up the valley?'

She swallowed. 'Firstly, there's nothing wrong.' She felt him relax. 'I need to ask something of you. It's important.' She looked up into those eyes that missed nothing, and silently begged him not to walk away as she deserved.

'Sure. Just let me tell the others we're taking a walk.' Was that hope lacing his words? Did he think she'd come to explain why she'd left his bed during the night last time they made love?

'Sarah, Sarah!' Leah exploded out of a tent, making a beeline for her.

Sarah's heart rolled over as she bent to catch the human speedball. 'Hey, gorgeous. How's my favourite girl?'

'Have you come to stay in our tent? Daddy takes up all the space. I have to curl up tight.' Leah's nose pressed into Sarah's neck, and Sarah inhaled her scent.

'It's so good to see you, sweetheart. I've come to talk to Daddy.' Then Sarah looked up and saw a shadow cross Dan's eyes. Had she made a mistake? Would he prefer she didn't act so affectionately with his daughter if she was leaving town? How could she not?

Within moments Sarah was surrounded by Bea, John and everyone else. It took a few minutes before Dan could persuade Leah to stay with Bea while he and Sarah went down to the river for a walk.

They sat on a large flat rock, their legs dangling over the water. Sarah batted away a mosquito and looked across at Dan. 'Robert's asked me to operate on his leg.'

'I knew you'd persuade him.' Disappointment and admiration mingled in Dan's eyes, making her feel sad and proud at the same time. She hoped he didn't feel peeved he hadn't been the one Robert had asked.

'No, you're wrong. He came to me.' She held his gaze. 'Dan, I need your help with this. Will you assist me? Tomorrow night.'

He looked away, looked back. 'Of course. But why? It's not difficult surgery.'

Everything her life had come to mean in Port Weston—friendship, love, belonging—was tied up in this particular operation. And, unusually, she feared failure. Sarah laid her hand on Dan's. 'Not difficult and yet the hardest I've had to do because he's a real friend. That's what this place has done to me. I know I'll be fine if you're there with me.'

His eyes sharpened, his hand under hers tensed. But he only said, 'I'll come back with you now. Leah will be happy staying with Bea. They're back the day after tomorrow.' He stood and looked down at her. 'We'll split tomorrow's theatre list so that you're not exhausted for Robert's surgery.'

He understood. He was coming to help her. And yet she knew she'd let him down. Had he been hoping for more? She wanted to explain her actions but couldn't without sounding like she was begging him for a place in his life. A place with conditions.

Because Dan had taken over half the surgical list Robert's surgery was brought forward to early afternoon. There were no problems, only one nasty surprise. When Sarah opened up the leg, she exclaimed in horror. The offending tendon had somehow got twisted before being rejoined.

'Working with you is a treat,' Sarah told Dan as they finished up. 'We seem to understand each other instinctively.'

'Not only in Theatre.' His eyes glowered back at her over his mask.

'I know.' But at the moment there were things they had to sort through to understand each fully.

In Recovery she told a groggy Robert, 'Your foot will take some work so you can walk without a limp, but at least the pain will be gone.'

Robert smiled the blank smile of a patient coming out of anaesthesia and promptly vomited into the stainless-steel bowl Jill held below his face.

'That's gratitude for you.' Sarah patted Robert's shoulder. 'I'll see you later.'

Outside in the waiting room she found Dan reassuring George that the operation had been a success and that there'd been none of the complications of last time.

There were tears in George's eyes when he gripped Sarah's hand to thank her. 'You don't know what this means to both of us.'

'Yes, I do. Great coffee, and lots of it,' she quipped, before giving him a hard hug. It was unbelievably good to have done something for people she had come to care about.

'I've got to go and pick Leah up from Bea's. It's been raining up the valley all day so they packed up camp,' Dan said.

'Give her a hug from me.'

'You can give her one yourself tonight. Unless you've now found somewhere else to stay?'

'Not at all. I'll see you later, then.' Sarah watched him go, her heart breaking. They were well matched, if only she could believe he wanted more than an affair.

'Sarah, we've got a man coming in from the mine.

Something about a head injury,' Hamish called from the door.

'On my way.' At least she wouldn't have time to think about Dan for a while.

Dan stopped in the doorway. His heart blocked his throat. Yearning stabbed him.

Sarah sat on the edge of Cathy's bed, baby Michael in her arms, a look of wonder on her face. Deep longing was in her eyes, in the careful way she held the precious bundle, in her total absorption with the wee boy.

Dan's feet were stuck to the floor. This was what he wanted too. With Sarah. He'd told her once she'd be a great mum, and he believed it even more now.

'I want to hold Michael.' Leah's voice cut across the room, jerking Dan's attention away from this beautiful woman to find Jill and Cathy watching him with smiles on their faces.

Sarah's head came up, her eyes seeking his. 'Hi,' she whispered.

'Hi,' Dan replied softly, love winding through his gut.

Jill sat Leah beside Sarah and took the baby, helping Leah hold the enfant. They all watched Leah, saw her face light up as she peered down at Michael. Then she looked up at Dan and Dan stared back. He knew what was coming, could see it in her innocent eyes. And, like standing in the path of an oncoming avalanche, there was nothing he could do to stop it.

'Daddy, why can't we have a baby?'

Dan stepped forward, not sure what to do, what to say. 'Leah, we just can't, okay?' And he glanced at Sarah.

Her face had paled. Her hands were fists in her lap.

'Why?' Leah persisted. 'I want one.'

Sarah turned to Leah. 'You've got to have a mother to have a baby.'

Leah's eyes widened. 'Why?'

'So the baby can grow in her tummy.' Sarah grimaced.

Leah gazed at Sarah, adoration in her eyes. 'You can be the mummy. Please, Sarah, please.'

'Leah,' Dan cut across the suddenly still room. 'That's enough.'

Sarah leapt up, her face drained of all colour, her eyes wild. She shoved past Dan in the doorway and was gone, tearing down the hall.

Dan snapped at Jill, 'Watch out for Leah,' and he was racing out after Sarah.

An ache grew in Sarah's chest. Mummy. That's the only word she could hear, bouncing around in her head. Bing-bong. Mummy. Mummy.

'Sarah, wait.' Dan's deep voice boomed out behind her.

She didn't slow down at all. Hauled the outside door open, charged out into the rose gardens.

Then Dan was running beside her, matching her step for step. His hand folded around hers, but he didn't try to stop her. Instead they kept running until they reached the car park on the other side.

'Sarah,' he gasped, and then he spun around in front of her and gripped her shoulders, absorbing the force of her forward momentum as she ran into him. His arms encircled her and he held her tight, his chin on her head, his fast breaths stirring her hair.

She tried to pull away. He tightened his hold.

'Let me go.'

'Only if you agree to come with me.'

What? Where? 'Why would I go with you? If you're gong to give me a hard time for getting Leah's hopes up then do it now, get it over with.'

'Sarah.' He leaned back at the waist to look down at her. 'I want to show you something.'

'Why?' She didn't understand. What did that have to do with what Leah had just said?

His finger lifted her chin so she had to look him in the eye. 'Will you trust me on this?'

Totally perplexed, she could only nod.

Within moments they were in the Land Cruiser, tearing down the drive and out onto the main road. She sat frozen while a million questions whirled around her brain. And then the vehicle slowed, turned in through a gate, the wheels bouncing over the rough terrain.

She jerked around to stare at Dan. His finger settled over her lips. 'Shh. Save all those questions. I asked you to trust me, remember?'

She nodded slowly. What the hell was going on?

Then he was delving into the back of the vehicle, bringing her gumboots to her door. 'Put these on.' He swapped his shoes for boots. He took her hand and began leading her across the ankle-deep, wet grass.

'Here.' Dan pulled her to a stop, turned her around and dropped his arm over her shoulders. 'Look at that view. Isn't it spectacular?'

The air was misty, and behind them the sea pounded the shore. Her breath caught in her throat. 'Simply beautiful.' But?

'Imagine a house built right here, a long house with this view from every room.'

Her heart began a steady thumping. 'A house?'

'Our house, Sarah. With lots of bedrooms for all those children we want. And a huge vegetable garden over there by that old pump shed. We'd have paddocks for horses, plenty of room for a dog to run around.' His hand tightened on her shoulder, pulling her closer to him. 'What do you say?'

The thumping got louder. Her tongue slid across her bottom lip. The picture he'd just painted was so real she could taste it in the air, see it in every direction she looked. It was everything she wanted with the man she loved. She wanted to say, shout, *What about those children?* What about the CF? But he'd asked her to trust him. And she knew deep down he'd never hurt her, never abuse that trust. And if she couldn't return that trust then she shouldn't be here.

She turned, slid her arms around his neck. 'I say yes. Yes, to all of it.'

Those blue eyes lightened, that wide mouth stretched into the most beautiful smile she'd ever seen. 'I love you, Sarah, with all my heart, and then some.'

'I love you, too. You sneaked in under my skin when I wasn't looking.' She stretched up on her toes, reaching her mouth to his.

Then he stopped her short. 'I had a sample taken and sent away to be tested for the cystic fibrosis gene the other day. The result will take a while to come through.'

Her heart slowed. She'd been right to trust him. He'd never let her down, never hide from his children's needs. 'Thank you,' she whispered against his mouth before her lips claimed his.

A kiss filled with promise. Not matter what the future brought them, their love would get them through.

EPILOGUE

SARAH stopped what she was doing to stare out across the lawn of their new home down to the pounding surf on the beach beyond. Those resolutions and new beginnings she had thought impossible almost a year ago had multiplied tenfold, making her happy beyond her wildest dreams. Today would tie everything, everyone, together perfectly.

A light kick on her hand made her smile, and she looked down at the most precious gift of all. 'Hello, gorgeous.' She bent over to kiss the fat tummy in front of her.

Davey gurgled back at her and kicked her chin.

'Thanks, buster.' Now for the job that had others in the house running for the beach. Holding her beautiful, healthy son's feet, she lifted his bottom and wiped it clean.

'Ooh, poo. That's gross.' Leah danced beside her. 'Boys are disgusting.'

Dan laughed from the safety of the doorway. 'We are not.'

'Not you, Daddy. You're not a boy, you're old.'

'Thanks a lot, missy.'

'Not as old as Santa.' Leah bounced all the way across the lounge to the huge pine tree in the corner, looking sweet in her lovely gold dress. She bent over, hands on hips, inspecting the bounty underneath.

Decorated in white and gold bows, glittering balls and

curling ribbons, their Christmas tree was perfect. Many presents lay around the base, constantly being shifted and sorted by a certain impatient young madam.

At a second change table Jill snapped plastic pants in place over baby Amy's clean nappy. 'Give Leah a few years and Dan will be wishing she still thought boys were gross.'

'I'm sure you're right.' Dan ventured close enough to drop a kiss on Sarah's brow and tickle his son's tummy. 'Can I get you two ladies a drink? One for the nerves, so to speak.'

'Oh, right, now he comes near. Brave man.' Sarah grinned as she handed him the bucket containing the offensive nappy. 'And by the way, my nerves are rock steady.' But her heart ran a little faster than normal, and she hadn't been able to eat breakfast. 'I'd love some wine but guess it will have to be OJ.' Breastfeeding had put a halt to some pleasures but had given her a whole heap of new ones. Four weeks old and growing by the minute, Davey had a voracious appetite for someone so small.

Dan didn't carry the gene but, while relieved, Sarah had discovered she'd have been more than able to cope if the test result had gone the other way. With Dan, anything was possible.

Jill lifted Amy into her arms and came to stand by Sarah. 'It's going to be a long time before I'll be touching anything remotely alcoholic.'

'I thought you were giving up feeding—' Sarah saw the glow in Jill's eyes. 'Oh, Jill. You're not? When?' She hugged her closest friend, careful not to squash Amy between them.

'September again.'

'You don't waste any time, do you? What wonderful news.' Sarah turned to dress Davey in a clean nappy, then tugged on his black pants and a white shirt to match his father's.

She glanced around, looking for Dan, expecting to see him caught up talking to a guest. But, no, there he was, walking towards her, two long-stem glasses held between the fingers of one hand. Her heart rolled over, her tummy did its melting thing. Dressed in new, fitted black trousers and a crisp white shirt, he looked absolutely wonderful. Mouth-watering. Sarah pinched herself, still struggling to believe how lucky she was that she'd found this man, the one man in the world guaranteed to make her weak at the knees. And even better, a man who loved her as deeply as she loved him.

He winked at her, a long, slow wink designed to make her helpless with desire.

'You shouldn't have done that.' She smiled back the kind of sweet, wide, tip-of-teeth-showing smile that got to him every time.

Dan laughed, loud and, oh, so carefree. 'Touché.'

Jill spun around to gawp at him. 'I still can't get used to you being so relaxed that you laugh at everything.'

Picking Davey up, Sarah glanced outside again. The lawn was filling up with people. The marquee to the side also contained its share of visitors. 'Who didn't Dan invite?'

'Old Joey.' Dan answered her rhetorical question from beside her. 'Actually, I did invite him but he had to catch a trout for Christmas dinner tomorrow. That's his way of saying he doesn't like to socialise.'

'That's sad.'

Dan raised those imperious eyebrows at her. '*You* think?'

She chuckled. 'Yes, I know. I remember that night I

came home to find a party in full swing. I wanted to head out of town.'

When she'd arrived in Port Weston she'd known no one and now look at all these people. She saw Pat, Malcolm, George and Robert. Bea and John. Family, friends, the new surgeon and his young wife who'd moved into the hospital house last week in preparation to working alongside Dan and her. Never in her wildest dreams, when she'd muttered 'new beginnings' that first day parked on the cliff top, had she envisaged being part of something so wonderful, of belonging to such an extensive and caring family.

And even more surprising were those two people sitting on the couch—at opposite ends—listening earnestly to Leah's explanation about how Santa would be squeezing down the chimney that night. Sarah gently nudged her son's cheek with her nose. 'Let's go and talk to Grandpa and Grandma.'

'Here you go, Dad. Your grandson wants time with you.' She handed her father the baby, and stood with her heart in her throat, watching the awe grow in her father's eyes. Her mother shuffled along the couch to be close to Davey. Or was it to be close to Dad?

They'd come separately, but were staying in the same motel in town. George had informed Sarah her parents had been for brunch at the café—together. And that they'd talked for ages. Good, happy talk, not acrimonious stuff. George's words. Sarah could only hope her parents might find their way back to each other.

Her father looked up at her, clearing his throat. 'I did my best for you at the time.'

'I know that now, Dad.' It had taken years, and Dan, for her to learn that.

He swallowed. 'But it wasn't good enough. I'm sorry.'

No, it hadn't been, but that was all behind them. Sarah

knelt down and hugged her father and son to her. 'I wouldn't change a thing, Dad. I really wouldn't.' Otherwise she mightn't have met Dan.

A warm hand on her shoulder. Dan's breath was warm on her cheek as he leaned down to kiss her. 'Have I told you today how much I love you?'

'Hmm, let me see. Once in the shower, again after breakfast.' She stood and slid her arms around his waist. 'And definitely when you were trying to get out of changing a particularly stinky nappy.'

Dan kissed her ear lobe. 'Are we ready?'

'I've always been ready.' It had just taken a while to realise that.

'Then let's do it, Dr Livingston.'

Sarah stepped back and smoothed her ankle-length white silk dress where it touched her hips. She straightened the gold sash around her waist and leaned down to do up the straps of her pretty, thin-heeled gold sandals.

'Leah, sweetheart.' Sarah held a hand out to her daughter. 'It's time.'

Dan lifted Davey onto one arm, and took Sarah's other hand in his. He led his family outside and down the lawn. They stepped over the scattered rose petals, heading to the marriage celebrant waiting for them. On either side family and friends cheered and clapped and blew them kisses.

Tears blurred Sarah's vision and she stumbled.

Dan tightened his grip, held her from falling. 'Silly sandals. What's wrong with a pair of gumboots?'

* * * * *

LET'S TALK
Romance

For exclusive extracts, competitions
and special offers, find us online:

f facebook.com/millsandboon
🐦 @MillsandBoon
📷 @MillsandBoonUK

Get in touch on 01413 063232

For all the latest titles coming soon, visit
millsandboon.co.uk/nextmonth